*Titles by Robin D. Owens*

**HEARTMATE**
**HEART THIEF**

# Heart Thief

## Robin D. Owens

BERKLEY SENSATION, NEW YORK

HEART THIEF

A Berkley Sensation Book / published by arrangement with the author

PRINTING HISTORY
Berkley Sensation edition / June 2003

ISBN: 0-425-19072-2

A BERKLEY SENSATION™ BOOK
Berkley Sensation Books are published by The Berkley Publishing Group, a division of Penguin Group (USA) Inc., 375 Hudson Street, New York, New York 10014. BERKLEY SENSATION and the "B" design are trademarks belonging to Penguin Group (USA) Inc.

PRINTED IN THE UNITED STATES OF AMERICA

10  9  8  7  6  5  4  3  2  1

*To all my friends online and off*
*who read and write paranormal romance.*
*From Australia to Manitoba our passion*
*transcends all boundaries.*
*Believe in magic and reach for the stars!*

*and to*

*Mistral/Samba*
*who sprawled at my elbow and told me her adventures*

# Acknowledgments

Since this book went through five major revisions, I have a lot of people to thank. Naturally, all mistakes are mine.

My friends and coworkers on the "project" for keeping me sane: Joanne, Meraj, Sharon G., Sterritt, Teri, Kay, Laura Kenny (actress), Bill, Carew, Bob, John, DK, Dennis, Judy, Cherie.

*In Memoriam: Sonya Roberts*

My first critique group, who suffered through three revisions: Anne, Diana www.dianarowe.com, Judy, Sharon www.sharomgnerey.com, Steven;

My other critiquers: Alice, Janet L., Leslee www.lesleebreene.com, Sue, Teresa, Monica, Linda H., Wendy, Eric, Charles, Joe, Margie, Donna, Chris, Stephanie, Tahtim, Janet M. www.millerclan.com/janetmiller, Margaret www.margaretmarr.com, Cate www.caterowan.com, Pam;

"Rough draft editors" who cut the manuscript by a third: Anne, Liz R., Kay (Cassie Miles), Peggy www.peggywaide.com;

My readers: Giselle and Morgan poodle experts, Anne Braude (Tal) for the brilliant inspiration of the mole; Ann (An'Alcha passion flower) http://members.aol.com/captnann/AnnJR.html;

Aryavarta Kumar who helped incredibly, and at the last minute, with nanotech data and brainstorming www.nanoapex.com;

My editor, Cindy Hwang, for buying *another* book;

My proofreader, Rose Beetem;

The cats: Diva, Mistral (Samba), Maddox (Zanth), Muse (Princess), Black Pierre, Pinky (who is not my cat), and Sabrina puppy who lived with me a while and thought she was a cat.

*Diva, I TOLD you I'm SORRY I had to cut your scene! I'll have Lisa, (www.lisacraig.com), put it up on my website, I promise! And Straif Blackthorn deserves a high-maintenance, nagging, Queen of the Universe Fam Like you . . .*

"Diva's Scene" www.robinowens.com

# *One*

## DRUIDA CITY, CELTA,
### 400 Years After Colonization, Autumn

*R*uis *'Llder stared out windows that faced the street,* checking as he did several times a day that no strangers loitered nearby. No assassins or guardsmen hired by his uncle Bucus.

Ruis's birthright had been denied him—his rank as the Heir and ensuing Lord of a GreatHouse, and the estate itself—something he strove to forget. To remember made him feel worthless. All he chose to recall was that he must always be on guard.

He went to his bedroom and reached through the open window. The wooden drying bar that extended into the courtyard from the rusty brick wall held his last good shirt. He plucked the red silkeen from the hanger.

The chill autumn air made him catch his breath. The deep blue of the sky with the distant small white sun dazzled his eyes. He savored the sweet-sharp tang of turning fall leaves as he turned from the window. The air felt good, and the silkeen shirt sliding over his skin felt better.

He'd moved into this apartment in the heat of late summer, and it was time to leave. He frowned. The intervals between his moves were getting shorter and shorter.

Stamping into new black boots, Ruis let his gaze linger on

the Earth Soil Analyzer, brought with the colonists to Celta.
The machine would take more time, money, and knowledge to
fix than he'd expected. He stopped himself from picking up
tools to tinker with it once more. When he worked on ancient
machines, he lost himself in the moment, able to forget his
wretched past and ignore his precarious future. His fascination
with artifacts that no one else cared about was his salvation.

He tore his gaze from the analyzer. Two Earthsun gems
shone in the sunlight on the table. Ruis grimaced. Stealing was
a fact of his life since his defect in Flair—psi power—pre-
cluded any normal work on Celta. When he was able to find a
job, it was as a common laborer. And laboring didn't pay
enough to rescue the past.

He took the jewels, placed them in a wall crack, and brushed
flaking grit from the surrounding bricks to cover the gems. One
Earthsun was for emergencies, for bribes and survival if his
murderous uncle Bucus found him. The second was to acquire
parts for Earth mechanicals, which Ruis collected from the corners of abandoned warehouses. Ruis thought he, alone in every
other way, was the only one on Celta who was interested in
saving and restoring the old machines.

The door burst open.

Guardsmen poured into the room; two stumbled over each
other, sprawling. Ruis lunged, aiming for a beefy man twice
his weight. Ruis slammed a fist into the guard's jaw. The man
staggered back.

"Get him!" cried a guard with chevrons on his shoulders.
The one in charge. Ruis spun to jump at him.

The two on the floor staggered to their feet. The one he had
punched lifted his staff.

It whistled through the air, hitting Ruis's head. Pain exploded
into white streaks, then darkness claimed him.

Sometime later the blackness receded and the buzzing in his
ears solidified into actual voices.

"Just a tap. It was just a little tap," the slack-faced guardsman
said in a whining grumble, rubbing his chin. "He'll wake up
soon, a minute or two—"

Someone grabbed Ruis's hair and yanked his head up. He
grit his teeth against the roiling pain. Sweat coated his body.

A stink of liquor and tobacchew swept over him, making his

senses whirl even more. He blinked and saw he was still in his rooms.

"Don' worry, Toady, he's comin' 'round. He's jus' a little more *delicate* a guy than you're used to tappin'. He's got noble blood in him, ya know."

Ruis was dragged to his feet with a clanking sound that hurt his head. He looked down in horror. Iron manacles clamped his wrists. He'd never seen such shackles—things from the ancient past. The smelly guard held a length of chain as a leash.

Ruis took a step and found himself hobbled by leg irons cutting into his new boots.

Bound and helpless again! His greatest fear. He shuddered, but reminded himself he wasn't a helpless boy anymore. Would the NobleCouncil torture him as Bucus had?

The fact that he even existed, a Null without the psi powers that every other Celtan had, infuriated Bucus. If Ruis had been normal, he would be GreatLord T'Elder, not Bucus. All the status, the power, and the estates should have been Ruis's. So Ruis had always been a painful thorn in Bucus's side. A thorn he'd tried time and again to remove and destroy.

Red-hot anger overwhelmed Ruis's pain. He lifted his hands to strike and was jerked off balance by the smelly one.

"None a' that." The guard grinned evilly, dropped the chain, and raised his fists. "Or mebbe so. You wanna fight some more? There are only four of us. Surely a *noble* like you can win against four. And I'd like to break that straight nose of yours, mess up that classy *noble* face." When he smiled, his teeth showed uneven and stained.

Ruis clenched his jaw and pushed the fury away—he couldn't indulge himself, not now.

Crashing erupted from the other room of his hideaway. He straightened to his full height despite the pain, several centimeters taller than the guards.

The other guards strolled into the room. The Petty Guardsman with chevrons on his sleeves scowled.

"Ya didn't find nothin'?" Smelly asked.

"Not the stuff *they* said he'd tooken." Petty scrutinized the room, then glanced at his wrist timer and swore. "I forgot my timer don't work around him. No spells work around him." Petty snorted, cursed, looked around again, scratched his big belly that hung over his guardbelt. "We gotta go. *They* only gave us a septhour to bring him to the Guildhall. Afraid we'll hurt the poor boy, mebbe." He passed Toady and Smelly and picked up the length of chain to use as a lead. "Let's go."

Two guards left. Petty tugged on Ruis's chain. He ground his teeth and followed, picking his way amongst the wreckage of his belongings. He'd seen his things gleefully destroyed before, especially as a child. Hiding his physical and emotional pain from his uncle Bucus had been the first lesson he'd learned.

*Crash!* He glanced back. The Soil Analyzer, so carefully cleaned and assembled, lay in a broken heap on the floor. Ruis fisted his hands, but kept hot, useless words to himself.

The last guardsman grinned. "Didn't like that, did you?" His voice held the trace of a good education.

Ruis kept his face expressionless as he battled rage. After a moment he shrugged and turned back to the door.

Surrounded, Ruis shuffled down the stone-paved streets of Druida. The NobleCouncil had caught him. It had sent louts for him, the lowest of guardsmen, ignoble bullies of brutish intelligence, with little innate Flair.

He stumbled, brought up short by his chains, forced into regarding the world around him—the stones under his feet, the squat old buildings of brick or stone set among mid-sized trees, and most of all, the people stopping and staring. The four guards pushed and prodded him, calling him filthy names.

Where *had* they found the manacles they'd slapped on his wrists and ankles? Ruis hated the constriction of his stride and the clanking that fascinated passersby.

He hid his anger and humiliation behind a casual, insouciant manner, and held his head at a jaunty tilt as if the chains were merely accessories to his fashionable clothing.

"The notorious Ruis Elder," one of the guards sneered, then belched. "Thief of T'Ash's HeartGift, thief of the Captain's Chalice, thief of Earthsun gems from Stickle's Shop, thief of the T'Birch emerald necklace, you think you're so smart, don't you?"

Ruis wondered which of the thefts had prompted his arrest, probably the T'Birch necklace, since he'd returned T'Ash's HeartGift. Rumor said T'Ash was downright affable now he had HeartBonded with his mate. Besides, T'Ash would have preferred to skewer his liver with a broadsword than have him hauled before a FirstFamilies Council for trial.

The guardsman hacked. "I spit on you." And he did.

Ruis flinched as the brown spittle hit his flesh exposed by the vee of his shirt. He straightened, glad the spit hadn't landed on his last good shirt and ruined the material. He wouldn't be getting a new shirt any time soon, and he wanted to appear before the most powerful nobles on the planet dressed as his former station deserved, dressed in the materials and styles they themselves wore.

Petty wrenched at the lead-chain. Ruis stumbled. The guard puffed out his chest as bystanders cheered. "He's worse than a thief," Petty imparted in a hoarse shout, "he's a *Null*."

Onlookers shrank from Ruis in horror. He ignored that, too. He was used to disgust and contempt, used to burying the insults deep inside.

"Yeah, this here Ruis Elder was once a GreatHouse Heir. Can you believe that? Thinks himself something special, he does. Thinks himself still noble, though his Family threw him out. Thinks himself more clever than guardsmen. Thinks he can steal all those treasures and not get caught."

Ruis clamped his jaw shut. He'd give no reaction to their words, wouldn't tempt the guards to abuse him, nor confirm their belief that he was subhuman. Despite what everyone thought, having no Flair didn't make him less than a man. Or even less than an honorable man.

True, his sense of honor had an unusual skew, but it was as strong and vital as anything else—except the smoldering rage that sometimes overwhelmed everything.

From under lowered eyelids, Ruis scanned the area, slowing his steps. The guards didn't object to his speed, no doubt thinking to extend their importance. The little parade moved from the narrow streets near the slum "Downwind" to the wider streets of middle-class commoners paved with squares of granite. Here houses and shops looked sturdy, respectable, and had more than narrow, stinking alleys between them. Tall trees lined the streets with rustling leaves edged in the orange and purple of fall. Public Carrier plinths stood at intervals. Traffic hustled with more people. A few personal gliders flowed by, but more often stridebeasts, long fur flying, headed toward NorthGate and out of Druida.

Ruis unobtrusively stretched the muscles in his arms and legs, rolled his shoulders, tested his neck with a wince. His head still hurt, but he could work through it.

He couldn't run, but he could fight. He'd take out a couple of guards and scrabble his way to a close hiding place. Maybe. He eyed the spectators again and took a step toward a cluster of them. They backed up as if he were diseased.

So, he just had to think of a bolt-hole near the route they marched to the Guildhall. He mapped out several pathways in his head. Perhaps there was a chance . . .

He jerked the chain from the loose grip of Petty but kept walking. The officer glared at him, then around at the crowd he'd been boasting to. Ruis gauged that the man wouldn't make a scene and show he'd lost control of his prisoner. Ruis smiled at him, baring his teeth, and reeled the chain leash up over his hands, feeling the weight, the use it might be as a weapon.

Petty darted looks at his fellows, two with guard-issued short swords and blasers, and the other with a staff. Petty loosened the haft of his own sword, glared at Ruis, then turned back to stride with out-thrust chest before his infamous captive.

A mistake. Ruis's smile widened into a grin.

Gold flashed at the edge of his vision. He glanced back. Narrowing his eyes, he recognized the jeweled pommel of a broadsword and the silver-gilt hair of the man who carried it. Ruis swore. Holm Holly, the best fighter on Celta, followed them, primed to thwart any escape. Holly hadn't forgotten that Ruis had stolen the HeartGift of Holm's best friend, T'Ash. Holly wouldn't underestimate Ruis, or take a chance he'd escape.

Holm was the Heir to the Hollys, a FirstSon, as Ruis himself was a FirstSon. But Holm was accepted and valued by his Family.

Then Ruis noted another blond head on a slighter form, keeping pace a block ahead—Tinne, the younger Holly son. He looked armed to the teeth, fast on his feet, and ready to fight if Ruis gave him an opportunity. There was nothing the Hollys liked better than to fight.

Damn! No out. No way out. Caught and trapped.

The surge of fury blinded him, made him stagger with its force. Shock sizzled through him at the realization of the depth of his corrosive rage—rage at the world for denying him his due, at his Family for shunning him, at others for not even treating him as human. That the burst of anger actually blinded him and stole his wits, shook him to his core.

He had to keep control.

Petty proceeded with his gloating spiel. "Yeah, this *thief* thinks he can steal and not get caught 'cause he's a *Null*."

Toady looked furtively around and lowered his voice. "What's a Null?" he asked.

Petty snorted. "A Null's a creature that don't have no magic, no Flair. And no magic will work on him or around him."

Toady's mouth dropped as his eyes widened. "No magic will work? Not even a 'light on' spell? Not even an 'open door' spell? Not even a 'protect house' Word? Not even—"

"Nothin' means *nothin'*." Petty shoved Ruis, who danced to keep his balance. "That's why we were sent to get him. He riles folk with good Flair somethin' awful. They's hair stands on end or somethin'."

As far as Ruis knew, he was the third Null in the history of Celta. Based on his own experience, he wouldn't have been surprised if others had faded away or committed suicide.

"Doesn't bother me." Smelly thumped his staff into Ruis's back with bruising force. Ruis was glad it missed his kidney. "I got little Flair, can just do the standard spells. I'm getting paid good gilt to pick this one up and haul him to Guildhall dungeon. Think they'll kill him after his trial?"

"Heh. Heh. Heh." Petty chuckled. "Mebbe."

"How do you think they'll do it?" Toady asked. "I've heard of no Council killin'—"

"Execution," Smelly corrected.

"—I've just seen some gang fights. And ten noble duels," Toady added with relish. "How will the Council ext—, exek—, kill him? Use some of those old ways in stories? Behead him? Hang him? Cut him up? Fry—"

"Turn here," Petty ordered. "Mebbe they'll banish him instead. Some o'those FirstFamilies are mush-hearts, an' that's who'll be tryin' him, those FirstFamilies."

Toady gulped. "Those great folk with lots of Flair are strange. Big and powerful and strange and weird—"

"Yup. The Council's gotta wait a coupla' weeks till all the FirstFamilies are there, but then he gets it."

"—I shure wouldn't wanna be in this guy's shoes." He

glanced at Ruis's boots. "Shure are pretty boots, though."

"Mebbe you'll get them after he's dead."

"You think so? Really? Really?" Toady got so excited he bumped into Ruis, pushing him off-balance.

Petty grabbed Ruis and jerked him upright. Manacles scraped his wrists, and blood stained the red cuffs maroon. How appropriate. The T'Elder GreatHouse color was bloodred. The leg irons slashed past the black dye into the leather, leaving white gouges in his boots.

"Hey, get smart," Smelly said. "Your feet are too damn big for his boots."

"Oh, yeah."

Ruis smiled ironically. Soon he'd be in the Guildhall dungeon. His concern to find a place to live was gone. No more worrying that the generational spells of old buildings would crumble at his long-term presence, that his neighbors would turn on him when they realized what he was, or about the ever-present threat of his uncle Bucus finding him to make him permanently disappear. Bucus, along with the rest of the NobleCouncil, now had him.

Some of the GreatLords and Ladies were out of town. As soon as the FirstFamilies Council had a quorum, he'd be tried. No doubt they'd take care of it before the Autumnal Equinox in a couple of eightdays. He wondered if he'd be executed— another rare occurrence in Celta, where duels were customarily used to settle differences. But he'd sinned against the First-Families.

Anger stirred, then subsided. Whatever happened, the life he'd known for thirty-five years was over. The crash of his world had been inevitable. The way he lived and his fury-fueled recklessness had guaranteed that. Though he'd stolen for survival and for objects to power his Earth machines, stealing from nobles had been enough to warrant death. Perhaps just being a Null was reason enough to kill him.

His anger had been just, but even justifiable anger was something he couldn't afford. He must master it, since it had determined his fate.

He hadn't seen this coming.

*     *     *

"*Of course the First Families Council will loan our Family* the 1,500,000 gilt," Aunt Menzie said from the front of the Family glider. "If they don't, it will be because *you* bungle the asking. You are far too young to be the Head of the Family."

"I don't bungle," GrandLady Ailim D'SilverFir replied with all the calm she could muster. "I have been trained from the moment I was born and have been a circuit judge for six years." She smoothed her brocade robe over her lap in a nervous gesture she was careful never to allow anyone else to see, then glanced through the spell partition separating her from G'Uncle Ab and his niece, Aunt Menzie. Ab drove the glider to the Guildhall.

Both of them sat stiffly, radiating anger and resentment.

Menzie snorted. "That didn't stop you from coming up with the insane idea of selling the D'SilverFir *Residence and ancestral estate.*"

"It would have cleared the debt once and for all." She'd hated the thought. It still brought a lump to her throat to consider selling her home, to be the first D'SilverFir to fail the Family, but it was the sole honorable option available.

"Utter nonsense. A good thing the Family convinced you otherwise, even though it took an eightday to do it." Menzie nodded sharply, not bothering to look back at Ailim.

Ailim clenched her hands. The confrontation with her Family had been ugly. Even after an eightday, emotions ran high. Her specific Flair was telempathy—being able to hear thoughts and feel emotions from others. She'd had to keep her personal shields at full strength, pulling energy from her body to bolster them. Emotions from her Family had pummeled her in waves, leaving discomfort and migraines in their wake.

"There is no reason to go over old ground," Ailim said, knowing it was futile, that Menzie would yammer at her during the entire drive.

"You—"

"Silence. I need to compose my thoughts." With a wave of her hand she thickened the shield between them until no sound came through. Menzie squawked in outrage, but Ailim didn't hear.

Menzie's mouth moved faster and faster. Ailim turned to

the passing city scenery. Autumn foliage melded into a
vivid blur that both comforted and hurt. Hurt because this
was the first fall her Mother and Mothersire would not see,
but comforted by the brilliant colors of her favorite season.
It was a blessing that autumn could lift her spirits.

Another blessing, Ab and Menzie wouldn't be allowed
to attend the FirstFamilies Council meeting. Her relatives
intended to wait for her. She longed to wash her hands of
the Family and all its responsibilities, but that would bring
a chaos of infighting amongst the others that would destroy
it.

So Ailim had bespelled the glider to return to the Residence as soon as she stepped from the vehicle. She'd face
the consequences of that later.

The vehicle stopped. G'Uncle Ab made no move to exit
and help her disembark. Ailim scrambled out and said the
Word that sent the conveyance away. She shouldn't have
enjoyed Ab and Menzie's startled faces as they were
whisked away, but she did.

Ailim stood before the doors of the Guildhall and sent
her mind out to brush against others for observers, but dusk
shadowed an empty CityCenter. She relaxed a little, pulled
a delicate handkerchief from the inner pocket of one wide
robe sleeve, and wiped her damp palms.

She set her shoulders and forced gray exhaustion from
her mind. She had to consciously lift each foot to walk. Her
feet wanted to drag, her eyes to shut. And she desperately
wished to escape into the oblivion of sleep. All eightday
she'd worked around the clock, fueling herself with
StayAwake.

The Family had decided she'd go to the FirstFamilies
Council and request a loan—in her mind, to beg. The
twenty-five Families who'd descended from the colonists
who funded the journey from Earth were still the most powerful in fortune and Flair. They'd judge her. She, who had
only been the head of the Family for little more than a
month and who had not yet formally been accepted into the
Council as D'SilverFir, would make her first appearance as
a supplicant.

She didn't want to beg.

She was going to do it anyway. Ask the Council for a

long-term loan at an absurdly low interest rate. The whole business left a bitter taste in her mouth.

To fail the Family would be to fail all her predecessors who had struggled to keep the Family together for four hundred years, and even before—to deny the colonists their great sacrifice in leaving their home planet. Ailim would not be the one who shirked her duty and allowed the Family to founder.

She stared at the large brass embossed doors and muttered the opening Words. The doors did not swing apart. Odd. She blinked—perhaps she'd misremembered the code, but at least the doors should be keyed to her touch. Sighing, reaching out with her mind again to check if she was still unobserved, she pushed against one door with all her weight, making sure her robe didn't touch the door coated with the day's dust.

Slowly the big door swung open and she entered the hushed silence of the Guildhall atrium. The quiet felt uncanny, as if all the myriad spells were stilled, and all the magical-technological machines were dead. She shivered and walked through the glass-domed antechamber and into the sky-lighted corridor, then turned left to the Council-Chamber and stopped.

Someone else sat—lounged—on the carved celtawood bench outside the rich Earthoakwood doors. Across the wide hall from him, in a tipped back chair, a guardsman snored.

At the sight of the handsome man on the bench, she summoned the last dregs of her energy to try and act like her normal self. How she wished she had his audacity, even though it was obvious that he, too, was a petitioner to see the FirstFamilies Council.

His long legs stretched well into the hallway, clothed in fine furrabeast leather breeches and black boots. His flamboyant red shirt with its bloused sleeves and tiny intricate embroidery on the cuffs that showed his Family made a bold statement Ailim wished she could follow. She smiled.

"Merry meet," she offered the formal greeting.

The man's red-brown head jerked up, and Ailim realized he hadn't heard her approach. She smiled again, in apology for startling him. "I see we are the two matters that the

FirstFamilies Council will consider tonight. I'm to be seen after you, I believe. I am here to beg." She felt a dull horror at such revealing words. She'd just opened her mouth and they'd emerged, without thought. But then she wasn't thinking much, with her brain clouded by fatigue. And there was something about him that innately appealed to her.

She lifted heavy eyelids to study him. His aristocratic features showed generations of noble breeding. His body was strong and well-formed, his chestnut hair wavy, and his deep brown eyes attractive. Yet it wasn't his appearance that so drew her.

Nor was it his casual manner that she sensed overlaid a naturally energetic individual. It was something else.

She couldn't quite determine the quality that pleased her.

He stood with a small clinking sound and she glanced at his boots, but no spurs gleamed in the dim light. His bow was graceful and elegant. He smiled, and a deep dimple showed in his left cheek. His brown eyes sparkled.

She felt her heart pick up pace. The sensations were new and unusual. And enjoyable enough to be dangerous to her peace of mind.

Peace of mind. *That* was what he gave her. Just being in his presence was soothing. No intrusion of his thoughts or his emotions impinged on her awareness.

A staggering thought.

Ailim faltered to the bench, sat, and slipped, prevented from falling off the polished wood by one strong, calloused hand.

"Thank you," she whispered, knowing she flushed.

He gave another half-bow and sat beside her. Again a metallic chinking came. She looked around, but saw nothing to explain the sound.

"Begging is wretched," he said, finally responding to her earlier comment. "I grew out of begging early. I'll never beg for anything from anyone again."

Her lips compressed. She hardly believed she'd told him. But she hated what she'd have to do for her Family. "Unfortunately this is my first experience. At least it's just the FirstFamilies Council and not the whole NobleCouncil."

He shrugged. "I don't care who hears my story."

She sighed. "Family business?"

The bitterness of his expression outdid her own. "Oh, yes."

Interested and curious, she moved closer to him, closer than she meant to when she realized their thighs touched. She started to shift away when his hand grasped her arm.

"Please. Stay," he said.

The stillness of the building and of the man himself lulled her. She fought to keep her eyes open. She would be able to sleep after the meeting, she told herself. Her gaze stopped on his fine hand that rested on her arm. She could sense his vitality, and wondered why she kept thinking of him as peaceful.

She dragged her thoughts back to the topic. "Families." She sighed again. "There are no more troublesome problems than those of Family. *They* made me come. To beg." She didn't like the petulance in her voice, but she couldn't seem to hide her emotions from this man.

"Oh, did they?" He glanced at the bright gold embroidery around her sleeves. "D'SilverFir," he mocked gently.

And it was that tone that won her. A sympathetic note in his voice that still poked fun at both her status and his own. She looked to his cuffs, but couldn't make out his embroidered rank and name in the low light.

"You're the Judge, aren't you? Why aren't you in the CouncilChamber with them?" He nodded to the ornate doors.

She managed to sit up straight but it took most of her energy. "I've only been D'SilverFir a month and a half. I haven't gone through the Loyalty Ritual with the Family or been confirmed and accepted by the Councils, yet."

"Ah. I heard of your loss and that you'd returned, but I've been occupied and didn't know the rest. My—condolences? Or congratulations?"

"Thank you for your sympathy." Unwanted fatigue crept over her, the long hours without sleep catching up to her. The potency of the StayAwake spellpill had diminished. "You don't think the head of a FirstFamily House has problems? I've been working for weeks to save my Family."

"The head of my House never acted as if he had problems. He removed all obstacles, including myself, quickly and efficiently. Some Families don't deserve to be saved."

His soft voice held anger. She wanted to comfort him, to find his difficulty and solve it, as she solved all the problems brought to her as a judge. So tired that words were beyond her, she could only pat his shoulder in support. Her eyes closed.

She felt an ease with the man that she'd never felt with anyone before, a complete lack of pressure from any of his thoughts and emotions ruffling her energy field. He must have an incredible natural inner shield.

The fact she couldn't read *anything* from him should have been frightening, but instead the silence was blessed. A peace and a privacy that she'd never known enveloped her like the softest cloak. She relaxed her own shields, both the instinctive ones and those built with experienced care. And as she loosened her mind's defenses, her body drooped. She found herself breathing deeply, sliding into sleep, resting against the man.

She jerked awake. "My apologies," Ailim muttered. Yet she'd never been so unself-conscious before.

He chuckled and his strong arm curved around her and pulled her to him. "As long as you don't mind your elegant dress brushing against my simple attire."

She sniffed. "My best begging clothes. I wish I could wear a bold red like you and tell them I had no need. You look like you'll stand in front of them and *demand*."

"I wish it were so. But I can stand in front of them and not care about their decision."

"Lucky you." His warmth encompassed her, adding to her serenity.

For the first time in her life, her physical senses were free from her mental telempathy. She'd never been aware of the scent of a man. Her nose twitched in appreciation of a spicy fragrance. There also came a hint of another aroma she didn't consciously recognize but which raised echoing genetic memories of metallic ships and the deepness of space. Surely no man would ever smell so good as this one. This incredible one.

Beneath her cheek the silkeen of his shirt and the firm muscles of his body felt warm. She appreciated the catch of his breath, liked hearing the strong and steady thumping of his heart. How wonderful. She couldn't remember having enough quiet to hear her own heartbeat, let alone another's.

"Nice," she said.

"What?"

"You're nice."

His laugh followed her into the darkness of sleep.

Marching footsteps woke her. Her companion set her from him with that odd clinking sound.

Heat suffused Ailim. "Forgive me." Her voice emerged strangled and husky.

"I'm glad to be of service." His eyes held a softness that hadn't been evident before.

He stood as the guard across from them woke and four other guardsmen marched in from an opposite door. A pair took position on either side of him.

Ailim blinked, trying to gather sleep-hazed thoughts. "What's going on here?"

A Petty guardsman inflated his chest. "Judgment of the Null, Ruis Elder."

"Null?" She tried to cope with the idea. It made no sense. Instinctively she looked to her companion. She licked her dry lips and tried out his name. "Ruis?"

"Yes." His smile mocked both Ailim and himself. "A Null is not an appreciated creature, but I'll wager that's why you felt so peaceful in my company."

The guard's word stuck in her mind. "Judgment?" Dread uncoiled within her. She, better than anyone in the hall, knew about judgment.

He shrugged. "You won't see me again. By tomorrow I'll be either banished or dead." When he bowed, the hidden chain tying his outside wrist to the wall and between his feet clinked.

She hadn't noticed the manacles. The black cuffs blended in with his boots, and he'd had enough inherent grace to manage to bow. Twice. Ancient chains to bind him, a Null. Her mind processed everything at triple slow speed. Of course, her StayAwake spell and pill would have failed around him.

"Now the FirstFamilies will decide my fate," Ruis said.

No hope, then, that she could do anything to put this right. Too late. Once again too late to stop disaster. She

rose and dipped a curtsy. "My thanks for your companion-
ship."

He stood proudly, ignoring the guards snapping the chain
from the wall to his other wrist. "I'd be glad to place myself
at your service, but all the spells of your Residence would
suffer. Even the great generational spells of your House-
Heart would wither and die." His mouth twisted. "My Family moved me from the ancestral Residence to a cottage on
the far edge of the estate before I was two years old."

She didn't need to read his mind or feel his emotions to
know his deep, caustic fury. It laced his voice, his manner,
his expression, everything she watched for as a judge.

"I'm sorry."

He inclined his head.

A guard snuffled. "Ain't you two going to give them noble goodbyes? You know, like 'Merry meet.'"

Ailim froze the man with a look. The guard snapped to
attention. She frowned. All the guards looked to be large
of muscle but small in intelligence. Not the usual highly
Flaired, trained, and shrewd guards assigned to the First-
Families Council, or even the Guildhall. Another indication
of Ruis's uniqueness. Lowly Flaired men to watch him.

She turned to Ruis and smiled. "It was merry met. You're
the most comfortable man," she murmured.

His smile became less bitter and more wry. "Thank you
for those gracious words." He shot a glance at the guard
and walked away, his natural pace restricted by the chains.

Ailim's heart contracted.

Ruis threw a smile over his shoulder. "But it's not a very
merry parting, and I doubt we'll meet again. I have 'business' elsewhere." He raised his manacled wrists. "Fare thee
well."

Ailim managed a sad smile. "And you."

He turned away. "I don't anticipate it."

# Two

❦

$\mathcal{R}$uis Elder sauntered into the CouncilChamber, head high, shoulders straight. His bootheels rang on the tile floor in counterpoint to the clanking of his chains. Each step seemed to echo, "Death, Banishment, Death, Banishment."

He wondered morbidly which would be worse.

Until this minute, he hadn't thought he cared about his fate. Now he knew.

He didn't want to die. Even though his existence had been a continuous battle, he still cherished life. Who would save the earth machines if he died? No one. Who would teach the nobles that Nulls were valuable? No one.

Yet he couldn't accept being banished. All the earth machines that still existed were here in Druida, so the GreatLibrary had told him a year ago. Without the occupation of restoring them, he'd be lost.

His heart thudded in his ears, but he refused to show any fear, any indication that the vital decision of the Council mattered so much to him.

He stopped on the colorful mosaic pentacle in the center of the large chamber. A couple of meters away, behind a long table, sat wood and ruby velvet chairs for the twenty-five FirstFamily heads of households and their spouses. All except two of the FirstFamily heads were there, the highest ranked nobles of Celta. The most dominant in Flair—psi talent. A shiver washed through him at the great power of the group. These were his judges, perhaps his executioners.

When he scrutinized the nobles, they appeared strained. His Null power definitely affected them. Ruis smiled. Some were pale, some flushed, some had a sheen of sweat on their faces. They didn't like being near him.

Danith D'Ash's nose twitched. He bowed to her. She blinked, then returned his courtesy with a nod. T'Ash, her husband sitting beside her, growled. Though he showed no outward discomfort, his expression was stern. His long black hair looked tangled, his blue eyes showed a fierce predatory awareness.

Ruis suppressed a grimace. It had been a real mistake, stealing that HeartGift from T'Ash—a man who'd grown up in the slums and had destroyed the killers of the T'Ash Family. But Ruis had been sure the roseamber gem in T'Ash's necklace would vibrate at the correct level to run the antique machine he'd been trying to save. Luckily, Ruis had found the gem useless and returned the necklace unharmed. Ruis met GreatLord T'Ash's eyes steadily. T'Ash, too, had known hardship.

D'Ash placed a hand on her HeartMate's tense arm and whispered in T'Ash's ear. The man relaxed a bit. Ruis wondered whether the pair would vote for death or banishment.

His gaze swept down the table. This year, GreatLord heads of households, like T'Holly and T'Ash, outnumbered Great-Ladies—such as old Muin D'Vine, the renowned prophetess.

D'Vine met Ruis's gaze and her eyes filled with sadness.

He flinched. They'd never met, but one glance at her tilted head, the sympathy that was not hidden by the crinkled folds of her aged skin, and he knew she'd had a vision of his fate.

Of the two chairs that were empty, one belonged to T'Blackthorn, the other to D'SilverFir. Ruis wished that the GrandLady in the corridor was with him, her compassionate blue-gray eyes looking at him from a heart-shaped face. Somehow he knew he'd feel steadier, despite the fact she was a Judge.

His stare snagged on a hate-filled black gaze—Bucus, head of the GreatHouse T'Elder. Hauling his wife beside him, Bucus went to the center of the long table. He sat in the Captain's Chair. He'd been elected the leader of the Council two years ago. When Ruis bowed to his aunt, she averted her face and stumbled into her chair. No help there. Never had been.

Ruis held his uncle's stare, revealing his contempt at the man who'd tormented him during his youth. Bucus banged a gavel. "Let this FirstFamilies Council come to order."

D'Grove, a matronly woman, shifted in her chair, frowning. She turned to stare at Bucus. "The invocation, Captain GreatLord T'Elder, if you please." Her voice was mellifluous, but insistent. Ruis could almost feel the rivalries that often divided the FirstFamilies more than their powerful Flair bound them together. If Bucus ran the Council the way he ran his household, there'd be plenty who despised him.

Ruis smiled.

Bucus narrowed his eyes, then nodded shortly. "You may say a blessing, but make it short. We have business to finish."

D'Grove lifted her eyebrows and intoned, "By the Blessed Couple—the Lord and the Lady, and under the auspices of Don, the patron spirit of Law, let this FirstFamilies Council do what is right."

Ruis noticed the faint odor of sage. It comforted him. He looked at his hands he'd folded and noticed, for the first time in many years, the multitude of small, straight scars on them. Scars made by a razorslit. The razorslit wielded by the man now sitting in the Captain's Chair.

He turned his hands over to stare at his palms, also showing scars. Scars covered his body. His uncle had liked the fact that one person he tortured, the boy he hated the most, would always be marked. Ruis couldn't be Healed by Flair. But his worst scars were inside and unseen. Would his uncle finally succeed in killing him? At least he was now sure he wouldn't be tortured again. The air of dissension within the FirstFamilies Council ensured that. A ripple of relief flowed through him.

When he looked up, he noted his uncle's increasing color, unhealthily red. Bucus snarled his words. "We know this man's crimes. The theft of the—"

"One moment," D'Ash spoke up.

There was a gasp around the table. The GreatLady was new, of common origin, and perhaps didn't know her place.

"Seeing the man in chains disturbs me," D'Ash said.

"Your husband forged those chains for the Null," Bucus said.

"And they've served their purpose. Holm and Tinne Holly

stand at the door." Ruis heard the men shift behind him as D'Ash continued. "Outside are stationed several more guards. Ruis Elder cannot teleport, no one can teleport."

Because of him, the Null. Ruis's smile widened.

"T'Ash alone could fell him—" D'Ash said.

Ruis's smile faded.

"—but there are three fighting Hollys."

"I agree," T'Ash said. "The chains are unnecessary. Our blasers may not work around him, but our swords can pierce him well enough."

"Vote," called D'Grove. "Let's vote. Shall Ruis Elder be freed during trial?"

Only the T'Elders voted to keep him manacled, his uncle shouting "Nay."

T'Ash rose and circled the table with a fighter's grace. He stopped two paces from Ruis. "Do I have your word that you won't attack when I remove the chains?"

Ruis couldn't prevent himself from a minor act of defiance and drama. He lifted an eyebrow and jangled the chains.

T'Ash gestured to the men behind Ruis. "Holm, Tinne."

Ruis heard footsteps. "You have my word," Ruis said.

The two men behind him retreated.

T'Ash took a key from his pocket. With three little clicks and a tug, the irons fell from Ruis.

Ruis stretched, easing muscles cramped for days.

As T'Ash took the chains and seated himself, Bucus said, "Ruis, calling yourself Elder, you stand before the FirstFamilies Council accused of the following thefts: theft of T'Ash's HeartGift, the Captain's Chalice, the T'Birch emerald necklace, and five Earthsuns from Stickle's Shop. How do you plead?"

Ruis rubbed his wrists, made a point of straightening the cuffs that still showed the embroidery of a GreatHouse Heir, widened his stance and replied. "I returned T'Ash's HeartGift—"

Ruis sent his most charming smile to Danith D'Ash. "I returned the HeartGift to D'Ash."

T'Ash growled again.

"That's true," D'Ash said.

"I would see proof that I stole the rest," Ruis bluffed.

"Arran of Mullin testified you bought an Earth Soil Analyzer for two Earthsuns from him, and Stickle says the gems came from his shop," Bucus said.

Ruis shrugged. "Two gems are not five."

T'Ash, the jeweler, curled his lip. "Stickle is the scum of my profession. We're taking Stickle's word about theft? He beats his apprentices, he weights his scales, and he sells vermeil— gold-coated silver—claiming it's pure gold."

D'Birch's high voice cut in. "I am missing a necklace, and I vow, this is the thief who stole it." She pointed at Ruis.

"Proof," T'Oak said softly.

Proof? Ruis stared, amazed. A GreatLord asked for proof. He'd believed that his trial would be perfunctory.

"I felt the drain of my Flair, then my necklace was gone!" D'Birch cried.

"Where was this?" Bucus appeared smug at her answers.

"In CityCenter Bazaar on Summer Solstice FairDay."

"You wore an emerald necklace to the bazaar on FairDay?" D'Ash sounded incredulous.

D'Birch looked down her aristocratic nose. "I had consulted with T'Ash to match the pattern for a bracelet."

T'Ash frowned.

D'Ash, his wife, nudged his ankle. Ruis saw her do it under the table. The Council had not bothered with damask table-cloths for him.

T'Ash muttered something.

She kicked him.

"The clasp to the necklace was faulty," T'Ash said, louder.

Bucus glared at D'Birch, then at Ruis. "Still—"

"No proof," said T'Oak. "The charge should be dismissed. Does anyone disagree?"

"I am Captain of this Council, I run—" Bucus started.

"You are biased in this matter," D'Grove interrupted. "Isn't this man before us the legitimate FirstSon of your brother, the former T'Elder?"

Bucus grumbled but didn't deny the statement.

"Let us dismiss the charge, then." D'Grove waved her hand.

A rivulet of sweat trickled down Ruis's back. He blinked. He thought he'd been cool, calm, composed. He rarely lied to himself.

But D'Birch lied about feeling him near her on the Summer Solstice FairDay. Not even the most powerfully Flaired sensed his nullness in passing, only after he lingered several moments.

As long as he stayed a meter away from strong spells and moved within a quarter-septhour, he was unnoticeable. Even during the night, when he slept, his nullness couldn't fill up the small apartments in the unspelled buildings where he lodged.

He hadn't stolen the ugly necklace, merely jostled D'Birch in the crowded square and caught the thing when it slithered down her silkeen gown. It had taken time to test the emeralds and find they were too poor to use as focal points for the lazer he'd been rebuilding. He'd planned to return them, but his arrest had prevented it. The gems were still hidden.

"Next, the Captain's Chalice, missing from the Colonist's Museum." Bucus glared up and down the table. "I have an affidavit from GuardsMan Winterberry, a man very familiar with this thie—person. He states that after the theft was reported, he used his Flair to scan the room and determined that a Null had stood in front of the glass display housing the Chalice. We only have one Null on Celta at this time, thank the Lord and Lady."

Ruis met his uncle's loathing gaze. "I visited the Museum on Discovery Day as part of my personal Ritual, as did others in Druida." He'd gone in the night, always preferring darkness. He'd stared at the cup and wished bitterly that he'd never been born on Celta, that his ancestors had not landed on the planet and bred for Flair. Ruis knew enough history to realize that on ancient Earth he wouldn't have been a detested outcast.

Beside the Captain's Chalice was a brass plaque listing all the FirstFamilies' lineages and Heirs. He, Ruis Elder, the first-born of his Family, had not been mentioned. His anger had ignited at the omission and hot sweat had coated his brow. Yet he would have left the Chalice alone except that he'd seen equations engraved in the gold that might help him in his quest to save the past. So he'd taken the Chalice, made wax molds of the equations, and returned the piece to the museum.

"That item, too, was recovered, was it not?" he asked in as calm a voice as possible.

Bucus pushed his chair back with a sliding rasp and stood. "Why do we try this piece of filth?" His face reddened, his nostrils widened and pinched with heavy breaths. "He is a NULL. Anathema to all of us. Threatening to all of us. Of no use to anyone. Less than a man, a Celta human. He has no respect for us or our traditions, and is filled with bestial emotions, not fit to live."

T'Ash rose, turned, and matched his gaze with the older man. "He's a GreatHouse FirstSon. Don't call him a feral beast."

"He is no son of ours. T'Elders cast him out long ago as repulsive, defective, and unworthy. An aberrant son of a sickly father. He is nothing to the Elders. Nothing. Death to him! I call for a vote of Death."

In the charged silence a little creak echoed as old D'Vine, the prophetess, rose. In hushed quiet she hobbled along the table, touching T'Reed's head, T'Ash's shoulder, D'Ash's hand. She came to stand before Ruis and peer up at him with milky eyes. When she laid her palm against his cheek, he jerked at her chill, uncanny touch. Yes, she must have had a vision.

A tremor shook him again when she stealthily slipped a note into his far trous pocket.

Her lips curved in a thin smile and she tilted her head at the table. Her whisper filled the room. "I have nineteen decades of using Flair, and not even a strong, young Null can suppress my wisdom. I am old, a crone—close to the cycle of death and rebirth—and my sensing of Mysteries is great. I have had visions of this young man—and of the fate of our Council, so I must speak. Events have already been propelled down a specific path. Be wary of trying to control the wishes of the Unknown, of usurping the strong Fate now in motion."

She dropped her hand and turned toward the FirstFamilies Council. "Not everything is predetermined in this matter, but be assured by seeking to punish Ruis, you will turn the river of Destiny to flood yourselves."

D'Vine continued. "I cast my vote. Life, as always. Freedom, cherished by us all. Respect—that which our ancestors sought when they cherished and nurtured their puny Flair, left their home planet to pursue their own Path of psi powers. I vote no death and no banishment. Blessed be." She shuffled, an eerie figure in black, to the doors. Before she reached them, the two Holly men, Holm and Tinne, opened the doors wide and bowed with perfect grace to her. She left.

Hope flared within Ruis. Could he be freed, simply freed? He hated hope. So much worse when it crashed into despair.

"The question of punishment for Ruis, once-Elder, has been called," Bucus said with relish.

D'Grove blinked. "The sole options before the Council are Death and Banishment, perhaps we should reconsider. . . ."

A flurry of words passed between T'Ash and D'Ash. D'Ash sat back with a huff and didn't meet Ruis's eyes. T'Ash scowled.

Bucus T'Elder glowered at his fellow nobles. "Do I hear any more options being proposed?"

Silence.

"Banishment will be from the major cities of Celta. If Ruis, calling himself Elder, is banished and later found within the walls of Druida, Gael City, Anglesey, or Lomand, he will be executed. Vote," Bucus ordered.

Ruis didn't want to care whether the FirstFamilies Council voted to banish or kill him. He'd convinced himself that he didn't care.

Had lied to himself again.

The room was hot. His lips were dry. His shirt stuck to his back.

T'Birch started. "Death."

T'Rowan followed. "Death."

D'Alder said, "Banishment."

Ruis's stomach clenched. The voices casting the vote floated to him from a great distance. His vision dimmed.

T'Ash's deep voice boomed, "Banishment."

More voices sounded. "Death."

"Death."

"Banishment."

Finally it was over.

Before she'd left, D'Vine had voted for Freedom.

Eight voted for Death.

Fourteen voted for Banishment.

T'Blackthorn was absent.

D'SilverFir was absent. The thought of her and the comfort they had shared earlier made Ruis's whole body tighten.

Banished.

*A*ilim *waited in the large corridor until the Council Herald* waddled to the double Earthoakwood doors next to her and consulted a scroll mounted behind glass next to the threshold.

"Prospective GrandLady D'SilverFir." His sonorous voice rolled through a hall filled with the dim emptiness of evening.

Ailim grimaced at his pomposity and rose. "I am present."

A patter of feet attracted her attention, and she looked down the hall to see GreatLady D'Holly exiting from the Council chamber by the unofficial door near the end of the corridor. She headed for the back exit of the building. GreatLady D'Vine, who had previously left the chamber, passed D'Holly and returned to the Council room by the same door.

The Herald ostentatiously swept the main doors open for Ailim with the help of Tinne Holly from the inside. He joined her in the passageway. She heard steady metallic clanks and caught a brief glimpse of a red-shirted figure, Ruis Elder, being marched out of the unofficial door in chains.

Her stomach clenched. Chains. Banished or death, he had said of his fate. She wondered which it would be, and prayed that he would live. Bonded together in the face of their own personal adversities, they'd shared hopes and fears.

She heard the sound of a blow on flesh and a surprised grunt of pain. Ailim leveled a stare at the Herald. "While they are in this building, the Council guards are under your authority. Do they make a point of beating a man before he is executed?"

The Herald's composure seemed to desert him. "Elder is banished, Lady, not to be executed. Execution would have been administered in the courtyard—"

"I am a judge of Celta. I do not accept the beating of prisoners under restraint." Ailim pivoted on her heel and marched down the hall.

Tinne Holly kept up with her. The Herald puffed behind them, protesting, "The Council awaits!"

She shouldn't keep the entire FirstFamilies Council waiting, but simple justice demanded that she not allow Ruis Elder to be harmed. The idea sickened her.

Halt! she sent mentally. Nothing happened. As she

caught a rushed breath, Ailim realized it was because of
Ruis Elder's Nullness.

The sounds of a scuffle and more blows made Ailim
break into a trot. As she rounded the corner she saw two
guards holding Ruis and another with his fist raised. A Petty
guardsman stood by, grinning.

"What's going on here?" she demanded.

The Petty guardsman tensed, then composed his face into
an ingratiating smile. "Nothin' to worry your head about,
M'Lady." He hitched his belt up his big belly.

A hiss of irritation escaped Ailim. Holly raised his eyebrows. Ruis Elder looked bored, despite tousled hair, a red
bruise on one high cheekbone, and a rivulet of blood trickling from the corner of his mouth.

"Release him at once!" she ordered the two holding Ruis.
They dropped his arms and shuffled away. Ruis straightened.

The grin faded from the officer's face. "M'Lady—"

"D'SilverFir," Tinne said softly.

"Judge SilverFir," panted the Herald, catching up with
them, "allow me to handle this."

The Petty guard's mouth fell open, then snapped shut.
He gulped. The other guards faded into the shadows. Ruis
stood with casual grace, adjusting his shirt cuffs, arching
his brows at the scene before him.

The Herald whirled toward the Petty guardsman. "I'll
have your chevron for this! All of you, listen to me, you
will . . ."

The others seemed to hear his fine tirade, but his voice
faded from Ailim's ears as her gaze locked with Ruis Elder's.

He bowed to her. His blasé manner was a mask well mastered, but his eyes leapt with wild flames of intense vitality,
recklessness. His glance seemed to dare her to take chances
and live life to the fullest. The Herald's voice became a
pattern of cadence. She heard the tiny clinks of Ruis's
chains and her stomach clenched.

She blinked and focused again on his face, and she understood that he hated her seeing him like this—a bound
captive, with blood oozing from his mouth, blood that he

wouldn't wipe away because he'd have to raise chained hands to do so.

Ailim looked back and forth between Tinne Holly and Ruis Elder, both sons of a FirstFamily, but how far apart in station! One was cherished, the other outcast. Ruis was taller than Tinne Holly, but with equally noble features and bearing. The injustice of the discrepancy made her dizzy.

"Elder's nullness affects you, GrandLady," Tinne said, steadying her with a hand under her elbow.

Wanting to wipe away Ruis's blood with a gentle touch and knowing she couldn't, Ailim shook her head. "No." She raised her chin and stepped away from Tinne. Now Ruis was scowling, his stare fixed on Tinne's hand.

"No," she said again, louder. "It is the flouting of the Law that I find distressing." She set her teeth, forcing herself to think beyond Ruis. He was going to be banished, not executed, but Ailim felt loss at the thought that she would never see him again. "Guards, accompany GentleSir Elder"—that brought a flashing smile from Ruis—"to Northgate. Master Herald, I expect you to check with the Northgate sentinel regarding the health of Elder and report back. Viz a full explanation of this incident to my collection box in the morning, understood?"

The Herald bobbed his head. "Indeed, Your Honor." He began talking again, reinforcing her orders.

Ignoring the other men, Ruis bowed, then lifted his manacled hands and blew her a kiss, followed by a wicked smile. Ailim blinked as warmth fluttered in her.

The guards sidled closer to him and muttered grumpily. Ruis pivoted and started down the hallway. Ailim released a long breath and turned in the opposite direction, walking down the hall back to the FirstFamilies Council and toward her own fate.

"You have a nice 'command presence,' Your Honor. I'm impressed," Tinne Holly said.

Though she trembled inside with the anticipation of her own judgment, Ailim kept her face serene, slipping her hands in her wide sleeves. "Thank you."

She thought again of the small bond that had spun between Ruis and herself. He'd been facing a death sentence, she the death of the Family line which had been entrusted to her care.

Who would she be if she failed her destiny and didn't obtain this loan? What if the Residence and estate were sold? Could she keep the Family together?

Her burdens and the long, hard road ahead made her shudder. Ruis had been banished. Ailim fought a twinge of envy. Ruis left the Council, and old Druida, free to explore and build his own future, with no duties or ties to the past, or the Council.

She wanted to see him again, to make sure he was all right. She wanted to experience being completely at peace and using her five physical senses. And she pondered what she might do to help him.

Now that Ruis was gone the hum of magical-machines and the inner tingle of deeply embedded spells welled to fill the vacuum his nullness had caused.

Thoughts and emotions crashed over her. She stumbled and would've fallen if Tinne Holly hadn't caught and steadied her. "Easy," he said with a charming smile.

Instinctive shields clapped around her mind, cocooning her inner self against the onslaught of telepathic noise. She erected powerful, conscious mindshields of her own until she could selectively practice her Flair.

She tried a smile. "My thanks." Then she freed herself from his light grasp, and for once ignoring who might see her nervousness, pulled her handkerchief from her sleeve and patted at her face. Squaring her shoulders and lifting her chin, she reminded herself that she was a Judge with six years of experience, that she was a FirstFamily Head, a GrandLady, D'SilverFir.

She mastered her anxiety and entered the Council-Chamber with a measured, serene step. Tinne escorted her to a chair facing the FirstFamilies Council. She arranged her gown in perfect folds, as she had so often arranged her judicial robes, and sat down. Tinne left the room.

It had been a long time since she'd visited this room as a very young woman. The marble walls with faint veins of rose and gold still gleamed. The council table was as massive as she remembered. Even the plump red cushions under her gave little ease as she anticipated the next septhour.

When she looked at the Council, several people were blotting perspiration from their skin and drinking water. All twenty-three of the House heads were there except T'Blackthorn. Instead of his spouse, T'Holly sat with his Heir, Holm.

Most of the faces were familiar from GreatRituals she'd attended in her youth, before she'd started her rounds outside Druida as a circuit judge. Ailim felt their thoughts as a heavy pressure like lowering storm clouds. The sensation wasn't as pleasant as the blessed quiet she'd experienced with Ruis Elder in the hallway, but something routine that she could dismiss. She could only discern thoughts from the new D'Ash who manifestly hadn't learned to completely conceal them.

D'Ash's thoughts were amusing. She worried about Ruis, not happy with his banishment and planning how to smuggle a rare cat Fam companion to him. Her strategy was amazing, particularly since she intended to circumvent her husband.

Bucus T'Elder, Captain of the Council, scowled at Ailim. He had insisted on the latest Family spreadsheets so he could study them before the Council meeting. Since Ailim hadn't been officially confirmed as D'SilverFir and accepted into the FirstFamilies Council, she could only respond to questions.

She received telepathic curses from him, due to the way the last decision had gone. He shredded some papyrus in front of him. Lust for Ruis's death flared around Bucus's mindshield.

Ailim shivered.

Bucus banged his gavel. "As Captain of this Council, I call the final item on our agenda; the request by Grand-House D'SilverFir for a loan from the Noble Treasury in the amount of 1,500,000 gilt, to be repaid over three generations." He stared at Ailim. "This is the first time since the colonists landed that a FirstFamily has asked for a loan from this Council."

Ailim flinched. All the other FirstFamilies who sat on the dais had prospered more than SilverFir. They were powerful in Flair and in wealth. SilverFir had already failed in their eyes.

Bucus droned on, listing SilverFir's debts, enough to sober her abruptly. As the itemization went on and on, people's faces clouded or went carefully blank. Ailim forced her hands to stay still, her teeth from worrying her lower lip. She fought a war against nerves. How could she bear to lose her Residence, the home she loved so much?

She sat stiffly; she must bear it. Better the loss of the Residence and ancestral estate than the fragmentation of the GrandHouse Family itself. Family was everything. She could hear echoes of her Mothersire's lectures about protecting the Family, keeping it safe. She could not fail her forebears, the relatives who supported her and worked as hard as she did, or herself.

Danith D'Ash focused her attention on Ailim and she tensed. How would this commoner newly elevated to the highest level of the nobility feel about loaning a poorly managed GrandHouse an outrageous sum of gilt? Suspicious? Contemptuous?

Compassionate. Danith D'Ash's warm hazel eyes met Ailim's. D'Ash, and her HeartMate, T'Ash, knew what it was to be needy.

D'Ash's mind became the cadence of calculation. *She needs a cat,* D'Ash thought.

Ailim hoped horror didn't show on her face. A cat! She didn't like cats.

*A Fam to be loving and supportive. T'Ash says her Family is nasty to her. Yes, a cat.* D'Ash stared at Ailim. *Which one should I give her?*

The woman's thoughts neared decision. Ailim had no choice, she had to do some telepathic nudging. *No cat,* her mind faintly whispered to D'Ash.

D'Ash showed no reaction. Ailim suspected she wasn't used to telepathy with anyone other than her HeartMate.

Ailim sent the insinuation a little harder. *No cat.*

D'Ash blinked. Blinked again. Her husband stirred beside her and grasped her hand. The sensual images flowing between the two made Ailim quickly withdraw from any touch of D'Ash's mind.

During the next septhour, one noble after another questioned Ailim, and in each question Ailim sensed doubt and wariness. Men frowned at her from under heavy brows, or thinned their lips. Women narrowed their eyes and made notes.

She could smell the faint tang of her own perspiration and wished she'd put a stronger cleansing spell on her robe. Time and again she forced her weary mind and dull tongue to answer a pointed remark.

It was as fine an interrogation as she'd ever seen, but never before received. She hoped that she answered all their questions with dignity, but felt wrung out when it ended, wiping the dampness from her palms on the softleaves hidden in her sleeves.

The emotions of the people seated on the dais lapped to her in waves of concern, unhappiness, refusal. Fingers tapped on the ledgersheets before them, mutters rose to the high ceiling.

She braced herself.

"I think we should grant the loan," D'Ash said, smoothing the account papyrus on the table before her.

Surprise filled the room. A couple of GreatLords started.

D'Ash continued. "As a former accountant, I believe GrandHouse D'SilverFir has much to offer, both in culture, services, and its members." She smiled at an amazed Ailim. "Further, I believe the Family has contributed much to Celta in the past." D'Ash looked at T'Holly.

"True," T'Holly said.

D'Ash nodded. "And Ailim D'SilverFir, here, previously donated her services as a traveling Judge to the people of Celta. I imagine the only reason she's asking for a salary now is because her household is in dire financial circumstances."

Heat rose to Ailim's face at the common speaking. "Yes."

D'Ash smiled again. "And it wasn't this D'SilverFir head that mismanaged the property. When one reviews the finances from the point this GrandLady took charge, one sees that she's balanced her budget and seriously slowed the debt increase."

"It's still a debt increase," T'Reed grumbled, stabbing at the papyrus. Financial genius was the Flair of the T'Reeds.

D'Ash raised her eyebrows. "True, but that's where we can help. If we appoint a good financier to overlook and

manage the GrandHouse D'SilverFir assets—perhaps one
of your Family, T'Reed—he or she could not only save the
Residence, but repay the loan quicker and ensure the
GrandHouse never suffers again."

Ailim stared at D'Ash. Ailim would have wagered the
woman had nothing more on her mind during the meeting
than the Null, cats, and T'Ash.

Old GreatLady D'Vine spoke in a wispy voice that yet
resonated in the large room. "The omens are propitious for
this loan. Giving it sets a precedent, but to let a Grand-
House suffer and perhaps fail due to lack of support from
the other FirstFamilies cannot be considered. What would
the rest of Celta think, the other noble GrandHouses,
GraceHouses, and the Commoners? Who knows when we
might need the succor of others?"

"I agree. Give GrandHouse D'SilverFir the loan," T'Ash
said. He looked at T'Holly, who consulted with his Heir,
both silver-blond male heads together. They straightened.
Holm Holly shot a glance at Ailim and winked.

She smiled. She had a soft spot for the Hollys; most
women did.

"I agree," T'Holly said.

Ailim's pulse picked up pace. Had they won? Would they
keep the Residence? Oh, the Family would hate a supercil-
ious Reed managing the gilt. But better a Reed than she.

She stopped herself from wetting her lips before she
spoke. "If the FirstFamilies Council is so gracious as to
grant the loan, D'SilverFir would be honored to have a
canny Reed adviser. He or she would be welcome to live
in D'SilverFir Residence and carry out his or her duties."
Ailim tried to sweeten the pot as much as possible.
"D'SilverFir has several marriageable members."

D'Ash's eyebrows dipped. "I believe in HeartMate mar-
riages, not alliances."

"Me, too," T'Ash said, twining his fingers in his Lady's.
T'Reed rolled his eyes.

"Let's loan the money with the proviso that a Reed administer the D'SilverFir finances," T'Holly said.

Captain Bucus T'Elder's heavy jowls quivered. Ailim
saw calculation in his eyes, felt a wave of greed from the
man. "This is too easy for D'SilverFir," Bucus said.

Ailim stared at him, barely keeping her mouth from falling open. Easy? All the mental battering she'd taken, all the talking and arguing? Showing up here and begging? Easy?

"We can't let anyone think that one merely requests"— Bucus snapped his thick fingers—"and gilt falls into their laps." His eyes narrowed. "Let's grant the loan and provide a T'Reed adviser." A sly smile lit his lips. "T'Reed, I think your grandson, my own g'nephew Donax Reed, would be appropriate."

Ailim knew then that Bucus T'Elder could control Donax Reed.

Bucus continued, "Let's also stipulate that the First-Families Council will review the matter in six months and must be satisfied with the performance of GrandHouse D'SilverFir. Should we not be satisfied, the D'SilverFir Residence and Estate will be forfeited."

Her heart thumped hard. The Family living in the Residence would be livid. Somehow she'd have to keep them all in line.

"The determining vote in six months will be by simple majority, not unanimous," T'Holly inserted.

A few more comments were made, with people leaning out over the table to catch the eyes of others, gesturing for punctuation. T'Holly's proposal was adopted and the matter—her future, the future of her Family and her Residence—was put to the vote.

She could not vote as D'SilverFir, and T'Blackthorn was absent. The loan was approved by eighteen to five. Ailim noted the five who voted against her, who would need to be considered in her every decision, who might have to be wooed into alliance.

Relief surged through her, leaving her weak. She leaned back in her chair. Inside her wide sleeves, she clenched her hands together to keep her composure. Ailim bowed her head in gratitude, but still felt as if she walked a tightrope. "D'SilverFir thanks you," she whispered.

"Humph," T'Reed, the financier, said.

The weight of T'Reed's measuring gaze bore on her and she looked up. He tapped a writestick on the desk before him. "Captain Bucus T'Elder prefers my grandson, my

Heir's SecondSon, Donax." T'Reed shrugged. "Donax is solid, but will take reasonable risks. He'll do."

"I'm sure," she murmured. Was Donax the short, stout one? How unfair to assess a man by his appearance, something she wouldn't dream of doing as a judge. But it seemed that appearance counted in her personal life. Her heart sank as she thought that from now on, every man she met would be compared to the bold, angry, but altogether attractive Ruis Elder.

She felt a penetrating stare from D'Ash. Ailim's heart jumped when she realized she'd let her mind wander at exactly the wrong time.

A dog, D'Ash was thinking. Yes, perfect. She needs an unconditionally loving Fam. A puppy.

Ailim restrained a whimper.

She got a loan.

She also got a puppy.

What would she do with a dog?

# Three

❤

$R$uis braced his shoulders against the city wall and let his head fall forward, surrendering to shuddering breaths that jerked through his body. The solid wall of the Guardtower just outside Northgate steadied him.

Only after the verdict had he realized the amount of adrenaline pumping through his body. His dry mouth, his damp shirt, his nerves shrieking for him to fight or run, then the abrupt light-headedness and euphoria—all belied his calmness.

He just hoped he'd managed to maintain his image in front of the FirstFamilies Council, so none of them guessed how frightened he'd been. He hadn't realized how scared he'd been, how terrible it was hearing people vote "Death" until it was over. Or how much he valued life. That last little sight of D'SilverFir had made life even sweeter, though it had rubbed his pride.

He'd even been wryly glad for the chains during the ceremonial parade from Druida and the reading of the Roll of Banishment. Heavy manacles around his wrists stopped his hands from shaking, the chains on his ankles checked his stride so he had to shuffle, and any staggering would be thought of as usual, not the reaction of a man flooded with relief. Even the beating from the guards had been welcome. He was used to blows and to using pain to focus his mind. It had cleared his head.

Now he waited for D'Ash, as she had requested in her note,

which D'Vine had slipped in his pocket. Ruis strove to gather his thoughts as his pulse steadied, his heart no longer racing as if it would burst from his chest.

He savored the myriad smells of the land outside the city, heavy with verdant growth dying in the autumn. The ground gently sloped down and was cleared of everything but fields fading from a brilliant green to green edged with brown.

With a new appreciation for life, his gaze scanned the undergrowth, bushes, and trees that marched across the land, blocking the sight of the Great Platte Ocean in the distance. Yet the scent of the sea drifted to him along with the fragrance of turning leaves.

He thanked the Lord and Lady that he lived. And he enjoyed every sensation—the green and purple and brown of the landscape before him, the distant sound of birds and other winged creatures, the touch of a freshening breeze drying the sweat from his skin, as well as the hum of the city that vibrated through the stone wall behind him. The wall that still carried the heat of the fall day.

The metallic tang of fear had faded. Now, life tasted sweet.

Almost, the challenge of Celta beyond the walls of the city tempted him to put the past behind him and stride into the wilderness to prove himself, as had many other Celtan men and women who had forsaken the cities.

But he was used to proving himself another way—pitting himself against the complexities of ancient technology and restoring machines that others feared, or despised, or ignored. When he restored a machine and it functioned, the pleasure at mastering a skill washed through him. He'd accomplished something no one else on Celta had—made an ancient tool operate. He proved to himself that his life was valuable.

He'd taught himself words of the antique language and translated old texts word by impossible word. Saving the past was his life's work, his passion. He wouldn't let the ruling of the nobles rip that from him.

Once again his gaze lingered on the natural beauty of this world. He dragged in another hearty breath, and shivered as if shaking the city off himself, finding himself liking the cool evening air. It seemed like freedom.

But it only seemed. Because wherever he would roam, he would take his Nullness with him. In dealing with anyone on

Celta, whether in Druida or the other cities and towns, or outside them, he would face the same fear and abhorrence.

In those last days of freedom, before his capture, when he'd given the slightest vent to the reckless anger, he'd taken chances a reasonable man would have avoided. Now he was banished.

He would master his anger.

The contemptuous and arrogant nobles weren't getting rid of him so easily. His life, his work and passion were in Druida City.

He would stay.

And Ailim D'SilverFir was in the city. Temptation to spend more time with her, the one person who didn't care how he affected her, drew him.

He would see her again.

To kill him, the nobles would have to catch him. He knew the perfect place to hide, and it was in plain sight in Druida. He just had to ignore the superstitious stories about the place.

There was a sleepy and careless guard at Eastgate. Ruis would return to the city by that route.

But now he felt scoured of extreme emotions, only able to enjoy each moment and breath.

His shoulder itched and he rubbed it against the rough stone wall, ruining the silkeen. He didn't care. He couldn't risk wearing a bright red shirt in Druida after being banished.

The note D'Vine had passed him was from D'Ash, asking him to meet her here one septhour after twinmoons' rise. His smile turned amused thinking of D'Vine and D'Ash conspiring to help him. Gentle ladies both.

As was D'SilverFir. Her image rose to his mind, sympathetic smoky blue eyes, piquant heart-shaped face, and fine blond hair. It would be wiser to imagine her in judge's robes, on the bench, a symbol of authority. Or to visualize her sitting at that FirstFamilies Council table, one of the nobles he'd always thought rapacious and dishonorable.

Staying in Druida and courting execution wasn't wise. But he'd decided not to be wise. Why not see the lady again, too?

"Ruis Elder?" D'Ash's soft voice called.

"Here," Ruis answered, fingering her note in his trous pocket. His eyes found her, passing through Northgate several meters away.

Behind her deep brown cowled caped figure followed another caped female. A flash of torchlight flickered on blond hair and a heart-shaped face—D'SilverFir. She walked slower, clearly not in D'Ash's company.

As D'Ash strode to Ruis, she didn't seem to be aware of D'SilverFir behind her. Since D'SilverFir didn't catch up with the other woman, Ruis could only believe Ailim had some private motive of her own for seeing him. His heartbeat quickened.

GreatLady D'Ash walked toward Ruis, carrying a huge calico cat. She looked fully recovered from the stress of his Nullness during the trial.

She met him with a smile. "Merry meet," she said. "Here." She gave him the animal. "She's yours."

D'SilverFir stopped some paces away and slipped into the shadows of the gate tower's walls.

Ruis opened his mouth to swear at the weight of the animal, but stopped as he met the eyes of the cat. They glowed like green jade. A ruffled purring rose to his ears and vibrated into his arms, a soft, mellow sound he'd never heard closely.

"Her name's Samba," D'Ash said. "She's a Familiar, bred of Zanth, T'Ash's Fam."

He grit his teeth. He wanted to give the cat back, but made no move to do so. Why was he having such a difficult time returning the animal? "I'm a Null. I can't hear telepathic communication from a Fam."

D'Ash raised her eyebrows in reproof and tickled the furred, round cat-stomach bulging between his arms. "She's lazy. She doesn't use telepathy, she talks instead."

Samba looked up at him and made a chirruping sound that he knew was agreement. He blinked.

"You'll soon understand her." D'Ash sniffed. "She's fat, but part of that is because she chose to be spayed. She didn't want kittens. She's also very curious and loves adventure. She'll make a good companion for you."

Samba's purring increased, then broke for a moment as her ears rotated. She strung a few syllables together in mews and rumbles that Ruis could have sworn meant *Fun! Adventure. Let's go play.* He stiffened in astonishment.

D'Ash smiled. "You see what I mean? She talks."

"I don't need a cat." But he didn't release Samba.

"Rrrfff." The muttering sounded piqued. *I am not Cat. I am FAM*.

D'Ash chuckled, then stroked the top of Samba's head.

"Hhhmph, rrrff, phsppth!" *Not your Family anymore. Finally I get the most attention. HIS. My FamMan. Take your hand away.*

D'Ash jerked her hand back. Ruis felt dazed that he understood the cat by the angle of her ears, the position of her body, her wordlike mews.

"You've won her already." D'Ash looked him up and down. "Handsome and a man of good character."

He laughed shortly. "There are few who believe so."

She sighed. "You've too much anger. Master it"—she smiled ruefully—"just as my T'Ash mastered his feral nature."

"Easier said than done." But as he stroked the cat—his Fam, he thought with wonder—he felt more peaceful than he'd been for a long time.

D'Ash glanced around and reached through the slit in her tunic to her wide-trous pocket and pulled out a fat wallet. "Here." She slipped it into his trous pocket.

He looked at her warily. "What is it?"

"Gilt."

The pouch weighed heavy. "So much?"

"Twelve thousand."

Shocked, he jerked. Samba jumped down and sat at his feet, curling her tail around her paws. He felt her warmth through his boot. He had someone on his side now. And twelve thousand gilt!

"I've never had that much gilt in my life." The words sped from him before he could stop them.

D'Ash stared. "It's a month of my noblegilt for being D'Ash. You're a FirstFamily FirstSon, you should've received noblegilt every month as a child—"

"I didn't."

D'Ash frowned.

Screeching broke the night silence. Samba arched her back and hissed.

A huge, battered tomcat jumped into the twinmoonslight. Ruis had tangled with Zanth, T'Ash's Fam, before.

Samba hissed again and took a stance before Ruis.

Zanth growled.

"T'Ash comes," D'Ash said. She stood tiptoe and brushed a
kiss on Ruis's cheek. "Go with the Lady and Lord. Start anew
in another place. Blessings upon you."

Samba jumped Zanth, her sire, and the cats rolled in a whirling, spitting ball.

"Zanth, come!" D'Ash ordered as she ran toward the city
gate. "If you don't come with me, right now, you'll eat no
cocoa mousse for an eightday."

Zanth hopped away from Samba, curled a lip and sneered at
her, then snarled at Ruis and spit on his boots.

Samba growled back and lifted a clawed paw.

Zanth disappeared.

Samba grumbled cat noises. *I showed him.* She glanced up
at Ruis, and a pink tongue came out and swiped blood from
her whiskers. Her smile held glee, undimmed by the red scratch
on her nose. Her gaze glittered with excitement, and she uttered
a string of murmurings Ruis had already learned. *Let's go play!*

"Not yet." Would D'SilverFir approach? To his surprise, his
spirits had lifted.

A moment later D'SilverFir stepped from the shadows of the
gate tower. The air seemed to shimmer around her, brightening
the stars in the sky as she moved toward him with inherent
grace and elegance.

She pushed the cowl back off her head with a fine-boned
hand and her serious blue-gray gaze met his. A touch of his
previous euphoria returned. She'd come to see him.

Samba moved closer to Ruis, setting a portion of her considerable rump on his boot-toe.

D'SilverFir stopped a meter from them. "Merry meet, Ruis
Elder," she murmured, "Greetyou, Fam."

Samba lifted her nose. *I am Ssssamba.*

D'SilverFir's brows lowered as she tried to decipher the cat's
words. "Samba." The GrandLady dipped her head politely.

Samba twitched her whiskers in regal response.

D'SilverFir studied the cat, and amusement flashed across
her face. "I'm glad D'Ash gave you the Fam," she said to Ruis.

Now he bent his head in courtesy. "Me, too." His sense of
drama and contrariness welled up. "Didn't you mean to address
me as Ruis, calling himself 'Elder'?"

A flush pinkened her cheeks. She stood straighter. "I reviewed your case, the Herald's report, and read the notes

T'Reed took of your trial—he has a famous memory."

"And you judged me guilty."

"No, no—" She stepped forward and placed a hand on his arm, then swayed.

Ruis grasped her shoulders, but to his amazement she leaned inward, against him. "D'SilverFir?"

She mumbled something against his chest.

"D'SilverFir?" he asked again.

She looked up at him with wide eyes and trembling mouth. "This effect— this thing—"

"My Nullness," he said harshly, tightening his grip around her shoulders to set her aside.

She clutched the wide lapels of his shirt, then shivered. "No. Don't. It's strange but comforting. Wonderful."

"My Nullness is wonderful?" he stated, expressionless, fearing to believe she meant her words.

"One moment." She sucked in a breath, then took a small step away from him.

He'd been stationary for several minutes, so his Nullness would be spreading out from him, affecting about a meter radius. She was within range, yet showed no signs of strain. Amazing.

"The effects of your Nullness are interesting," she said.

He crossed his arms. "And terrible."

"No."

"As I am terrible."

"No," she said.

He raised his brows. "So you didn't judge me guilty?"

Her gaze searched his face. "Did you steal?"

"To survive. Always to survive."

Though her features froze into a sterner aspect, an aspect natural to a judge, her voice was soft. "I understand."

"No, you don't." He uncrossed his arms and stared down at her. "You can't possibly understand my life. You're D'SilverFir, chosen to be the head of your Family when a baby. That means you have exceptional Flair—because that's how heirs are designated. So you're very powerful."

An unamused smile twitched on and off her lips. "In Flair, yes. Nothing else. I've always known my duties and responsibilities to my Family as D'SilverFir must come first."

"What kind of Flair do you have?"

"Telempathy."

"I understand," he replied, using her own phrase. He could no more understand her Flair—feeling the emotions and thoughts of others—than she could understand his life without it.

Her eyes met his and he thought of mist, and the loneliness of being lost in it.

"Intellectually," she said, "I know being a Null molded you, how it defined your life, the hardships you must have faced."

He shrugged, but was impressed she was still with him, and showed no indication of being disturbed by his Nullness.

She leaned in and sniffed at the skin exposed by the open collar of his shirt, shocking him. She stooped to pet Samba, and it seemed as if her nostrils widened again and she savored the feel of Samba's fur.

"Why did you come?" he asked. "To make sure your authority wasn't denied?" He touched his sore cheek. "To determine whether your orders were carried out and I was in sound health when the gates of Druida closed behind me?"

With one last pat on a purring Samba, Ailim stood. "I did care what happened to you," she said with simple dignity.

Ruis shook his head, winced.

She frowned and touched his swollen jaw. "Move your face into the light. I want to see how much you're hurt."

"Not much."

"It looks awful." She sounded angry. Odder and odder. He let her soft fingers turn his head. She inhaled sharply and whipped out a linen softleaf from one of her large sleeves. Just before she touched the corner of his mouth with it she seemed to see its crumpled state. She started to lower her hand, but Ruis had caught her scent and wanted nothing more than to have her palm on his face and the fragrance of her deep in his lungs. He stopped her hand and brought the softleaf to his mouth. His wits swam as her touch and scent dazzled him. How he yearned to kiss her fingertips—but didn't dare.

Ruis kept her hand against his jaw for a long moment before her fingers slipped free and left him holding the linen square.

"May I keep it?" His voice sounded husky, but he didn't care.

Her eyes widened, but she nodded. She didn't look like a stern judge now, but a vulnerable woman. A woman he ached to take into his arms, to learn, to cherish. Instead he tucked the softleaf into his pocket, more valuable to him as a gift than D'Ash's gilt.

Samba mewed. Ailim dropped her gaze and stooped to resume petting her.

"So you feared for my safety and came to see if I was healthy?"

She looked up at him, continuing to caress Samba who purred her approval. "I came to see if I could help. I'm a judge. Injustice bothers me."

"So the guards did me an injustice."

"Abusing a restrained person is not lawful."

"What of our so-noble FirstFamilies Council? Did they, too, do me an injustice? How could that be?" he mocked.

She stiffened her spine. "I can see how you might believe nobles are base and corrupt," she said carefully.

He pressed the idea. "And false to their stated ideals and vaunted self-proclaimed values of honor and respect for all." Ruis thumped his chest. "They didn't act with honor to me. And I can measure in my smallest fingernail the amount of respect I've received from anyone, especially nobles." His anger surged, lacing his words, pouring from him without his consent, but he couldn't stop it.

He despaired. This one woman had shown him more than kindness, and he would drive her away with his burning fury.

Samba growled.

D'SilverFir studied him, then she reached up and set her hand on his shoulder, as if testing him, or his Nullness, or the connection between them. "The nobles did not treat you right. Nor did your Family. You are the son of a former GreatLord, you could have been his Heir, a GreatLord yourself."

Ruis shook his head. "The Noble families prize Flair above all else. Of course I couldn't be named Heir." He was disappointed but unsurprised when she withdrew her hand from him.

"The Council didn't listen to you. You had no advocate. That was wrong."

"And who would be my advocate? You?"

She met his gaze. "Your trial is done. For the moment we will have to accept the ruling. In a while I can start a judicial review by a panel of judges. We wait for now."

"We?" He couldn't stop from goading her. Did she mean

them both, himself and the GrandLady? Together? He liked the thought of them working together, though he'd long ago abandoned the idea of fighting Bucus. The man was too powerful. And to try and fight the FirstFamilies Council itself . . . He found himself shaking his head.

"Don't look so doubtful. There are things that must be investigated, and I'll do it. I heard you tell D'Ash that you had never received noblegilt."

"True."

Samba stood and wound around his boots, grumbling low cat-sounds as if in sympathy. Ruis couldn't quite catch the meaning. From the way D'SilverFir tilted her head, she couldn't, either, but his Fam was comforting. Her complete support siphoned off his anger. He smiled down at his Fam. "There's my advocate," he said.

D'SilverFir looked at Ruis, her body relaxing a bit at the new lightness in his tone.

Perhaps he hadn't disgusted her or pushed her too far. She might accept him. He scrutinized her, her lovely features and innate grace. Lowering his voice, he asked, "Is injustice the only reason you came to see me off? Nothing more personal?" He wanted words of reassurance that she, too, felt the bond— no matter how fragile—that spun between them. Yet he held his breath, dreading the truth. She'd always tell the truth.

Again a flush blossomed on her cheeks. "I think you know that I find being in your company—pleasant."

"Pleasant?" He wanted more than that, wanted to hear again that his horrible Nullness was "wonderful."

Her shoulders shifted beneath her cape. "Restful."

He decided he'd settle for "restful." For now. He lifted her right hand from her side and pressed a kiss on her fingers with as much panache as Holm Holly could have shown her, and with far more emotion. He liked the feel of her smooth skin under his lips, the undertone of something rich in her natural scent. Reluctantly he let her hand go and swept her a bow. "Thank you. I appreciate whatever little you can do for me."

She wet her lips. Something tightened inside him.

"Do you go far from Druida City?" she asked.

He smiled with real amusement. If only she knew! But he dared tell no one. "Not far," he said softly.

She gave a short nod and swept an arm around them. "You

might go to Auray on the Bay of Fin, or Alfriston."

"I might go to Alfriston." It was a farm town no more than an hour by glider to the south.

At the thought of Auray's fish stink, his nose wrinkled. "I think Auray is too conservative for the likes of me." Ruis flicked his fingers at his full red silkeen shirtsleeves.

A gurgle of laughter flowed from her.

He inclined his head in polite farewell. "Thank you for your intervention with the guards and coming to see me off." Ruis glanced down at Samba, who had perked up. They started to walk around the walls to the Eastgate where they could slip back into the city unnoticed.

"Ruis Elder," D'SilverFir called.

He looked back at her and his heart clenched at the enchanting picture she presented, a small noblewoman of great gentleness, dignity, and beauty, her face and figure lit, then shadowed by flickering torches set in the city wall. The dark greenery of the Celtan landscape lay on one side of her, the bustling city to the other.

It was an image he'd always remember—of this woman, this night, this moment. The first moment of his new life.

"Merry meet," she said.

"And merry part."

"And merry meet again." Though spoken lowly it reached his ears. She drew her cape around her and walked to the city gate.

Before she vanished from his view, he turned and continued down the path circling the city walls. Mentally he charted a route to his new home, a place he could live forever inside the city of Druida and never be discovered, the perfect place to continue his work to save Earth technology. He didn't believe anymore in the tales of a curse. Ruis wished he'd thought of it sooner, but he'd been as blind as the rest of Druida.

Banished. If he were caught, he'd be executed. But he was sure he could cheat death for a long, long time. Life was going to be very exciting.

He looked down at Samba, whose jade eyes gleamed as she strolled with him, sniffing at the beltway around Druida. The walk to Eastgate would be long.

The Earth people had planned the city and walled a circular area, omitting the West wall where the sea and cliffs protected

Druida. He was going there, to the western edge of the city. The colonists had expected Druida to grow large based on cities they'd left behind. But such growth never came. Life was still a struggle on Celta due to low birth rates and failure to adapt.

Yes, Ruis knew the city. Banished or not, he'd still live within the walls.

Samba mewed. He looked down at her and smiled. She glided beside him, tail waving. Warmth unfurled in his heart. A companion, a Fam. Someone of his own, at last. "We're going to sneak back into Druida at Eastgate," he said.

Samba chirruped, *Fun!*

He took longer strides. "Let's go play."

*A*ilim *should have gone to bed. She was beyond exhausted.* But after speaking with Ruis Elder in the shadows of evening, she'd wanted to search her ResidenceLibrary. She needed the intricacies of inheritance spelled out in exact detail. To help Ruis, she needed all records of previous Nulls. And she needed every piece of information she could get on Ruis Elder himself.

The man had become a priority.

So she'd retired to her ResidenceDen. She hadn't shielded the door, a mistake she wouldn't make in the future.

She'd already broadcast the results of the council meeting to all branches of the Family, but those who lived on the estate—those who preferred to be supported—barged into the room, disrupting her peace. They didn't like the orders she'd left.

Now her relatives milled around the den, throwing off as much anger and demands in their auras as in their verbal comments. The light paneled walls and plaster-molded ceiling of the chamber closed in on her. The glowing yellow spell-lights wavered. Ailim banished the illusion. It wasn't the charming room that oppressed her, but the turbulence of her D'SilverFir relatives.

Ailim stood behind her desk, and wished the solid piece of redwood was even more massive to deflect the ill-will hurled at her. Her fingertips touched the satin wood edge and it steadied her. The desk had sat stolidly in this place for over five decades, and through the wood she sensed the durable bones of the Residence, and even beyond, to the island the Residence was built upon, the fertile planet of Celta itself.

She hadn't wanted this confrontation, but she'd handle it. She'd do her duty—save the estate and hold the Family together. "One at a time," she gritted. Her tiredness faded as the adrenaline of conflict shot through her system.

They ignored her, all speaking at once.

"You threw me out of my suite!" G'Uncle Ab thundered, waving his arms.

"You took my housekeeping nestegg!" Aunt Menzie shrilled.

"You stopped my Tranquil Treatments!" Second-cuz Canadena whined as she wiped tears away with a fine linen handkerchief.

"You stripped my rooms of all their comforts!" Portly Uncle Pinwyd blustered.

"You canceled my party!" Cuz Cona stamped her foot.

"We will not tolerate it!" Aunt Menzie's piercing tones rose above them all in finality. The others looked at her, then echoed the sentence. "We will not tolerate it!"

The cool tones of the Residence announced a visitor, one already cleared for admittance, and a request from Danith D'Ash to teleport to the entry hall. Distractedly, Ailim touched the blinking crystals and lowered the Residence shieldspells.

Her relatives' minds howled and hounded her even louder and stronger, including Uncle Pinwyd's, whose useless cheaptin antitelepathic crown sat tipsily on his head.

Ailim cupped her hands and clapped them, sending out a sphere of silence and raising a silver shield deflecting illwill between the line of her live-in relatives and her desk.

She refrained from rubbing her temples. "G'Uncle Ab, the suite you recently moved into should be assigned as a matter of Family honor to the Reed Financial Adviser, who will arrive soon. It's being furnished with items from the entire Residence, including those from your rooms, Uncle Pinwyd."

"Those music, holo, and scry systems are mine!" Pinwyd yowled. "You have no appreciation of the finer things of life, and had no right to take them." The bright yellow lapels of his silkeen shirt flapped as he shook with emotion.

Ailim tried a smile. It twitched on and off her face. "How clumsy of me. I thought they were purchased with GrandHouse D'SilverFir funds. I'm very sorry. Please give me your personal receipts and I will replace them."

There was a moment's silence as fulminating gazes passed back and forth.

Cona stepped forward, heels clicking from the pine floor to the rug, rudely breaking the deflection shield and slapping her hands down onto the desk. "You canceled my party! How can we keep our reputation if we don't entertain?"

"The only celebration that will be scheduled in the near future is the Loyalty Ritual, where you can all vow your allegiance to me. This is tentatively scheduled next week, on Mabon, the celebration of the Autumnal Equinox. If the Reed adviser agrees, perhaps we can have a small New Year's party at the beginning of Birch, two and a half months from now."

Cona squealed. She fisted her hand and pounded the table. "No! You have no right. I'm the most beautiful, the one who'll make the best marriage, I decide about the parties." She lifted her perfect nose, set in a perfect face, atop a perfect body.

"I am D'SilverFir," Ailim backed her quiet words with steely Flair, making them reverberate on both the physical and mental planes. Everyone faded away from her a step or two.

Ailim considered her cousin. "Ngetal T'Reed will be sending one of his Heir's-Sons to us. Perhaps you should speak to him about the cost of any entertaining in addition to the Loyalty Ritual." She studied Cona's expensive embroidered gown, fine cosmetics, and elaborately braided hair. "I am pleased that you wish to make a good impression upon him. An alliance with T'Reed would be very helpful for the Family."

Cona hissed. Her bright blue eyes darkened and she tossed her head. "I marry how I want, whom I want. A Reed—" She lifted a shoulder in dismissal.

Ailim merely smiled and turned her gaze to Aunt Menzie.

"A housekeeping nestegg? I'm not sure I understand what you mean."

Aunt Menzie drew herself up to her full height and glared down her aristocratic nose at Ailim. "You are impertinent to your elders. I had a cache in the kitchen . . ."

"Why would you need a cache? Is our Word no longer good at the merchants?"

Red slashes appeared over Menzie's elegant cheekbones. She walked, stiff robe rustling, to stand with her daughter, Cona. "You are letting a Reed run our finances," she accused.

Cona started talking at the same time. "A Reed, they're so ugly, not even their money can recommend them!"

"In my FatherDam's time we feuded with them." Menzie drew in a breath, and Ailim knew she was in for a long, piercing, mindshield-battering tirade.

"Ahem." A slight cough came from the open door. A man about Ailim's own age with the firm jaw and bluntly plain features of a Reed stood on the threshold. He looked stolid, but a flushed face accented his straw-colored hair and pale green eyes. Ailim felt sure he'd heard Cona's insult.

He gazed cautiously around, then squaring his blocklike shoulders, he strode into the room and bowed neatly. "GrandLady D'SilverFir, allow me to present myself. I'm Donax Reed. My FatherSire said my skills and Flair might be useful to you."

Very prettily said by a not very pretty man. Donax was more attractive than Ailim remembered. He was fitter, with no bulge around his middle. Yet he'd never be as appealing or tempting to her as the banished Ruis Elder who ghosted through her mind.

Ailim made introductions. The women dipped barely polite curtsies, G'Uncle Ab inclined his head, and Uncle Pinwyd stared at Donax with protuberant eyes.

Ailim said to Donax, "I've placed all the ledgers in your room. The ResidenceLibrary has now memorized your voice, and will give you our financial information for the last three decades. If you've any other requests, please see me. I consider you a member of the Family during your stay, GreatSir."

Her relatives mumbled imprecations under their breath and shot vitriolic glances at the young man.

"Merry meet!" caroled a voice.

They all turned. GreatLady Danith D'Ash smiled in the doorway. She was dressed in a blue commoncloth trous suit and held a tiny golden pup with curly hair.

Ailim suppressed her shock at the sight of Danith carrying the puppy. The GreatLady worked fast.

Danith's smile spread into a grin. "I brought you a gift; her name is Primrose." Danith traipsed into the room, ignoring the others with a lack of self-consciousness Ailim envied.

"You are a friend of my niece?" Menzie's voice held brittle coldness at the sight of the young woman in middle-class clothing. Cona sniffed.

Danith stopped. When her stare met Menzie's, it was even more freezing. "I'm Danith D'Ash. You are?"

Menzie goggled at her title. Cona gave an unbeautiful squeak.

Turning back to Ailim, Danith smiled again.

It was as if the GreatLady had completely dismissed the tense, nasty emotions in the room as of no more importance than the people. An interesting trick. Ailim noted the woman's attitude and deportment as one Ailim could model in the future.

The puppy wriggled in Danith's hands, and Ailim knew they both were very aware of the strained atmosphere.

"A Family meeting, D'SilverFir? I'm sorry I interrupted, but the door was open. Here." Danith set the puppy in the crook of Ailim's left arm. Primrose's tiny tongue darted out to dab at Ailim's face. Ailim shut her eyes and hung on to her composure.

When she opened her lashes, it was to see silky puppy ears and big, brown, liquid eyes. *Me love You. Yes. Only You*, the puppy murmured in her mind.

"I—" Ailim started.

"Good, you've bonded. Primrose's a teacup poodle. You'll find her a very loving Fam Companion. She's eight weeks old and only needs to be fed four times a day. I've sent a light-globe with other information. Please scry with any questions."

"A puppy! From D'Ash!" squealed Cona, all her surface charm back in place for this important Lady. "The most prized gift one can have this season. Why, Earthpets are so scarce, particularly dogs. We're so honored." She clapped, then clasped her hands, sending D'Ash a melting look. "Could I dare ask—"

Cuz Canadena whiffled and snuffled.

"The beast irritates Canadena's allergies. Ailim can't keep it," Menzie said with satisfaction.

Primrose made a little growling noise. Ailim sensed her simple thoughts. The puppy wanted desperately to run around the room. The puppy needed desperately to gnaw at something smelly and tasty. Primrose eyed Uncle Pinwyd's natty shoes.

"Aunt Menzie," Ailim said, "you know we're not a Family prone to allergies. Canadena is just upset, not suffering sinus problems. Perhaps she should receive a Fam, too. It would give her something to focus her attention on outside of herself."

Danith looked at Ailim with raised brows.

Ailim nodded.

Moving to Canadena, Danith took her hands and stared into Canadena's sad slate-blue eyes. Canadena's lips trembled. "D'SilverFir canceled my Tranquility Treatments." Her heartbroken whisper lilted through the room. She sniffed.

"I'll send you a kitten. It will soothe you and be Primrose's playmate," Danith said. "They're at an age to accept each other."

"A kitten!" Canadena gasped.

Danith dropped Canadena's hands, turned to Ailim, and inclined her head, one FirstFamily Lady to another, then left.

Danith made dealing with hostile people look easy. Of course, they weren't her relatives. Still, the GreatLady's secure self-confidence was something Ailim vowed to learn.

*Want down. Down! DOWN!* Primrose insisted.

In a moment. Ailim cuddled her new Fam closer.

"A kitten." Cuz Canadena drifted out the door.

"Cona, please show GreatSir Reed to his new suite in the northwest round tower," Ailim said.

Cona glared at her. "You've not heard the last of this." Cona pasted a smile on her face and simpered at Donax. He looked stunned at her liveliness.

Ailim sighed.

Primrose licked Ailim's chin. *Down!*

Ailim placed the small energetic bundle of fur on the area rug. The puppy took off at a run. Cona sent it a repugnant glance and hastily moved away, her hand on Donax's arm.

"Awful thing!" Backbone stiff, Aunt Menzie marched away, trailing the men in her wake.

Primrose nipped at their heels, and they sped their retreat. The door slammed behind them.

Primrose sat on the floor facing Ailim, tongue lolling. *Love You.* The puppy's eyes filled with adoration. She puddled on the pine floor.

Ailim collapsed into her chair.

*B*efore *Ruis reached Eastgate, he took off his red silkeen* shirt and dragged it through dirt until no bright color showed.

He opened the arched door in the guard tower wall and ducked into the small building, crouching under the sill of the large window of the guardroom to his left. Due to his Nullness the spell-light wavered. The guard's snores hesitated. Ruis hurried through the tower to the door opening into the city. He sighed with relief as soon as he shut the portal silently behind him.

Druida had quieted into night's slower pace, but Ruis kept to the shadows. A fine tension imbued him, sharpening all his senses. Whispering, he sent Samba ahead to scout for any danger. Stealthily he followed.

A septhour later he walked into the large dim park at the southwest part of Druida. This was the last area before the cliffs. Leaving the nightpoles that framed the park on the city street behind him, he glided through tall trees, avoiding the crisp leaves underfoot. He strode past the Summer Pavilion. Samba bounded beside him.

Then he stopped and looked up and up and up at his new home.

It loomed above him, dark and massive, blotting out the starbright sky and even the radiant twinmoons' light. It blocked the horizon on both sides.

The only whole spaceship left. *Nuada's Sword.*

# *Four*

$T$he ship filled Ruis's vision.

Stretching six kilometers in length, two in width, and twenty-five stories high, it was too huge for the FirstFamilies to protect with shieldspells. By law no destruction or pilfering was allowed, and none had taken place.

Celtans were superstitious about the ship. The technology that had brought the colonists had long been superseded by the combination of psi power/technology developed by the Celtans. Preferred by the Celtans. Now the old mechanical and nano-electron engineering systems were almost lost. The texts Ruis had managed to glean from T'Elder ResidenceLibrary and the public GreatLibrary were nearly impossible for him to understand.

Deep silence pervaded the night. No noise drifted from the city beyond Landing Park. Between midnight and dawn, nothing stirred here, except Samba.

She danced around his feet, traveled the few meters to the spaceship in leaps, and sniffed along a portion of its length, paying attention to the outline of the hatch.

A few rooms of the ship were open near the main landing ramp three kilometers away, but fewer and fewer Celtans visited the museum each year. The metal spaceship seemed alien to the descendants of the colonists, sterile when compared with the verdant Celta, claustrophobic to a people who still had most of a world to explore and tame. The chambers contained strange machines that didn't work with the common spellwords.

Lights flickered inside and out in strange patterns. There were rumors that if a Celtan stayed in the ship for more than a few hours, he or she would go insane. School groups hurried in and out of the museum rooms through the main landing portal.

Ruis had chosen his route and this door as the most inconspicuous.

*Here? Our new home?* Samba's sounds rang like words. Ruis marveled again that he could understand her perfectly.

"Yes." *Nuada's Sword* was still inside Druida. If he was found on her, he'd be executed. Yet everyone believed he'd left the city. A slow smile filled his face as he considered the nobles' shortsightedness. They didn't take care of the starship, thought of it as a lump on the horizon. But for Ruis, it was perfect. He would do what no one else on Celta had done—he'd attempt to restore the colonists' most important machine.

His new home.

His new life.

It must be better than the old. He'd work on the ship, master its systems. Even more important, he'd master his own anger. Most important of all, with care, he'd be able to see Ailim D'SilverFir again.

Going to the hatch, he watched as a tiny green light flickered, then shone steadily. He picked up Samba and positioned them both in front of a smooth, black glassy-looking plate, nothing like the faceted scrystones Celtans used at the entrances of their homes.

"Request permission to board the ship." He said the odd-sounding words. He'd constructed the phrase from several sources, and learned the strange pronunciation through trial and error from ancient audios. The sentence was referred to once as "Standard Portal Acceptance Command for Entry." A bright yellow light flashed from the plate and disappeared; clicks followed.

Samba pressed her nose to the plate and hummed.

"Feline. Some traces of sentience," a mellow voice intoned.

"Her name is Samba," Ruis said.

"Acknowledged. Status?" asked *Nuada's Sword*.

"She is a crew member." Ruis held his breath, hoping his

poring over tomes of archaic information would pay off.

The plate hummed. "An overabundance of rodents in the Greensward has been verified. Samba accepted provisionally, upon determination of the human male status."

"Yesssssss," said Samba.

Ruis shifted his grip. Samba's fur felt slick under his sweating palms. His heart thudded with anxious anticipation.

The ship rumbled, the light flickered from the plate and over him once more. "Human male primarily of the genetic code of Elder and Oak, with traces of the Houses of Comfrey, Rose . . ."

Ruis's mouth fell open; even he didn't know that.

". . . some slight mutation as expected over time. Status?"

Ruis gulped. "Of Command Officer rank."

Dead silence. Ruis stood, every muscle tense.

Samba rubbed her head against the underside of his chin and began a quiet, soothing, rumble-purr.

"It is noted that Our last Captain was an Elder. However, in accordance with Our programming, a sufficient time has elapsed that a new Captain may also be appointed from the genetic code Elder. Acknowledged and accepted. Welcome aboard, Captain."

Captain? Ruis stood, stunned, as a square silver door rose upward with a quiet *whoosh* and a ramp angled out and down to his feet. He'd had no notion he could be named Captain, still the highest rank in all of Celta. The highest rank ever held by any ancestor. Captain.

*Let's go play.* Samba wriggled in his arms.

He'd wanted to be of a Command Officer rank to access as much of the ship as he could. He'd thought he'd be a Lieutenant.

Ruis walked up the incline of the short ramp into a small spherical room. He looked around the tarnished metal interior as the ramp retracted and the door closed behind him. Then he followed the ship's directions to the omnivator and took the box to the Captain's Quarters. The metal wall beneath his fingers was warm to his touch. Too warm for regular metal, more as if it were truly alive. He curled his fingers and pulled them away.

Ruis squinted at the golden insignia on a gleaming wood door of the Captain's Quarters. "Too dim," he murmured.

The light brightened.

Ruis shivered. He'd just been reminded that the colonists had come from a yellow-sunned, dimmer world.

The quiet was incredible. No night noise. No wind. No insects. No animals.

No people.

His ears strained to hear sounds other than his own breathing and Samba's. Nothing. He squared his shoulders. This was what he wanted.

"Request entry," Ruis said.

*Let's go IN!* demanded Samba.

"Place your hand on the palmplate," the deep, reverberant Ship's voice said.

He put his hand against the slot.

"Align your eyes in relation to the retina scan," Ship said.

Ruis shifted and let a light sweep across his eyes.

"Captain Elder examined and data stored. Initiate Password Sequence of three words."

"Machine," Ruis said, thinking of the Earth Soil Analyzer that had started the whole thing. Machine was a word that defined the inner creativity that kept him sane, his quest to restore Earth technology.

Excitement made his voice higher than he liked, so he cleared his throat. "EarthSun," he said. That word symbolized his past—the anger that burned, the restless life he had to lead, his thievery to survive and elude Bucus.

Now he needed a third, something special and precious. Before he knew it, he'd said, "Ailim."

"Ailim," the Ship repeated, pronouncing it differently. "You mean the sixteenth letter of the Ogham alphabet?"

He meant the GrandLady who haunted him. The one he yearned to meet again. The only reason the origin of her name mattered was that it marked her as a GrandLady, a woman who should have been far beyond his reach. But Ruis began to believe that as Captain of *Nuada's Sword,* he might dare anything. "Yes."

Ruis and Samba stood before the doors to the Captain's Quarters. He traced the ancient Earth symbols: "Captain of *Nuada's Sword.*" From what he understood, the Captain had a suite with visual and audio access to the entire ship, a tradition the GreatLords had continued in their Residences.

"The chosen passwords of Captain Ruis Elder are: machine, EarthSun, and Ailim," the Ship intoned. "Accepted."

Samba yowled. *And Me!* She jumped to Ruis's shoulder and planted a paw on the palmplate, blinked as her eyes were scanned, and mewed the familiar *Let's go play!*

The plate closed. With a swish the door opened in the middle, sliding to each side.

*Home. How fun, a new place. We will play well here.* Samba set her claws into his shirt, pricking him, as he strode inside.

She jumped down and strolled through an entryway into a large room. The walls were blue-gray, austere and empty of ornament. The furniture was square and functional, built into the walls. The seat coverings and the cloth over what Ruis thought was the bed shimmered blue and silver. Wooden trim seemed the sole natural touch in the quarters.

Samba sniffed and Ruis noticed the faint metallic odor permeating the suite. She rubbed against the furniture to mark her scent.

"All automated systems are in need of priority lists. Does the Captain wish to review current shipboard specifications?" the ship asked.

A thrill ran through him at the title. He grinned. "Yes."

Huge three-dimensional holo diagrams appeared. "The Ship's outer hull. A crack in the northwest quadrant upon landing. The Ship's energy reserves: energy acceptable for planetside, our stellar-solar radiation collectors in our skincells are at sixty percent efficiency, additional catalysts to repair them are needed. Ship's weapons are depleted since rerouting to general maintenance. Ship's communication system: acceptable. General maintenance includes testing of all lights at intervals . . ."

Ruis swallowed and struggled to keep up with the information. He darted glances around, looking for papyrus and writestick to take notes, but saw nothing recognizable.

Finally the ship ended its report. "The personal DaggerShip is ready for spaceflight, as is a glider for land transport."

Ruis's jaw dropped. He had personal transportation other than his feet. He controlled the ship, its energy, its weapons. The idea sent tremors up his spine.

Better than anything, he had knowledge. With the things this ship could teach him, he could become as mighty as any GreatLord. Even more.

Power. Immense power, and all his. Energy. For anything he wanted to do.

He was the Captain of *Nuada's Sword.*

*A*ilim struggled to keep her eyes open as dawn lightened the windows of her den. She sipped caff and concentrated on the numbers of the ledgersheet on her desk. The numbers in all the tiny rows blurred except the huge, red negative total.

At least she had a new, substantial income to place in the "credit" column. Her judicial record had been reviewed and she'd been appointed the SupremeJudge of Druida. There were few telempathic judges, and she was the most powerfully Flaired.

She'd hoped for the post. But she had doubted the appointment. Before her mother's death, she would have been sure of her vocation and her world. But when she'd returned from her circuit rounds and discovered the Family's financial mess, she'd been shaken. The problems demanded desperate measures and her utmost of effort. She couldn't ignore the smallest detail or take the tiniest possibility of income for granted. She'd worried about whether she'd be named SupremeJudge.

Ailim gazed at the golden pine walls and their paintings. She lost herself in the still-lifes of D'SilverFir symbols, wandering through the fir grove to a meadow of cowslips. She imagined the warm texture of a glowing stone huddled with eggs in a nest—the magical Quirin. Just sitting in the ancestral chair caused her grief to surge.

When her Family problems crashed down and she'd realized she hadn't the time or the luxury to grieve, she'd gone to a MindHealer who'd distanced the emotional storms. Little by little the grief worked itself out of a huge tangled knot into the small, even threads of memory and life.

Ailim bent again to the figures, trying to make sense of them. She was expected at JudgmentGrove by Eighth Septhour chime as the new SupremeJudge. She'd already reviewed her cases. Those were understandable and interesting and resolvable. These numbers weren't. She couldn't do anything more to make them better. She gulped and put them in a drawer.

Unfolding a papyrus, she frowned at the sketchy information, every official record about Ruis Elder before his trial. There was no mention of him as a child or a young man; no birth data or the report of a Flaired oracle that attended every noble birth. Nothing showed the man he had become—the fascinating man that she'd been drawn to in the hallway of the Guildhall.

The new puppy-flap in the den door banged as Primrose hurled through to zoom under Ailim's desk and land panting on her feet. Then the door slammed open and Uncle Pinwyd stalked in. He scanned the room with an angry scowl then dumped an armful of shoes—a single shoe of ten pairs, on her desk.

"My ex-footwear wardrobe," he said through clenched teeth. "The puppy chewed everything. I demand redress!"

Red anger blasted from Pinwyd. Ailim rubbed her forehead. "I will obtain matching shoes for you." How and with what funds, she didn't know.

"NOW!" he shouted.

"I will take care of it promptly," she said.

"That miserable cur!" He kicked the desk, then swore.

*Bad man chases me!* Primrose shot from under Ailim's desk, zipping through Pinwyd's ankles.

He windmilled, then fell, yelling in fury.

Ailim clapped hands over her ears and shut her eyes, erecting her strongest barriers. As a greatly Flaired person she could, and did, teleport her Uncle to his room. She didn't care that most of her energy was drained. It was worth it to get him out of her presence. She massaged her aching temples.

The scent of dog pee permeated the air. *Uh-oh. Sorry. Accident,* whimpered Primrose from a corner.

Ailim wondered if the Chinju area rug was ruined. She bit her bottom lip and stared at the puppy. Big brown eyes peered at her from an adoring, furry face. *Accident. Yes. So sorry.*

Ailim's anger drained. She stood and walked over to the dog, then picked her up. "Don't do it again." She pointed the pup to a thick pile of papyrus. "There are newsheets in every room. Run there if you think you're going to have an accident."

Primrose hung her head, then peeked up from under heavy lashes. *Love You.*

Sighing, Ailim petted Primrose. Ailim couldn't do anything but return the little dog's love. And nothing could make her give up her Fam now. The puppy wriggled happily against her and licked Ailim's chin.

"ResidenceLibrary, is the Chinju rug in the den spelled against puppy 'accidents'?" Ailim asked.

A soothing voice answered. "The Chinju rug of a lapwing and her eggs, woven for the den two hundred years ago, contains a simple cleaning spell. The words are 'Dog Begone.'"

Ailim looked down at the damp rug. "Dog Begone!"

The carpet dried before her eyes. Then the rug rippled in a wave. When it finished the colors showed brighter and a fresh scent of herbs hung in the air. Ailim frowned. How long had it been since the rug had undergone a complete cleaning? Just what was Aunt Menzie, the ostensible D'SilverFir housekeeper, who only had to activate the various household spells, doing to occupy her time?

A rap came on her door. She turned with the puppy in the crook of her elbow. "Enter."

Cona swept in, garbed as usual in an exquisite and expensive robe. This one was of midnight chiff with sapphire embroidery.

She sneered at Ailim and Primrose. "That Donax Reed's a pest," Cona hissed, pacing. "I spoke with him last night. He's given me a pittance of an allowance. How am I to dress? Or to entertain? How am I to keep up appearances?"

Ailim set her teeth and twisted her fingers in Primrose's fur. "All Druida knows of our financial woes. The most we can do is hold our head high and work to solve our problems."

"I don't want to live like this!"

"Then you may leave." Hearing her own words shook her. Ailim couldn't believe they came from her mouth. Her duty to her Family, to guard it and lead it, came before everything else. But her temper had frayed with the incessant demands of the resident Family.

Cona paled. Her mouth fell open, but nothing emerged.

Ailim found her voice first. "We must take desperate measures or the Residence will be lost. I'm expecting everyone to help. If that is beyond you, go. You may set up your own household, as other D'SilverFirs have done, and live on your monthly GrandMistrys Noblegilt and a Flair career. One tenth of those funds will be taken for upkeep of the estate." She continued in her judicial mode, laying out the options, refusing tumbling emotions. "Or you may disassociate yourself from the Family and your Flair income will be entirely yours. You haven't pledged your loyalty to me. You are free." She waved a hand.

Cona stomped from the room, trailing images of a tortured Ailim in her wake, outlandish mean-spirited plots. Her thoughts leaked, *She will pay for insulting me.*

*A* noise jolted *Ruis awake from his first night's sleep in the* Captain's Quarters. He blinked his eyes open to an odd light that never existed under the Celtan sun, Bel. The blue of the walls held an unusual tint. His heartbeat picked up pace.

With the inrush of his waking breath he tasted a metallic tang and his nostrils flared at the equally alien scent. Sterile. Absent of any life. The only natural odors were his own and Samba's. He didn't like it.

He strained to listen, only his breathing broke the quiet.

"Good morning, Captain Elder," Ship said in deep male tones, spacing the words in a strange rhythm and accent.

Ruis jerked upright in the bed. "Ship?" His voice sounded hollow. It didn't matter that the furniture was trimmed in wood, or that fabric quilted his bunk and the chair he saw in the den, Ruis knew metal surrounded him. It shouldn't have set off a creeping apprehension, but it did.

"Yes, Captain. We are implementing your initial orders. Additional priorities can now be accepted for future restoration of Our systems."

The statement nearly distracted Ruis from the realization that the fine hair on his body stood on end. He looked for his clothes he'd folded on a nearby chair. They were gone. "What happened to my clothes?" The morning harshness in his voice should've faded by now, but his throat was tight with anxiety. He reached for Ailim D'SilverFirs's softleaf that he'd tucked near him while he'd slept.

Her scent had triggered his body into full arousal, leading him to impossible imaginings of them together. The fantasies had kept him awake long into the night. In the wee hours it didn't matter that he hung under the threat of execution, an outcast, and that she was a Judge. All that had mattered was that she was a woman and he was a man and they fit together as if they were legendary HeartMates. He snorted. To find your HeartMate you needed great Flair. He'd never know one. But he couldn't imagine any woman who could please him more than D'SilverFir.

He shook his head at the stupidity of his nocturnal fancies.

The Ship recited the systems that needed correction.

"Ship. What happened to my clothes?" The thoughts of Ailim had diverted him, but now the tension he'd awakened with rushed through him stronger than ever.

"We requested crew member Samba place them in the cleanser. They will be ready tomorrow. The cleaning system is being overhauled."

Ruis looked for Samba. He didn't think she was in his quarters, but she'd slept near him all night. The idea sent warmth through his increasingly chilled body. "I want clothes, now." He recalled the antique texts he'd studied and the most important phrase. "That is a direct and immediate order."

A panel slid open across the room from him, showing an outfit of tunic and trous that looked more feminine than his own breeches and shirt. Neither the trous nor the tunic contained much material. The tunic ended at his waist and had no collar. The trous had no belt. Even the color, a dark off-blue, irritated him. He couldn't go outside dressed that way.

This was his new home. He should be fascinated, exploring the Ship, learning its secrets. Yet he hurried to get out as soon as he could. Of course the rumors of madness after a few hours in the Ship were superstition, Ruis reassured himself. He wasn't mad. He hadn't planned on departing the Ship for a while, but a wave of uneasiness rose in him, making his skin tingle and his insides quiver.

He had to go out. Into the light he'd been born in, into the scents of Druida and green Celta. Again the image of the delightful D'SilverFir came to his mind and he grabbed at it for comfort. He needed to see her.

"Get me something green. Or brown. Now."

When he threw back the covers, they slithered across his skin like nothing made in Druida. Ruis shuddered.

He stood, naked, and walked into the den, then leaned over the desktop that was a maze of buttons and lines, some lit, some dark. With a forefinger he traced a circuit, frowned, knowing he should recognize it. He sank down into the chair and opened a drawer in the right pillar of the desk. There he found books and some delicate tools of a foreign material nestled in a flat box with a clear cover. Carefully he reached for the container.

Even in the den, the most protected place of the quarters, Ruis heard the main doors swoosh open. Cat sounds and meows came to his ears. *I'm back!*

The desktop was cold under his left hand, as if it were made of glass, but it wasn't. The drawer by his right hand was shaped subtly different from any on Celta.

The air wasn't right.

He was panting again, and his teeth hurt. Even while he'd been concentrating on the technology, he hadn't relaxed. His jaw ached as did the tendons in his neck. The trepidation that crawled through his belly intensified.

Ruis shot from the chair and into the bedroom.

Samba sniffed at the open panel displaying the same poorly cut tunic and trous, this time in a nondescript brown. Ruis grabbed them from a hanger and put them on.

The clothes weren't constrictive, just more form-fitting than he liked; the stretchy material was unexpectedly warm and comfortable.

Samba sniffed at his ankles and sneezed. *Funny smell.*

"Yes."

He turned from the closet and sat on the bed. For some cat reason, last night Samba had retrieved his liners from his boots and put them on his bed. He wrinkled his nose at the foot smell, but pulled his last remaining Celtan clothes on his feet. Then he stamped into his scarred boots and walked to the door. Samba trotted beside him. *Where are we going?*

"Out," he replied, unused to having anyone ask anything of him. An old phrase came to mind about something giving you the "creeps," and he noticed his goose-fleshed skin. The Ship gave him the creeps.

Samba's nose twitched. *I have been out. Much gossip.*

Ruis scowled. "You went outside the Ship?"

Samba lifted her muzzle. *Ship food is not good. Ship says I catch mice as a duty. I don't eat mice.*

"Ah," Ruis coughed to cover his laughter. "You have to be careful; those who know you're with me think we've left Druida."

*Yesss. I ate crunchies at Clovers, friends of Ashes who feed ferals. No one saw me.*

Ruis knew nothing of the middle-class Clovers except that they were one of the few Families on Celta with high birth rates.

"Gossip, eh? Tell me about Ailim D'SilverFir."

*She got loan for Family. Bucus Elder appointed his nephew Donax Reed as financial adviser.*

Ruis couldn't prevent an involuntary jerk at the sound of Bucus's name. "Donax isn't Elder blood. He's my aunt Calami's blood nephew."

*You are Bucus Elder's nephew by blood,* Samba said.

Ruis looked down at his scarred hands. "He did this to me as a boy."

Samba's eyes slitted. *Bad man.*

Ruis rolled his shoulders, refusing to think of his childhood. "Tell me more about Ailim D'SilverFir."

*She is new SupremeJudge.* Samba sat on plump haunches and lifted a paw to lick it. *She in JudgmentGrove today.*

Hearing of D'SilverFir cheered him. JudgmentGrove was directly in line with the Ship, two kilometers away. The old grove had been planted with Earth trees to frame the Ship in the distance, something that Celtans preferred to forget. Now he had a destination and a goal in mind after escaping the Ship. "We'll go see how she handles her duties."

Samba stood, planted her front paws and stretched luxuriously. *It's cool outside. You need a cloak.*

Ruis stopped before he exited his quarters and scowled down at his clothes. "Damn."

Turning his head, he said, "Ship, I need a cloak." It would provide protection from the weather and hide his clothes.

"Cloak?" Ship asked.

If he couldn't get something to put over his outfit, he'd have to be very, very careful and lurk in Landing Park until he could persuade himself to return to the Ship.

"There is one 'cloak'," Ship said. "An experimental light-bending cloth, designed by Our last Captain. Due to the unique properties of the material, it was decided to keep the pattern simple and shaped in the style of a cape."

"Light-bending?"

"It was constructed to make the wearer nearly invisible."

Better and better. Satisfaction infused Ruis. "Great." He nodded. "Please provide it."

Now the machinery showed its age with a clanking and a clash of parts that made Ruis wince. He wondered where the problem was and if he could fix it manually, then took a deep breath to even his breathing again. Ruis went back to the bedroom closet. After staring for a moment, he caught a glimpse of cloth. He reached out and touched a tissue-thin handful of material. Its texture felt more like scales than weaving. Without further thought he swirled it around him.

Samba jumped back, hissed. *Your body gone!*

"No, I'm here," Ruis said.

She stalked around him. The cloak fell to just above his ankles.

"This will be very useful." He'd have to watch the wind, though.

*I don't like.*

"Sorry." He felt slits inside the cloak and fumbled to insert his arms through them. When he lowered his arms, the cloak fell in deep folds, hiding even his hands. He pulled the roomy cowl over his head. His hands twitched and Ruis knew he had to get away.

They passed through the quarter's doors and Samba trotted ahead. A few moments later Ruis walked towards the northeast portal of the Ship. "Open the doors, please."

Nothing happened. Ruis stopped, all senses on alert.

"Ship, open the doors."

Silence.

"That is a direct and immediate command. Open the doors."

After a long moment, the doors slid open a millimeter. A crack of gray light slanted across the floor, and the scent of Celta, heavy with the fragrance of autumn, filtered in.

"What's wrong?" Ruis asked.

A slight chittering came. A whisper of sound.

"Ship!" Ruis demanded.

The voice that sighed in answer was not the authoritative masculine one Ruis had heard before, but more like a thousand small voices merged into one. A tentative voice. "People come and they go away again," it soughed. "They don't stay."

Pity rose in Ruis, but his apprehension spiraled since the opening between the doors was even too small for Samba.

His throat tightened. The Ship was an outcast, too, and knew it.

"You came. You wanted command rank. You brought a pet. You listened. You acted. Now you go. So soon. Will you return? I cannot take the chance." The mournful sounds whistling in the airlock must come from a breeze of the dying year outside, not from some burgeoning sentience inside.

Ruis licked dried lips. "I command you to open the doors!"

Nothing happened.

# Five

As Ruis stood in the Ship's airlock, hair rose on the back of his neck. Anger turned his vision red. Remembering old diagrams, he pivoted and banged a fist on an indentation in the wall of the airlock.

"No!" cried the Ship.

Switches and buttons showed in the control panel, along with a large red oval hand-pull that would fit around his fist. Ruis thrust his fingers into it and pulled a little, testing it.

"NO!" The Ship's shriek reverberated through his head.

He tightened his fingers on the handle. "I am the Captain of this Ship," he managed as pain speared his ears. "You will let me come and go as I please or I will institute all the manual overrides of your systems."

"Agreed!" The doors flew open. All the pressure pounding at him ceased. Ruis shuddered, then closed the control panel. In the background, almost beyond his hearing, he thought he heard sobbing.

Outside showed the last of the green summer grass, faded from its former glory. Trees blazed with bright leaves, purple and maroon and rust and red and orange and yellow and pink. He cherished the sight. The big-boled trees of Landing Park, and the other groves and parks would hide him. Buildings and alleys would provide shadows for him to slide into.

Ruis didn't need to look at the Ship. It surrounded him. Big and steely.

He lingered in the airlock. If he stayed in the city, outside of the Ship, he'd die. And if he left Druida and the machines he had restored, the craft he'd acquired after long hours of patient work, he would leave the best part of himself behind—his passion and his one contribution to his own world. His soul would die.

The atmosphere of the Ship had returned to what he'd experienced since waking. It seemed to seethe with bitemites. "There's something in the environment of the ship that disturbs my nerves. It probably irritates other Celtans as well."

The Ship hummed as if with new determination. When the voice came, it was smooth and male once more. "We have never been told this. We have no orders for observation of visitors."

Ruis blinked. "You have orders to observe, now."

"Yes, Captain. However, under standard operating procedure, we have been monitoring your life signs since you have arrived, particularly the slight energy field that surrounds you, and will compare your vital statistics to our database. We will also review previous vids of visitors to Our museum rooms. An initial hypothesis is subsonic vibrations. . . ."

Ruis blinked. The Ship worked fast. Behind him, he thought he heard whirring, and some sort of rush of air that made the muscles between his shoulder blades twitch. A non-sound pierced his head, dizzying him. Samba screeched. He reached out and grabbed a metal handhold for support. "Stop that!"

"Subsonics," Ship said, "some vibration that affects humans more than felines."

"Continue with your tests to find the problem. I'm leaving," Ruis said. "I'll return near sundown."

As he walked from one tree to another in the empty park, he thought of Ailim D'SilverFir.

Yesterday evening she'd come to him. He couldn't prevent satisfaction, and other rare emotions—joy, hope—from singing in his veins. That she'd come to see him again after his banishment was a sign that she cared about him, no matter how little. And she was the first person he could remember to care for him as an individual and not an object of pity.

He smiled. He knew nothing about the ways of men and

women in courtship except what he'd overheard now and again in low-life taverns. Men boasting or complaining or venting anger about the women in their lives. Ruis only had women when his physical need was great and he wished to pay the price.

D'SilverFir had promised to help. Perhaps she would. Hope. It was such a new and tender emotion, so light and effervescent bubbling through him, that he couldn't bring himself to crush it. For once, he'd let himself indulge in optimism.

The walk to JudgmentGrove was peaceful. Ruis kept to meandering pathways through a series of parks and groves. Only the Downwind area of Druida was crowded together without greenspace. He stood still behind a tree when he saw others, women with children, brisk walkers and runners. When he came closer to JudgmentGrove he took great care, pulling his cloak around him. His blood fizzed with adrenaline at the risk and the push to take chances. He found a tight way between tall bushes that were planted just beyond the staggered four-deep trees on the west end of JudgmentGrove.

His mouth twisted and hands clenched as he saw the line of bright purple Flair denoting a closed sacred circle. The band was just a meter and a half from where he stood. Bitterness rose through him, coating his mouth.

If he touched the pulsing band of light, his Nullness would break it, alerting the guardsmen to his presence. He'd be caught and executed.

The pulsing bond before Ruis seemed to mock him. Even in this, the basic religion of Celta, he was nothing.

He looked through the Grove and the atmosphere grew wavy before him. He knew what that meant, too, and folded his cloak around him, against the cutting autumn breeze that could lift it and reveal him. A weathershield had been invoked.

He saw people a few meters ahead who had come, like him, to watch the new SupremeJudge. But they were inside and could hear her words, while random phrases came to his ears. They were inside, able to see her and hear her and be warm.

He was outside, ignored, outcast, and cold.

*A*ilim settled her morning cases with speed and ease. She used minor Flair, reading surface thoughts and emotions to determine guilt, not forced to intrude otherwise. Once or twice she adjusted the punishment based on her detection of contrition, but otherwise followed standard judgments proposed within the Laws.

By noon recess she realized that her new bailiff, Yeldoc, had set the docket in order of difficulty and knew she could trust the fussy little man.

Most of the nobles who'd come to watch—and judge— her left when the circle was opened for midday break. But the representatives of the five FirstFamilies who had voted against the loan to D'SilverFir stayed.

Second nature had Ailim using Flair to check on the state-of-mind of the gathering. Everywhere she'd visited on her circuit rounds held a distinct cultural bent, and she factored that into her rulings. The murmuring of those milling in the grove was accepting and appreciative.

Ailim rose from the ornate Sage's Chair behind the rainbowstone desk placed in the center of a stone-paved stage that stretched between two towers. The front of the stage was curved, with shallow steps leading down to more pavement, then to the huge grassy glade between two lines of trees that were in the grove. People stood in colorful groups. Blankets and smallchairs dotted the lawn.

She crossed to the far tower and with a low Word opened the door. This tower was larger than the other, meant to be the Residence of the SupremeJudge of Celta. The room was empty. But here, where even Yeldoc didn't come, Ailim could finally relax.

All her actions, every decision, would be scrutinized and critiqued by the ruling FirstFamilies Council, the NobleCouncil, and the GuildCouncil.

She couldn't afford to make any major missteps. While she was confident in her skill as a judge, she was ambivalent about her ability to keep her live-in Family in line, as the head of a House should be able to do.

And she knew she couldn't let the emotional woman inside her surface, the one who yearned for another chance to speak with Ruis Elder. To associate with him would mean ruin. Last night she'd stood at her bedroom window and looked out across the glittering water in the moat into the darkness, wondering where he was in all the huge world

outside Druida. For a moment she'd hungered to be with
him away from the city. Close to him. Close enough to
experience the marvel of her senses freed from her Flair
and her shields.

Her shoulders slumped and she leaned her forehead
against the cold stone. For an instant it shocked, then felt
wonderful. She stayed that way for several breaths before
raising her head.

Bel streamed sunlight into the many-paned window, giving the room of golden stone a cheery aspect. For a moment
Ailim contemplated how it would be to live here, away
from her relatives at the Residence, then set the unattain-
able notion aside with a sigh.

The bell tolled once. "Two minutes before the sacred circle is closed and Grove begins," announced Yeldoc.

Ailim did a quick mind-sweep. Throughout the morning
she'd felt two distinct currents of antipathy. One was hostility and resentment with a known pattern, Aunt Menzie.
The second force-stream contained a repulsive taint of evil.
She had an enemy.

An enemy stalking her!

Ailim pressed her hands together and sucked in a deep,
controlled breath, sending her mind into a spiral that would
deflect panic. She didn't know why she had a deadly enemy, but there was no doubt that was the case. A bitter
smile tugged at her lips. Politics as usual.

Her psi-sense whisked through the Grove as she struggled to discover him, to no avail.

Yet she sensed a blankness at the far west end of the
Grove. She hesitated, thinking Celtan plant or wildlife in-
terfered with her Flair. But the image of Ruis Elder rose in
her mind. She wished she'd known him better. He was the
most complex man she'd ever met. It would be interesting
to depend upon her powers of observation when with him.

She suspected he could teach her a great deal about living
in the moment, not always expecting perfection from herself.

Yeldoc rapped on the door. "Time, SupremeJudge
GrandLady."

She reeled in her Flair and shook her arms to release the
tingling energy coursing through her. Straightening her

robes, she opened the door. "Call me Ailim," she said to Yeldoc.

His eyes rounded. "I can't do that."

"Of course not." A corner of her mouth lifted.

He marched ahead until he stood on the outermost curve of the stage, then banged his staff on the pavement. "JudgmentGrove is now in Session. SupremeJudge GrandLady Ailim D'SilverFir presiding. All rise."

"You may close the sacred circle," Ailim said before walking to the Sage's Chair to sit.

When mid-afternoon came and with it her last case, Ailim was ready to be done with the day.

She looked at the boy before her. The weathershield cast shadows over his face, making him quite unprepossessing. He stood petrified with fear, clutching a small cream-colored cat.

Antenn Moss, no older than nine, was held in place by a DetainSpell. His eyes looked wild.

"The next case is the People of Celta and the Maidens of Saille against Antenn Moss, juvenile," Yeldoc announced.

The Maidens of Saille was a religious order of celibate women who ran the sole orphanage. Several Maidens, from teenage novices to elders, stood near the edge of the terrace.

"This Antenn Moss is accused of assaulting a Maiden of Saille, in the Maidens of Saille House for Orphans," the prosecutor declared.

The boy's mouth opened and closed without a sound. *No!* screamed his mind.

Ailim saw it all unroll before her. Antenn had been part of a group of boys living Downwind, along with his brother, an older boy who'd renamed himself Nightshade. Nightshade had joined a mind-bonded triad and abandoned his younger brother, but Antenn tagged after the triad's gang. When the gang disintegrated, Antenn had been sent to the Maidens of Saille Orphanage.

He'd tried to fit in. Ailim saw how desperately the Downwind youth had tried, but the confinement and the rules had been too much for him and his cat. He'd decided to escape.

Two nights ago he put his plans in effect. They'd sneaked into an empty room and run for the window over the bed.

He'd miscounted the doors. Ailim felt him writhe at the

stupidity of his mistake. He'd hit the bed fast, and there was a Maiden in it!

"I am requesting the maximum penalty for Antenn Moss," said the Prosecutor.

"No," Ailim said.

A surge came from both the auras of Aunt Menzie and the vague presence of the evil one who'd watched her. Ailim repressed a start when she understood that the two people were together. She tried to see them, but the layered shadows of the trees hid them.

"No? SupremeJudge, the crime is loathsome!" The prosecutor demanded her attention. Ailim wanted to concentrate on finding and naming her enemy. She couldn't. Her duty to this boy and the laws and people of Celta came before personal problems.

She addressed the Grove. "There was no crime. There was a mistake by a wretched boy. He wanted out of the House for Orphans, and thought he was escaping through an empty room."

She heard approving murmurs from the crowd, as if finally understanding the matter. It had been an awful accusation. Tears ran down Antenn's cheeks. He hid his face in the cat's fur.

"SupremeJudge, are you positive?" the Prosecutor asked.

"I believe it has been some time since Druida had a telempathic judge, GrandSir Prosecutor, but I just told you the truth."

Gleeful satisfaction leapt from her enemy. Ailim froze, as quiet as hunted prey. Her mouth dried and her stomach clutched. She'd always used her Flair when necessary in her work. But she'd just revealed the extent and skill of her power. She hadn't needed even the most minor probe of any mind during the day, and in Antenn's case, the truth was right before her eyes—obvious to her as it had been obscure to everyone else. Despite the bright sun stinging her eyes, she felt cold.

The Prosecutor bowed. "As you say, SupremeJudge."

Ailim again wrenched her attention back to the trial. Anger stirred in her that she should have to deal with others' hostility and her own fear in her JudgmentGrove.

But the boy's trembling body focused her. She raised her chin. "However, Antenn did hurt the Maiden, even if inadvertently, so I do have a judgment." Ailim narrowed her eyes. The boy was reaching puberty and she caught the faint pulsing shadow of incipient Flair. She chose her words. "I request that Antenn be tested for Flair. . . ."

"I'll donate T'Ash's Testing services," GreatLady Danith D'Ash called from the grove's edge and hurried to the center clearing.

"T'Ash is going to love this," the Prosecutor muttered, too low to be heard by anyone except Ailim and Antenn.

"T'Ash?" the boy squeaked, and shivered.

"He is a wonderful Tester. I'm sure he'll find exactly what you're suited for." Danith beamed.

"And after Testing," Ailim instructed, "Antenn will apprentice to an appropriate Family and live with them. He will pay the cost of Healing Maiden Fern from his wages. Until then he is to be housed in the First Downwind Boys Center." Ailim clapped her hands and made it echo through the Grove. "That is my judgment. Also, Maiden of Saille Fern is here and I require Antenn Moss to apologize to her. Detention spell dismissed."

The boy was freed. He dropped the cat and wiped his nose on his sleeve, then set his narrow shoulders in the plaid commoncloth shirt. Antenn walked over to the small, elderly Maiden who leaned on a stick. She was still taller than he.

He fell to his knees, shocking Ailim. "Please, Maiden Fern. Sorry. Didn't know you were there. Didn't mean to hurt you."

"Stand up, boy!" the Prosecutor shouted. "We kneel to no one here on Celta."

"I forgive you, Antenn." Maiden Fern laid a wrinkled hand on the boy's head. "Blessings upon you—and Pinky."

Antenn rose, snuffling, and wiping his nose again on his arm. The Prosecutor sighed. "I'll take you both to the Center."

For the first time Ailim picked up her gavel and banged it. "Grove is done. Now the closing prayer: By the Lady and Lord, let us give thanks that these actions have been resolved. Let us believe that our proceedings have pro-

gressed for the good of all and according to the free will
of all. Blessed be."

"Blessed be," echoed from around the Grove.

Ailim glanced at Yeldoc. "You may dissolve the sacred
circle and dismiss the weathershield." She hoped to glimpse
her enemy as he left.

Aunt Menzie sidled from the Grove. She wore dark gray,
not D'SilverFir light blue, and blended into tree shadows.
Ailim bit her lip and backtracked to where her aunt had
emerged from the trees, but saw no one, only felt the baleful presence. A shiver rippled through her and she murmured a Word of protection.

She dismissed Yeldoc and told him that she wanted to
walk the Grove, learning the trees, the small glades set
amongst them, and reacquaint herself with the location of
the brook that burbled in the background. But when
JudgmentGrove was empty and Ailim sensed no other
minds, she dropped her head to her arms folded on the desk.

She couldn't remember a longer day than yesterday in
her life, a culminating blur of the last two eightdays. The
sole vivid moments were her conversations with Ruis Elder.
Even the arguments with her Family smeared into one large
altercation. She had the depressing feeling that her domes-
tic life would continue to be a long battle with a few tiny
moments of respite. Which is why she hadn't gone home.
D'SilverFir Residence didn't feel like home anymore. Before she could shake the self-pitying thought, her vision
grayed and she dozed.

The atmosphere changed around her. She was conscious,
but too tired to do anything but distantly observe the sharpened fragrance of dying grass, hear the creek increase its
burble and every chirp of the crickets, even feel the small
delineation of the different colors of the stone beneath her
fingertips. All her senses sharpened. The air on her left side
stirred.

Scents teased her nose, ones she'd smelled just the day
before, but she refused to catalogue them and accepted the
easing of tight emotions. She knew who stood next to her,
Ruis Elder, the Null.

She could not acknowledge him.

He was banished from Druida on pain of death. As a

Judge it was her duty to report that he was flouting the will of the Councils and the Law of Celta.

She could not betray him.

She kept her mouth from forming his name, just heard it echo in her mind. Tentative fingers brushed against her hair once, twice, as if they had never stroked someone in comfort—or had luxury or permission to touch. Ailim's throat tightened.

She could not resist him.

At her stillness, the soft touches stopped. Ailim's thoughts scrambled at how to let him know she treasured this moment. She relaxed and snuggled her face deeper into the crook of her arm. "Mmmmmmmm," she said, hoping he would not leave.

A moment later his palm curved around her head. "Mmmmmmm," she approved.

His trailing fingers grew bolder, stroking her head again and again, then stopping at the rapid pulse in her neck.

Only the tension between them, his movements, led her to guess at his feelings. She felt no emotions or thoughts from him. For the first time in her life she wondered what another felt.

She concentrated on what his movements might mean—the hesitation of his hands as they smoothed out the waves of her hair that had been strictly bound in braids and tied with spellthreads. Ailim guessed that he was inexperienced in tenderness between men and women, and her heart ached. What had his life been like?

She sought to think, but his hands upon her drowned any thought. She could only feel.

Warm palms touched her shoulders, fingers found the knots in her muscles. Awkwardly, with several shifts of position, he began to massage her. Nerves within her prickled as the gentle touch continued, then increased in pressure as if his fingers were learning a new art. Wetness dampened her eyes and Ailim realized that her tears weren't solely from released pain.

She blessed them anyway, since they kept her eyes from seeing what they shouldn't.

Thumbs brushed at her neck and she tipped her head to give him access to her tight muscles. She enjoyed being at peace and without any thoughts or emotions intruding on her own. If she listened, she might even be able to hear herself think over the pulse of her heart.

Except the delightful massage took all thought away. Her physical senses bloomed and her sheer awareness of everything fascinated her. She thought she could hear the trees drawing in an interminable breath, withdrawing deep into their bark to slow and prepare for winter. A small breeze rattled leaves, and she imagined them swirling and dancing in joy of being free from twigs and branches. The leaves and the grass and the brook scented the air with layers of fragrance she'd never experienced.

She recalled the fingers moving down her back were long. They hesitated to pursue a tangled spot of muscle or sinew, then continued. When she was utterly relaxed, hands stroked, comforted and discovered the shape of her back.

Heat rose within her, languidly unfurling from low in her torso to spread throughout her body. Tingles pulsated out from her temple along her nerves. Her blood pulsed low and steady, carrying the throb of desire. A unique desire flowing so sweet and heavy that she felt caught in a spell, too drugged to move, aching for the next caress of his fingers. She wanted more, to hear and feel and smell and touch and see. The way she had experienced all her senses yesterday when her Flair had been suppressed by Ruis Elder's Nullness.

But to break the spell would be to set a lightning bolt of duty and danger against the cobweb of ease and comfort surrounding her. Better to doze and be dazed.

The light of Bel was blocked an instant, and something softer than fingers grazed her temple. Mint, another scent she remembered from before and ignored. This time when she sighed out her breath, it was of yearning, of a great need that had opened inside her. He was giving, of his time and himself. Tears backed up behind her eyes that a simple touch of comfort could so move her. But she hadn't felt a gentle touch for more months than she could count.

His hand tangled in her loose hair again. One sifting of fingers and a harsh sound as he started to move away.

She couldn't let him go without acknowledgment. With sheer instinct, she flung out her hand, caught his hand and clung. She did nothing else, just held on to him, savoring his strength.

For a moment they stayed that way, then she felt the brush of his lips on her fingers before her hand was replaced next to her face. Then his footsteps strode away.

Ailim shut her eyes tight, and wetness overflowed. She could not look, could not openly declare the lovely feelings that passed between them. It had to be Ruis. But if she didn't see him, couldn't swear that it was a banished Ruis breaking the laws, she couldn't be forced by her vows as Judge to report him.

When he left her, he took all the new brilliance of her senses with him.

She sat up and removed the tracks of tears with a spell-word, then began to braid her hair again. Tight.

*The hallway to his old apartment was as dark and dank as* ever. Even several paces away, he could see that the door to his old rooms stood splintered and tilted in the corridor.

He hesitated, sure he wouldn't like what he'd see beyond the door. He strode to the door, grabbed it, and heaved it aside.

A stench hit him and he breathed through his mouth. He forced himself to enter. The mainspace was a wreck, and someone had relieved himself on what had once been a chair.

Something was wrong. He stopped as still as the dead door, then pinpointed why his heart sped and his throat closed. Another scent lingered, a whiff of an expensive men's cologne. The odor of Bucus.

Ruis swallowed, and swallowed again, pushing away images of his uncle leaning over him with a razorslit. Smiling. For some reason GreatLord Bucus Elder had visited his nephew's lair. Ruis relaxed his tensed muscles, lifted a shoulder, and let it drop. So his uncle's presence still triggered physical reactions, so what? He'd live with it.

His eyes went to the hidden cache in the far wall. If Bucus had found the T'Birch necklace or the gems, they'd be gone, secreted away by fat greedy fingers into a secret treasure box. Bucus might someday sell the Earthsuns, but would hoard the necklace to use it against Ruis.

He scuffed through the mainspace, kicking up debris at each step. He licked dry lips. The last time he'd been here, the earthmotor had been the size of his head. Now he couldn't discern the remnants. Not one piece of the shabby furniture was whole. The odor got worse as his meager food rotted where it'd been thrown from the coldbox. Ruis counted bricks to the cubby. He pulled the brick out and reached inside. His fingers touched the rough leather of a satchel, and as he drew it out a metallic clink told him the T'Birch necklace was still safe.

Moving to an empty wall-shelf, he opened the case. Two uncut Earthsuns stuck into a fabric pocket now gleamed golden, picking up Bel's final rays.

He'd spent the day outside in his old world, in a culture that reviled him. He'd seen and touched his Lady. It had been a good day, better than many he'd had.

The cloak had hidden him from observation, and he'd taken care not to break any spells or stay close to anyone.

He closed the satchel. After one final look around, red tinted his vision and he shook his head, struggling to clear it of wild ideas of vengeance. His body trembled with the urge to lash out at Bucus.

When he sucked in air, the scent of Bucus came again. And anger won. Whirling, he slammed a fist into the wall. Old brick crumbled around his knuckles, pain shot up his arm. He stilled until the sweat beaded on his forehead dried, then withdrew his hand. The cloak caught on shards. He froze. He couldn't afford to damage the light-bending cape. He lifted the odd cloth bit by bit until it was free and flung the cloak back over his shoulders. He shook his hurt hand and swore. The injury wasn't as bad as it could have been, the wall was too rotted for that, but it hurt. Once again he'd given in to anger, and once again the only one he had harmed was himself.

"Ruis," a voice hissed from the doorway. "Ruis Elder."

Ruis spun, swinging the satchel. A slight form darted into the room and past him to hover by the window.

"Ruis Elder." A young man of about nineteen grinned at him, showing canine teeth filed to points and gilded with the iridescent Celtan metal of glisten. He jittered with twit-

chy energy, shifting often, darting glances around. He wore
black trous and shirt, cuffed at ankles and wrists, of good
material but oversized for his body.

He held up both hands, palm out. "Truce, quarter-
septhour?"

Ruis needed to find out how much the youth knew. The
boy's eyes were dark with an edge of something disturb-
ing—madness or viciousness or desperation.

"You want to talk to me?" Ruis kept his voice low and
menacing.

Light flashed off teeth again. "Watched you, before you
caught." He spoke the rough short-speech of Downwind.
Twitching his shoulders, he cocked his head toward the
open door. Glisten-capped teeth spoke of a triad—three
boys linked by the Flair of them all into one mind, functioning as one person. And the unstable triads ran with
gangs.

Ruis had never tangled with a triad and wondered how
his Nullness would affect them. Would there be some sort
of reverberating shock? Or would he break the triad bond?

Nerves and discomfort bordering on paranoia showed in
the youth's rattled state. With T'Ash's new Downwind
youth centers, the gangs were slowly dissolving. Testing
for Flair was common now, and the young men were being
directed into careers. Only the worst gangs remained.

"Heard you banished, but didn't think you coward to
leave." The youth smiled with more amusement now, and
Ruis liked it even less. "Didn't think fliggering nobles scare
you. Hee, hee, hee," he wheezed. "Watched this old hidey.
Heard you. Came."

"Who—" Ruis started.

Loud male voices interrupted. "Did you see where the
kid went? Let's check the Null's old place again."

There came the sound of spitting. "Those rooms stink!"

A rumble of laughter answered. "Yeah, noble piss don't
smell no better than any other."

The other man snorted. "Imagine wanting to do that to
your nephew's place. I can't stand the stench."

"Huh! We're gettin' paid to watch the building. I saw the
kid come in."

"The kid is just a kid. There's no sign of him now,

prob'ly got his own burrow somewhere else in this lousy building."

The boy swore under his breath and swung out the window into the courtyard. Ruis gathered his cloak around him and settled into a crouch, one odd shape among many. Cold air poured in from the open window.

Loud steps paused outside the threshold. "See? Nothin' there. Can't figure out why T'Elder'd think the Null bastard would return. Nothin' for him here."

"Pew! Almost puts me off my feed."

"Yeah, it's time for dinner, awright." Lips smacked.

"Come on!"

"I want some clucker with noodles."

"You always want noodles, but I'll let ya have some if we play Dice later."

The other snorted. "Your gamblin's gonna get you in trouble someday, Sloegin."

The footsteps faded from the hall.

Ruis waited until silence shrouded the building before standing, then slipped from his old apartment into the alleys. If Bucus's bully-boys found him before the guards, Ruis would disappear quietly and permanently. He'd fight and die before he fell helpless into his uncle's hands again.

Adrenaline flooded his bloodstream. Danger from the guards. Danger from his uncle. And now danger from the youth. But Ruis was willing to bet that the teen would be known to the guardsmen, too. A chill slithered down Ruis's spine, cooling his ire. He'd never quite figured out why Bucus had wanted him dead.

The sun had set and the afterglow was fading. Ruis rubbed his jaw. He saw no signs of the two other young men who were linked to the teenager who'd spoken to him. The youngster's flight bespoke a criminal wariness. Ruis vividly recalled how it felt to be young and nervous and hunted. His first year on the streets of Downwind at fourteen was imprinted on his brain in horrible vignettes that could still sweat him awake.

The satchel with the T'Birch necklace and gems bumped against his leg. The necklace was the last of his thefts. The emeralds had been useless in focusing his reconstructed lazer. Now all he wanted to do was restore them to the Birches.

His mouth tightened as he thought of D'Birch and her lies at his trial. The Birches had voted for his death. His gut burned.

Think of something else. Something pleasant. D'SilverFir came to mind and his temper dissipated as he recalled the silky mass of her hair under his fingers, her skin pale and beautiful and soft, how her body had relaxed and yielded under his hands. Without trying he could remember her scent, her lovely features, and the thrill of knowing his touch was welcome. Not flinched from, not endured, but welcomed. There was a true Lady, a woman of honor and integrity, one who cared about others. He'd learned that much when he'd listened to her decisions in JudgmentGrove.

Holm Holly had watched her for a septhour in the Grove, noticing her as a woman. Holly could be looking for a wife. Ailim D'SilverFir would be high on any noble's list as a good alliance. Ruis sucked in cooling air.

But she'd been aware of Ruis. He knew she'd sensed him when he'd dispelled her Flair, and he knew she'd liked his company.

Ruis draped the cowl over his head and made sure he was covered before stepping out of the alley.

# Six

*S*amba bumped into *him. She hissed and batted a paw at* his boots, leaving new scratches on them. Ruis grimaced.

*I don't like this cloak. Hard to see you. Have to smell for you, and smells around here are not good.*

Ruis noted the odors of rotten garbage, urine, and vomit. He'd lived amongst those smells most of his life. The recollection of the metal odor of the Ship hit him with a longing for cleanliness, privacy, and safety.

"Let's go," he said.

*Let's go PLAY,* Samba corrected, turning to prance down the cracked sidewalk. *In the Ship. Much to explore. I went back and Ship said it found the problems with sound.* She sniffed. *We will listen to noises, then Ship will make awful feeling go away.*

"An experiment," Ruis said, cheered at the idea of a little scientific work. He rubbed his hands.

*Look under My collar.*

He bent down and stroked her. She purred. He saw nothing under her collar, but his fingertips tingled as he touched the same scale-like substance of his cloak. He tugged. Two pieces of cloth flashed, then vanished as they hit the ground.

Samba delicately lifted something up with her teeth. Ruis took it and pulled it through his hand since he was having trouble seeing it. "Gloves."

"*Yessssss.*" She picked up the other one and gave it to him. He donned them. They sagged around his fingers and the length was almost too short. The previous owner—the last Captain?—must have had wider, more workmanlike hands.

Ruis and Samba passed through a series of parks on the way to the Ship.

*I went to your old place, like you said.* Samba sniffed again. Ruis had heard that her Sire, Zanth, was prone to sinus problems; he wondered if Samba was, too. *It was a hole. I have never lived in such a place. Looked bad. Smelled bad. Felt*—

Ruis winced. "I'm a Null, Samba, without Flair. I lived where people would let me pay good gilt for holes."

Samba stopped and looked up at him. *Flair interesting,* she meowed matter-of-factly, *but sometimes puts My hair on end.* She lifted her nose and flicked her tail back and forth. *No more living in holes. Now We have Ship.*

"Yes." They'd walked through a shabby Downwind park, through one middle-class grove with play areas, and were traversing a long, thin green in "noble country" that would lead to Landing Park. Between bare branches, Ruis saw the bright lights from the multistoried castles—noble Residences.

Silence broken by the sounds of nightwings and insects, the rustling of dry leaves and the soft sound of a brook, enveloped them. No one was out in the darkening night. Everyone else was with Family or friends or even strangers in taverns. He was alone again. As always. And now lonelier than ever before, since he'd known D'SilverFir's smile. He wished the D'SilverFir Residence was on his way to the Ship.

Samba snuffled beside him and his spirits lifted. He wasn't alone. He had Samba, his Fam. He had the Ship, his home.

*A*ilim sat behind her desk in the *Residence Den,* staring impassively at her aunt Menzie. Ailim needed to discover the name of her enemy and what plots might endanger the SilverFirs. She felt just as much a judge as if she were hearing a case. A nasty tang coated her mouth. She shouldn't have to judge Family—and find them wanting.

Aunt Menzie sat ramrod straight across from her with bright spots of color on her cheeks. Her eyes narrowed and she sneered.

"I saw you at JudgmentGrove," Ailim said.

Menzie's face went blank as if disconcerted. Now Ailim had the advantage. Menzie hadn't been smart enough to realize Ailim had spotted her.

"You are wrong," Menzie said.

"No, I'm not. I must insist that you tell me who you met."

"Don't take that tone of voice with me! I met no one. I wasn't near the grove. How dare you call me a liar."

Ailim opened her shields, but no emotions or thoughts came from Menzie. Wisping out tendrils of Flair, Ailim still couldn't sense anything from Menzie, who until now broadcast with a ferocity that gave Ailim headaches.

Since probing was futile, Ailim concentrated on the odd, low hum with Flair-distorting waves that came from Menzie. The strange effects emanated from the center of Menzie's thin chest where something looked lumpy under her bodice. An amulet—something darkly powerful, not like the useless cheaptin crowns that never blocked Ailim's Flair.

Ailim concentrated on the fetish. Demons whispered in her ear that she would fail, fail, fail and the Family would shatter and the Residence would be lost—her deepest fears. Terror grabbed at her, spiking high, making her breath stick in her throat, slicking a fine film over the nape of her neck.

She snatched back her awareness and built additional barricades until she received nothing on the psychic plane from the malefic charm. But she trembled. Menzie's eyes held malice and her lips went from sneer to smirk.

Ailim was tired of confrontations, all the balancing she needed to do to keep the Family together, but she couldn't let that show. She straightened her spine. For simple pleasure, she nudged her feet beneath Primrose snoring under the desk.

"The new amulet you wear is a bane," Ailim said.

Menzie looked shocked, her hand fluttered to her chest.

"A Family heirloom," Menzie said with stiff lips.

"I don't think so. It reeks of newness." And was tuned to specifically block Ailim's Flair and project negative energy.

"You can't know—" Menzie snapped her mouth shut.

Ailim was too tired to do anything but show a polite mask. "Which heirloom?"

Menzie's lower lip protruded.

"I don't like playing these games. ResidenceLibrary, list the Family heirlooms in Menzie's possession," Ailim ordered.

The strong female voice of an ancestor answered Ailim. "The emerald beads carved like pinecones; the ancient gold pin in the shape of an evergreen with jeweled ornaments—"

"Enough!" Menzie ordered.

The ResidenceLibrary stopped. Menzie lifted her chin, color still blotched her cheeks. "The amulet is an heirloom of my late husband's Family."

"Ah. You don't lie well, you shouldn't try."

"I'm not lying." She shifted in her seat.

"No?" Ailim frowned, trying to determine how dangerous the fetish and Menzie could be. "Please give the amulet to me."

"No."

Ailim gathered her Flair, feeling her braids lift. Psi action against a Family member wasn't easy.

"No!" Menzie clutched at the piece again. "The fetish is a gift to me and I value it. You can't take it from me. Try and I will cry abuse to the NobleCouncil. You don't want our quarrels to become public, do you?"

Ailim had already decided that she didn't right now, but couldn't let Menzie know that, couldn't back down. "If our quarrels become public, you have more to lose than I. We will all lose."

Menzie tossed her head, looking for an instant like her daughter Cona. "I don't believe that. You exaggerate everything—the debt, the danger, even your silly feelings about my new charm—just to make yourself more important. I knew you were too young and immature to be GrandLady. The Council won't take the estate from us. It's not done."

Ailim gritted her teeth.

Menzie stood and walked to the door, sneering again. "You can't take the amulet from me."

"Perhaps not. But I can confine you to your room if you insist on wearing it. And I can dock fifty pieces of gilt a day from your housekeeping salary until you give the

charm to me. ResidenceLibrary, note the reduction and forward the information to Donax to take into account for the
budget."

"Done," said ResidenceLibrary.

"You can't!" screeched Menzie.

"I can. No matter how young and immature you think I
am, I am in charge of the Family and our finances. Com-
plain to the Council if you want. Residence housing and
wages given to Family members for their services are at my
discretion. Further, I can prove that you have been derelict
in your duties. The carpet in this room, for instance, hadn't
been cleaned in some time."

Menzie stared down at the carpet with a puzzled expression.

"As I told Cona, should you care to move from
D'SilverFir Residence and set up your own household—"
Ailim started.

"You can't make me. You wouldn't dare." Menzie trembled with fury. "This is my home."

"Which we will lose if we don't work together."

Menzie whipped the door open. "I don't believe you."

"Leave the amulet on my desk when you've decided it's
too expensive a bauble to keep," Ailim said, her voice cool
though a hot wave of frustration swept through her.

The door slammed behind Menzie, making Ailim's incipient headache bloom into full pain.

Ailim locked the door with a Word and let her head rest
on the chair back. Primrose whimpered in her sleep and
Ailim stopped a sigh of exhaustion and futility from breaking free.

She didn't know how she would cope with the Family.
The Council had granted the loan because the SilverFirs
were a FirstFamily, but should the Family splinter, there
was no reason to let them keep the Residence and the estate.
She could fend for herself, but she'd have to live with her
failure.

How could she deal with the problem of the amulet? Con-
fining her aunt to her room was a stopgap measure. Ailim
sensed that destroying the horrible thing would take energy
and skill, skill that she didn't have, nor did she have gilt

to pay a master to disarm or destruct the fetish. That left an alliance, and with D'SilverFir as the beggar again.

Her head pounded. Her muscles had tightened into knots once more. No one would come here to soothe and massage her, not even the outcast Ruis Elder.

Ruis Elder—a Null who could handle the amulet without harm. Ailim had already promised to look into his case—something simple justice demanded—but perhaps he could help her. If she could get the amulet away from Menzie. If she could locate Ruis.

She rolled her tense neck and shoulders. His long fingers and stroking hands weren't here to ease her turmoil, nor was his tender touch that assured her that she was valued and cherished. The loneliness hurt worse than her head or her body.

She picked up Primrose and buried her face in soft puppy fur.

$T$he next morning Ruis and the Ship designed a psychology program to help him rid himself of the fury at being born a natural outcast. The procedure included interactive role-playing with various Celtan models—a brutish supervisor, the Petty guardsman, a haughty GraceLord. Ruis was pleased that he managed his anger as often as he failed the exercises. But he preferred the other portion of the program—hard work and anger diversion into the mental challenge of restoring Earth objects.

That afternoon, he studied the Ship's blueprints in his workroom. On a side table was his latest project, a nano-assembler the Ship was teaching him to repair.

"We've repaired and reprogrammed all our stellar-solar collecting skincells for better efficiency," Ship said.

Ruis smiled. He was getting used to the Ship speaking in the plural. When asked, Ship stated it was an amalgam of departments integrated to communicate with him.

"We request further orders."

"List priorities," he said.

It did.

"Repair additional maintenance androids," he decided.

"Yes, Captain," the Ship replied.

Ruis whistled through his teeth. He was Captain. He tapped his finger on the map where the DNA Room was located. It was a huge room filled with samples of all the life of Earth, information on papyrus and film and "bubbles." Encyclopedias of instructions and diagrams.

A tingle of awe ran up his spine at the thought of all that knowledge available to him. So many options for his learning and his life to follow that he struggled to choose what to do first.

But he knew what he wanted the most. He wanted to see D'SilverFir. The feel of her body under his hands had only made him want more.

Samba entered and jumped onto a cabinet. She hooked a paw in the door and something fell out. She peered down at it. When Ruis saw the satchel from his old rooms, he scowled. That was his shame. Heat flooded him as he flushed with guilt. He didn't like the way his gut twisted, either.

*What's this?* She jumped down.

The two Earthsuns rolled out. Ruis grimaced. He'd have to return the gems to Stickle, the man who mistreated his apprentices. No way to avoid it. But the jewels had meant a lot to Ruis—they had meant safety from Bucus, days spent working with his mind and hands instead of his arms and back, being beaten by his supervisor.

He glanced at his watch. It was an ancient thing he'd found and fixed when a youth, depending upon a tiny spring to work. Ruis had replaced the insides many times, altering it and the face to reflect the seventy minute septhour and twenty-eight-hour days. A Celtan "timer" used Flair technology to measure time, impossible for him to wear.

Evening was falling. Soon he could leave the Ship and use the shadows of the autumn dusk to augment his cape.

He was taking a chance in returning the T'Birch necklace. His jaw clenched at the thought of the noble. The Birches had voted for Ruis's death. He could feel the red tide of anger rise.

Ruis swung a fist at the wall, and it connected with an absorbent panel the Ship had fashioned for him. He pummeled the strip until his breath came fast and his fury died.

Then he showered, grimacing wryly. Outside the Ship he

couldn't afford to be reckless and vengeful against the nobles. That was a battle he could never hope to win. Outside, all the power was with them.

But here, he ruled. His lips curled back from his teeth as he thought of the vengeance that he could have on the nobles, on all of Druida, if he liked. For a moment glittering temptation beckoned. He liked the feeling of power, let it flood his body and surge through his blood.

A moment later he set aside the false lure. His culture had abominated him, but he'd developed good qualities: pride and honor, love of the ancient Earth technology. The cost of vengeance was much too high. His image of himself as different and better than the nobles would be shattered for all time.

On the Ship he knew the folly of revenge, but when he was outside with a price on his head, moving in a civilization that despised him, his anger would strike again. He would have to be more careful of his own emotions than of the guardsmen of Druida.

A clank came from the workbench. Samba trotted along it, a silver necklace in her mouth. When she reached him, she dropped it and spit out some shiny pieces of Earth mechanicals.

Ruis raised his eyebrows. "Yes?"

Samba sat on her haunches and moved the pieces around, setting them in a line near the necklace. *Tonight we go to the big playhouse.*

"Yes."

She lifted her chin regally and stared at Ruis with green eyes. *All Cat Fams have necklaces—*

"Collars." His brows drew together as he ran through the Fams he knew. She was right.

*Jewelry. Is a Rule. D'Ash says so.* Samba sniffed.

"I see." He looked at the silver chain he'd found broken in the dirt and repaired. Neither the chain nor the little bits of metal and colored enamel were valuable to Celtans. Samba would be safe wearing them.

"All right." The same pride that demanded he dress like his true status required that his Fam have a collar. Ruis wiped off the Earth parts with a rag, then strung them on the chain that was slightly larger than Samba's neck. He loosened one link in the chain. "I'm going to make it so if it catches on anything, you'll break free."

"Yesssss," she vocalized. *My price for doing what you want tonight.*

Shocked, he started, then laughed. He'd heard rumors that cats charged their FamPeople for errands.

"Agreed." He smiled. He wouldn't indulge in physical revenge, but a little embarrassment of his enemies was another matter.

GreatLady D'Birch was going to the opera tonight. Before he was caught Ruis had strategized on how to return the necklace. He knew the T'Birches's habits. Right now the gown D'Birch would wear tonight hung in the empty bespelled T'Birch laundry shed, being restored and freshened. It was simple for him to enter the shed, loosen a sleeve seam, and slip the necklace inside.

How everyone would stare when the loose threads of her sleeve pocket broke and the emerald necklace she'd accused him of stealing tumbled out!

Samba purred as he fastened the collar around her calico neck, smoothing fur under the piece.

She pranced around the quarters, tinkling. His heart tightened. He loved her, this plump cat. She was beautiful in her collar, and enjoyed it more than D'Birch would ever prize her emeralds.

That thought led him to the image of GrandLady D'SilverFir. He needed to see her, just to remind himself that not all nobles were arrogant, overweening, and selfish. Anticipation lodged in his bones. He was sure she'd be at the opera.

Enough thinking. Time to act. Ruis went to the closet and took out the light-bending cloak. Just like himself, it contained no psi-based spell. Just like himself, it was made of interesting stuff. Just like himself it was something Celtans didn't comprehend.

*You and I go play.*

He glanced down at Samba. "You know the plan."

*Yessss.* Her whiskers bobbed in satisfaction.

Pausing beside the intricate Captain's desk, he scanned the functioning lights. Each day the Ship brought a new program on-line. He was learning the technologies bit by bit. A blue holo light glittered. Ruis ran a finger through it. "The prophecy program has been initiated," a low, sultry female voice said.

Ruis jumped back, then laughed shortly. Prophecy! The whole world revolved around psi powers he didn't have. He snorted and reached through the holo of a whirlwind of cards to cut the light beam and abort the program.

One card spun in the holo, enlarged, then became animated. A man and a woman walked hand-in-hand. Ruis froze. The man looked a bit like him and wore what Ruis recognized now as a lieutenant's uniform with pentacle shoulder patches. The woman was small and voluptuous with tumbled black hair and a heart-shaped face.

A wall near them toppled.

Ruis cried out.

The man grabbed the woman and jumped aside. They stood, disheveled and with minor, bloody scratches.

Ruis noted their blood looked darker than his own.

"Love and Danger walk the night. Be careful, Captain," the female voice said.

Prophecy. He didn't believe in it.

Samba sniffed. *Cards are the old-fashioned suits.* She looked up at Ruis. *We be careful.* She planted a paw on the door button and marched out ahead of him, tail swaying. She glanced back with slitted eyes. *I watch. Let's go play.*

Ruis followed slowly. Prophecy. It wouldn't work for a Null, would it?

*A*lone in her den, *A*ilim dropped her head back against the chair. She rested her eyes until duty nagged her and she looked down at the wretched ledger sheets on her desk. Primrose whined to be lifted to her lap. "Be careful of my gown." Ailim lifted Primrose eye-to-eye.

*Me love You. Me go to opera?*

Ailim groaned. She preferred instrumental music. Lately she'd been listening to new artists that mimicked the sounds of the Colonists' journey to Celta, "spacewave" music. The odd bells and bongs, a trifle metallic, pleased her and fed some deep need. Her liking of the strange music was her little secret.

Primrose's eartips quivered as if trying to lift. *Me go in Your sleeve pocket. Me be very good. Me not snore.*

Ailim laughed and petted her Fam. "Your snore won't drown out this sort of music. It's some ancient incomprehensible Earth thing, high-pitched singing by a bunch of rotten characters about their miserable lives and nasty plans."

"I have never heard Das Rheingold described in such a way," Aunt Menzie said coldly from the doorway. "I trust you aren't taking that disgusting furry object." Not bothering to close the door, she advanced until she was in front of Ailim. Hectic color mottled Menzie's cheeks, yet shadows rested under her eyes.

Primrose whined.

Ailim gathered her thoughts to reply to Menzie's last question. "Yes, I'm taking Primrose with us to the opera. As Cona says, it is the fashion to parade Earthpets."

Menzie snorted. "Fashion can be awkward. Ah, I wish to drop a word in your ear."

Ailim stared. Aunt Menzie trying to be tactful? The woman had never bothered to be anything but rude. Ailim lifted her chin. "Yes?"

As Menzie smoothed her damask skirt, her ring-encrusted fingers flashed in the light. "I want my daughter Cona to make a HeartMate match."

Impossible. Who would HeartBond with a woman like Cona? "Oh? Have you had indications in your divination system that such a union is upcoming? You use runes, do you not?"

Menzie frowned. "There is evidence of an impending important marriage—"

"Perhaps it is Cona and Donax."

"I don't like that match. He is beneath her—"

"They are nearly equal in status. He is the son of a man who will become T'Reed. She is the great-great-niece of a former T'SilverFir," Ailim pointed out. "Donax has tested high in financial Flair and will be extremely wealthy one day. So will D'SilverFir if we keep him in our Family."

Menzie's eyes glittered. She clutched her pursonal that Ailim sensed contained the baleful amulet. Since they were leaving the Residence, Ailim said nothing.

"Hmmm." Menzie stroked her bag and she shook her head.

"What does Cona's divination system say?" Ailim asked.

Menzie stared down her nose. "Cona leaves her prognostications to me."

"She doesn't practice daily divination and meditation?" Ailim was aghast.

"And you do?"

Ailim flushed. She'd been conscientious in her meditations, but her auguries always showed responsibility, duty, financial worries, burdens, and Family quarrels. The prophecies had been too depressing over the last month to face anymore. "I meditate in the HouseHeart," Ailim said.

"Ah, yes, the HouseHeart, the most sacred place in the Residence." Menzie's voice became more guttural. "I wanted to talk to you about it. Cona was lucky and had quick and easy Passages, so she didn't connect with a HeartMate."

In other words, Cona's Flair for dress design wasn't great enough to trigger the deep emotional traumas. Each of the three Passages tested an individual to the core before freeing major Flair. Ailim's had come early and she'd barely survived.

"I want permission to use the HouseHeart to determine if Cona has a HeartMate," Menzie said thickly.

"No." The word spurted from her lips before Ailim could frame a more diplomatic reply. She petted Primrose, tangling her fingers in the puppy's silky hair. Tension hummed in the air. "So long as you have the amulet, the HouseHeart is closed to you. As is the D'SilverFir ritual grove by the river."

"You can't forbid me. It's my right to use the HouseHeart once a year for three and a half septhours!" she screeched.

"True. But I can set conditions. You must leave the fetish outside the gates of D'SilverFir estate before you will be allowed in the HouseHeart. I will not have an alien object tainting D'SilverFir sacred space, particularly since I will be visiting the HouseHeart every day until my title confirmation and loyalty ceremony next week."

"No." Menzie fisted her hands and pounded on the desk.

Ailim stared. She'd never seen Menzie so out of control.

"You are not yourself. Perhaps you should stay home to-night."

Menzie shut her eyes and shook her head as though shaking insects away. When she opened her eyelids, the blue looked faded. "I'm going."

Ailim lifted Primrose and tucked the pup deep into her sleeve. "Very well. But I am concerned for your health. I'll call a Healer to examine you."

Glaring with her usual vigor, Menzie curled her lips. "No."

"Yes. I am responsible for the health of my Family."

Donax put his head inside the door. "Our glider is here."

"Thank you." Ailim rose.

Primrose wriggled and popped her head out of Ailim's sleeve. *Out. Singing. Fun.*

Menzie turned on a precise heel and stalked from the room, not deigning to notice Donax.

When Ailim drew up to him, she asked, "Are you interested in marrying Cona?"

He nodded.

"I don't suppose you would care to make a HeartGift?" Ailim asked.

"For Cona?" His snort was deeper than Menzie's, but just as disdainful. "Not likely. I don't have a HeartMate this lifetime. No suggestion of it during my Passages to free my Flair, so I didn't make a HeartGift then. And I'm not a damn fool like T'Ash to suffer through another Passage."

He sounded far too cheerful about not having a HeartMate, a partner to love and cherish. Ailim would have been depressed at such news. That realization startled her. Had she such romantic notions, still, at her age? She did.

But she didn't know whether she had a HeartMate. Her Passages had taken place early in her childhood, before puberty, so she'd never felt any sexual or love connection with another.

Donax escorted her from the room. "I'll settle for a wife, not a HeartMate." He grinned. "A marriage alliance will suit me fine."

Ailim sighed. "You'd best invest in some jeweled baubles from T'Ash."

His scowl gratified her.

* * *

*R*uis and Samba stood in the shadow of the Opera House's huge pillars framing the edge of the large terrace. He'd chosen the spot carefully. The oldest stones would bear his Nullness for a couple of septhours before the first few layers of spells were affected. He'd also calculated the distance between himself and the opera-goers. They'd feel a low irritation, but wouldn't be able to define it as Nullness impinging upon their auras.

Large family gliders belonging to nobles whispered to the curb on their cushions of air. Naturally, Ruis had never ridden in one. He stared, wondering about their working parts. Vehicles came and went as he focused on their manufacture and propulsion, ignoring the people who disembarked.

Ruis petted Samba as they waited for the D'Birch glider vehicle to arrive. At the appropriate moment Samba would jump at D'Birch, tear her sleeve, and the emeralds would roll out.

A corner of Ruis's mouth quirked. It had been as easy as he'd planned to insert the necklace into the thick hem of the dress sleeve. Now his own play was about to begin.

He knew that the "found" emeralds wouldn't change his own circumstances. He'd been banished more for being a Null than for his breaking of any Celtan law. So embarrassing D'Birch was the sole satisfaction he'd get from this night's work—and the knowledge that he'd kept his own code of honor.

Samba fluffed her tail up, arched her back, and hissed. He followed her gaze to see his uncle a few meters away, lecturing his head-bowed wife.

Ruis's gut clenched. His body jerked in checked movement as he stopped himself from instinctively plunging forward to bury his fist in the man's soft belly. Except for the trial, Ruis hadn't seen Bucus for years. His uncle was overweight and out of shape. He never had to fight for food scraps and make do with whatever diet he could scavenge. He never had to keep a sharp eye out or maintain a honed body to run from a murderous enemy.

The idea of pouncing on Bucus like Samba pounced on

a mouse in a park sizzled through Ruis. He could see his
own fists pummeling the man, hitting him until each and
every one of the razorslits, each backhanded slap, each
hurtful blow to Ruis as a boy was paid for in full. The
image was so sweet he could taste it, rolling around in his
mouth like the richest candy.

He took a step forward. Samba grabbed his trous leg in
her teeth. The little ripping sound sobered Ruis. To attack
his uncle would be suicidal. There were guardsmen near
the door, and most nobles had their own Family guards.

In the past, assaulting Bucus might have been worth punishment. But not now. Not when Ruis had the Ship. And
Samba. And the thought of more moments with D'SilverFir.

Ruis slid back into the shadows and steadied his
breathing from the ragged panting of anticipatory battle.
Cool air settled his hot blood. He looked at his uncle and
knew that someday Bucus would fall under his vengeful
fists. Ruis smiled.

"MMMrrrffoww," Samba growled, then spit out cloth.
*D'Birch comes*.

So she did, sweeping up the stairs in an overdress of
white and gold, stiff with embroidery and the twinkle of
small gems.

Ruis smiled again. His pulse sang in his ears. A little
payback would come due tonight. He'd taken the D'Birch
necklace when it had slid off the GreatLady's neck, but now
he could return it. The damned necklace that the noblewoman believed was worth his life.

"Ready?" he asked Samba.

"Yesssss," she said. She flexed her claws, hopping a bit.
The light in her eyes matched that which might be in his
own.

As D'Birch climbed the last step and lingered to see who
was on the great portico and who was arriving, Samba
moved. The cat streaked across the marble-squared pavement to catch the lowest drape of the woman's left sleeve
and tug.

Silkeen ripped. D'Birch screamed. Samba flattened her
ears. Tumbling from the gown, jewels flashed green and
gold.

A jolt of exhilaration arrowed through Ruis. Done! The

plan carried out, GreatLady D'Birch caught in a malicious lie. She hadn't been able to sense him when she'd lost the emeralds, but had blamed him anyway. Now they were returned and her words at the trial would mock her.

Samba gazed at the gleaming stones against the pristine white marble of the Opera terrace. All talk stopped as everyone stared at the circle of dazzling emeralds.

"Thief! Thief!" cried Uncle Bucus.

Ruis pulled his cloak around him, then saw Bucus was pointing at Samba.

"Samba!" Ruis hissed.

She started, then threaded through legs, hobbling people. She dashed in front of Bucus and spat at him. He kicked at her.

"Thief!" Bucus shouted again.

Ruis gritted his teeth.

Now Bucus rocked on his heels. "That cat. She's a thief. I've heard she belongs to—" He snapped his mouth shut. Ruis knew then that somehow Bucus had found out Samba was Fam to his loathed nephew. In a temper, Bucus had almost revealed that Samba might lead him to Ruis.

Ruis had no doubt Bucus still wanted him dead. The hair on the back of Ruis's neck prickled, yet he wanted to jump into the milling crowd and protect his Fam. He dared not. Certain death. "The cat's a thief," Bucus said.

"Is that so?" D'SilverFir asked coolly.

Ruis started. He hadn't seen her arrive. His glance fixed on her, slender and elegant in a simple pale-green gown shot with silver. His thudding heart missed a beat, his breath lodged in his throat. She was the epitome of graceful breeding, everything a noble lady should be.

Bucus went motionless. "Judge D'SilverFir."

Ailim studied portly, red-faced T'Elder. He obviously was hiding something, as well as scrambling his surface thoughts so she couldn't read them. "You call a feral cat a thief?" she asked. But anticipation shimmered in her blood. She recognized the cat—the Fam—as the one that had bonded with Ruis Elder.

T'Elder's eyes shifted. He knew the cat, too.

"Very well, I'll set the guardsmen on the animal." Ailim

lifted a hand and sent a mental command to two uniformed men standing near the door. *Catch the cat.*

They stared in disbelief, exchanged glances.

"T'Elder wants that cat," Ailim called above the renewed hubbub of the crowd.

Chuckles and laughs rippled around the Opera portico. The guards jogged after the cat. The feline stayed in the light of the night glows, weaving in and around people as if it were a game, fat and sassy and appearing thoroughly delighted.

T'Elder turned a deep red. "Stop the guards," he choked.

Ailim lifted her brows. "Of course. Stop guardsmen!" *Stop*, she reinforced the order mentally. Everyone turned their attention to her. Damn. She'd overdone the mental call and drawn notice to herself. She suppressed a sigh.

*We hear and obey,* the guards replied, with a hint of panting in their thoughts.

Ailim nodded severely to Bucus T'Elder and his wife, who stood before her. "It is done. If you need my services, please don't hesitate to contact me."

A screech focused all notice on D'Birch. With one last ebullient run, the calico zoomed back past D'Birch, who stooped to pick up the emerald necklace. One black, orange, and white paw flicked an expensive comb from the woman's hair. D'Birch tottered and the jewelry fell from her grasping fingers.

Holm Holly stepped forward to steady the lady. A circle of nobles gathered again to stare at glittering gems.

"Interesting," Holm said. "I believe these were the subject of some controversy not too long ago. I rather thought the thief Ruis Elder was supposed to have taken these. Then again, T'Ash said the clasp was loose. . . ."

"They're mine," D'Birch said.

"Oh, indubitably." Holm stooped and picked up the shining necklace. With a sweeping, elegant bow, he gave it to her.

A high-pitched yapping caught Ailim's attention, and she looked over to see Primrose struggling in Cona's hands. As a sop to Family peace, Ailim had let Cona carry the pup as the most fashionable "accessory" a lady could have this season. Now the "accessory" was making her liveliness known.

*Friend. Friend. Play friend,* Primrose squealed. She jumped down and tore past several clusters of nobles, all with pets. *Let's play! Play! Play!*

Her invitation got immediate results. Kittens poked heads out of long sleeves and jumped nimbly to the steps, dogs started barking. One thin, aristocratic but stupid-looking hound took off after Primrose in a run. The air filled with animal sounds, the steps became a whirl of furry bodies.

Silky ears flying, Primrose bounded down the stairs toward the busy, deadly street after a supple calico tail.

"Primrose, stop!" Ailim sped down the steps, heart pounding with fear for the puppy's safety in the street. She'd reached the last tread when a foursome of young dogs hit her ankles.

She pitched forward, arched to miss the gliders, but two crashed near her anyway. Their forcefields collided, sparked, promising death. She shut her eyes as she fell.

*Jerking his light-bending cloak close,* Ruis jumped, grabbed D'SilverFir, and dived, twisting, under the bumpledges of the glider vehicles. He grunted as he struck the ground.

The gliders's forcefields, already weak from the collision, fizzled when his Nullness hit them. Their stands clattered down. The transports rocked back and forth above him, the flowskirts ringing the bottom of the bumpledges fluttered down, hiding Ruis.

He heard the hiss of emergency mechanics opening the doors. An argument started between the drivers.

Danger feathered up his spine. He'd saved D'SilverFir from death, but his discovery was a few seconds away if he didn't get out of here, fast. "GrandLady," he panted.

She didn't answer. Her body was limp atop his.

# Seven

❦

$\mathcal{F}$*ootsteps came close.* "*Hey, you blithering idiots,*" Holm
Holly said. "The opera is starting. Are you going to stand here
and argue, or take care of this mess?"

Ruis should leave D'SilverFir, let the eminently noble Holm
Holly rescue her. But he couldn't give her up to another man,
especially Holly, noble and charming and in need of a wife.

Ruis's arms tightened around Ailim. All the nerves in his
body went on alert. The feel and scent of her dominated his
senses.

He had to protect her.

Holly and the drivers discussed what was to be done. Other
nobles talked loudly and gathered their pets, scolding the animals. Ruis got an impression of confusion, with no one missing
one small GrandLady new to society.

A cold nose pressed against Ruis's cheek. Rumbling and
"pprrps" told him Samba had returned. A chirrup. *Good playing. Chase. Hide-and-seek. Slink and Evade. All good games.*
She snorted. *Dogs are not as smart as Cats.*

Harness jingling mixed with animal whuffling protests.

*Riderbeasts. They don't like Our smell. Come, now.*

Ruis's arms tightened reflexively around GrandLady
D'SilverFir. He didn't want to let her go.

He had to let her go.

She was a SupremeJudge. He was a condemned man.

She opened her eyes and gasped when she found herself nose-to-nose with Samba.

Samba sniffed her. *Verrry nice smell. She can come with us.*

"No," Ruis murmured, releasing her hand and rolling away.

Too late. Her eyes met his and went wide.

"Look at this traffic," a disgusted Holm Holly said above them, blocked by the metal of the glider. "And it's taking far too long to be cleared. Hey!" he shouted.

D'SilverFir jerked her head up, banged it hard on the underside of the glider, and went limp once more.

Ruis cursed under his breath.

"Tinne, brother of mine, come help me 'port this mess to T'Furze's Courtyard. He can sort it out later," Holly called.

A young man's laugh answered him.

*We GO!* Samba hit Ruis in the cheek with a sheathed paw. *I'll make more trouble. You play Slink and Evade.*

Ruis grunted.

Samba shot out from under the glider to zoom around the Opera steps.

"It's that damn cat again! Does anyone know who it belongs to? Or is it feral? Is it wearing a silver collar?" Holly shouted. More gasps and shrieks and shouts.

Ruis slid through the flowskirt and from under the glider's far bumpledge, pulled D'SilverFir after him, lifted her into his arms, and crouched below the glider's top. He muffled himself and her in his cloak, then drifted away like a shifting shadow.

Samba joined him. *Are we going home?* The angle of her whiskers showed she was very pleased with herself.

"No. We can't take Lady D'SilverFir to the Ship."

Samba grinned. *We play hide-and-seek?*

"Yes."

*My Sire, Zanth, has many hiding places in the City. Downwind—*

"Nothing Downwind. She doesn't belong Downwind."

*I don't belong Downwind.* Samba sniffed. *Downwind smells. But I know a place near here. Clean and dry and pleasant.*

The thought prodded Ruis's recall, of a place that had once welcomed him, and where he hadn't returned for many years since his Nullness harmed it and he had prized it so. "Follow me."

Samba, ever curious, rotated both ears, flicked the tip of her tail and pranced to his side with a purr of approval. *I will follow you to a new and interesting place. Fun.*

Ruis and Samba hurried from CityCenter and down ever quieter streets. He worried about the too-limp woman in his arms.

After a few moments he stopped at a tall, crumbling wall of a GrandHouse estate. The Family had died out, an all-too-common occurrence on the yet untamed Celta. Like the Blackthorn estate, this, too, was reputed to harbor a curse.

Ruis knew better.

Potent illusions surrounded the property and the rumor of a curse guarded a natural wonder: the first Healing grove of the colonists. Many generations of Healers had been taught here. They had reinforced the first, ancient healing spells in the naturally curative spring and the protecting trees. But as the Nobles became more powerful, only the greatest of Healers were allowed in FirstGrove, and then, through secrecy and mischance, the location had been lost.

When Ruis had deciphered the ancient words on the ruined stones, he'd researched FirstGrove. It held a powerful gatespell, keyed to let the most wounded and desperate in.

His lips twisted in an ironic smile. The spell had no effect on him—none of the illusion spells, nor the gatespell, nor even the healing spells. But he couldn't deny that he'd been heart wounded and desperate when he'd found it at fourteen.

D'SilverFir shifted in his arms, moaning a little.

Ruis cuddled her closer and made soothing noises, noises he was aware that he'd never heard himself and that were echoes of Samba's to him. He only hoped that they translated into something that might reassure a lady.

When she settled, he felt triumphant. He found the pointed-arch door in the wall and showed Samba how to use the lever. The cat did so with great smugness. They walked through a maze of vine covered lattices, hedgerows, and tangled brush until Ruis ducked and entered the long leafy tunnel to First-Grove itself.

He pushed past the last veil of vines and stopped at the beauty. The twinmoons had risen and gleamed three-quarters full on opposite sides of the sky. Cymru glowed dull gold, Eire a rosy pink.

Dark trees thrust into the sky, huge and sheltering the soft, mossy ground below. Unlike the other trees of Druida, they still held their leaves. FirstGrove lagged behind the year; it was still summer here. Some of the great trees were old Earth oaks mixed in with large boled trees native to Celta, and hybrids that had bred in this special place.

Ruis carefully lowered himself and D'SilverFir down to the thick, fragrant grass, close to the shallows of the spring.

Samba squealed, her green eyes bright. *Verrrry interesting place. I go play.* She trotted off, tail waving.

D'SilverFir groaned and raised a faltering hand to her head. Then she jerked upright. "I can't feel I can't read—" she cried in panic.

He thought of leaving her; he couldn't. "My fault, I think," he said, surprised at how low and rough his voice was.

She lifted glazed eyes. Blinked. Stared. "You!"

"Me." He began to withdraw his arms from around her slender body.

She grasped his shirt. "No."

Tremors ran through her. She was reacting to her close brush with death.

He kept her close and murmured into her hair. "No?"

She shut her eyes again and relaxed against him. "No," she whispered.

"You're a SupremeJudge and I'm condemned to death if found in Druida."

Now both hands clutched at her head. "I can't think. My head hurts."

He sighed inwardly. She didn't want to face facts. He'd been doing his best to ignore the deadly facts himself, but was always aware that each time he stepped from the Ship to roam Druida, he placed his life in danger. She turned her face into his chest and his thoughts scrambled as he tightened his hold on her. She trusted him. She liked being in his arms. The attraction he had felt, had thought she'd felt the times they'd met, was definitely mutual. His spirits rose.

"This is a healing spring, GrandLady. There's a head-depression carved in the soft stone at the edge of the water. Would you like to try it?"

"A healing spring?" She opened her eyes. Her breath caught as she took in the loveliness around them. Fascination appeared on her face. Slowly she sat up. "Where are we? Where is the HealingHall attached to the grove and the spring?"

Ruis smiled. "We're in FirstGrove."

"FirstGrove." She looked around the trees and the pool, the summer roses still blooming in autumn. "The fabled First-Grove?" She sighed, her shoulders slumped, then squared, as if accepting all her usual responsibilities. Then she sat, spine straight, away from the curve of his supporting arms. Ruis reluctantly moved so they no longer touched. She released deep, unsettled feelings in him, brought a great yearning for a normal life. He suffered through it, gritting his teeth. He wasn't normal and never would be.

"Why don't we try the healing spring on your head?" He stood and held out his hand.

She stared up at him, and he saw a reflected flicker of longing cross her features, only to be supplanted by guilt and duty that made her thin her lips and raise her chin.

They both knew they were worlds apart, worlds that couldn't ever be reconciled. But she placed her hand in his and he slowly drew her to her feet. He guided her a few steps to the pool and indicated the depression shaped in the marble, surrounded by a lacy stonework crown to direct the flow and ensure the patient could not drown. Water bubbled through the intricately and beautifully cut masonry, but would not touch her face.

She stooped and trailed her fingers in the spring. "It's warm."

He squatted and put the tip of his little finger in the pond for an instant. Then he stood and backed away. "That's me. It should be hotter than this, but I'm in the vicinity."

"Hmmm." She eyed the water and stone crown. "Time in the Healing Spring couldn't hurt."

"And your head does."

"Oh, yes." She looked up at him and her face softened. "You are always taking care of me."

He cleared his throat. "My pleasure, GrandLady."

Her delicate skin flushed. She lifted her chin. "And it has been my pleasure, too." Raising her hand, her fingers brushed against his face. "Call me Ailim."

Ruis's heart pounded. He wanted her in so many ways, so he stepped aside. "Let's take care of your head . . . first."

She reddened more but nodded, then winced. Moving warily, she went to the pool, lay flat on her back, and began lowering her head into the water.

"Wait. I'm going to the other side of the spring so the Healing spells and heat will return fully. I'll keep a lookout."

She was so dignified. Didn't she get tired of being so proper all the time? He wanted her relaxed, smiling. He grinned at her and thought of teasing a little. "All you have to do is squeak and I'll come running."

She blinked, then her lips curved. "Squeak?" she asked, as if such a sound had never issued from her lips. Probably not— she must have been taught the dignity, decorum, and propriety expected of a FirstFamily Heir since she was a toddler.

He cocked his head. "Squeak. Why don't you try it?"

She stared at him.

"I can't hear you," he said.

She started squeaking with low and short sounds, then as Ruis stood back, hands on hips, her squeaks became long and high, then with complete abandon.

He laughed.

She stopped, raised her chin. "I can squeak if I want."

"You certainly can."

D'SilverFir sighed. "At least here."

"Don't limit yourself."

She shrugged and lowered her head into the pool. Small lines of strain smoothed as the water rose to frame her beautiful face. She wriggled a bit, breasts and hips moving in a way that made Ruis suddenly aware of her femininity and his very masculine reaction.

He nodded to her and flipped a hand in the direction he would be going. She smiled again.

Ruis set off around the pool, keeping the glittering silver threads of her gown always in sight. He reached the other side of the spring and stared at D'SilverFir. Her hands were folded, her sliver slippers pointed. Serene and ladylike, as always. Yet he sensed that if he had her truly alone and in an intimate setting, he could coax her to abandon herself to passion.

She adjusted her head and her pale braids rippled around her face. Her expression showed enjoyment.

He wanted to be with her, next to her, but here he was, across the entire pool. His mouth twisted. It was symbolic of their relationship.

A few moments later Ailim rose and started to dry her hair with a spell. Her fine blond tresses had been freed from their elaborate plaits in the form of Celtic knots and floated around her. When Ruis got within a few feet of her, the drying spell died, and her hair subsided back onto her head.

D'SilverFir put a hand to her temple, tilted her head, and narrowed her eyes. She was obviously trying to use her Flair. She shook her head.

Ruis tensed.

The slight curve that graced her lips faded and her expression became solemn. "You saved my life."

"Did I?" Ruis smiled ironically. "My Nullness short-circuited the glider forcefields."

She took a small step toward him. "You kept me from falling between them. You brought me here to Heal."

Ruis shrugged.

Again she stepped forward, staring, her eyes moving as if trying to gauge his motives. Ruis realized that, probably for the first time since she'd experienced her full Flair, she had no telempathic clues to what another person was thinking. His own gaze sharpened. As usual, she didn't look frightened or distressed—she seemed intrigued, perhaps even fascinated?

When she came another half-step forward, his nostrils widened as he caught her scent, something deep and rich and sweet, completely tempting. The fragrance insinuated itself inside him and twined through his blood until it picked up pace.

"Will you turn me in?" he asked.

Her mouth pinched. In her eyes, duty and responsibility warred with gratitude and interest. Ruis was glad to see the conflict. It fed his starving ego.

"Are you going to leave Druida?" she asked.

"No."

Impasse. She huffed out a breath and shot him a disgruntled look. "You could have lied," she murmured.

"I want every word, every action between us to be honest."

She raised her eyebrows. "The honorable Ruis Elder. I knew it, but couldn't find proof." She bent down and scooped up a handful of water. Watching him, she spread her fingers and the water sieved away, tiny droplets clinging to her fingers. "You are like the water, flowing through all the official papers of Druida and Celta. A mention here, a hint of someone who might be you there, but no solid records.

"You were a FirstSon, entitled to an allowance from your

birth. The papers are muddled, the bookkeeping odd." She set her hands on her hips and tapped her foot. "It can only be extrapolated that your allowance was actually paid. But no receipts are on file written in your hand and independently verified that you, personally, ever received the funds."

"A Null isn't a person in Celtan culture or to those who comprise the GuildCouncils. That's a statement of fact."

She gave a ladylike snort. "Not acceptable."

He shrugged again. "It hardly matters. I'm a convicted thief, now. I'm sure that according to the law of Celta, any monthly noblegilt due me is void upon my banishment." He lifted his eyebrows. "You might want to ensure that no noblegilt is paid out in my name," he said, a slow smile touching his lips. One stream of funds to Bucus cut off, at least.

She nodded shortly. "I'll take care of that in the morning."

Ruis liked the way authority sat upon her. Liked her obvious competence. And knew he liked it because it warmed him to think of someone such as she respecting him, valuing him. His gut clenched and he battled back weakening emotions. "So, are you going to turn me in, Judge D'SilverFir?" He was sure he knew the answer—it lived in the thread of attraction that spun between them, but he wanted words. He found that he was greedy for solid words that she esteemed him, not merely indirect hints. He needed a declaration that he was of some worth to someone. Finally.

Her eyes narrowed. "I am not in the habit of ingratitude. Of course I will not turn you in. You saved my life." She might be trying to keep her face impassive, but Ruis had long experience in measuring the expressions of others, and there was no hardness in hers.

"We're even," he said.

She tilted her head. "I don't think so. I don't know that we will ever be 'even' and . . ."

"And?"

A slight flush pinkened her cheeks. "I dislike thinking that we might be keeping track of favors. There is too much between us and time is too short, that we should tally courtesies."

"I am banished from Druida," he said softly. "I am breaking your precious laws."

Her fingers tunneled through her hair. "They *are* precious

laws. The rule of law is paramount in keeping humans civilized. Without law, people would act on whim, with no thought of the consequences. The powerful would rule without recourse."

"Oh, and that doesn't happen?" His sarcasm made her color. But she lifted her chin.

"Not always. And not forever. No one is above the law. No one."

Ruis laughed. She closed her eyes as if pained and that stopped him short.

Her breasts rose as she took a deep breath. "I know that you, of all people, have trouble believing that, but it is the cornerstone of my life. What has happened to you is—" She shook her head, raised her hands, then dropped them in a futile gesture. "It should not have happened to you, to anyone."

He shook his head in disbelief at her idealism.

She stiffened her spine. "I will undo the tangle of records around your life, and when I do—"

He took one of her waving hands and raised it to his lips. Again she pinkened, but this time he was sure it was not from misguided guilt or shame. This time it was because of his touch. His. Touch. He, Ruis Elder.

"So you will not turn me in," he whispered against her hand. "Because I saved your life. Because I came to you after your JudgmentGrove and massaged the wretchedness from you."

Her fingers fluttered within his own as he admitted what was true and real between them aloud.

"Because I have been wronged and you revere the law and strive to correct any injustice. Because my existence is tangled in missing pages and incomplete documents and raises many questions. Do I have all this right?" He kissed her hand now, grateful to her for all the good emotions she'd set blooming in his life. "And what of this wonderful sharing bond we have between us?"

"I will fight for you." It was barely a whisper, but it sounded like a vow.

"What's past is past. I don't dwell on that which is gone. I'd rather you kiss me," he said, and held his breath at his impetuous words. A glacial ice froze him in place. He'd left himself completely vulnerable to her rejection. Something he hadn't done since childhood.

She stepped up close to him and her hands went to his shoulders. He wondered if she could feel the tremors coursing through his body. Her expression turned to longing, matching the need twisting inside him. Rising to her toes, she brushed her mouth gently across his. Too gently. He ached desperately for more, but fisted his hands at his side to endure the exquisite pleasure, more emotional than physical, of a woman kissing him. A groan of delight mixed with need tore from his throat.

She settled to her feet, but instead of leaving him, she rested her head and palms against his chest, breathing deeply. Ruis closed his arms around her.

"I can't read you," she murmured against him.

"No." He wanted to string some charming words together, but his tongue stuck.

"All my senses open up when I am with you. I experience so much of the physical world without any tinge of the mental. It's wonderful."

She looked up. Her breasts pressed against him as she breathed, and Ruis could not turn away from either her soft body or the bemusement in her eyes. He could only stand and let her feel the pounding of his heart and the gathering sexual tension of his muscles. "You open up the world to me, yet you keep my mind quiet and safe and—restful."

She stirred him up to storm, yet smiled calmly at him.

He set one hand at the back of her waist and cradled her head with his other hand. Lifting her slightly, he placed his lips on hers.

How soft! He inhaled and her natural aroma settled into his memory until he knew he would never be free of it. His lips parted and the merest wisp of a tantalizing feminine taste teased him.

He wanted more.

Thought fled. He gathered her closer until all of her pressed against him. Only the delight of her full bosom soft on his chest, her firm bottom under his hand, moved him.

He flicked his tongue across her closed lips. "Open your mouth for me."

Her lips parted and he delved. She tasted dark, rich, sweet. Desire erupted through his veins. He savored her, drawing into himself all the essence of her taste, her scent, her self.

Her hands slowly brushed up his arms to settle on his shoulders, accepting the kiss and accepting him. Need grew for this delicious woman.

He wanted to touch her everywhere, but could not bear to separate himself from her, even to caress a breast, a thigh. The pressure of her body along his ignited sensation in every nerve.

She plunged her fingers into his hair, her tongue tangled with his and made him groan. Arching to him, her hips rocked against his throbbing arousal.

He lowered them to the ground. The light impact of her softness on him fed his fever.

She gasped, moaned. An odd sound.

He drew back.

Her eyes were dilated black. She panted. Her delicate lips trembled. He was hurting her! He'd paid no attention to her head. He tore himself away, staring at her heart-shaped face and lovely features, her fine-boned body with full breasts and curving hips.

This was no tavern girl to tumble in heedless lust. This was a GrandLady. A FirstFamily GrandLady. A woman who had been kind to him.

Now and then, at his most optimistic, he dared to hope he could court her, win her, ignoring that she had great duties and status. Those last words of hers vowing to help him bolstered his hopes. He could give her something no one else on Celta could—relief from the mental battering of others, an exploration of her physical senses.

Realistically, he could see no good end to their association. She was not his woman. The most they could have was a short affair. His life was too opposite hers, and he now held secrets of the Ship that he didn't dare let anyone—even her—know.

Ailim rose to her feet, her hands clasped at her waist. She looked a trifle mussed from his hands, but not in pain. In fact, her expression was more carefree than he'd ever seen.

"Did I hurt you?" he asked.

She raised perfectly arched brows. "Is that why you stopped? No. You didn't hurt me. I enjoy being with you."

Samba strolled from some bushes and came to sit beside him. Both her ears moved forward, her whiskers quivered with her subvocal growl. *My FamMan*.

D'SilverFir nodded at the cat, but fear crossed her face. "My Fam, my Primrose—"

Samba snorted beside him. *Young, stupid puppy.*

D'SilverFir winced.

*Puppy fine. Ran to Holm Holly.*

Ruis blinked. The name was clear in Samba's meows.

"Holly?" he said.

*Holm Holly. Hollys have kept Fams all through the years. Hunting Cats.* Samba lifted her pointed chin. *My Dam is Holly.*

D'SilverFir sighed. Her hands tightened. "I'm sure D'Ash will have something to say when I have to pick up a prized puppy from the Holly household." One of her shoulders hunched, then she angled her chin. "Nothing to be done about it."

"You're very conscious of appearances."

D'SilverFir gestured gracefully. "Appearances, manners, propriety, duty. All are scrutinized in a Judge."

The fact that she was forbidden to him crashed down on him. Anger surged through Ruis. Why had he thought he could ever have this woman? He had been given the Elder Heir's name of Ruis. He was a FirstSon. Without his Nullness, he would be equal to Holly, a match for even D'SilverFir. But not now. He staggered a step and accepted the pain in his heart.

She moved to him, wrapping her fingers around his arm as if to steady him. She frowned up at him, and her other hand touched his jaw. "You have scratches, and bruises. You saved my life and hurt yourself—the spring—"

"Is imbued with healing spells. No healing spells work on me."

She looked horrified. "Then how—"

He folded his fingers over hers. "I'm careful." He raised an eyebrow. "And I use herbs. Isn't that how everything started?"

She pulled her hands away to whip a softleaf from her sleeve, then carefully patted his face. "Herbs, yes, of course. This has a little healing spell—"

"Which I have just negated—"

"But it also has an unguent for minor scrapes."

Taking the softleaf in one hand, he grasped her fingers and held them to his mouth in a brushing, tender kiss. She hesitated and pulled her hand away. Again attraction spun between them, desire—then even more, something he'd never known from a person of any Flair—simple affection.

Now he raised the cloth to his nostrils and sniffed. "It doesn't smell of unguent. It smells of you."

She flushed and looked down, gathered handfuls of the fabric of her gown and shook it so bits of grass and twigs that had clung to it fell free.

Ruis harkened back to their conversation. "It seems to me that you've always lived a restricted life, not only now. You should enjoy the present moment more. Cherish the now."

"You saved my life." She smiled. "Some would say that gives you infinite rights to advise me." She turned and hesitated at the branching of three paths.

She didn't want to think of reality, either. Ruis walked to her. He wanted to offer his arm, but it would be better to not touch her.

She wobbled on shoes that were fashionably high. He shot out a hand to steady her, and when she curved her own hand above his elbow and hung on, he said nothing. He cherished her touch. And her scent. And the lingering taste of her. The memory he would never forget of her body atop him. His own body tightened.

Samba smacked his boots with her paw. *You are ignoring Me.*

Ruis looked down at her. D'SilverFir's steps didn't falter. She was too close to him, connected to him. He halted the woman and waved to a proudly preening Samba. "GrandLady D'SilverFir, my Fam, Samba, and I are honored by your presence."

Samba snorted.

D'SilverFir looked at him, then the cat. She stooped and tentatively patted Samba's large head. Samba rumbled a purr. "She looks quite the huntress."

Samba's purr went up a notch. *I am great huntress. I am wonderful Cat and Fam.*

Ailim frowned as if she had trouble picking out Samba's individual words.

"Samba is a good Fam." Ruis held out his elbow and D'SilverFir tucked her hand into the crook of his arm. They began walking again.

*I am also smart.*

"She's smart."

*Unlike the puppy. Puppy will never be smart.*

Ruis didn't translate.

They stopped at the edge of the FirstGrove. Selfishly, he wanted to give her a token to remember him by. Looking around, he saw a lush plant twining up an arbor. Though only a few of the trumpet flowers still bloomed, he could make out their heavy scent—An'Alcha—passionflower. Just thinking of passion caused blood to pound through him.

Just beyond the An'Alcha he saw a bush of delicate BalmHeal, rare and beautiful, a plant to heal any lingering trace of Ailim's headache.

He hesitated, then chose.

Walking past the An'Alcha, he addressed the BalmHeal in Celtan tradition. "Forgive me, I need a spray of your blossoms." He snapped a small branchlet off. "I will not forget your generosity. Thank you."

When he turned to D'SilverFir, she was smiling. "Well done."

He bowed. "For you."

"Thank you." She tucked it carefully into a loop near her shoulder, made for displaying flowers.

Ruis couldn't help but smile. It was the first time he had ever given a lady flowers, and to have pleased a woman with so small a gesture made him feel strong and confident.

She smiled back at him, and he realized it was the first carefree smile he'd seen grace her face. For once she must not be thinking of duty and responsibility, of what her station, as a FirstFamily head and a SupremeJudge, demanded of her. He slowed his steps. If this was the last time he dared spend with this woman, he would completely enjoy it.

They came to the wooden door in the dilapidated wall, and D'SilverFir traced a finger in the cracked stone plaque next to the portal. "GrandHouse BalmHeal," she mused. "How long have they been gone, I wonder."

Ruis's smile twisted. "They didn't make it two centuries. I researched them."

When she looked surprised, he straightened. "D'Licorice, the Public Librarian, allowed me use of the system and the archives." She'd set up a special room for him so he could be comfortable and not affect the collections with his defect.

He looked down at D'SilverFir and smoothed a wisp of

blond hair back from her face. The last touch, before they faced the outside world.

She smiled and turned aside.

He nodded to Samba, who opened the door. The hush of the garden was broken by city sounds.

D'SilverFir withdrew her hand and stepped aside. "I can find my way home."

Ruis followed her through the gate. "I'll make sure you get to D'SilverFir Residence."

She whirled on him, looking angry. "You've tempted fate too much this eve. I'll—"

"—accompany me when I walk you home. We'll be safe." He took her arm, then dropped it. "Unless you tire of my presence. My Nullness wears on you."

Her head jerked up. "You know the reverse is true." She set her hand back between his side and elbow and sighed. "Very well, but we must be careful."

Half a septhour later Ruis opened the huge greeniron gate of D'SilverFir estate for her. She led him down a side path toward the castle.

It stood regal in the twinmoonslight, ruddy stone with round towers capped in greeniron that reflected in the lake around it. Like many FirstFamily Residences, it copied some ancient earth castle.

He looked down at her, her blond hair pale in the moonlight, framing her heart-shaped face, and he didn't want to leave. He wanted to be with her, for the evening, for the night, and even for the morn to come—a strange, impossible fantasy. Ruis framed her face in his hands and brushed his lips across hers.

Her mouth trembled against his, and she returned his kiss, pressing her soft, warm body against his. His mind swam with colors and sensations as his body tightened in the urge to mate.

A siren screamed from the castle. A few seconds later the door flew open.

"Intruder alert! I'll send a scan out!" a male voice shouted.

"I must leave," she said.

Her gaze searched his face, but he saw only yearning in her eyes.

"Run," he said.

"You, too."

He grinned and she sucked in a breath.
Before temptation to kiss her won, he said, "Go!"
They ran.
In opposite directions.

# Eight

*All* the serenity her time with Ruis had brought vanished when Ailim entered the GreatHall and found her Family waiting. She intoned a Word, canceling the alarm, and a HouseHold wind pushed those who had hovered near the entrance firmly into the Hall and slammed the door.

Face flushed with anger, Aunt Menzie rounded on Ailim. "Where have you been?"

Ailim drew herself up to her full height and raised haughty eyebrows. "My actions are my own."

"There are certain rules that all of this household are to follow—" Menzie started.

"Yes, and the first rule is that D'SilverFir makes all the rules. I will not be questioned regarding my whereabouts, my schedule, or my private life."

"You owe the Family an explanation." Menzie's voice spiked even higher. She and the others—Ab, Cona, Pinwyd, and even Canadena—surrounded Ailim in an accusatory circle.

She snapped up her personal shields, hard, but not before she had seen mixed with their anger their deepest, unconscious ugly hope that a fatal accident might have occurred to her.

That hurt. Terribly.

Ailim stared at them. Who were these people? She shook her head to banish the discomfiting thought. They were her Family.

Breathing deeply and controlling her voice, Ailim answered, "I owe the Family my allegiance, my protection, and my best efforts to preserve it. I am endeavoring to fulfill all my duties and responsibilities, but that does not mean you can poke into my private life—"

"Private life?" Cona stared as if the concept was inconceivable.

"We were afraid for you." Canadena's voice wavered. She clutched her Fam kitten close, heedless of its little claws snagging the expensive fabric of her gown.

Ailim managed a smile for her and softened her tones. "I thank you for your concern, Cuz."

"Yes," shrilled Cona. "Very afraid." She patted a hand over her heart as if she still suffered from palpitations.

Ailim leveled a glance at Cona. "Were you? And here I thought that you and I are linked on a health knowing level so you would know whether I was ill or well."

"I felt danger, then hurt, then unconsciousness. Then *NOTH-ING.*" Cona lifted her hand to her head and swooned toward Donax Reed. He scooped her into his arms and onto a plush sofa.

Being with Ruis had blanked the minor connection with Cona, and Ailim was glad. Her wondrous moments with Ruis were hers alone, private and not to be shared with anyone.

"As you can all see, I am well." Ailim sent a cold glance around the circle. "I went after my Fam, but didn't find her. I've heard that Primrose is with the Hollys, and I'll pick her up tomorrow. Primrose wasn't in my care and got lost. I trust that you understand better care from all of you is necessary in providing for the GreatHouse Fam."

"Of course, of course," G'Uncle Ab said.

Ailim turned on her heel.

"You listen to me, Ailim—" Menzie said. She stopped as Ailim walked to a small, ancient door set in a dim corner. "Where are you going?"

Ailim looked at her in disbelief. They all knew the door led to the sacred HouseHeart. Ailim needed refuge, sanctuary, time to sort out her thoughts, and the HouseHeart would give her that.

Menzie actually stepped back at Ailim's gaze. She waited, unyielding, until her Family filed from the GreatHall. Then she opened the door with a spell, summoned a lightball, closed the door and locked it with a powerful chant. She wended her way deep into the bowels of the earth below her home.

The last passage had the curved walls of a tube, and Ailim's footsteps echoed uncannily on material never forged on Celta. She hurried through the cylinder, SilverFir's deepest secret— their HouseHeart was connected to the Residence by an ancient Earth tunnel through the lake.

She took a moment to scan the walls for cracks. Tiny threads laced the end of the tube. Much of her personal energy and the energy of the Residence was used to keep the passage stable. Other Noble households could run their entire Residences for a year on the energy the SilverFirs used just to maintain the corridor. So other common spells had to be purchased at a high rate.

Ailim sighed. The only way she could reveal this to Donax Reed so he could work with good figures was to get his consent to a selective "forget" spell. Then he'd know that a certain amount of personal and household Flair must be allocated to a powerful spell, but not exactly what the spell was. She hoped to wait until his own goals aligned with the SilverFirs and not the Reeds—or his uncle, Bucus Elder.

At the end of the tunnel, beyond several illusions, she faced the huge stone door of the HouseHeart. Again she breathed deeply, preparing herself. She had only visited this place once since becoming D'SilverFir, to affirm to the Residence that she was now head of the household and to set her own personal lockwords and preferences. Earlier it had been too difficult to admit that she now led the Family, not her mother or MotherSire. At the moment the HouseHeart offered blessed peace from the rest of her live-in Family.

The stone door was different from the redstone of the castle, made of black and white marble—Earth marble—set in an intricate pattern. She touched a black square and the door opened with a soughing. Warm air issued from the chamber, bathing Ailim in the sharp scent of pine with a dark underlying note of resinous amber.

Hesitantly she slipped inside. The door shut behind her. Before she stepped from the square threshold, she disrobed. A gentle breeze caressed her, a welcoming touch from all the shades of her ancestors. The HouseHeart beat in a rhythm Ailim had felt since before she was born.

"Blessed be," she said.

"Blessed be to us all, and to you D'SilverFir," replied the rich tones of the HouseVoice, the voice of a FatherSire gen-erations gone. Like all the D'SilverFir Heirs and the heads of households, he had been called Ailim.

"Thank you," Ailim said, and the HouseVoice subsided until she wished to address it again.

She looked around the HouseHeart, her glance touching the four elements: the everlasting fire in a small sconce; the puri-fying waterfall that rushed in from the lake; the thick, soft moss that comprised the floor; and up to the wind chimes that tinkled before the main air vent.

One by one, Ailim let her inner shields down, until she was only aware of the life pulses of her Family and the ancient beat of the Residence itself. Thoughts and feelings were distant, though not as wonderfully absent as they had been with Ruis Elder.

Heartache twisted inside her. How could she be so attracted to the man after so short a time in his company? He had placed his own life in jeopardy to rescue her. He had saved her life. He had cared enough to do that. She owed him gratitude and more.

Here, at the core of her Family Residence, she could concede that she'd found being with him exciting and touching. But there were many facts to consider.

He was kind to his Fam and to herself. He was handsome, and charming, and virile, and just thinking of him caused her blood to simmer through her veins. The time she spent with him, not being able to feel anyone's thoughts, yet able to ex-plore her physical senses, was completely relaxing, energizing, and fascinating. Better than even being here, in the HouseHeart. He treated her with such gentleness and respect—her, Ailim SilverFir, not thinking of her only as a judge or a telempath or a GrandLady, but as the individual she was.

Ailim sensed a deep anger in Ruis. She shivered. And he was banished from Druida. She'd sworn to uphold the laws of Celta, and if she told of his presence, when he was caught, he would die. But if she didn't tell of his presence in Druida and this was later discovered, the FirstFamilies would be enraged.

She'd be disgraced and her career as a Judge ended. But worse, the FirstFamilies Council would cancel the loan to D'SilverFir and take the Residence estate. The Family Ailim was fighting so hard to bind together would be shattered.

She moaned.

She yearned to spend time with Ruis, unburdened by any press of emotions and thoughts of others, not only to explore her physical senses, but to be completely free in her own emotions, knowing that whatever she felt was true and real and came solely from her.

A thin gold chain caught her eyes, and she glanced up to where it fastened to the ceiling. The chain was the original and best D'SilverFir divination device—a pendulum. Her breath stopped. Her knees gave out and she plopped onto the moss. She sat and looked at the chain with unfocused eyes, wondering if she had the courage to see what it would prophesize and whether she had the energy to use it.

Finally she crawled over to the end which suspended a "bob" made of obsidian about twenty centimeters from the floor. Embedded in the floor was a large square piece of cream-colored eternastone with the words "Ready, Yes, No," and ancient signs to be used for interpretation of the prophecy, and letters. Circling around the square were the eight different colored sliding Subject Question Wheels.

The atmosphere of the HouseHeart throbbed. The chimes tinkled in a sudden gust of air, the water tumbled with an increased flow, the scent of rich moss saturated the air. Small tremors spread from inside her, and Ailim knew she'd utilize the divination device. A true moment of foreseeing enveloped her.

She stood and went to the altar, opening the small door with a mighty Word. She got the large silver band and held it between her palms—the programming ring for the D'SilverFir Pendulum, set to her own vibrations. After licking her dried lips, she murmured a chant to set word/synapses into the ring. It updated the connection between her conscious mind and her unconscious.

When she returned to the chain and the stone, she slipped the thin band in to frame the Question Wheels. With a metallic snick, the divination device was ready.

The outermost royal blue Wheel showed the Celtan year. Automatically Ailim adjusted the wheel so it aligned with the greeniron pointer. Today was in the middle of the month of Ivy, a few days before Mabon, the Autumnal Equinox. The Wheel was old enough to call the first day of the New Year, Samhain, by its ancient Earth name of November 1.

She firmed her jaw to keep her teeth from chattering and folded her hands over the chain and the bob stone. Muttering a brief prayer, she held her breath until the chain vibrated between her hands, and the Divination Spell hummed around her.

Her fingers brushed the light-blue Family Wheel, to also align it with the Pointer. The chain slowly stopped and changed direction to swing over the "Ready" indicator.

She breathed deeply and cleared her mind. "I think I will see Ruis Elder again," she whispered, stating what she wanted, and what she thought he wanted also, aloud, safely here where all the secrets were kept. "Can I trust any of the Councils to give him justice?" It ached in her, this conflict. Her true belief in the rightness of Celtan law versus her intuition that Ruis would never be judged fairly. No one could see past what he was to understand who he was.

The chain started swinging slowly.

Ailim shivered, knowing her subconscious was connected with the ALL that contained every answer. Her brain formed the question, but the ALL funneled through her to guide the minute energy in her hands into small motions that directed the chain.

The bob settled into a pattern over the "No."

Ailim shuddered. "What should I do regarding Ruis Elder?" The words tumbled from her lips without thought.

The pendulum swung long and energetically over a symbol. "Two paths," murmured Ailim.

"An irrevocable decision must be made," said the House-Heart.

Tremors started deep inside Ailim. "Show me the first path," she rapped out.

The pendulum swung over the diamond-shape. Duty. Duty was diamond hard. She knew what that meant. She bit her lip. The chain jerked into a different motion and began tapping against a small metal pin Ailim hadn't noticed before. *Ping. Ping. Ping.* Then harder. *Ping-ping-ping-ping-ping-ping.* Her eyes widened.

"Danger to the family and the House lies down this path."

The HouseHeart intoned, "Do you hear, Ailim D'SilverFir?"

"Yes." She clenched her hands.

"The second path," she whispered.

The bob slowed, then changed direction again, until it slowly swung over the heart-shape.

"What?" she asked, surprised.

The obsidian pendulum-bob circled the letters, spelling: "Follow your heart."

The chain picked up speed and changed angles. *Ping-ping-ping.*

"Danger to you and the House lies down this path," the HouseHeart intoned.

Ailim clutched her head, trying to formulate the right question. "What is the best possible outcome!"

The stone began to glow with dark inner fire, sparking black. Then the pendulum swung over the "I" ancient Celtic ogham letter, which meant Ioho, Yew, representing rebirth.

"Great Changes for the Family," the HouseVoice said.

The altar fire popped. The chain leapt in her palm. Ailim snatched at the stone, but the black bob hit the outer edge of the Question Wheels with a clack and rolled. It paused and wobbled on the rose colored Heart Question wheel, then continued to the eternastone, stopping on "Yes."

"A matter of the heart will bring great changes to the Family," HouseVoice said.

"Great changes for the Family," Ailim said. That usually meant transitions—a completely new direction, or a new head of household. With all the danger surrounding both decisions could it mean absolute destruction?

Follow your heart.

Her body wanted Ruis. She ached for him.

But what did her heart want?

*R*uis *found himself whistling as he opened the door to his* quarters. His spirits had revived. He would not think of the future—GrandLady Ailim D'SilverFir could never be his in the long run. So he would concentrate on the now, when he could be in her life.

And what a lady. She looked like icefroth—too cool and reasoned to be passionate. A lady who would always put duty first. Yet she tasted of dark, rich sweet cream—and she trembled with passion in his arms.

He shucked the light-bending cloak and carefully examined it for tears. It was solid, so he set it in the cleaning closet.

"Samba," he called. No answer. His Fam cat was nowhere to be seen though she'd preceded him to the Ship. He believed she sometimes enjoyed being in the great artifact alone, and being the Queen of All She Surveyed. He felt sure her curious nature had lured her into surveying much more of the Ship than he.

"Captain?" the Ship questioned.

"Yes?"

"Your energy levels are slightly high, the innate field that surrounds you has expanded to a meter and a half from your skin—"

Ruis flung up a hand. "What field are you talking about?"

The Ship replied in its usual courteous tones. "We have perceived that you have a personal energy field. This is not the same sort of psi manifestation that others who visit Us in our Museum Rooms evidence. We understand that the other natives vary from Our colonists by the encouragement and mutation of psi powers. This is not the case with you."

"I know," Ruis said with a clenched jaw. He took off his clothes. When he found the softleaf Ailim had used, he sniffed at it, smiling. It held her scent. His body tightened with desire. He set the cloth aside, and tried not to be distracted. "You mentioned an energy field?"

"Indeed. We have measured it to be a standard sixty centimeters surrounding you. It moves as you walk. It affects Celtan made energy-objects and Celtan psi powers, and the effect is exponentially cumulative. That is, the longer you are stationary, the larger the area your forcefield affects and the stronger it grows—"

"I know this."

"Your field promotes more efficient connections in Our trons and so causes smoother transitions in the workings of Our mechanical parts. In five Celtan decades all Our levels will be affected."

"Oh," Ruis said blankly.

"We perceive that you have minor scrapes and bruises.

This is new to Us. . . ." There came a pause that for any other being, Ruis would have called embarrassment. "We regret to say that We have requested, and received, orders from you in general housekeeping and processing Our engineering sectors and that We have proceeded to stock and repair these areas. However, We have not yet recommissioned the sick bay or the small emergency medbeds in the escape pods for the crew."

Ruis blinked. "Ah—"

"But We will make that Our highest priority."

"Be sure to include supplies and information for Samba."

"Of course. Though sick bay is not functional, perhaps in the interim, you could visit the herbal gardens in the Greensward and the stillroom you set up."

"Good idea."

The Greensward held a fascination for both Ruis and Samba, with its tangled Earth plants, insects, small animals, and even birds. The horticultural expanse comprised fully a third of the Ship, a huge natural area designed for the mental health of the crew, the production of necessary gasses and nutrients, and the genetic stock of Earth plants to be used by the colonists.

Ruis had a direct private portal from his quarters. "Do you sense my Fam?" He'd grown used to having a companion to share things with. He'd shared much with Ailim this night and wanted to share more, much more.

Having his Fam had spoiled him for a solitary existence. Being alone no longer appealed. He realized that he'd never been alone by choice. His isolation had been forced upon him, as most everything else in his life. Now he had command of the Ship, that was power. He had its respect, and status as its Captain, but he began to feel that without others, living would be just as sterile and intolerable as before.

"Through Our cameras, sonar and infrared, we have located the crew in the Greensward, immersed in her duties."

"Hunting rodents." Ruis went to the washroom and used the flowing water to wipe away dirt and blood, then changed into fresh clothes.

"We will take this opportunity to remind you of your anger-management program," Ship said.

"I know, I know." Ruis hit a button and an iris-door opened in the back wall of his study.

"Increasing levels of hard physical exertion . . ." recited the Ship as it had every few septhours.

Ruis grinned, shaking his head. "You mean tramping through the Greensward to locate the ninety missing maintenance robots." He slid down a tube to the Greensward.

Ship's voice followed him. "Alternating with intense mental concentration . . ."

Ruis landed lightly, but still shook the creaks from his bruised muscles. ". . . which means learning the intricacies of Earth nanoelectron tech and repairing the 'bots when I find them." His gaze lingered on the wildly intertwined plants around him. A many-tentacled robot chugged past, clearing a path centimeter by centimeter. Ruis patted it.

Filling his lungs with the sweet atmosphere thick with humidity and scent, he looked around him and grinned. Lord and Lady, what a profit he could make from this natural Earth abundance! Many plants had not managed the transition to Celtan soil. Many others had mutated since. He wondered what he could charge for a genuine Earth lily, or original plants for which the FirstFamilies were named— Birch, Rowan, Alder, Willow—

"We are concerned about your mental health," Ship continued.

Ruis snapped up straight, dragged from pleasant thoughts. He grabbed a machete and went off at an angle from the robot. Sweat coated him quickly. Increasing levels of physical exertion. He grunted. There were Healers that dealt with the mind. They couldn't help him, though, their Flair didn't work around him, and it wasn't as if Ruis had an illness that could be cured. His Nullness was bred in his bones, never to be removed.

"Every time you return from Outside, your endorphins have spiked. We speculate that your anger is exacerbated when you are Outside."

"So?"

"If you intend to continue visiting Outside, We must insist that you follow the psychological program precisely."

Just that quickly fury slammed into Ruis. He strapped it

down. Frustration and hurt that even here in the Ship, he was not to be left alone to be what he was.

Samba nipped at him.

"That's a nice 'greetyou,' cat," he growled.

She slapped her tail against his boots.

"I'm working on my temper. I will continue my morning role-playing exercises," Ruis said between clenched teeth. "But here, on the Ship, I am Captain and I insist on a modicum of serenity. I will not allow nagging."

"What will you do about Outside?" asked the Ship.

Ruis snorted. "I'm an outcast in my Society, a criminal, with a death warrant on my head if I'm found in Druida." All the ills of his situation crashed down on him. He could never claim the Lady he wanted, the one he ached for.

The Ship emitted high-pitched noises that resonated through his bones. Samba flattened her ears and shot into dense bushes.

"Stop!" The noise ended, but his ears still rang.

"Captain, We are gathering information about your situation, and tabulating it to postulate additional hypotheses and options for the psych program. With the synapsis connections you recently reconstructed we can access Our old contact with the main Library as well as other archives."

"Other archives?" Did that mean the ship had now had access to Family ResidenceLibraries? Incredible.

There was a whir, then the Ship spoke again. "We request that when you are Outside you wear a communicator-throat band in the future so that you may contact Us and We may keep track of your location."

"Maybe."

Another whir. "The throat band can be modified to appear like the Celtan jewelry called torques. You will find several new bands in the Captain's quarters."

"I'll consider it." It could be useful if he was abroad and wanted information from the Ship.

A small maintenance robot came clanking up, Samba followed, sniffing at it.

"PEEP!" it announced itself, clinked, gestured with three flailing tentacles at the heap it had dragged behind it. Another broken garden robot.

Samba swatted the 'bot. It rolled away. Ruis surveyed

the broken thing before him that Samba was nosing. "Ship, I suppose you want me to fix this."

"We would appreciate it. We cannot maintain the Greensward without them. We have catalogued new plant species, and kept records on others, but it is not a complete listing. Our information is deficient." Something the Ship apparently considered appalling verging on inconceivable.

"Very well."

Samba came back and climbed into the breached interior. His job wouldn't be made any easier by removing cat hair. Ruis bent and picked the whole thing up, grunting, until it was chest-high.

Samba, now being carried, sat upright like a queen and increased her purring.

"We also wish to caution you to be extremely careful Outside. We have determined that you are Our best hope for future refurbishment and survival.

"The scholarly Family of Astragalus, who previously studied Us, expired four generations ago. Celtan culture is focused on the future, still exploring and colonizing the planet." In any other being, Ruis would have called the tone a pitiful plea. "No other Celtans have expressed any interest in Us," Ship ended, almost in a whimper. "We do not wish to see you harmed."

Samba swiped a rough tongue under his chin in agreement.

Ruis was touched. He needed the Ship, but not, it seemed, more than the Ship needed him. "I'll keep that in mind," he said, walking back to his portal.

Weariness fell upon him. The night's experiences had been incredibly interesting. He'd saved and kissed a Lady. He'd returned to FirstGrove and felt a small tendril of rare connection with his home world. But most incredible of all, he hadn't had any upsurges of blinding anger. Despite the danger, Ailim D'SilverFir tempted him. She was good for him. He would not give her up.

*The* small canvas tent attached to the large Celebration tent was blessedly silent. Ailim let every muscle of her body loosen for the first time in days. Finally alone. Ever since the night an eightday ago when she came in late with no explanation, one of the Family members she lived with was constantly with her—or watching. Except when she slept. But her days had been longer and longer and her nights so short she stumbled to her bedsponge and fell asleep as soon as she touched the soft permamoss. She hadn't even managed to meditate in the HouseHeart. Ruis Elder had hung on the edge of her senses, but not approached. Only Primrose had given any comfort.

At least when the outlying SilverFirs trickled into Druida and the Residence for the loyalty ceremony, she had different faces around her—and some genuinely interested and interesting people to talk with. The resentful relatives had been diluted remarkably with those approving of her and her leadership. It lessened her burdens.

Now she was alone, aching with the sheer relief of being solitary. She grinned. No one would bother her here in the meditation tent where she was to keep vigil in the septhours between midnight and full morning. If she knew her fellow nobles, and she did, they would all be considering the impression they would be making on each other and the commoners in the event of the season—her loyalty ritual, followed by formal acknowledgment of her status in the FirstFamilies Council. Both had been scheduled to take place the day of the Autumnal Equinox. The public ritual of Mabon would flow into the annual citywide festivals, parties, and harvest bonfires.

Ailim flopped back on a stack of thick chinju rugs, as soft as a bed. With a spellword, she set her hair free from tight braids and bared her feet.

A slight rustle was the only warning she had before her Flair failed. She opened her eyes and squinted but just saw a moving shadow darker than the rest. The spell-lit candles had died. The drifting tendrils of smoke filled the tent with rich amber fragrance.

"Ruis?" she breathed his name.

"Here." The blackest shadow moved, something clicked, and a tiny flame illuminated his elegant hand as he touched fire to several of the candles. She saw a gleam of metal cradled in his fingers.

"What's that?"

He smiled, and her heart thumped harder. She wondered how often he smiled so, and who had ever seen it.

"It's called a 'lighter.' You don't want to know where I got it." He shrugged out of a cloak and she blinked. Suddenly she could see him better, dressed in a tunic and trous of an odd cut. He folded the eye-confusing cloak and set it aside.

She shut her mouth against curious questions and felt oppressed because of queries that never could be asked or answered. She wanted to warn him, but those words, too, stayed in her throat. He knew the danger of staying in the city and seeing her. Yet he came anyway. "I missed you."

"I was near."

"I know. I can feel your—absence—at the fringe of my mind." Again she felt impelled to mention the danger. Again she refrained.

He nodded. "My Null field. I'm honored you thought of me—maybe even sought me with your Flair."

She didn't tell him how often she had probed for him, and how comforting it felt when she found a suspicious blankness.

"I wanted to see you again. To talk," he finally said, then hesitated, "to ease your day with a massage, perhaps."

"I would have liked that." Ailim scooted back to lean against huge pillows set around the edges of the tent. The body-sized cushions were also chinju, brighter in color but softer and lighter of weave.

Ruis sat opposite her, stretching out his legs and crossing them at the ankles. His boots were as black as ever, but the old gouges still showed in the furrabeast leather. No polish shone—to keep him safe, Ailim knew. Lady and Lord, keep him safe. His trous and tunic were black, too.

She stared at him, and he returned the examination. She knew she searched for all the small indications of difference in him since they had last met, and thought that he might be doing the same. Ailim sighed. He looked relaxed and at ease, more carefree than the last time she'd seen him. The fine lines in his face seemed gone, and she knew it wasn't simply the dim light. He had changed for the better. She was sure she hadn't.

"You look tired," he said.

She shrugged and smiled wryly. "This Loyalty Ceremony has had the household in an uproar, getting ready for a large gathering of all branches of the Family."

He glanced away. "I wouldn't know."

She searched for some other topic, but he spoke first, softly, gazing at her from those intense eyes. "And how do you find my Nullness tonight, D'SilverFir? Interesting? Wonderful? Terrible?"

She blinked, and became aware of the soft night noises outside the tent, the steady, loping tread of one of the D'SilverFir guardsmen who had arrived from a frontier estate that so trained their sons. There was a chirp or two from night birds and the rhythmic rasping of crickets. Beyond that, there was silence that held expectation of a busy day once Bel rose.

Breathing deeply, she inhaled the fragrance of amber and pine and even a faint tantalizing scent of man and most especially, Ruis.

But she could not take her eyes from him—his noble features and the clean, muscular lines of his body. And though she had no Flair to sense his thoughts or feelings, the atmosphere between them thickened with unspoken emotions. She tried to recall what he'd asked her and tore her gaze away from him. She had to think instead of feeling the heat of his body radiating desire and stirring her own yearnings. Cravings that seemed so futile, yet so limitless.

What had he asked? She didn't remember.

His voice broke her thoughts, and this time it lilted with male satisfaction, as though she'd already given him his answer. "How do you find my Nullness tonight, D'SilverFir? Interesting? Wonderful? Terrible?"

Ailim let her eyes go back to where they wanted to rest, on Ruis Elder. "I asked you to call me Ailim."

"And you called my name when I entered. Say it again."

"Ruis."

He closed his eyes. His chest rose in a deep breath and shuddered out. "That sounds so wonderful it's terrible. Terrifying."

Her throat closed and she could only nod. But he couldn't see, and she couldn't speak to him mind-to-mind, so she forced the words out. "Our plight is scary, but I want to continue."

Bright brown eyes pinned her. "I waited in the Grove every day for your followers to leave. But they didn't. I wanted to massage you again. Touch you." His eyes gleamed flames in the candlelight. Then he shook his head. "That strange Family of yours hedges you around. You're never out of their sight. You have small time alone, no wonder you are so self-conscious."

She hadn't been until he'd said it. Now she could feel her shift tangled around her, exposing her legs to his view. His gaze slid over her millimeter by millimeter, from her toes up to her wild hair. Her nipples hardened at the desire in his eyes, the flaring of his nostrils. He'd sparked a pooling fire in her lower body as expertly as he'd lit the candles. Her breathing quickened and his gaze went from the shadowy apex of her thighs back to her breasts.

He knelt beside her and his unforgotten scent wafted to her, bringing memories of comfort, of his lips on hers, of his hands on her. She trembled, but did not move, waiting, wondering with exquisite blindness of Flair what he felt, what he thought. What he would do next.

His face had tautened, his lips thinned. The low light burnished the red in his mahogany hair to copper. She heard his ragged breath. Ruis touched the center tab groove of her shift. With one long stroke he separated the material.

Ailim could barely keep still, she wanted to fling herself at him, wrap her arms and legs around him, please them both with rocketing pleasure. The very thought shocked her, but didn't stop the daring images from flashing through her mind.

Yet something stopped her from acting on impulse. Something she hadn't felt in a long, long time—sexual anticipation.

The yearning in his eyes made her want to extend the pleasurable tension. His mouth had softened and his expression held more than lust. Need marked his features. Need for intimacy.

Without Flair, without words, she knew that this passion that spun between them had little to do with healthy sexual drives and everything to do with how they valued each other.

The moment stretched until she felt herself arching toward him, offering herself, everything she was. She could not wrench her stare from his.

She'd never felt so aroused. Her senses, so overwhelmed by inrushing sensation, narrowed to the visual. Sight. The sight of his long fingers gently peeling back the two panels of her shift to expose her to his probing gaze. A small moan whispered from her lips, and he looked into her eyes. His hands stopped.

"Don't stop." Hadn't she said that before? Again and again before? She knew she'd say it again and again and again in the future.

He smiled once more, tenderness touching his mouth as he smoothed her shift on either side of her body. His fingers trailed heat to the side of her breasts, the inner curve of her waist, the sensitive flesh of her thighs, and all the way down touching her knees, feathering against her feet.

"Lady," he said thickly, then touched the peaks of her breasts. Her body undulated. He gasped, pulled his fingers from her, then firmed his jaw and set his hand on her stomach, his thumb close, so close to where she wanted to be touched. "Ailim," he said.

She wet her lips. She should have felt vulnerable, but instead felt cherished. He stared at her as if she were a prize he'd always sought and never hoped to obtain. His mouth touched hers. Convulsively she entwined her arms and legs around him, seeking to align the most needy part of her against his sex. He withdrew his hand from between them, and when she shifted, she was where she wanted, her woman's flesh cradling the thick, long ridge that she craved. She moaned again.

He chuckled, but did not move. His lips dipped to her neck, her shoulder. His tongue flickered against her skin. "So rich and sweet," he muttered. The edge of his teeth scraped her, bolts of fire arced through her.

"Come to me," she said, amazed at the need for this particular man.

His hands tunneled through her hair, separating strands still twisted together and the tingling sensation shivered through her and she gasped. Thought spun away.

Rough-padded fingers brushed over her ears, traced her jaw, then framed her face. His lips touched hers, tongue questing and she opened her mouth eagerly. When she sucked on his tongue they both moaned in pleasure. The taste of him speared through her. Heated fire flickered on the inside of her eyelids. Her breath was ragged, her hunger avaricious.

His long-fingered elegant hands slid to her back, between her and the shift, again the callouses roused sparking excitement until she was a mass of unsatisfied need.

He enveloped her . . . the scent of spice and man, his warmth, the sound of his quick breath. Blind with pleasure and seeking tactile sensation, she flexed her hands against his back enjoying the firmness of muscle, learning the wedge shape of his back. She curled her arms around him touching the nape of his neck and laughing lowly as he shuddered. She petted him there, playing with wisps of hair.

His large palm found the roundness of her bottom, and she quivered, then gasped as he pressed her closer and the strange texture of his trous teased her. Now his tongue roved through her mouth, claiming her taste, knowing that portion of her thoroughly, intimately.

"You! Guard!" Aunt Menzie's high voice from outside the tent whipped against her ears, striking her like lashes on tender flesh.

# Nine

♥

The sensual moment of loving disintegrated. Ruis whisked Ailim's shift together with a fast jerk. He retreated to the darkest corner of the tent, but not before Ailim noticed his hands shook.

Ailim strained to see him. She was cold, bereft, mouth swollen and trembling. When she breathed, the lingering scent of him dizzied her for one more instant before she relinquished all the delectable feelings of desire and caring. Frigid duty mixed with simmering resentment flooded her. Was she never to have any peace?

"Yes, GrandMistrys Menzie?" The guard outside the tent answered coolly, with just the barest respect. Ailim grabbed at self-control, levered herself up, shook out her shift, finger-combed her hair, and donned a nightrobe. With a glance at Ruis, who looked at her expressionlessly—he couldn't think that she would ever betray him?—Ailim went to the tent flap and opened it only as wide as her body.

The draft slapped cold air at her and she chilled. "Is there something wrong, Brant?" she asked the guard, a distant cousin.

He turned and bowed. "No, Lady, don't be disturbed, go back to your thoughts."

Aunt Menzie marched forward, one hand clutching her ugly, evil amulet. "Of course she will not be disturbed. I have a night-drink to help you focus, Ailim." Menzie presented an ostentatious silver goblet.

Ailim forced a smile, knowing Menzie must have an ulterior motive, but what? "Thank you, but I am fasting."

Menzie stared, blinked, moistened her lips. "Fasting? Fasting is not required!"

Ailim lifted her chin. "Nevertheless, as a SupremeJudge and soon-to-be confirmed GrandLady, I wish to set a good example. Menzie"—she smiled wryly—"I have never had any trouble with focus."

Menzie frowned, her free hand clutched her amulet, and a look of confusion crossed her face. Her hand fell from the necklace and she sniffed. "I think you should drink."

"No," Ailim repeated. "Water is enough." Whatever the potion was, it no doubt would affect Ailim adversely . . . probably cause her to humiliate herself in some manner before the whole world.

Even in the twinmoonslight Ailim could see her aunt flush with anger. "I insist."

"I am set on my fast. You look ill. Perhaps you should use that drink to help you swallow one of the pills the Healer gave you to steady your blood."

Menzie's mouth opened and closed.

Ailim inclined her head to Brant. "Please escort her to the edge of the square and tell one of our kinsmen stationed there to accompany her home."

He scowled and rested his hand on his sword hilt. Ailim made a show of looking around. "I sense no threat." That was true. With Ruis so near, she couldn't even read Brant, who was only a few steps away.

Brant jerked a nod, then grasped Menzie under the elbow and swivelled her. "Come, GrandMistrys, I wager there's still plenty of work for the D'SilverFir housekeeper before the ceremony."

Menzie snorted. "Housekeeper. I'm not a mere housekeeper."

"Your daughter might need you," Brant said.

Their footfalls moved away.

Ailim dropped the canvas flap and turned to face Ruis. He lounged against a solid post, a small smile curving his lips. He looked dangerous—reckless. Ailim bit her lip to keep from warning him of his obvious peril at being in Druida.

She looked closer and saw that his fists were clenched, and something about the skin around his eyes spoke of vulnerability. A lump inside her melted. "Ruis," she said.

His smile turned lopsided. "We have come full circle to the start of our conversation." His gaze drifted to the chinju pillows that showed the deep indentations of their bodies.

Ailim felt heat rush to her face, but she didn't falter. She didn't regret her passionate response to him. "Ruis."

When he looked at her again, softness moved in his eyes. "I like hearing you say my name."

She swallowed.

His shoulders squared. "This is not the time or the place for lovemaking." Yet his voice held a strained note, as strained as her nerves.

"No." She sighed. "No. I am supposed to be preparing myself for the responsibilities of my new status and rank."

"You have been D'SilverFir a couple of months now, haven't you?"

"Yes."

"And a judge for how long?"

"Six years."

Ruis looked her up and down and she became aware of her rigid stance and her hands folded at her waist.

"It seems to me that you've been responsible all of your life. Maybe you should consider some alternatives."

She raised her eyebrows. "During the time I am meditating before the loyalty ritual?" But she was glad to see the twinkle back in his eyes.

"RRRRRRoooooowwwww." Samba kicked the flap aside and strolled in. She went over to Ailim and licked her ankle politely. Ailim, now used to such damp shows of affection from her puppy Primrose, didn't even flinch.

Samba sauntered over to Ruis and looked up at him. *Dawn is coming. Much is happening in the square and market. Today is a big holiday with bonfires and free food for Cats. Let's go play!*

Ruis rolled his eyes.

Ailim hurried to update him before he left. "I put together an official file about you for the Council's records. My clerk was as displeased as I about the lack of information, especially

regarding whether you ever personally received the noblegilt
due to you as a FirstSon of a noble Family. My clerk comes
from the Licorice family."

He blinked. A slow smile curved his lips. "What relation to
the head of the PublicLibrary?"

Ailim smiled, too. She liked that they shared simple amusement at the ingrained D'Licorice Family traits. It was so rare
for her to share anything at all with anyone these days. "Daughter'sDaughter."

"Ah." He lifted his eyebrows. "And?"

"Under the seal of the Supreme Grove, we have asked for
an accounting from the T'Elder bankers, as well as from
GreatLord T'Elder of his household ledgers regarding your expenses."

Now his mouth hardened and sharpness came to his eyes. "I
thank you for your efforts."

"But you don't think they'll be fruitful?"

"No."

"You don't care?"

He shrugged. "I can't afford to care. There's nothing I can
do to unseat my uncle Bucus. He is solid in his ambitious career
and holds all the power, as usual."

Ailim wet her lips and his gaze focused on her mouth. To
her surprise, he relaxed a bit and the smile that returned to his
face seemed genuine. She continued, "Rumor has it that you
left T'Elder household when you were young."

Again his smile faded. He sank to his haunches and petted
Samba, face averted. "I was fourteen." He glanced at his hands,
at the candle, and with a grunt pulled Samba closer to him,
into deeper shadows.

Ailim strove to look at his hands, but they were lost in the
dimness. An unexpected yearning came to see those hands
closely, against her bare skin. She blinked the erotic image
away and concentrated on what also mattered deeply to her—
the law and justice. "If T'Elder continued to draw the monthly
noblegilt allotted to you as a FirstSon after you left his Residence, he has swindled the Councils and the people of Celta."

Samba sprawled on her side rumbling a purr.

"And I'm so concerned about the Councils and the people
of Celta," Ruis said.

Before she could find words, he looked up, his expression

one of mild interest. "But I know that it matters to you, and if it casts a slur on Bucus's name . . ." Ruis shrugged. "So be it. Even Bucus might have a problem explaining taking years of noblegilt for my care as a little oversight. Odds are, though, he'll blame it on the household bookkeeper, or even his wife Calami." Ruis snorted. "As if he didn't keep track of every silver sliver in the Family coffers."

"I've only been back in Druida for a couple of months, but I've heard rumors. . . . I don't usually repeat them. . . ."

"Of course not. Don't think you need say anything now."

Ailim sucked in an audible breath. "You should know the way the wind blows. Your uncle Bucus, as Captain of the NobleCouncil, is not respected or liked."

"Imagine that." Ruis scratched Samba's ears.

"Apparently he had a sheen of smooth affability combined with common sense that allowed him to win the vote for Captain's Chair two years ago."

"Not to mention the all-important FirstFamily heritage," Ruis continued, keeping his attention on his cat. "Even I know that the NobleCouncil would prefer T'Holly as Captain."

"The two strong rivals, T'Holly and T'Hawthorn," Ruis said. "Ally with one and you alienate the other. Everyone streetwise knows the Holly-Hawthorn feud is heating up."

"Surely not," Ailim protested.

Ruis shrugged.

"Back to your uncle Bucus," Ailim plodded on. If she was going to start repeating rumor, she would tell the whole of it. "The nobles believe his surface persona is eroding, showing the true man." She licked her lips and cast her mind back to words she'd overheard at a mandatory social gathering. "He's called rigid and unpleasant. There have been uncontrolled outbursts of temper." Breath rushed from her as she finished her report.

Ruis only continued to stroke his Fam, looking up at her with acceptance. "He's still in power. And I've heard that he doesn't favor the D'SilverFirs."

Ailim shivered. Bucus T'Elder could squash the hopes of D'SilverFir GrandHouse with one fat finger. "I wish the D'SilverFir estate didn't border with T'Elder's."

Ruis frowned. "That's a concern, too."

"You don't hide on T'Elder land, I hope!" That thought scared her more than the idea of Bucus as an enemy. Whatever malice he had for her was small compared to the malevolence he bore for his nephew.

"No. I don't stay on the T'Elder estate. It's big, but not large enough to hide me from Bucus. And I never prized it." He rose to his feet. "The Family means nothing to me. They could all perish like the FirstGrove BalmHeals and I wouldn't care."

Ailim just stared at him.

"Family has been nothing but grief for me," he said softly.

She pushed her hands through her hair as if to slow her flying notions. How contradictory was Ruis's and her own views. She had been willing to sacrifice her ancestral estate to save her Family and struggled every day to keep her Family together. He cared nothing for a Family who'd repudiated him. Yet she could not fault him for it. Again she brought her mind back to the topic—Bucus T'Elder.

"It might not take much to topple Bucus from power, a vote of 'no-confidence,'" Ailim whispered.

Ruis shot her a glance. "Don't plot against him. He's mean. He doesn't play fair, and I don't want you hurt. No matter what you do, my banishment will not be rescinded."

Ailim started stubbornly, "There are ways, a panel of judges to overturn the Council—"

Ruis cut her off with a sharp gesture. "Don't endanger yourself for me. It's a battle that has already been lost. If I didn't think so, I'd try for him with my own hands."

Ailim pressed her lips together. She knew the law, knew there was a method to overturn his sentence, but also knew that right now, Ruis would not listen.

He stared at her from under lowered brows, but when she said nothing more, his tense muscles relaxed and he gave her a smile that spun her wits. "You listen to me." He shook his head. "You can't know how—pleasing—it is that someone actually considers my words and treats me decently." He gently nudged Samba with the toe of his boot. "Come on, Fam cat, let's go play."

Samba heaved a sigh, opened her green eyes, and hefted herself to all fours. *Let's go play!* Ailim rated the barest dip of the Fam's head as she trotted from the tent.

Ruis watched his Fam leave. Time for him to go, also, but not before a farewell kiss. Two strides brought him to Ailim and his long, strong arm swung her into the cradle of his body.

His mouth was on hers in a soft, sweet kiss before she could blink. Her mind whirled once more, reason threatening to desert her. She wanted to say something, but only a moan emerged as she flattened herself against him. A thrill ran up her spine when she realized he was still aroused. Her heart thudded hard.

Again it was he who broke the embrace. He lifted his head and his fingers came up to feather across her cheekbone. His eyes burned with desire that weakened her—physically, emotionally, mentally.

"I'll come to you tonight. After the great public ceremony, you'll need me," he said matter-of-factly. "And I'll massage you." His eyes crinkled, and his even teeth gleamed. "Then we will make love."

"You can't!" Ailim gasped. She wanted nothing more than to have him in her bed—in her. She could barely think, but there was no thinking involved when danger always shrouded them like a thundercloud about to spit lightning. "You can't continue to visit me, to be in the city. You can't come tonight, my Residence is full of people, crammed to the eaves with Family. You mustn't—"

Ruis's lips pressed on hers again, moved against her mouth. She melted, surrendering to him.

"I'll come." He stepped back, grabbed the odd cloak and swirled it around him. Everything but his face and hands disappeared.

Ailim gasped again. "How can you do that without Flair?"

"Don't ask." He lifted a cowl and draped it over his head, moved his fingers as if he put on gloves. He vanished.

A surprised sound broke from her. She could only see the drape of the cowl and shadow inside. She shuddered as primitive superstition prickled at the base of her spine. No matter how deeply her culture was based on Celtic beliefs, the image of that hood brought back the ancient symbol that everyone knew of, the Grim Reaper—Death.

The shade of darkness that was Ruis glided to the tent flap and lifted it. "The way's clear. It seems GrandMistrys Menzie has kept Brant talking—scolding him, no doubt."

The words she'd managed to suppress all the time he was with her tore from her heart and mouth. "Be careful, Ruis."

He nodded in courtesy. Then the flap fell on nothingness and he was gone. When she peeked out the tent, he'd disappeared.

She retreated back inside, and with a small spell she lit all the candles. Before she could stop herself, she'd tidied all traces of Ruis from the tent, marching over to the fat pillows and plumping them, even smoothing the faint indentations of his large feet in the thick rugs. The action kept her busy, but she winced inwardly, knowing that it wasn't entirely fear for him that prompted her. It was habit, and responsibility, and in-grained self-consciousness. As her hands passed over the pil-lows, her fingers stirred a vestige of his scent from the cushions, his fragrance that she had noticed from their first meeting.

The respect she'd felt when she'd seen how uncaring he was of the Council's opinion still lingered. All her life she'd con-sidered the opinions of others: during her childhood when she followed the Family rules for an Heir, in her first years as a judge, and even more so now, as she watched her every step so she could keep the Family together.

Ruis Elder could teach her to be free. If she let him. With fantastic speed her mind blazed images of the self she could be if she learned to be so self-confident that she would never think other's opinions more important than her own needs. She could openly express her emotions.

She knew if she spent time with Ruis, she'd learn how to relax her guards. With him she would need no guards, would have none—that was a trifle frightening, but when she recalled how her senses expanded under the influence of his Nullness she thought she'd dare to be with him anyway.

Her memory played back every pass of his hands, the sen-sation of his body on hers. The banked fire of her desire blazed once more, the low heat deep inside her flowing to warm her.

There was no denying the sexual heat between them.

Ruis's clever hands incited exquisite feelings and she wel-comed the ache of unfulfilled passion because it was different from the other emotions that usually plagued her.

And he had given her a respite she was grateful for. Even though he'd been with her only a short time, the fact that he'd completely blanketed her Flair had eased the tension of her always raised mindshield.

Ailim rubbed her temples. She felt better, but there was no chance of any deep meditation. Her entire body quivered with anticipation of the coming night. She wanted him, would not deny him, would not betray him, but the danger for them both was so extreme . . . death for him if he were caught in the city, destruction of everything she cherished for herself.

She wanted Ruis, but he was forbidden. Her passion could doom them both. Their passion. Ailim was clear-headed enough to see that not only did each of them bring solace to the other, but because of their very circumstances, there was an inner rebelliousness in them both that increased the desire. Ruis wanted to prove that he could walk where the nobles had decreed him banned, that he dared to touch a Lady of the highest status. She—well, Ailim tired of always being responsible. Why could she not take something she craved for herself?

She sighed. Their emotions tangled together in a knot she feared was past smoothing. They could only go forward. And she could pray.

*"Careful, you clumsy oafs!"* A Hawthorn houseguard blundered against Ruis. Ruis huddled in his light-bending cloak, cowl pulled low. The Hawthorn looked for him, then shoved others in the square aside with a pointed staff.

A block of red rose before Ruis's eyes. He sucked in his breath. Let it out. Turned aside and away. A moment or two later he was completely in control again. Though the fierce anger left a tinge of nausea, still a feeling of satisfaction blossomed inside him.

The fury had not blinded him or made him react with reckless disregard of his own skin. Back to a wall, he breathed the cool air of the day, taking it deep into his lungs to banish the last trace of any resentment.

Though he knew he shouldn't have returned to the city to watch Ailim's Loyalty Ceremony, now he was glad he had. This moment, this first step, was triumphantly his. From one step he could forge a whole new path of reaction, of change. For once, he had fought the ire and won.

The wind flattened his cloak around him as he hustled through the square to a rickety balcony where he could view the ceremony. A few moments later he was the balcony's only occupant.

It looked as though all of Druida had turned out to view the spectacle. The sun's watery blue light gave him reason

to be bundled up, but more and more he disliked skulking
around.

Trumpets split the air and processional music started.
Slow and solemn, there was still an underlying theme of
flutes that should have been uplifting. But the nobles
sweeping into the square, elegantly and expensively
dressed, gold and jewels glittering, attention focused on
themselves, only left Ruis feeling sour.

Ailim was formally seated in an elaborate chair by Bucus, Captain of the Council. Ruis found himself growling
in his throat as his uncle's hands lingered on her arm.

The scent of rich incense drifted in tiny streams across
the square as blessings were invoked. The ceremony was
magnificent, full of pageantry, color and four centuries of
Celtan tradition. Ailim clasped hands with each person, ex-
changing her oath of protection and patronage for the Family member's pledge of loyalty. It was one of the most
sacred bonds in the Celtan culture. He only hoped that the
members of her Family who tormented her daily would
cease after this event. He snorted. Not fliggering likely.

Even as he thought that, Ailim's cuz Cona sank gracefully on her knees before Ailim. With the sharpness of a
former thief, Ruis noted that both Cona's dress and her
accessories were more fashionable and costly than Ailim's
GrandLady accoutrements. Ailim said her words, but her
lips appeared to move stiffly. Her feet nudged under Primrose as if in comfort. The puppy Fam must have been bespelled to keep quiet. When Cona rose she sneered down
at her cuz. Heat burned a little brighter in Ruis's blood.

He uncurled his fingers from fists. It had been a mistake
to come. He skulked in a place no one else wanted, watching others touch the woman he wanted.

Ship had been right. It had issued dire warnings, but Ruis
could not check his innate recklessness and his need to see
Ailim. The time in the tent that morning had only whetted
his appetite for her company.

Samba had been eager to leave the Ship, too. She'd
wanted to play. He caught sight of his Fam slinking around
the edge of the ceremony, weaving amongst noble ankles.

After all the heads of the outlying branches of SilverFir
swore their oath of loyalty to Ailim, the entire Noble-

Council would induct her into their membership as a
FirstFamily GrandLady—the most powerful and elite group
on Celta.

Again the scent of pine and amber wafted to his nostrils
and he waved it away—he much preferred remembering the
personal scent of Ailim, the woman.

Trumpets blared and Ailim rose slowly from the ornate
chair to accept the cheers of the crowd and the symbols of
her office from the Captain of the Noble Council. She bowed
her head to him, and the delicate nape of her neck appeared
too fragile for the responsibilities she now formally bore.
Anger sparked in Ruis as Bucus again touched her with
sausage-like fingers, stroking her nape as he placed her
necklace of rank around her neck. His hands slid down her
shoulders along her arms until Bucus raised her hands to
his lips and kissed the backs. Red tinged Ruis's vision.

She swept a glance around her Family pressing close, the
other FirstFamily Nobles near, the outlying onlookers, then
finally her gaze steadied in his direction.

But Ruis's calm vanished when Holm Holly swept her a
flamboyant bow as the representative of the FirstFamilies
and placed Ailim's hand upon his arm. He led her into a
feast at the grandest tent set up at the end of the square.

Ruis narrowed his eyes. Information about the First-
Families was generally known—Holm Holly did not have
a HeartMate. That meant he would make a dynastic marriage.

Holly could never understand her like Ruis. Ruis wanted
Ailim, planned to love her into insensibility in the night to
come, yet he couldn't see how he would be able to truly
win her—and keep her.

Still, he needed to be closer to her, perhaps meet her
blue-gray gaze with his own. Let her know, not merely
guess, that he, too, was here to support her.

Ruis slipped from his lonely balcony down into the milling crowds. It wasn't often that commoners got to see
something of the Noble ceremonies, and the fact that it was
also Mabon, the Autumnal Equinox holiday, made everyone
boisterous.

With ease born of a lifetime, Ruis wended his way
through the crowd to the large tented pavilion hung with

banners of the FirstFamilies. But she was already inside. His lips tightened and he told himself he wasn't disappointed. His expectations this moment had been too high. He could ignore the small hurt in the anticipation of tonight.

Before he could leave the vicinity of the FirstFamily tent, he spied something rare—his uncle Bucus's wife Calami Reed D'Elder, alone and unprotected. He sidled up to her and pushed his hood back.

"Well, Auntie Calami. Merry meet." He showed all his teeth in a smile.

Aunt Calami started and squeaked. The little woman, wizened beyond her years, shrank back to the fabric of the tent. "Ruis!" She put her hand to her throat. "I never meant to betray my oath, my solemn vow! I tell you, I never wanted to be foresworn By the Lord and Lady, not that sin. But Bucus made me. He is so strong. He made me, all of us. I can't—" Now she wrung her hands and avoided Ruis's gaze.

What was she talking about?

"I'm feeling odd," a man close by said. "I can't seem to concentrate. Something awful—"

Ruis knew he'd been still for too long; his Nullness had expanded from his body and was now making itself felt. But he couldn't leave yet. He grasped Calami's shoulders. "What do you mean? What oath?"

"The Elder Oath of Loyalty." She looked frantically around, then began to screech.

Swearing under his breath, Ruis ducked and yanked the enveloping cowl over his head, fading into the folds of a nearby banner.

Aunt Calami stared open-mouthed in his general direction, but her gaze went past him.

"Can't I leave you alone for a moment! Enough of this fake sensitivity, fading away for 'a breath of fresh air.' Time for you to get back in the tent and act like a GrandLady." Bucus closed his fingers roughly over his wife's forearm, yanking her into place behind him. "Come on. And no more babbling about what happened thirty-five years ago. Forget that. Forget it once and for all." He scowled, then his eyes lit and his mouth twisted in a gleeful smile. "I'll punish you later."

She shuddered.

They passed close enough to Ruis that he smelled the rancid sweat that sheened his uncle's reddened face.

He couldn't help himself—he kicked the feet out from under his uncle.

Bucus bellowed. His eyes narrowed as he scrutinized his surroundings. The cloak didn't really make Ruis invisible, just hard to see, but possible if someone looked intently.

Bucus was. His stare fixed on Ruis. He grinned in triumph. "Guards!" he yelled, and lunged at Ruis, throwing a clinging Calami aside.

Guards came running, shoving, pushing. Ruis pulled his cloak close, hunched over, and let himself disappear in the whirl of bodies until he stopped once more in the folds of clustered banners. The guards circled around Calami.

"Not her, you fools!" Bucus screamed. "My—" He broke off, then swore luridly as he realized he'd lost Ruis. "I'll get you!" he shouted above the noise of the crowd.

"A problem, Captain of the Council?" Tinne Holly appeared at Ruis's elbow.

"That cat!" Bucus pointed.

Ruis noticed his uncle's hand seeped blood from scratches. Ruis followed Bucus's outstretched fingers and caught a glimpse of Samba's waving calico tail.

Apparently so did Tinne. "You do seem to have trouble with that cat. The same one that was at the Opera the other night, hmmmm?"

"Guards! I want a quartering of this area, inch by inch."

"For the cat?" asked Tinne.

"T'Elder!" T'Reed joined Bucus and Calami. "You're needed inside for the food blessing. What is all this commotion?"

Bucus opened his mouth, sent another fulminating glare around the area, grabbed Calami hard enough to leave bruises, and marched off to the FirstFamilies Feast Tent.

Ruis eluded the guards who were discussing their orders, and drifted away, keeping close to clumps of people. He frowned, his mind turning over the words of his aunt. An event thirty-five years ago would have been when he was just a babe, not yet a yearling. That was when his father, the older Ruis, had died and his mother had followed quickly. HeartMates invariably did.

Making his way to the booths set up in an adjoining square, he didn't realize his hood had fallen back and his cloak was pushed behind his shoulders until a shopowner asked, "Kabob, sir?" The shrewd brown eyes of the merchant surveyed him.

He couldn't afford to be recognized.

Lady and Lord, what had he done? Presented himself to his aunt, revealed himself. He wanted to hurt his uncle and took a chance. Just when he thought he was making progress, old wounds flared and made a mockery of his control. What a fool he was!

Ruis flipped a twelve-sliver to the food seller and took the four offered meat-sticks. Automatically he bit onto one, delicious juices flowed into his mouth. He chewed and swallowed, and strode away from watching eyes.

Samba joined him. Her purr rolled above the hubbub of the crowd. Her whiskers twitched. *Some for Me!*

Ruis tossed her the rest of the stick and she gobbled. A familiar platinum head caught his attention—Tinne Holly. Ruis faded from the Holly's line of sight, frowning. No doubt inside the main, luxurious tent, Holm Holly, the young man's brother, was flirting with D'SilverFir even now.

Samba finished with a slurp, a burp, and a quick lick of her whiskers. *More for Me!* She snagged the bottom of Ruis's trous and dug in. He barely noticed the prick of her claws.

A cat bottom landed with a thump on his shoes. Samba walked herself up his legs to plant her forepaws on his knees, and tilted her head up at him.

Ruis heard a giggle and saw some girls who had been playing with a handheld folding-oracle drop the pointed papyrus and stare at him and Samba. Tinne's head turned.

Ruis scooped Samba up and shoved another bite in her mouth. She hissed and thumped her tail against him. When he ducked into a hidey-hole away from curious eyes, he dropped her. She darted back out into the square.

He pulled the hood back over his head and the cloak

around him, hoping Tinne hadn't seen him. Ruis didn't dare look.

He mulled over Calami's and Bucus's words. What had happened when he was a babe? Could it be, could it possibly be, that his Nullness hadn't been evident as a baby? If his father had died, and Ruis was still believed to be "normal" he would have been considered the Heir. That raised many thorny issues.

Ruis believed he was the rightful heir, Nullness or not. But his Family and uncle had not agreed. He'd been forced by abuse to run away, then disinherited by Bucus.

Samba appeared with the colorful folding oracle in her mouth, dropped it and batted it around a little. She peered up at him. *I'm still hungry.* Samba's plaintive mew rose to a whine. *You promised furrabeast steak. I get no furrabeast on the Ship. I want some. Now.*

"Right." He gave her the other kabobs. He had to regain his control. He could not afford to think about his aunt's words now. He adjusted his disguise once more, pulling his cowl over his head and his cloak around his body.

Samba grinned as she chomped. *Yum. We eat.* She pounced on the folded square of paper. *My toy. You take back to the Ship for Me. Then let's go play.*

He bent down, wiped the cat-spit from the pointed papyrus with a softleaf and pocketed it, still thinking about his uncle. Bucus had tortured Ruis until he fled. Now he began to think that was exactly the result his uncle had wanted. All the blame was on Ruis that way, as an ungrateful and ungovernable boy who could not and would not try and fit into normal Celtan life.

The thoughts tormented him almost as much as the strap and the razorslit had years before, so Ruis hurried back to the crowded square and ducked into the nearest booth. It carried clothing. A few months earlier he would have been driven to outfit himself like the richest of nobles.

He eyed the high-quality goods. They were actually sewn, something necessary for Ruis to be decently clothed. He could not wear garments seamed by Flair, they simply fell off him.

Looking around, he decided the light was dim enough that he could take a risk, particularly since the shirt before

him was a shade of electric blue that flattered him. He'd
look good in it. He could wear it tonight. He tossed back
his cloak and hood.

"There you are. Psst, Elder, Ruis Elder."

The sound of his name made Ruis freeze, then casually
glance around. The Downwind youth Ruis had met in his
old apartment earlier grinned at him, showing canine teeth
filed to points and gilded with iridescent glisten.

His eyes were dark with an edge of something disturb-
ing—madness or viciousness or desperation.

"Yes?" Ruis kept his voice low and menacing.

# Ten

*"We talk."* The teen fidgeted, flicking his fingers over the texture of the shirts, tapping his fingers on his thigh, rubbing them up and down the frayed seam of his own commoncloth coat. "We alike, we twinnies."

Ruis didn't like the thought that he was anything like this youth. He hoped with all his heart that Ailim didn't consider him that angry, that rough, that rude.

He took the shirt, tossed coins for the price onto the counter, and left the booth, tugging his cloak around him, knowing the youngster would follow.

They halted in a crack between two buildings, barely wide enough for Ruis's shoulders and dark enough that he squinted at his unwanted companion.

Ruis stared at the young man's wrist. A raw red wound ran beneath his right hand. It didn't look right.

"Your hand."

"They made me cut it off, them fliggers. Healers at All Class not good, 'cept Lark Collinson. She recognized me, asked too many questions. She's noble, too." Gleaming teeth flashed again. He rubbed the scar. "Nobles. Treat us like scum. You. Me. I have plan. Get even."

"Where's the other two of you?" Ruis asked.

The young man angled his body so they could watch the square. His eyes darted to Ruis and back to the opening. "You have rep Downwind, Ruis Elder—TopDiss." His nervous grin flashed again.

Ruis shrugged. He was beginning to feel old and conservative.

The triad member laughed, short and harsh, jerked a thumb to himself. "I'm Shade. Nightshade. Triad brothers gone. Nobles killed." He spat, pointed. "Look."

Following his bony finger, Ruis saw a line of nobles exit the colorful tent and form a parade. Since it was the month of Ivy, T'Ivy and D'Ivy led the stream. The FirstFamilies followed in month order, then the rest of the GreatHouses, the GrandHouses, and the GraceHouses, all in order of rank. Bucus would be the last of the GreatHouses, as his month was the last, the thirteenth. Ailim D'SilverFir would be third after the Elders, no doubt still paired with Holm Holly.

Gold and silver and jewels glittered, the scent of perfumes, the ancient incenses of noble houses, and the odors of expensive food wafted to fill the square with fragrance. Ruis's hackles rose at the opulent display of wealth. A visible sphere of Flair surrounded them, glowing bright in the dimness of the evening, as if marking them favorites of the Lord and Lady. As if they were Chosen, as he would never be chosen.

Shade murmured in his ear. "We talk. Twinnies work together. You will like. Get your due."

The smile Ruis felt twist his lips had nothing to do with humor. "No one works with me."

Feral sparks lit Shade's gaze. "We work together. Or I tell guardsmen you in Druida. Dawn tomorrow, DownwindGrove."

"Oh?" Ruis clamped his hands on the boy's thin shoulders and felt a wiry strength. He held him still for several moments.

"Let me go. Let me go!" Shade whipped out a knife.

Ruis knocked it from his hand. "I thought so. You have Flair. It bothers you to be near me. How can we work together?" Ruis stepped on the knife blade and released Shade.

Shade narrowed his eyes. "My plan. We work together. Or else. Dawn tomorrow. DownwindGrove."

"Wait! I know a better place, a deserted Healing Grove that will help your hand."

Shade stared at Ruis, hesitated.

Ruis couldn't stop himself from trying to help the desperate boy. "I know where FirstGrove is, and it will welcome you."

Shade blinked, disbelief and hope warring on his face.

Ruis knew those emotions. It was awful to hope, because when the hope died, you felt all the worse. He gave Shade directions to the FirstGrove. "I'll meet you there at dawn."

When the boy slipped into the shadows of the darkening night, Ruis drew his cowl and cloak around him and followed. The young man headed straight for FirstGrove. Ruis circled back uptown.

A few meters from the Ship's entrance he heard a soft meow. He looked back. Samba wavered to him on unsteady, drunken paws, her plump figure swaying. Intermittent mews issued from her until she collapsed, soft and warm on his boots. She blinked slowly up at him and smiled. *Greetyou, FamMan. You got My toy?*

Ruis lifted her bulk with an exaggerated grunt. "Greetings, drunk cat. Yes, I have your toy."

Samba rumbled a laugh, then stretched sinuously in his arms. *Catnip bonfire very good, D'Ash is good person. All feral Cats in Druida were there. Fifteen. D'Ash Healed them.*

"Yes, D'Ash is a good woman." Though not as wonderful as Ailim D'SilverFir. The thought might have calmed him, if he hadn't thought of her laughing and dancing with Holm Holly. He brooded as he approached the Ship.

A few septhours later in the Greensward he wiped his arm across his brow and surveyed a new clearing with satisfaction.

"Your emotional state is now within average ranges," the Ship said. "After reviewing your records since you first boarded, it has been observed that you are making considerable progress in overcoming your problems. Your mental health is gauged to be approximately forty percent better."

Ruis mumbled a curse.

Samba trotted out of the brush with a dead mouse in her mouth that she dumped in a small pile. *Ship's right. You not as angry. You think clearer. You don't make as many mistakes. I am good for you.*

Ruis considered this new information—more new information that was being crammed into his brain every day.

He was changing.

The man he'd become was being peeled back layer by layer so he could see how life had shaped him. He also admitted that, deep inside, despite everything, he held an inherent belief that everyone was essentially good. He groaned in disgust.

The Ship acknowledging his worth, and his feelings for Ailim and Samba, had changed him.

He glanced at his watch and his heart started thudding faster. Time to prepare for his night with Ailim. He ordered a maintenance 'bot to "recycle" the dead mice. "I'm going to shower and dress."

A few minutes later Ruis pulled his cloak and gloves on under Samba's watchful stare. "I'm going to D'SilverFir's, to help her. I'll be back just before dawn."

*I will come, too. D'SilverFir has puppy and Kitten.*

"It's dangerous outside. My uncle's guards know you're my Fam, and you're easily recognized."

Samba lifted her upper lip at the mention of Bucus, then her expression became smug and she slicked down a bit of hair on her shoulder. *It is true. I am most Beautiful Cat.*

Ruis shut then opened his eyes. "Your collar's unique, too." She just lifted her nose.

He cast his mind around for some way to deflect her. "How about playing with your folding-oracle toy? See what your future is?"

Samba sniffed. *My future with you and Ship is good. Toy made for fingers and thumbs.*

"I've seen you bat it around until it opens and shuts, peel back a corner, and have Ship read you your future."

"Your language has mutated," Ship said. "And the proper name for the toy is a 'cootie-catcher.' "

Ruis stared, but when Samba trotted to the door, he grabbed the pointed-cornered piece of papyrus. "Here."

She swatted it halfheartedly, then indicated Ruis could peel back the folded corner and reveal the fortune.

" 'You shall save the world and be a heroine in your own time,' " Ruis read, and frowned.

*That's Me,* agreed Samba. *Time to go. Let's go play!*

In desperation, Ruis addressed the Ship. "Ship, do you have a program that will amuse Samba for the evening?"

"We always have proper entertainment for any crew," Ship said.

Suppressing a sigh, Ruis ordered, "Please provide, immediately."

A colorful holo the width of the room began to play. "The History of Cats on Earth," Ship announced.

Samba's tail waved and her eyes widened. *History of Cats!* Samba trilled.

The regal history of cats unrolled in colorful scenes. Samba looked riveted. Her purr rose to new levels. *I will tell Ship of My History, the best. And of My Sire and Dam and T'Ash and D'Ash and Princess and My littermate Drena, and the new kittens coming.*

"We would appreciate the information for Our archives," Ship responded.

Awash with nervous anticipation, Ruis smoothed his clothes under the cape and adjusted the cloak. Impulsively he pressed the Prophecy program button.

The bright blue light stream flickered on. The low, lilting female voice curled around his senses. "Program starting, please interrupt the ion stream for your reading." Hating what he was doing, a stupid divination, but wanting to believe the night would go well, Ruis slashed his hand through the beam.

Cards fluttered and fell in a colorful heap to disappear and leave only one holo image. The Captain who looked like Ruis and a small rounded lady with long dark hair and dancing gaze toasted each other with a gold and silver cup. After they drank, the Captain took the goblet from the Lady and placed both cups gently aside. Then he picked her up and whirled her around and around. They laughed together, a set as matched as the cups. Ruis tasted bitter envy at the couple in love. He could never be so free with his own lady.

He narrowed his eyes. At first the setting looked like a Grove, but he could see shimmering, slightly curved silver walls through the leafy branches. It was the greensward on the Ship.

"Follow your heart and you will triumph." The breathy female voice said, still holding a hint of laughter.

Ruis's insides contracted. How he wished it were true. But he watched the image cycle again and again until he knew he had to get out. "Prophecy program dismissed."

"Blessed be, Captain Ruis Elder," the Lady said.

He sucked in a breath and left his quarters, striding to the door to Landing Park. He was the Captain of *Nuada's Sword,* not merely the despised Ruis Elder.

The Ship was helping him with the anger. He was growing in skill and confidence.

Who was he becoming?

He didn't know.

But he would learn.

Maybe he could even save Shade.

And Ruis vowed to follow his heart. The first thing it demanded was that he make love to his lady. Tonight.

*With a wave of her hand Ailim extinguished the glowlights* in her bedroom. She didn't know how she'd managed to survive the day. Because she was D'SilverFir, no doubt. She'd been trained to survive days like this, but sincerely hoped there wouldn't be many more of them in her future.

She shuddered. Always mindful of the strings to the D'SilverFir loan, she had agreed to the public show. Let the other nobles observe Ailim D'SilverFir and regard her as a GrandLady worthy of respect and consideration. The more nobles she could win to her side, the better.

She undressed and put her casual dress into the cleanser, then took out the shift and robe she'd worn early that morning. Lifting the cloth to her nose, she inhaled deeply and imagined that she could smell a whiff of him—the outlaw she wanted.

Her heart sped with giddy delight that he might come to her, touch her, help her, love her.

Or perhaps it wasn't delight that thundered through her veins, but apprehension.

Sex was not something she'd often enjoyed. Not since she realized that if she lost herself in passion, her Flair spiraled wide. Then she knew exactly what the man she was being intimate with thought and felt.

She shuddered as memory spun out her first sexual encounter. She'd believed her first man was making love with her.

But in uncontrolled passion, she'd found out otherwise. He was just taking the edge off a physical hunger. With a jerk of her head she banished the past. No need to think of that man—who had considered her strange and not nearly as beautiful as the woman he really wanted. At least the old emotions of shock and shame were mostly gone.

But Ruis would be different. Though she couldn't read him, she sensed that he was an honorable man, obeyed his own rules. That those rules might not march with the standard laws of Celta bothered her, but she couldn't fault him for acting outside them since they had never protected him.

Now he was banished. When she shivered again she knew it was fear at his daring, at the thought he might be caught.

Unable to stop her shudders, she donned her shift, then went to glance out the French doors that opened onto the terrace over the music room. The moons were high and would be full the next day. Nothing moved in the grounds.

He shouldn't come. He couldn't come. He wouldn't be able to avoid all her relatives or reach her rooms. With that gloomy conclusion she walked over to the platform of the huge four-poster bed draped with curtains and canopy—the empty, lonely bed—and climbed the small steps to get in.

Primrose lingered downstairs in the GreatHall soaking up admiration and love. Ailim smiled. It was so long since she'd spoken with a member of the Family who approved of her that tears came to her eyes. She shook them away— merely tiredness and self-pity. Now she'd formally sworn to lead and protect her Family. It was her duty, and hopefully her duty would transform into pleasure once she made this transition and the Family's loan was completely approved in six months.

The only part of the day that had been enjoyable was the evening Mabon ritual she'd conducted with her Family in the sacred Grove on the estate grounds. She'd chanted incantations and gathered the combined Family psi power to fashion spells for prosperity. During the ceremony soothing renewal had flowed into her, uplifting and inspiring her. The Grove had shimmered with magic and holiness, and she wondered how she could have considered selling the home that called to her heart.

Ailim drifted to sleep and dreamt again of Ruis Elder. She became aware of his scent first and smiled, knowing she dreamed, for his scent wasn't the one she recalled.

His aroma had changed, the spices were still there, but subtly different, the obscure undertone was the same, but intensified. So she knew she dreamed, and she sighed as his fragrance enveloped her.

She could feel his body heat as well. The air outside her covers held the cool of autumn and the first bite of winter, but next to her was warmth, and she imagined the steady thudding of his heart, strong and comforting.

The warmth enclosed her and gradually transformed into heat, almost as though she felt a hard body a hair's breadth away—muscled thighs, a wide chest. Sensuality uncurled inside her and built into taut desire.

Soft touches brushed over her cheek, an airy wisp trailed across her collarbone, and she thought of Ruis's elegant fingers. Her breathing sped.

A firm, moist pressure came against her lips and stoked her twisting hunger. She knew this taste, Ruis, and his kiss.

His dream kisses had never felt so real, but this one demanded she respond. She opened her mouth and whimpered when his tongue glided into her mouth and explored. She slid her own tongue against his, teasing herself and him, sucking, touching, then withdrawing, feeling coiled tension wind even tighter.

Her body arched in passion, came up solidly to his, so she rubbed herself against him. Her fingers sought the silkiness of his hair and tangled in it, bringing his head closer, deepening the kiss.

The slight nip of his teeth on her bottom lip brought her eyelids flying open.

He was here!

In the solid flesh. The heat of his desire transferred from his skin to hers. She felt the tautness of his muscles, the heaviness of his hands splayed on her back and the rigidity of his sex near the apex of her thighs.

His scent became muskier; the raggedness of his rapid breath fanned her shoulder, bringing tingles. Candles brightened the room and flickered over the taut planes of his face.

She tasted.

All her senses, freed once more from the oppression of her Flair, exploded until her wits spun, and she could not bear to deny herself, or him. She sucked his lower lip inside her own mouth.

He drew away and she could feel his piercing stare. He'd lit two pillar candles that provided a soft glow.

Her lips throbbed from the passionate kisses. Her body throbbed with unfulfilled hunger.

"I had to come," he murmured. "to make love with you. Also . . ." He stopped, mumbled, "to ask—"

His fingers pushed hair back from her face and trailed down her cheek. "You are beautiful, and so special." His head angled to kiss her again, but his lips only brushed hers as if now he was hesitant. "Roll over and I shall massage you."

"Only a massage?" she murmured, trapped in a honey golden moment, unable to free herself from drugged desire.

The flash of vulnerability in his eyes almost made her think, but instead, she tucked the expression away in her memory so she could savor its sweetness later.

His hand curved around her cheek and his pupils dilated. "We'll love?" he asked with a raw note in his voice.

"Yes." She brought his hand to her mouth and placed a dozen butterfly kisses on his fingers, then licked his palm. His whole body jerked and she laughed.

Ruis couldn't believe his eyes. Ailim's face was totally open and expressive, with no hint of any shield or mask that she wore for the world.

Her mouth was lush and tempting, her cheeks a deeper shade of rose than he'd ever seen, but it was her delighted smile and the sparkle in her blue eyes that transfixed him. He knew that no one, and especially no man, had ever seen her so spontaneous. A precious gift for him.

Blood pounded hotly through his veins but he couldn't move. He hardly dared to move, wanting nothing more than to give her the most beautiful night of loving she could ever imagine. And he didn't know how.

With a shake of his head he flung doubts from his mind. It didn't matter that he'd never experienced loving sex. He could give her tender passion. The emotion welled through him; there was no way he could fail.

He sucked in an unsteady breath, and rose to his knees. With a smooth pull, he slid the bedcovers from her, then slipped her shift open with one glide of his thumb. Just as

he had that morning, he spread the shift open and laid her
bare before him.

"Ruis," she said, and he shuddered. She lifted her hands
and drew them down his arms. The silkeen of his shirt felt
fine against his skin, but her fingers against his muscles
sparked a pulsing hunger that he couldn't deny.

One hand went behind her head and he lifted her so he
could take her mouth. For only an instant she held her arched
and still in a sensual curve of beauty he'd always remember. Then her arms went around him, and pulled him down,
her tongue penetrating his mouth and claiming him as her
legs twined around him until his throbbing shaft lay against
a warm moistness.

Passion sizzled all thought. Only the texture of her
tongue against his, the ripeness of her soft curves mattered.
He luxuriated in the heat between them, and then pulled
away to slip her arms from her shift and wrestle his own
clothes off.

As he fumbled, her small hands glided over him, squeezing his biceps, smoothing over his hipbone, curling around
his waist, as if she was free from all bounds to explore him
and satisfy her curiosity.

He returned his attention to her, groaning, and kissed her
lips once more, memorizing the taste of her mouth, then
went on to sample the taste of the angle of her jaw, the
salty dip in her collarbone, the succulent side of one plump
breast.

She gasped and her pale body trembled. The rose-colored
tip of her breast lured him. He circled around her nipple.
At her urging he took it into his mouth. The best taste of
all, exploding through him. Her softness pillowed his
mouth, her small, wild cries incited him to suckle deeply,
hardening his sex to the point of pain, sending him into
pure wondrous exultation that he pleasured her so.

His skin burned, barely able to contain his blazing
arousal as if he were a creature of pure fire. His teeth
clenched against the hard need to pound into her, to take
her with all the strength and passion at his demand.

"Ruis, Ruis, Ruis," she chanted, twining her fingers into
his hair. He lifted his head and found a sheen of sweat
dewing her skin. More tastes. More. Forever more.

"Ailim," he rasped.

Her eyes focused and fixed on his face. She gasped, her mouth opened wordlessly, moved, then she cried, "Ruis!"

He shuddered with the effort to hold his craving in check, and his name on her lips gave him a tiny shred of control. No woman had ever called his name in her passion. Sucking in his breath, he lowered his head to her collarbone and traced it with his tongue.

She tugged his hair and the sweet pain shot lightning through his blood. He didn't know how long he could last. With every breath he fought for restraint, to taste her again in special spots, at her sweet delta where the scent of her drove him mad.

He pressed a kiss on her dark blond curls and she rose against him, keening. Her fingernails bit into his shoulders. "Yesssss!" she cried.

His mind spun with dizziness and pulsing arousal. He tore himself from her clutching hands and one last sight of her torrid beauty pierced him before he took her.

Her satiny skin slid against his. With one plunge he was inside and surrounded by her, clasped in her tight, heated moistness. So exquisite he thought he'd die. Mind, body, soul connected to this one woman.

Ailim thrust against him, her inner muscles clamped and she tensed, and one last drawn-out moan came from her lips.

He exploded into flames and emptied himself into her, fragmented, unknowing if he'd ever be whole again.

Their breathing sounded loud in the room, though he thought his ears still rang with her last cry. He wondered if she'd released a burst of Flaired energy when she climaxed but understood he'd never know, though the room was much warmer.

A moment later her delicate fingers touched his chest. She caught a few of his hairs between her fingers and rubbed them.

He grunted.

She chuckled. The tip of her tongue laved the base of his neck. He shuddered as another bolt of lust sizzled through him, but managed to roll so they rested on their sides. His eyes were closed, streaks of fireworks still blazing on the inside of his lids.

"Uuhhn . . ." he stopped, tried again. "Ahhh." He hitched a breath. "That was too fast. Next time, I'll do better."

She choked.

He smoothed her hair from her face, enjoying how the fine strands clung to his fingers, but still didn't open his eyes.

Ailim spoke first. "What are you doing here? I told you not to come."

He sighed. He would have liked to pretend a few seconds longer that they were normal lovers.

When she tried to roll away, he pulled her close, opening his eyes to scan her face for any regret. She looked well-loved, delectable, but concerned.

"How did you get in here?" She stroked his face and the pleasure that speared him held nothing of lust, only encompassing tenderness. "What am I going to do with you?"

Ruis cleared his throat and achieved a steady whisper. "Anything you want to, Ailim. Talk to me, play with me, bed me. Or turn me in to the authorities."

Her eyes went wide and she snorted. "As if I could ever do that after what we've shared." She averted her gaze. "What I want to happen again," she ended on a murmur. Her lips firmed and she met his eyes. "I could never betray you."

His heart clutched. His entire life had been a series of betrayals, but he knew she meant what she said. He lifted her fingers to his lips and kissed them. "The noble and most honorable GrandLady D'SilverFir."

She reclaimed her fingers and her cheeks reddened. "I'm not going to turn you in."

"GrandLady D'SilverFir," he repeated, knowing his next words would remind them of the barriers between them. "Oathbound to lead and protect your Family."

Her face crumpled. "Yes, I swore, just this morning. How can this ever be between us?"

She could give him her body, and her respect, and her affection . . . but she couldn't give him her future, and he ached. "We live in each and every moment. In the present, so long as we can." He smiled crookedly. "I'm good at that, I'll teach you."

Her smile was as lopsided as his. "I can learn so much from you. And in being with you, I can live in the moment, but otherwise . . ."

He sighed and rolled onto his back. "I know, you're the head of the Family and must plan for their future." The deepest bedrock of Ailim's character would be honor; without that she wouldn't be the woman he cared for. He almost grasped what it would have been like to have been born into an honorable Family, accepted, then stacked his hands under his head as his imagination failed.

He looked up and saw the SilverFir Crest embroidered into the canopy above. A corner of his mouth hiked. She would never escape reminders of who she was, who she'd been taught to be. Nor would she ever betray her oath—as a GrandLady or a Judge. So Ruis had to recognize that.

"Speaking of Family, my aunt wears an evil, Flaired amulet. Could you help—"

"Yes."

She shook her head, her eyes holding wonder. "Just that quickly."

"Tell me how I can help you get your aunt's amulet."

"In a minute." She scooted close to him and put her hand on his chest, then smiled as if she liked feeling his heart's vibration. "A long time ago you said you wanted to ask me something. I was too dazed to pay attention." She chuckled.

Heat came to his face and he kept his stare fixed on the cloth above him.

Her finger touched his cheek. "What is your question?"

Stupid to feel foolish and insecure after what they'd just shared. Awful to feel a surge of jealousy. Ruis licked his lips and said, "I watched the ceremony in the square today. Very impressive. You hardly seemed to be the same woman I'd met. I wanted to find out—"

Ailim tensed. She could read body language and knew when someone thought they'd said too much. She scowled. "Exactly what did you want to find out?"

"I wanted you to be with me, part of the crowd, not one of them—the elite, the nobles, the FirstFamily GreatLords."

"And?"

He propped himself up on one elbow and again she felt the intensity of his gaze. She matched the steadiness of his stare. "What did you want to find out?" she repeated.

One of the moons broke from behind clouds and silver rays illuminated the room enough for Ailim to see the clenching of Ruis's jaw. "Tell me you had no pleasure in the company of the Holly," he said.

She blinked, sure it wasn't the question he meant to ask, or only a question that reflected a concern of his that went much deeper.

Her mind scrambled a bit, grasping for the memory he wanted, so long ago—this morning. "The Holly? Do you mean HollyHeir? Holm?"

"Yes, Holm. The FirstSon. The man who will be T'Holly. He of the silver-gilt hair and charming smile. He who led you into the banquet."

"Uh."

"Yes?"

She shrugged. "You said it. He's charming. Amusing."

"He can't give you what I can, stir the feelings in you that I do."

She didn't know if he was stating a fact or voicing a hope, as he grasped her and pulled her close.

Before his lips even touched hers again, she surrendered to him. The red heat of desire rose once more. She wanted, she yearned. Her mouth opened against his questing tongue. His spicy scent enveloped her, and then blossomed into taste.

Her blood raced. He pulled her closer still, and the whole of his body cradled hers. Once again, his heat and strength and hardness whirled all thought away. She entwined her arms around his neck and returned his kiss with all the fevered desire that had built in her over the last few weeks. She accepted the thrusts of his tongue, the rocking of his hips, the caress of his hand on her bottom, and returned them with passion. She drank his taste deep into her being, where she could always cherish it. Her palms smoothed from his neck to his arms.

He pulled her skin-to-skin, as if he wanted every inch of her skin touching his.

She slid her hands to his broad back, testing each straining muscle, each sinew, kneading and learning his essential shape. He rolled until he lay panting under her and she broke the kiss to study his face flushed with desire.

How dear he was. She stared at him, his face that spoke of noble blood. He should have exuded the ingrained arrogance that all the male nobles of her acquaintance bore, but his eyes told another story. Their expression held shadows of a lifetime of pain, of the expectation of cruelty, and to her gaze, an open vulnerability.

Her throat tightened. How wrong they were to pursue this. Yet how right they were for each other. But she didn't want to think, so she lowered her mouth to his, preparing to dive once more into pure sensation.

A cat hissed. *Ssssamba is here!*

Primrose yipped and bolted through the small pet flap set in Ailim's heavy bedroom door. The puppy leaped up the small set of steps to the great bed and shot across both of them to the pillow next to Ruis and licked his face. Ruis ducked.

Primrose was probably broadcasting a stream of eager, happy thoughts at great speed and loud level, but Ailim couldn't hear them. A small blessing.

Low menacing cat growls came from the doorway.

"What?" Ruis said, rolling so that he and Ailim were both on their sides.

The angry cat-rill sounded again. Ailim almost caught words, then Primrose was licking her face. The dog had eaten furrabeast mixed with raw eggs not too long ago. Ailim gently pushed her away, toward Ruis. He swept covers over him, to his waist, disappointing Ailim. Primrose whuffled at him and snuffled in his ear. He automatically picked her up and cuddled her, stroking her long, soft fur.

Samba began to curse. Cat-obscenities sounded worse than human swearing. Ruis chuckled.

"You really can communicate with her without telepathy," Ailim said, slipping off the bed and walking toward the door. "Samba?"

Snarls greeted her. *I'm stuck. Stuck in puny dog hole. NOT acceptable to a Cat of My high-degree or My substance.*

"You certainly are a cat of substance," Ailim replied. Of course, some of that was the volume of calico fur on-end sticking out across her body, except where it was pushed aside by the square frame of the pet door. Ailim winced. It looked painful. She hesitated to try and help, seeing bloodily scratched hands in her future.

Ruis, still holding and petting Primrose, joined Ailim.

Samba looked up at him and her frustrated face turned lethal. *You will smell of dog.*

"That's too bad," Ruis said blandly. He seemed to be trembling with suppressed laughter.

A low rumble started deep in Samba's throat. From Ailim's experience with her cousin's new kitten, she knew exactly how high and piercing the sound could escalate. "Quiet!" she commanded. "Do you want to get him caught and killed?"

Irregular, hard thumps hit the door from outside. Cat tail lashings.

Ruis squatted out of striking-paw distance.

Much too close to Samba, Primrose quivered and jumped from his arms to streak away. Ailim heard the scritch of claws on steps and the rustle of covers. Glancing back, she saw that Primrose cowered in a corner of the bed, curled on Ailim's pillow. Primrose belched. Ailim looked down at Ruis and Samba. He wasn't touching her, but murmured soothingly. It didn't seem to have any effect.

"I think," Ailim bit her lip and tried to keep a straight face, "that it would be best if you go, Ruis. After the House spells revive from your presence, I'll teleport Samba to the coordinates she gives me."

He rose and gazed down at her. "What of your aunt's amulet?"

She rubbed the back of her neck. Ruis pulled her in front of him and started massaging her nape. Ailim struggled to think past the pleasure of his touch. "The Residence is too full for us to wander around tonight. Menzie keeps the thing somewhere in her rooms, and hasn't been leaving them very often. I worry about her."

Ruis's hands progressed down her shoulders. "Mmmmmmm," Ailim hummed.

Samba hissed, set her claws in the ancient carpet and ripped.

"Stop that!" Ruis ordered.

Samba narrowed her eyes and hissed again.

Ailim stepped away from him. "I don't think Menzie will do anything soon." Ailim prayed not. "Go." A tingle went up her spine. "You've lingered too long. Get back to safety."

To her surprise, Ruis bent and kissed her brow, then swept her a bow as gallant as Holm Holly. "I'll be at JudgmentGrove this afternoon—"

"No. It's too dangerous." She bit her lip, shook her head. "Come to me tonight," she whispered.

Ruis's smile was brilliant, lighting his eyes. He lifted Ailim's hand and kissed her fingers. His low voice emerged with a rough note. "I'll be here. We'll solve the problem of the amulet."

Ailim nodded. Samba had started a sub-vocal rumbling again.

Ruis pressed a quick kiss on her lips and dressed.

"I'll send Samba along shortly," Ailim said.

"Teleport her to Landing Park."

"Landing Park is a big area."

*Needs to be big to hold*—Ailim made out Samba's words.

"Quiet," Ruis ordered.

Ailim's stomach knotted. She felt as if icy bone fingers shredded her heart. Ruis didn't trust her to know where he hid.

He gathered her close, but she didn't soften against him. Second thoughts poured into her.

# Eleven

"**D**on't," *Ruis said to Ailim. "Don't draw away. I can't* tell you where I hide. It isn't solely my secret."

She rubbed her temples. "Someone hides you, then? I thought you lacked good friends."

"You are my best and first friend, as well as my lover. But—another—could be harmed."

Lover. The word rocked her, and the feel of his body began to ignite insidious licks of banked desire burning low within her. She shook her head so she could think, kept her breaths shallow, so she wouldn't inhale the scent that whipped her wits away.

"Teleport Samba to the Summer Pavilion at Landing Park," Ruis said.

"All right."

His lips molded hers and she relented, leaning against him. She could understand his protection of someone else. Wasn't her whole life about just that? His hands stroked her back. "It was worth every danger to come to you. I won't be stopped, and I will return."

"Be very careful—"

*You are forgetting ME, and My problem,* Samba insisted.

Ruis released Ailim. He took a step away from her, two, then gestured to the bureau.

He'd brought passionflowers tonight. An'Alcha. The trumpet

like blooms showed pale peach at the edges shading into dark red at the base. A large bouquet sat next to the spray of BalmHeal he'd picked for her in FirstGrove, and which she had placed in a transparent no-time egg.

Passionflowers. Ailim felt a blush heat her face. Suddenly she was aware of their heady fragrance, something she hadn't noticed, as concentrated as she'd been on Ruis's scent.

"An'Alcha and BalmHeal still bloom in the FirstGrove?"

"Yes, a gift. I'm no longer forced to steal. I am not a thief."

*Anymore.* The word hung between them, but it was of no importance.

As with her sense of smell, Ailim became aware of other sounds in the Residence including the muted bellow of G'Uncle Pinwyd. She clutched at Ruis's upper arms, tried to give him a little shake. He stood like a rock. "You must go. Hurry, quickly and quietly."

He didn't move a centimeter, but smiled his crooked smile, and kissed her again. Then he picked up a bundle of something that she couldn't quite see. To her utter astonishment he went to the corner of her bedroom and flipped the latch that opened the secret door to the staircase.

"No one knows of that door but D'SilverFir Heirs and heads of household," she whispered.

His teeth flashed in a grin. "I got it from the plans."

"No plans are on file, anywhere."

"There are plans, back even to the last plans of the Earth castle, Egeskov, in Den-Mark."

Ailim's mouth fell open, but before she could grope for a reply, he was gone, the panel closing without sound.

She stood there for several moments, and let her mixed emotions flood through her as she stared at the An'Alcha, the rumpled covers on the bed, the place where he'd disappeared. Finally she figured out what she was feeling. Joy. Tenderness. A sense of being valued.

Friend. Lover. He'd called her both of those, and right now, both of those were incredibly essential to her.

But he'd lied.

He was a thief.

She was very sure a piece of her heart was missing.

*       *       *

*R*uis *was dozing when Samba jumped on his belly. His* breath whooshed out and she pricked his stomach with sharp claw-points. "Ouch!"

He'd learned by now that, as a very proud cat, she hated being embarrassed and would slink away or sulk until she got over it. Obviously, she'd decided that her getting stuck in Ailim's pet door was Ruis's fault.

"Rrrrowww!" It reached the supersonic stage, vibrating his eardrums. *I am back. Had to slink and evade My sire Zanth.*

A frisson of warning crawled up his spine. Ruis opened gritty eyes. "Do you think Zanth is suspicious?"

Samba rolled her back. *He just out hunting celtaroons.*

Ruis hoped so. "Zanth could be dangerous."

*Nothing to worry about.* Samba sniffed.

Ruis turned over, enduring the pain of Samba's claws scratching across his abdomen to his hip as he dumped her. "The way you carried on tonight at D'SilverFir's, you wouldn't care if I got caught."

He ignored her small apologetic mew and pretended not to hear her tentative sounds to attract his notice, but watched her from the corner of his eye. Finally she spoke in a subdued fashion. *I would miss you. You're my FamMan. We're companions. FAMily.*

Ruis grunted, then felt little licks of affection from her rough tongue on his hand. "Hhhn. I guess you're right."

*I'm always right*, she replied, but with only half her usual smugness. *Time to sleep.* She moved down to the end of the bed and curled in her usual place around his ankle.

Some septhours later he was awakened by an odd creaky noise. He blinked and as his mind cleared, he realized the Ship wasn't making the noise. It was natural. It was coming from Samba. Not quite a purr and not one of her cat-laughs, a mixture of the two.

Only the glow of machine lights brightened the room, leaving it dim. "Lights," he said.

Samba hovered in front of him. He gasped and rubbed his eyes. His heart jolted as he hazily saw Samba sitting straight—and floating at eye level. He gulped. "Wha—? What?—"

Samba lifted her nose, and a hum got louder and she

lifted even higher until he saw the color of the floor reflected in a curved surface above him. He blinked.

*Mine. Mine. Mine! MY flying saucer!* Samba squealed, her long whiskers twitching madly, her tail hanging over the rim of the thing as she rocked it back and forth.

Ruis's eyes widened.

Samba grinned, little white fangs showing. *My toy. You have lots of toys in Ship. This is mine! I found in storeroom. Perfect condition!*

Ruis grunted.

Gurgling deep in her throat, Samba swerved figure eights throughout the quarters. *Wheeeeeeeeeeee! This is BEST play!*

"You can play all you want with that saucer in the Ship, but it would be deadly for both of us if you took it out."

Samba sniffed. *If I fly high, no one can see.*

"Let's not test that."

Samba played with her saucer while Ruis took a shower in herbal-smelling water, dressed, and put on the light-bending cloak.

"Nearly dawn. Time to meet Shade."

Samba snorted. *He Downwind scruff, no good. He tell nobles and guards about you.*

"Ship, transparent window, please." The Captain's Quarters had a huge window, fully four meters square, in the sitting room. Ruis glanced out. Bel, the small blue-white sun, was beginning to light the sky. Many of the brightest stars still shone, as well as both moons. An unusual number of people dotted the large Landing Park. Small campfires still burned, and couples lay entwined. It looked more like Beltane, which the Ship called May Day, instead of the Mabon harvest.

When he reached the den, he found that Samba had played one of her tricks, and activated the Prophecy Program. His body interrupted the light beam and a swirling column of cards appeared. Two cards fell, to be fixed and magnified by the holo.

The first card stunned him. A man dressed in gray, with scuffed boots and enveloped by a cloak, pulled a hood to shadow his unshaven face. As Ruis watched, he slunk from the background of tents with pennants flying, to scale a wall. Tucked under both arms, he carried a wealth of swords with various shaped pommels studded with jewels. The bright sky behind him turned gray with black edges of an oncoming storm.

"Seven of Swords," the program's throaty female voice said. Ruis translated the "swords" of the Earth cards into Celtan "blasers." In a contemporary deck, the sneaky bastard—a thief!—would be carrying a basket of seven rich, noble-crested blasers. Ruis grit his teeth, remembering what he had been. Even as he watched, the thief slipped from the holo.

The program continued, "This symbol indicates unreliability, betrayal, spying, the failure of a plan. An undesirable action. Beware."

Ruis stopped in his tracks as he saw the next card. "Where did you get that image?" he croaked. A blond maiden with a heart-shaped face sat with a unicorn's head in her lap. Ailim D'SilverFir, shown in the vision as the GreatSuite card, Lady and Unicorn.

Ship answered him. "We obtained it by holos of yesterday's Mabon festival and OathTaking. We must comment that the ceremony has changed—"

"Stop," Ruis said.

"Lady and Unicorn, a good omen. She brings blessings, power that guards, nourishes, empowers. Your constructive creativity develops, especially at home, in orderly, serene surroundings. Healing and recovery."

*Mmmmrrroww? Are you coming?* Samba asked. The saucer settled gently to the floor. Samba was wearing a huge cat grin. She pressed a round green paw-sized button. *I stick good inside saucer. And the bigger I am, the better I stick.* She raised her nose smugly.

Ruis smiled halfheartedly. "End program." He was glad when the holos vanished. "We have to hurry." He stepped over Samba, left his quarters with her trotting beside him, and took an omnivator to the northeast portal, thinking of the divination.

Uneasiness filled Ruis on the way to FirstGrove; he thought he'd seen the flash of the first sunlight on a silver-gilt head, a Holly head, either Holm or Tinne.

He waited until he was sure he and Samba were alone,

then continued. Bel was just sending blue-white rays over
the tops of the trees surrounding him when he entered the
Grove.

The Ship had discovered some interesting information on
Nightshade. As the boy stated, his triad brothers were
dead—after tangling with T'Ash. Shade was nearly as
"wanted" by the guards as Ruis. Shade had escaped All-
Class HealingHall before answering criminal charges. At
the time he'd had a "DepressFlair" bracelet melded permanently around his wrist by T'Ash. Shade had severed his
own hand to remove the DepressFlair cuff and regain his
psi power.

Ruis shivered from the chill of the morning, the idea of
crossing T'Ash, and Shade's desperation. No doubt Shade
believed that T'Ash was Ruis's number-one enemy, since
Ruis's stealing of T'Ash's HeartGift necklace had led to
the Council taking notice of Ruis and Ruis's subsequent
imprisonment and banishment.

Ruis had automatically followed Samba, who now sat at
the bottom of an oak, looking up and lashing her tail. He
was unsurprised to see Shade stretched out on a huge limb
a meter or so above his head.

Shade scowled down at them. "Send Fam away. Don't
like fliggerin' cats."

Ruis noticed thin scars of cat scratches on Shade's face,
and Ruis gestured to Samba to go.

Samba whipped her tail back and forth and lifted her
muzzle in disdain. *I never "fliggered" in My life.*

Ruis believed her. She was neutered.

*Boy is Downwind scruff. He's fliggered plenty. Probably
with Triad brothers.*

"Go," Ruis said to Samba.

She let out a nasty little chuckle. *I go. I talk better than
him. Only young Fams of Zanth breeding, or stupid pup-
pies, talk in Downwind shortspeech.* She tilted her head.
*puppy might learn. This scruff, never.* With tail high and
curved haughtily, she strolled away.

Shade narrowed her eyes. "She talks? You understand."

"She's my Fam."

"You're Null."

Ruis bared his teeth in a grin. "That's right, Flaired boy.

I'm a Null. Can't you feel it?" Knowing Shade could, Ruis saw tiny beads of sweat at the youngster's hairline.

Shade scrambled down the tree. He might have had the genetic potential to equal Ruis's height, but a Downwind childhood of poor nutrition made him several centimeters shorter. He cradled his injured wrist with his other hand, and Ruis was glad to see all Shade's fingers occupied. No doubt the youth had a concealed knife, throwing star, or razorslit.

"I'm not a boy. You think I can't plan, can't fight, can't follow vengeance stalk?"

"No. I think you can do all of that." Ruis had to ensure Shade didn't betray him. Perhaps he could somehow rehabilitate the youth. Ruis stared at him, wondering if there was anything below Shade's driving need for revenge that could make him into a decent human being. All Ruis could see was the power of Shade's rage, a wrath that had once mirrored his own.

He, too, had been considered unredeemable.

Ruis nodded to the moss-encased poultice around Shade's wrist. "Is that fresh?"

"Within the septhour."

"Better stay a little distance from me, or your Healing Waters, poultice, and spells won't work." Ruis walked a meter to a stone bench and sat. "Now. Tell me about your plan."

"You Null. You can get in anywhere, anytime. Like the FirstFamilies Council Meeting, even Ritual in Guildhall or GreatCircle Temple."

Ruis stiffened, but kept his voice mild. "That's right. After a few moments the spells in my immediate area falter, then fail. I can forge a path anywhere, but only my body-width. If the spellshields are automatically renewed, they'll regenerate behind me. Anything around me is affected until I leave."

"Gossip says when you were locked up in Guildhall gaol all spells failed. All."

"I was there two eightdays." He grinned with real amusement. "They had to move the record-keeping to a building across the street."

Shade grinned back and almost looked his young age.

Ruis frowned. "So, you're thinking of confronting the nobles in the Guildhall. A full Noble Council? FirstFamilies Council? Or GreatLords and Ladies Council only?"

Shade made an awkward movement with his hurt arm. "FirstFamilies most important."

"FirstFamilies, then." Ruis watched as the boy unwrapped his arm. The reattached hand appeared much better than it had the night before, but Ruis doubted if it would ever be right. "Don't bother to try and renew the Healing Spells on yourself until I'm gone. What's your Flair?" If the young man was a Healer, there might be hope for him yet.

"Fire."

Ruis sucked in a breath. He tried to gauge how powerful Shade might be, but had no way to measure it. "I like the architecture of Guildhall, and would hate to see it burn."

Shade scowled.

Ruis rose and strode away.

"Wait," Shade said.

Ruis leveled a stare at the youth. "I've business and no time to play games. Get to the point. I won't be a party to burning the Guildhall down around a FirstFamilies Council."

Shade met his gaze with a deceptive innocence. "Only want to play a trick. Set off one little firework, make big stink. And you remember, you walking deadman if any catch here in Druida."

Ruis narrowed his eyes. "I know that the guards want you, too. You left the HealingHall while under charges of assault."

Shade snorted. "Assault. Fights called assault when winners whine on losers. Fights, noble duels, noble melees, all legal."

That hit a nerve. "The strong win, the weak lose."

"We work together," Shade pressed. "Teach fliggerin' nobles they not safe, not even in NobleCouncil Hall, not even at Council." He shot Ruis a sly look. "Council tried and judged you."

Another good hit by Shade. Anger flashed at the memory. Ruis beat it back. He set his teeth to keep from responding to the bait. They could trade histories of noble insults for hours.

Ruis had already talked to the Ship and Samba about his life and the way he had scrambled to survive. He stared at Shade. Who could the youngster talk to? It was a sure bet that he'd never be welcome in one of the youth centers T'Ash had founded for Downwind boys. His triad brothers, closer than friends, closer than brothers, boys who had often shared the same thoughts, melded into one unit, were dead.

Perhaps Shade could be retaught. Perhaps listening would lance his pain and lead to the acceptance of his grief. Perhaps.

Since Ruis had never been given a second chance by anyone, he was willing to give this lost boy one.

"Don't blackmail me," Ruis warned. "Don't try and set me up. I have proof that you've been mugging noble-bloods—the young GrandSir Lotus, the brothers Chicory, and old Sassafras." Ship had provided records.

Shade jolted, then mustered bravado. "My plan. You get me into NobleCouncil, I hu-mil-I-ate all nobles, BroadcastScry the scene. Much laughter by commoners." His narrow face contracted in a blissful grin. "Oh, yeah. Fab."

For a moment Ruis indulged in the fantasy. It would be very interesting to see how the nobles would handle the incident—who would carry on with grace, who would fall apart. With luck, Bucus could actually die of sheer outrage.

Even as Ruis smiled, he knew he'd come too far along his own path of recovery to do such a thing.

Ruis considered Shade. How dangerous was he? Could he be redeemed? Still, it would be better to keep an eye on him. "Don't trap me, or betray me. Samba and all the Fams and feral cats can keep an eye on you. A short, anonymous note to the guards will take care of you. If I don't get you, the Guards will. If they don't get you, Samba and her friends will."

*Will eat your balls from your live body*, Samba purred, loudly and distinctly, plunking down from a tree branch.

Shade staggered back. The cat scars turned red against his sallow skin. "I understand."

"Good," Ruis said.

"Send it away," said Shade.

Ruis jerked his head. Samba deigned to acquiesce. Tail flaunting, she strolled into the underbrush.

Ruis studied the boy. The desperate, friendless boy. "This afternoon is full twinmoons. There's an altar in a ritual grove in the southwest corner of this property. We can celebrate the Sabbat there at dawn. Merry meet."

Shade's mouth fell open. Ruis knew then that the young man had never been given the courtesy or respect of the most minor Celtan greeting. Had he ever been to a true Ritual, ever participated and felt the inspiration? Could giving him these very important and intangible things instill a sense of honor in him?

"Merry part," Shade croaked.

"And merry meet again." Ruis grinned. "When you wish to contact me, just say so to a feral cat."

Samba crawled out from the brush. *We are very smart,* she said smugly. *Ferals playing Hide from Zanth.*

"Cats not obey well," Shade said.

"Which of us here does?" Ruis said. "But the cats know they'll get a good reward for bringing a message to Samba." Prime earth catnip from the Ship. News of the excellent drug was already making the feline rounds.

"Goodbye, GentleSir Nightshade." Ruis bowed, keeping his eyes on Shade, then left.

*A*ilim's last case before noonbell at JudgmentGrove was allocating the Residence, funds and possessions of the late, last member of the GraceHouse Asphodel. The whole business was conducted with a note of melancholy. The Asphodel Family had been one of the first GraceHouses founded, by one of the technicians of the starship *Arianrhod's Wheel*. The Family had never proliferated. The HealingHall diagnosis was that some gene which was dominant and essential on Earth did not allow the Family to adapt well to Celta.

As the last bong echoed through the ancient grove, Ailim stood. "I have an announcement to make. Most people celebrated both Mabon and full twinmoons yesterday; however, the exact time of the full moons is in two septhours. As is standard practice, JudgmentGrove is ended today at noonbell and will recommence tomorrow morning at workbell." She said the closing prayer and Yeldoc ended the weathershield and cut the sacred circle.

Ailim watched her kinswoman, Caltha of Woodpine, stride through the center of the Grove.

The moment crystallized. Time seemed to stretch. Every action moved with infinite slowness around Ailim while her senses sharpened preternaturally. Her Flair coalesced in an oppressive bubble indicating a moment of great decision.

She studied Caltha, the head of a cadet branch who ran one of the outlying Family farms. She was the reason for the odd atmosphere. A tangle of light-brown hair curled about Caltha's round face, her eyes were the same blue-gray as Ailim's. The long tabard Caltha wore over her blue gown emphasized the ripe breasts and hips of a thirty-seven-year-old woman. She looked the epitome of the Lady in her aspect of Matron. But Caltha's physical characteristics dimmed before her personal qualities. Ailim saw generosity, shrewdness, and integrity. In that moment Ailim saw more. She saw her Heir.

The strange time-stretch snapped and Caltha stood in front of Ailim. Caltha curtsied.

"Greetyou, Caltha," Ailim said, slipping her Flair-chilled hands into the opposite wide sleeves of her robe.

"Greetyou—Ailim," Caltha replied. "This is the first time I've been to JudgmentGrove."

Ailim smiled. "Everyone is welcome."

Caltha looked around. "It's a place everyone should visit, but I doubt it's a very popular attraction, like the ship, *Nuada's Sword*. I took the younglings there and, you know, we didn't even want to go inside and visit the museum rooms. It is very impressive, but"—she shrugged—"just utterly different."

"It is part of our past," Ailim chided, but struggled to remember when she, herself, had last visited the starship. When she was a child, she thought. *Nuada's Sword* was ever-present. Huge as it was, it loomed in the skyline, visible from every part of the city, yet everyone took it for granted, only showing the thing to out-of-towners as an odd site.

Caltha shrugged. "True, it's our past, but I prefer to focus on the future." She nodded to a plump merchant who rubbed his hands and beamed with happiness, being slapped on his back by friends. Ailim had determined he was the best candidate to win and care for the old Asphodel estate. "Like the new GraceLord T'Goldthread, there. An excellent choice. He'll cherish the grounds and the Residence. Under his hand, new traditions will be made, a new Family dynasty founded. He'll bring vitality and spirit to the old place. The future is very important."

"Of course. Speaking of which, when did you plan to leave?"

"This afternoon. We have several days' journey to the plantation on Huckleberry Finn River."

"Stay."

Tilting her head, Caltha raised her brows.

"We haven't had time to talk, and there are things to discuss," Ailim said.

Caltha frowned. "I've been keeping track of the Family's financial problems, but I really need to get back—"

"Stay, D'SilverFirHeir," Ailim said softly.

Shock flashed in Caltha's eyes. Her cheeks reddened. "I . . . I . . . I can't think of what to say."

"Young as I am, I still need an heir. We must discuss this. I would prefer you keep your Family here, too. Have your children been Tested for Flair?"

"Not . . . not formally." Caltha sucked in a big breath. "Can we do it here? With the D'SilverFir testing stones?"

"Of course."

"I am appreciative of the honor you do me, D'SilverFir," Caltha said, formally bowing her head.

"But you are not going to say you are unworthy."

Caltha raised her chin and met Ailim's eyes. "No, I'm not. Until you have children of your own, I'm glad to be your Heir."

The thought of children gave Ailim a twist of pain. The man she wanted was not the man who could father her children. She pushed the thought away. "Stay, please."

Again dipping her head, Caltha said, "Yes, D'SilverFir.

I'll go and inform my husband and children that we'll remain. There's much to see and do in Druida; we should take advantage of the opportunities." A gleam came to her eyes. "Isn't Cona going to be fussed? She's been boasting she's your Heir, you know."

"Oh, has she?" Ailim said coldly. She gestured to Yeldoc to come over. She wanted a witness to her intention, and fussy Yeldoc would do very well. "D'SilverFirHeir, I would like to introduce you to my bailiff, Yeldoc. Yeldoc, please make sure my heir has access to my chambers and me whenever she wishes."

"I am honored," Yeldoc mumbled to Caltha, obviously impressed with her figure.

Caltha nodded regally and strolled away.

Ailim swept a glance around JudgmentGrove. She loved the place, the grassy green, the huge trees, the small stage with the Sage's Chair and rainbowstone desk. This, more than her Residence, was home. She wanted to spend more time with Ruis here, but it was best to limit his visits to nightly passion.

A nasty odor hit her nose and it twitched. Then she realized it was just a reminder of the evil amulet Menzie wore. The effect seemed to be growing, feeding off Menzie's energy, but Ailim could not convince her aunt to give the wretched thing up. At the idea of Menzie, a waspish buzz filled Ailim's head. She couldn't bear to see Menzie now.

Ailim sent her robe to her chambers and went into her private area behind the stage, then left the grove. She dreaded returning to the Residence. She needed time alone. She wanted to walk.

*R*uis stood in the shadows of a doorway and watched as Samba walked her paws up the side of the impressive marble building across the street, a bag clamped in her jaws. She pressed a button to open the collection box of "Cascara Bank and Financial Services." Ruis grinned to himself, feeling a fizz of happiness. He'd never had a bank account, let alone one at such a firm as Cascara's, second only to

GreatLord T'Reed's. Now he, Ruis Elder, was a valued client.

Not that they knew who he was, of course. They thought he was some old, feeble offshoot of the Elder Family.

The firm was efficient and quick. Ruis was pleased with their service and would not hesitate to give them a recommendation.

The collection box slowly opened; Samba placed the satchel inside. The box closed.

Ship had decided that an additional component in Ruis's anger management would be a sense of financial security. Always one to have a stash, Ruis had opened an account at Cascara's. Originally he'd thought of marketing the plants in the greensward, but decided it was too risky.

There were plenty of objects on the Ship that were extremely precious. He and the Ship had concluded that several ancient coins, actually minted on Earth, would provide the security Ruis needed. Ruis had also hidden a few coins in various parts of town in case of emergency.

Through correspondence and Samba's willing paws, Ruis had hired Cascara's to receive a long-lost bounty—three Earth coins—sell them, and keep the funds in an account. Samba was delivering the final papyrus connected with the sale . . . authorization of the commission.

Samba sharpened her claws on the stone building as she waited for a receipt. Her ears pricked. Ruis heard the clucking tongue at the same time. He dared not speak. Samba looked up the street. Ruis huddled in the doorway between two bow windows and crouched down, pulling the light-bending cloak around him so none of his skin showed.

"Here, cat. What a beautiful, lively puss," said a lilting male voice that Ruis recognized, Holm Holly.

He ground his teeth; surely Samba wouldn't be lured away by such a compliment.

Of course she would. She pranced up the street, out of sight.

"What a beautiful puss, what a clever Cat. Look at that pretty silver collar," Holm flattered.

Ruis hunkered down further. He caught a glimpse of Holm approaching in an angled window.

Cascara's collection box opened to emit a scarlet receipt.

Ruis cursed under his breath, waiting, assuring himself that all was not lost. Samba was not recognized. If she were, Holly couldn't connect her to him, but the Elder name on the receipt could be damning, could start already suspicious minds thinking.

It could be worse.

It got worse.

Zanth, T'Ash's Fam, swaggered up the street from the opposite direction. A huge cat, he could easily reach the receipt. He'd recognize his daughter, Samba. Zanth had mated with Samba's mother, Tinne Holly's Fam, so Zanth knew the Hollys well. He knew Samba was Ruis's Fam. Zanth hated Ruis.

Zanth lifted his muzzle, sniffed, spied the open collection box, and trotted over. He pulled the receipt from the box with his teeth.

Samba's yowl of outrage split the air. Her papyrus was being stolen by her sire!

Zanth whirled and bounded away, obviously recalling his fight with his daughter. Samba sped after him. Holly laughed.

Ruis gritted his teeth. This could mean discovery. It could mean life or death. Who would the Fam give the receipt to, D'Ash or T'Ash?

Less than a septhour later Samba materialized outside the gates of T'Ash Residence. Ruis had waited out of sight in a spot where his Nullness affected no inherent spells.

"Well?" he asked.

Samba scowled, then burped. *Slip is shredded.*

He sucked in a breath. "Tell me."

*Zanth 'ported here. I followed. He ran into D'Ash. She took slip. I jumped, got slip, shredded.*

"That's all?"

Her muscles rippled from neck to tail in a feline shrug of irritation. *Slip is gone.* Her long wet tongue swiped her whiskers. *Best food in Druida for Cats, here.*

"Did D'Ash read the slip?"

*Don't know.*

He looked down at her. She looked away, embarrassed at her failure. He wanted to shout at her or punch a convenient hedge, or swear. He didn't. He loved her, this vain, precocious, often maddening cat. She'd been the first being who had ever loved or trusted him. He sighed and reached down to pick her up. She looked at him with wide green eyes and began a rough purr.

Carrying her, he strode back to FirstGrove to set up the twinmoons ritual for himself and Shade.

*R*uis let *Nightshade dismiss the Guardians of the Watch-* towers and extinguish the four directional candles. The ritual had gone better than Ruis had expected. Since he had no Flair he couldn't call upon psi power to manifest his will and prayers into concrete events, but he'd found peace in the actions.

Nightshade no longer jittered. His expression held an underlying serenity so Ruis considered the ceremony a success.

Ruis had stood before the simple, ancient altar in FirstGrove and named aloud resentments and hatreds he intended to release for all time from burdening his soul. He trusted the boy enough to let him hear some minor sins and secrets.

At one moment during the prayers, when Shade was on the opposite side of the circle, Ruis sensed Nightshade had experienced a small pulsing of Flair he could learn to use to fashion his own rituals. Ruis felt a small flicker of hope that he'd turned Shade onto a path other than the vengeance stalk.

Shade cut the Circle, and the ritual ended.

"Good job," Ruis said. He clapped a hand on Shade's shoulder. The boy started and tugged away. Ruis's mouth tightened, but he banished the hurt. People would always pull away from him.

"Shade," he said.

The youth looked up from dousing the candles set at the compass points. At least there wasn't a wariness in his stare, the young man trusted Ruis—a little.

Ruis swept a hand around them. "This is the FirstGrove." His voice naturally lowered. He wanted to extend the feeling of serenity as long as possible. Being on the Ship usually energized him, thinking and working; being with Ailim

D'SilverFir usually made his thoughts and body concentrate in a different, carnal, direction; but being here in First-Grove gave him a calm he'd rarely experienced.

"It will let you in. I've given you the dismiss illusions spell and the gatespell." Ruis nodded to the edge of papyrus sticking out of Shade's pocket. Ruis hoped soon Shade would need those spells to enter, that he wouldn't be admitted because he radiated desperation.

"Use this place to heal. In the gardenshed are fresh herbs and recipe books for poultices you can make for your wrist. If you use your hand, it may Heal better. I'm leaving the altar, tools, and candles in place. When I'm gone, consider doing a ritual of your own, using your Flair."

The boy blinked and an arrested expression crossed his face. He grinned and almost looked young. "You think?"

Ruis smiled back. "You won't know what you can do unless you try."

Shade looked around the grove then up at him, brows lowered. "You mean what you say during Ritual? Ill-will to T'Ash gone?"

Ruis nodded. "Yes. Not only has that GreatLord forgiven me, but it's damned dangerous to hold a grudge against him." He stopped himself from adding that Danith D'Ash had helped him, leading to the lightening of his resentments. When Shade was further reformed, they'd talk of Danith D'Ash.

"Ill-will, pitti-pat word." He sent Ruis a sly look. "Dangerous to cross T'Ash, dangerous as crossing a Holly. You didn't release no ill-will for Hollys."

"No, I didn't. Some emotions take longer to let go. Like your hatred for T'Ash."

Shade's glistened teeth flashed, and again he was the cunning, feral, blood-lusting gangmember. Ruis wished he hadn't spoken.

"T'Ash killed my triad-brothers. He noble. Go unpunished."

"Who attacked first? Your gang. Who threatened his HeartMate? Your gang. Who tried to kill D'Ash? Your brother, Nettle. What was he supposed to do?"

Shade shrugged. "He chose. He will pay."

"His choice was forced upon him, by you."

Shade began to walk away. Ruis grabbed him by the shoulders. A tremor of shock went through both of them at the contact, Shade reacting to Ruis's Null touch, Ruis realizing he defended nobles. The teenager was too taut and thin under his hands. He gave Shade a little shake. "Who started the fights? What would you have done if you were T'Ash?"

Shade jerked from Ruis. "She in our territory, Downwind. She ours. We many, he one. We take what is ours."

Ruis squeezed the boy. "Listen to yourself! You sound like a wolf, not a man. Think of what you were and what that brought your brothers—death." He let the young man go and gestured to the altar, shining with small gifts from Ruis and Shade, symbolizing the shedding of old, bad habits. "Think of the man you can become. A man of talent and Flair and worth who can make a good life for himself. Think, damn it, don't just react!"

Shade stared at him for a long moment, then turned and disappeared into the tangled brush of the FirstGrove.

Ruis stood in shock, his own words reverberating through his mind. He'd come a long way since the day he'd been led in chains to the Guildhall gaol. Samba had helped him become a new man. The Ship had made him think and develop his own skills and intelligence. Ailim had given him her respect and her body. He now had pride in himself, goals, and a good life. After long last, when his reckless anger was scraped away, he saw he was a mature man.

"I think that the 'Rule of Three' is what brought about Shade's triad's downfall and your own," said a calm voice.

He spun to see Ailim D'SilverFir standing in a tree shadow, her arms at her waist, hands concealed in the opposite sleeves.

# *Twelve*

♦

"*A*nother basic tenet of our culture," Ailim continued. "Whatever you do comes back to you tripled."

A corner of Ruis's mouth twisted. He'd botched the moment with Shade. He didn't have the experience to deal with the youth, but no one else was around to help. Ruis's shoulders tensed at the thought. He crossed to D'SilverFir, standing respectfully outside of the circle. Taking her arm, he led her away from the Grove and toward a summerhouse at the far corner of the estate. Her eyes lingered on the spot where Shade had disappeared, then she gazed up at him and smiled.

He felt a hot pulse in his heart.

"I admire what you are doing for that youngster," she said.

Ruis bent closer to hear her, but her eyes and smile distracted him from her words. Her lips were a tentative curve and her blue-gray eyes looked huge. She glanced away and blinked rapidly and he could think again.

"You don't know what I'm doing for—the young man."

"No?" Now her eyes slid his way as they ambled down a path once the width of a glider. Bushes encroached until it was just broad enough for the two of them. "I can guess that he's an ex-gang member, I saw the sheen of glisten in his mouth. I doubt he is welcome at one of T'Ash's Downwind Youth Centers, so he must be a very rough case."

"As I am."

She made a sound of exasperation and stopped to angle her head up at him. Now flame touched the depths of her gaze. "No, you are not. You've been more transgressed against than have transgressed yourself."

"Ha. I've stolen." His throat dried at the admission. Once again words slipped from his tongue that could ruin everything, this time with Ailim. His gut tightened. He knew their liaison would end, probably before the first snow, but not now. Please, Lady and Lord, not now.

They'd reached the summerhouse, a pavilion built of sturdy, beautiful reddwood. Dirt smudged the steps and ledges of the open arches. Ruis suspected grime would coat the benches inside.

Ailim frowned, studying the building. Ruis thought his heart would fail if she didn't comment on his confession soon.

"This looks familiar," she said.

"It's a copy of Summer Pavilion in Landing Park; they're much the same age," he said. He grasped her shoulders and swung her toward him, scowling. "I said I've stolen."

"I'd imagine you'd have to," she replied. "We'll talk about it in a bit. Go away a little so I can clean this place."

Muttering to himself, Ruis strode away to find the last of the flowers for another bouquet. She always appreciated his gifts so. He looked at the sky, a deep clear blue that bespoke a fine day. No wind cut the air. To his ears came a faint phrase or two of halting speech. He strained to hear. A few more words drifted to him and he stilled. As the twinmoons were rising, on the other side of the grove, Shade was once again engaged in a Ritual. Ruis closed his eyes. Perhaps he hadn't erred too much with the teenager.

A clap of air and a whoosh stirring fallen leaves into a small whirlwind drowned out Shade's low chant.

"Ruis," Ailim called.

He bowed and explained his need to the BalmHeal bush, then snapped off a branchlet that held three blossoms and hurried back to Ailim. She was inside the clean pavilion, leaning against an upright, looking pale. Her hands were clasped in her lap.

"You're doing too much." He thrust the flowers at her. She sniffed and color tinged her cheeks. "How much energy and

Flair are you expending daily? How much sleep are you getting?"

She stared at him and chuckled. Heat crept up his neck. Their loving the night before had made sleeping time short. Again she buried her nose in the blossoms. When she took them from her face, she still smiled.

Ruis sat next to her. "There's something you don't know about me."

Ailim huffed a breath and shook her head. "There are many things I don't know about you."

He nerved himself again. "I stole."

Her brow furrowed. "Are you stealing now?"

"No. But I didn't just steal for food." He stood, went to one of the octagonal corners and pressed a hidden latch. When the bench cupboard opened, he pulled out a metal cylinder with nodes and buttons. He crossed and gave it to her. She turned it over in her hands, then looked up at him.

"What is it?"

He sat, reached across her and pushed a button. The little machine whirred and peeped in her hands, then lifted from them and flew around the pavilion, avoiding the walls.

"It works without Flair!"

"It's an ancient Earth device. I find old Earth machines and fix them. I used to steal to buy parts or make them. Sometimes I stole jewels because our ancestors used them in their tools."

"Oh," she said, focused on the little toy drifting with the air current. It blinked bright blue numbers. "What does it mean?"

He glanced at it and the numbers changed. "It's a weather-station. It shows the temperature, barometric pressure, humidity, wind speed, and elemental composition of the atmosphere. We can read the sunrise and set, the season." He didn't take his gaze from her face. Her absorbed expression held curiosity, probing observation. She returned her stare to him.

"No one else on Celta cares about these old things. They don't save them, they don't study them. They don't value them!" Ruis said.

She wet her lips. "True. Who would want something so odd and intricate and strange when your personal infodeck could tell you with a simple inbuilt spell?"

Ruis croaked laughter.

Ailim watched the machine whir through the summerhouse.

"But you are right. The past must always be preserved. There is a very, very old saying: Those that forget the past are doomed to repeat it.' "

"And that applies to little Earth machines?" he mocked, as he had so often been mocked. He raised his hand and snapped his fingers. The bright numbers stopped and the little device shot through the air to smack into his palm. Ruis rubbed his thumb over the irregularly molded surface, as he had long ago, and felt a similar comfort.

Ailim touched a finger to it, drew back. "It's warm."

He grinned. "Yes, energy generates heat."

She tilted her head and looked straight at him. "All knowledge is important and should be cherished; that includes the history of our kind, their machines, the first crude spells. We have museums of the first magical tools, but I don't recall—"

"No. We don't have very many of our ancient artifacts." He studied the weatherstation. "I restored this. It's also supposed to detail the time of moonrise and set, but Earth only had one moon. I was trying to alter it, but couldn't—then. Hmmmm. Perhaps now."

Ailim put her hand over his. "You value the past, but not your past."

"My past can't be changed."

"I think—"

Ruis cut the air with his hand. "Tell me about your aunt Menzie's amulet."

Ailim's lips thinned, but she pressed her hand against his. "You've been helping that boy and now will help me. And I will help you. D'Birch's accusation of theft against you has already been proven false. I'll clear all the charges against you."

Ruis snorted. "I was in the square that day. When I saw the Birch emeralds, I thought they'd be a good foci for a lazer. I jostled D'Birch and picked up the necklace when it fell. The emeralds weren't right. Before I could return them, I was caught. I put the necklace in her gown yesterday."

Ailim took her hand from his and rubbed her temples. "Why do you make this so complex?" She sighed. "Because you are a Null, the situation itself is complex. So what else did you steal?"

"The only other things were T'Ash's HeartGift. . . ."

Ailim winced.

Ruis shrugged again. "Some items that might have helped me with my quest, some gems to help me survive. I always returned the unique. Before I met you, restoring Earth machines was my sole passion. The only thing that kept me sane or made me happy." He grasped her hand and lifted her fingers to his mouth, kissing them with all the tenderness he was capable of, keeping his eyes on hers. "Anything else I stole was to survive or buy parts, like I said."

Her gaze softened. She believed him! Relief loosened the tightness in his chest.

"Oh, Ruis," she said. "Your banishment will be hard to re-voke, but I vow—"

He put his palm over her lips. "No. We've had this conver-sation and the discussion is ended. Nothing you can do can clear my name. I don't want you going against Bucus. You can't win." Her mouth frowned under his hand. "Bucus is cor-rupt and ruthless. You can't fight fair with him and win, and I know *you* won't fight dirty." She scowled, nipped at his palm. He dropped his hand and gripped her shoulders again. "Tell me you won't pursue this."

She pursed her lips.

He gave her a little shake.

"I will reconsider my opinion." She lifted her chin and folded her hands in her lap, sounding like a judge.

"Let's talk about the theft of an amulet."

Her hair had fallen from her be-spelled braids at Ruis's touch, she swept her hand through the strands and closed her fingers around silver and gold pins, then put in a sleeve pocket. "It's not precisely a theft . . ."

"No?" He grinned.

"Tell me your plan," he muttered, and turned her to massage her tense shoulders.

"I thought you'd come after midnight, we'd go to Menzie's rooms, I'd dismiss the housespells on her door, and you'd take care of those she's added herself. Then we'd go inside and take the amulet."

"Do you have any idea where she keeps it? What if she sleeps with it on?"

"She's been drinking a medicinal potion every night—due to the bane of the amulet. I have a new beverage from a Healer that includes a sleeping draft."

"A drink rather than a sleep spell, which I'd nullify. All right, I'll be in your rooms tonight after midnight."

Her muscles were now warm and loose, while his were hot and tight. He slipped his hands from her back around to cup her breasts. "Let's talk about now."

"Let's don't talk." She leaned back against him and looked up. "You are so very special."

The corners of his mouth turned up. "Quite unique, in fact."

Her palms reached to stroke his face. "Don't mock yourself. It's a testament to your spirit that you've survived so well."

"I'm outcast and banished." He turned her and took her mouth.

Ailim sighed as her nipples hardened under his hands. Her lips moved under his, nibbling at his own, her tongue flicked across his mouth, then inside as if she yearned to taste him.

Hot blood pooled in his groin. The position was awkward, so he set her aside, got to his feet. "Stay there," he said between ragged breaths. Flipping open a bench-top, he pulled out cushions and woven throws. He eyed the narrow window seats and dropped the makeshift bedding onto the floor.

Ailim laughed. She'd risen and stood backlit by an arch. Her amusement died on her parted lips and her hands froze on the tabs of her gown as she saw his yearning passion.

He couldn't take his gaze from her, the lady in elegant dress, blonde hair loose, blue eyes gentle, cheeks rosy with incipient desire. She stunned him. Who she was, how kindly she treated him. Intelligence shone in her gaze, but so did respect. "I need you," he said. He strode to her. When he curved his hands around her shoulders, she stiffened. He liked that her spine had straightened and lifted her breasts.

"Let me," he said thickly. He ran his thumbs under the tabs across her shoulders and separated them, then pulled the top of her dress down, smoothed it over her curving hips and let it fall in ripples at her feet. The sight of her body in a thin shift over a white undergarment that covered her from the top of her breasts to the crease of her thighs strained his control.

He swept the shift from her with one swipe. The color of her nipples were hidden from view but little nubs showed. He wrenched his stare to her face. Now her eyes were serious, questioning—wary? He shook his head in denial. Lifting his hand, he skipped fingertips across her cheek. "Do you fear me?"

Her tongue darted out to wet her lips, make them a deeper rose. Slick, dark, moist. He groaned.

"No," she said. "I don't fear you. All these feelings are so intense—all the sensations. I don't know what to think——"

He smiled wryly. "You think too much. Now's the time to feel. Please yourself and me, concentrate on your senses."

"Yes."

Her hands came up to rest on his shoulders, but he caught them and put them back down to her sides. "I need to see you. See all of your loveliness. Appreciate you." He had no words for what he wanted—to cherish this moment and embed it in his memory for all time, how she looked, how she awaited his touch, how she trusted.

He framed her face, brushed the lightest of kisses on her mouth, trailed his fingers down her face, across her collarbone, and rested his hands on her flesh above the undergarment. She trembled, swayed a little to him and his body tightened. A pulse pounded in his ears until he thought his restraint would shred with the next instant. But he held on. There would never be another moment like this, and the sting of anticipation was too good to be eased quickly.

He molded his hands over her breasts and she gasped. Her garment was satiny and soft under his palms. He pressed where her nipples were, circled them, rubbed.

Then his hands slid down her sides until he felt the roundness of her hips under his fingers.

A little cry escaped her and she fell against him. He caught her up, took a step to the heaped tumble of blankets and cushions and set her down into the nest. Now her underwear was a barrier, an ugly thing that kept her body from his gaze. He reached down to the tab low on her stomach and whisked it open, pulled the flap back to see the dark blond curls of her mound and her plumped, darkened flesh beneath. A rasping groan came from his throat. Perfection. Paradise.

His knees weakened and he knelt beside her, then slid his hands under the garment around her bottom and she shuddered. He peeled the cloth from her and tossed it aside.

Her eyes were closed, her breasts rose and fell quickly, their centers tight. She shifted, opening her legs slightly, and his breath caught hard in his throat.

He flung his clothes off, set his hand on her skin, marveling at the whiteness of it, then slowly, exquisitely parted the petals of her flesh to learn her readiness.

Moistness dampened his fingers and the rich scent of her desire exploded his last thoughts. He grabbed her hips. Set his sex at the gateway of hers. This last waiting, the heat and slickness of her against the head of his shaft made him dizzy, but this, too, was too luscious to rush.

"Look at me."

She opened her eyes and they looked dazed. She licked her lips again, and her mouth turned the same color as her womanhood.

"You're beautiful," she sighed. "So beautiful. Big and comely. I can smell you, and me, and us. And the last remnants of summer gardens and beginning of fall breezes. I can hear my heart pound and your breath, and birds—"

"Me!" he said gutturally. "Me, only me. Only know ME!" He plunged into her and her hips arched, her hands flew to his shoulders and clamped.

He couldn't last more than a few strokes. Her inner tremors signaled she was on the brink. "Scream for me." He surged in and back, delirium twisting inside him to the peak of pleasure. He yelled. Mixed with his shout was her scream. "Ruis!"

Shattering climax tore him into a thousand pieces. He pulsed long and hard within her, his body folding on hers. They were damp with the sweat of deep pleasure and release.

Some moments later he stood and stretched. Her widened eyes followed his movements so he flexed a little longer.

He grinned. Gathering their clothes, he bundled them and held out his hand to Ailim. "There are hot springs a few meters away. Let's go soak . . . and play. You don't play often enough, SupremeJudge."

A genuine smile slowly bloomed on her face, delighting him and winding around his heart. He was getting in too deep, nearing the point where he could fall in love with her. He wasn't sure where that point might be in his loveless life, but knew it loomed. He shrugged inwardly. His time with Ailim was worth any pain. He was accustomed to pain: mental, physical, emotional.

Her fingers curled around his hand and he pulled her up.

"Weren't we just playing?" she purred.

"No. We were communicating, dancing, loving . . ."

She looked around the gazebo, then out the open sides. "It is so lovely here, and so like the last summer days."

"The miracle of FirstGrove." There wouldn't be any other garden or grove in Druida that still held the scents of summer— except the Ship's greensward. "Don't you have a conservatory at your Residence?" he asked idly as he led her down the steps and to a nearby hot spring.

She stiffened. "We have not been able to care for it."

"Pity." He gestured to wide, shallow steps leading into the deep green pool. He let go of her hand and threw their clothes on a large flat-topped boulder landscaping the spring.

She turned to him, brows lowered. "Will your Nullness have any effect on the pool?"

Smiling, he shook his head. "It's for bathing with natural heat and no spells. Our ancestors were practical, using hot springs as a basis for a HealingGrove—the First HealingGrove would be logical to them."

"Of course," she said, observing the bushes with fading blossoms and trees just beginning to turn color. She dived in.

Ruis plunged in next to her, and shot a spray of water over her lovely breasts. "Tag, you're it!" he called. He'd never played the game, but had watched children.

Surprise and glee swept over Ailim's face. She laughed, then sucked in a breath and submerged. Ruis was too busy admiring her grace and the flash of her bottom to realize he stood still. Small hands grabbed his ankles, jerked, and he fell heavily into the pool, swallowing water. Her delectable distraction and his lack of experience cost him. He sputtered to his feet and shook his head. Droplets flew.

Ailim laughed, her eyes sparkled. "You're it now!" She disappeared, her pale legs scissoring away.

They played with abandon. Ailim's ease in the water balanced his greater reach and strength. Finally, through a devious bit of strategy, Ruis captured and caged her in his arms.

She flung back her head and laughed. His pulse stuttered. He'd seen her laugh more in this last half-septhour than in the eightdays he'd known her. She was loveliest when she laughed up at him, her eyes darkening to deep blue without any hint of the normal, judge-like, gray.

"Oh, Ruis, you are so good for me!"

He kissed her, broke it off before pure lust stole his wits. "Yes, I am. You need to play, to relax, to learn to live from moment to moment."

Shade appeared. "Finished my Ritual. It was good," he said flatly, standing well back from the spring, his wounded hand tucked under his opposite armpit.

"Know you, you're a judge," he accused Ailim.

Her face fell into responsible lines, her eyes dimmed. "That's right. Ailim D'SilverFir."

"Why you with him?" Shade jerked his head at Ruis. "He banished outcast! You should tell on him. That he's in Druida. Good rep for you, catching him."

"I will never betray him." Her gaze locked on the ex-triad member.

Ruis didn't feel he should interfere. The boy trusted him, perhaps. It was obvious that Ruis trusted Ailim with his life. Could the teen understand that sometimes trusting others was a necessity of a decent life?

"You don't betray him 'cause you like to fligger him."

Ailim didn't flinch. Ruis's respect for her grew.

"That's part of it," she said. "But more. I'm an empath. He's a Null. When I'm around him, I don't have to build mind-shields. It's a great relief. I enjoy his company. Something I don't think even you do."

Shade scowled, looked away. "Maybe not." He dropped his hands, revealing the bloodred line at his wrist. The small, unconscious gesture spoke of an equally small amount of trust in Ailim. "You SupremeJudge. You helped my brother, Antenn."

Ailim's head came up. "Antenn Moss is your brother?"

Shade gazed into the distance. "He run with triad." Pain edged his voice. When he looked back, his eyes burned. He pointed at Ailim. "If you hurt Antenn." His finger swerved to Ruis. "If you hurt Ruis, I hurt you. BAD."

Ailim inclined her head as she'd acknowledge one of her own rank. "I understand and accept. I will not harm him."

Ruis decided it was time he spoke. "I trust her."

The boy narrowed his eyes, jerked a nod, and loped off.

Ailim drifted to the far end of the pool, her gaze on the steps leading to the ground.

Ruis frowned. Shade had reminded her of her responsibilities. The laughing, uninhibited lady who'd played with him in the pool had vanished.

She stopped at the bottom of the steps and turned large, sad eyes on him, eyes that held the same yearning he felt, but contained even more hopelessness for their doomed affair. One side of her mouth lifted in a wry smile. "I have to get home."

"Is it a home?"

She averted her face. "No. But it is all I have. And visiting with the Family from the distant manors has been good."

He yearned to kiss her tears away, but sensed she didn't want to reveal her vulnerability—her love and duty for a Family who didn't return those feelings. So he came up behind her, drew her close and wrapped his arms around her. She felt cool against him, her skin chilling in the autumn breeze. His body heat would keep her warm for a short while, but for her own sake, as always, he would have to let her go. Once she was away from him she could use a weathershield spell to protect her from the harshness of the day outside the grove.

He bent and kissed her head, skimmed his lips against her temple, so she felt his mouth on her skin. "Wait for me tonight, I'll come to you."

Her shoulders lifted and slumped. "I'm sorry we have to deal with the wretched amulet."

"If I could, I'd make all your dreams come true."

She stiffened and stepped away. "That's not possible." She hurried up the stairs, dried quickly, and donned her clothing. With quick, efficient hands, she braided her hair.

"There is something I'd like you to check for me," he said. The episode with Calami and Bucus had nagged him until he'd researched the Loyalty Oath and asked Ship to request information from all the Residences and the PublicLibrary. Ship had not yet established an interface with the Guildhall Records.

When she faced him, her gaze had lost the touch of despair and she looked curious. She folded her hands in her opposite sleeves. "Yes?"

"I'd like you to research the events around my father's death and Bucus becoming T'Elder."

Her eyes widened. "You believe there was something illegal in the transfer of power?"

The possibilities made his teeth clench. "I don't know."

"Did you have an oracle at your birth to forecast your future?"

"I don't know." He strained to recall any mention of that Celtan tradition in relation to himself. "I think so. But I don't know the prognosis, I don't know whether they knew right away I was a Null."

Ailim held out her hand. He lifted his own and put wet fingers in hers.

A reverberating gong echoed through the grove. Ailim jerked. "What's that?"

Ruis smiled humorlessly. "Shade's wound the clock in the old stillroom." Ruis glanced at Ailim. "I'm sure he's a wanted criminal."

Her tongue touched her lips. "You're doing good, trying to steer him into a better way of life."

"I'm hopeful, but the death of his triad mates . . ."

Ailim whitened. "Terrible. I'd imagine it would be almost as bad as losing a HeartMate."

Ruis couldn't bear to think of HeartMates. "Losing you would be terrible."

Strain shrouded her features. "I can't afford you."

"I know," but hearing the words stabbed like a knife. She didn't let go of his hand. "I accept that," he said. "We'll live in the moment. Enjoy every second." He kissed her fingers.

She withdrew her hand. "I must be going. I'll set the GrandHouse Library to check the Guildhall records regarding the accession of your uncle to the T'Elder title. I won't look into the dossier of one ex-triad member called Nightshade."

Ruis pulled himself from the pool and stood next to her, glad of the cold breeze. "Thank you." He caressed her cheek with his knuckles. "I'll see you tonight. Merry meet."

She smiled and dipped her head. "And merry part."

He inclined his own head. "And merry meet again. Until later." He blew her a kiss.

Her cheeks tinted rose and he won a true smile from her before she spun and ran down the path to the exit gate.

\*       \*       \*

*A*s soon as *Ailim* returned, the *Residence informed her that* Bucus T'Elder visited with Donax Reed. Her mouth flattened and she cursed inwardly. She should have been here when T'Elder arrived, to keep an eye on him.

"Yip!" Primrose bounced down the stairs at the end of the GreatHall and ran through the room, braking a few feet away to slide the rest of the distance to Ailim. She laughed and scooped up the pup to hold her close. Ailim went into her ResidenceDen.

Primrose tugged a rag knot from her basket beside Ailim's desk, and worried it with pointy little teeth. *Man came. New smells.* She stuck out her tongue and wrinkled her face. *Nasty.*

"Residence," she said.

"Here," it replied in her ancestor's calm voice.

"Lock, guard, and alarm all the doors to the HouseHeart and my suite."

"Done," said the Residence.

"Augment all illusions that camouflage the hidden doors to the secret passageways."

"T'Elder is aware of the large passage bisecting the Residence."

Ailim drummed her fingers on her desk. That particular passage was common knowledge.

The Residence said, "GrandMistrys Menzie SilverFir Cohosh admitted T'Elder and led him to Donax Reed's tower through the inner hallway."

Ailim sighed. "Don't spell the halls and doors Menzie is aware of. She doesn't know more than most Family members, does she?"

"She is unaware of the doors FirstSon Ruis Elder uses."

That jolted Ailim. When she didn't reply, the Residence continued. "I was assured before he came that he is acceptable to you. His Nullness is discomfiting, but tolerable. Do you confirm his access? I can alert you or the guardsmen when I first feel his presence upon the edges of the estate."

"Ruis Elder is welcome here."

"As you say, D'SilverFir."

"Mention his visits, past or future, to no one."

"Your order is acknowledged."

"Residence, can you replay the conversation between

Donax and T'Elder in the chamber assigned to Donax?"

"Not possible. The Captain of the Council invoked a hush spell. Words did not reverberate to my walls or floors or ceilings."

"Are any images available of the two men in the last septhour?"

"No. They entered a cone of light, then bespelled darkness outside the cone."

"Thank you."

"I will keep in contact with T'Elder Residence. It is a haughty House, like its owners, but it will share minimal information."

"I didn't know that Residences shared information."

"It is a relatively new process. We did not have the means or know how to communicate until taught by *Nuada's Sword*."

The notion stunned Ailim. "The starship?"

"Yes. It approached us and set up a network. Despite the fact that our basic energy and fuel is the psi-Flair of our Families, and the technology built on that, we still have ancient systems that correspond to the Ship's science."

Ailim tried to bend her thoughts around this news and what it might mean, but didn't have enough information.

Primrose distracted Ailim. *Love YOU*.

"I love you, too." And she came dangerously close to loving Ruis Elder—a futile love, bound to break both their hearts if he cared as much as she.

Just the thought of his long fingers caressing her heated her blood. She should make him go, stay far from her and her life, but she couldn't. If her Family had been even a little supportive . . .

She had been a good, dutiful, responsible person. Now she struggled with all her might to save the Family, to reform the finances, to lead them into a better future. Was she never going to have something for herself? Was she never going to have one shining, reckless moment in her life? And she knew, with all the Flair that had been bred into her genes through the centuries, that she would never meet another man who would affect her like Ruis, who would encourage her to be free, who would look at Ailim and see Ailim, not D'SilverFir. Who would treat her like a desirable woman for herself alone.

Primrose flopped over so Ailim could rub her tummy. She opened her big, brown eyes wide and made them mournful. *Sick today. No more Catfood. D'Ash told Canadena.*

"Poor puppy, you need a treat." Ailim got a brush from her bottom desk drawer.

*Brush me! Yes, yes, yes. Me be beau-ti-ful.* She sat, then moved for Ailim to groom her. She tried a small rumble, then a series of yips.

Ailim finished one last sweep of the golden coat and shook her brush at Primrose. "Stop that."

*Me purring.*

"You've been spending too much time with cats."

*D'Ash has many Cats. Samba comes to play. Samba is big, beau-ti-ful, smart, won-der-ful Cat. Me will learn to purr.*

Ailim smiled, until an insinuating feeling crept over her. Loud thoughts rapped at her mindshields, thoughts that attempted to hide themselves. She caught a tinge of danger, a broad flash of greed, and glanced at the holo above the desk, showing the hallway outside Donax's rooms. His door opened. Bucus and Donax stepped out, wearing identical smirks. A few minutes later they were at her door.

Ailim rose to her feet, shook out her dress and adjusted the long sleeves. She glanced down at Primrose. "You can hide or not as you please."

The puppy cocked her head, letting her tongue loll. *me not hide. me be Fam, good companion.*

Ailim clenched her hands and opened them, saying a Word to release her disquiet.

When Donax knocked, she bade them enter. Bucus T'Elder's eyes gleamed with calculation as he scanned the ResidenceDen, tallying the value of every stick of furniture. His sharp stare narrowed as he looked through the windows at the moat and the large, rolling green lawns of the estate.

Ailim curtsied. T'Elder sucked in his gut. She made the formal gesture simply because she didn't want to offer her hand.

He nodded. "I thought it was time to review the

D'SilverFir estate. It has been some years since I've had a tour, and now with the loan . . ."

"Of course." She smiled politely, seething that Bucus took advantage of her absence. "I didn't know the First-Families Council wanted a tour. Are you the sole representative?"

"Yes."

Ailim gestured to Primrose. "My Fam, Primrose."

His gaze lingered on Primrose. He smiled and the puppy shrank into the folds of Ailim's skirts.

"A Fam," he said smoothly. "I hadn't thought of a Fam for my own before."

Ailim kept a smile on her face as she picked Primrose up. "Telepathically bonded animals can be a comfort. I'm sure D'Ash would be pleased to find a good Fam for you," Ailim lied.

His fleshy features solidified into a rigid expression. "Fams. From D'Ash, of course."

"GreatSir Reed must have reported on our financial progress. We are all very pleased to be ahead of schedule in our recovery," Ailim said.

"Hmmph," grunted T'Elder. "I saw the latest reports of the other four D'SilverFir estates."

"They're very good. I'm sure you approve of our progress. Was your tour satisfactory?"

"I saw enough."

Enough to estimate their assets, their finances, their standard of living, and the current inhabitants of the Residence.

She squared her shoulders. One last thing to do. She mentally contacted Caltha. *Ready?*

*As I'll ever be*, came the reply and the feel of Caltha straightening her spine.

Ailim smiled. *Get used to it. I'll meet you in the GreatHall in two minutes.*

# Thirteen

♥

Ailim had the image of Caltha swishing through her bedroom door in her most elegant gown—the one purchased for the D'SilverFir Loyalty Ceremony. Caltha hoped T'Elder would be man enough not to notice she'd worn it before.

*May you live a long, long life,* grumbled Caltha.

At the loud voices of the men, signifying the private meeting was over, the rest of the Residence inhabitants converged on Bucus T'Elder and Donax. Canadena, holding her kitten, hovered on the edge of the group. All were dressed in their best—this year's costly fashions.

"I hope you found everything to your liking," Aunt Menzie simpered. "It isn't easy making do on a strict budget." Her smile might have been meant to be indulgent. It looked sour.

Donax stiffened at insult to his financial cunning.

T'Elder grumbled, "The way this household ran through gilt a year ago was criminal. No thought to the future. Only interested in present gratification."

Cona batted her eyelashes at T'Elder and Donax. "A woman feels better when luxuries surround her—more loving. We are a FirstFamily, after all. We have tastes and standards Commoners can't appreciate."

Ailim grit her teeth. She replied only to T'Elder's remark. "Our gains are heartening. Thank you for sending us Donax."

Steps echoed from the marble stairway. Ailim crossed to the

end of the GreatHall and held out a hand to Caltha. Caltha
joined hands and they returned to the others.

"I want to make known to all of you, my choice of Heir
Caltha of Woodpine, former Lady of Woodpine estate on the
Huckleberry Finn River."

For an instant there was stunned shock.

"Heir!" Cona shrieked. "I'm your heir!"

Caltha ignored the outburst, curtsying to T'Elder.

"Ailim, you must be—" Aunt Menzie started.

*Quiet!* commanded Ailim telepathically, following it with a
disciplinary mind-shock.

Menzie's words strangled in her throat; her eyes bulged.

The SilverFir men stirred uneasily and Canadena faded up
the stairs.

T'Elder bowed jerkily to Caltha. He eyed her bountiful
charms with approval, then looked at Cona. "The Council, too,
was under the impression that GrandMistrys Cona SilverFir was
your heir, Ailim."

She met his eyes limpidly. "You know yourself, T'Elder, that
people don't always choose Heirs. Oracles do at birth, Flair
does at other times."

"I've seen enough," Bucus T'Elder said and left.

*A*ilim *was listening to* SpaceMusic, *petting* Primrose *and*
dozing in the waning day when the Residence spoke. "Menzie SilverFir has left the building."

Ailim hopped off her bed. "Does she have the amulet?"

"Yes, the great evil energy of the bane travels with her."

"Has she crossed the drawbridge yet?"

"No."

"Follow her progress by scry as long as possible." Ailim
ran to her closet and pulled on her old riding trous and
heavy travel tunic. It fell to her knees but was cut up the
sides for easy movement. Swearing, she hunted for her battered walking boots in the messy tumble of shoes Primrose
had made of the bottom of her closet.

Primrose darted into the closet and began tugging out
footwear. Ailim swore under her breath.

"Most of the far-scry stones in the estate and linked to

the Residence are not in working order. The spells were not renewed," Residence said.

Every second counted. "Boots!" she cried, holding out her hands. The tough furraleather footwear smacked into her palms. With each little use of Flair, her energy diminished.

"I thought the various far-scrys were set for renewal in a cyclical manner." She grunted as she tugged on her boots.

"They have not been renewed for the last three years. Therefore three sets are out of commission."

"Cave of the Dark Goddess!" Ailim stomped until the worn leather cupped her feet. She let out a little moan, they felt so much better than the fancy shoes she'd been wearing.

Primrose panted, tongue hanging, before Ailim. *me go too!*

Ailim closed her eyes, sought the simple puppy mind. *Sleep.* She sent the order low and soothing. Primrose yawned and circled herself, dropping into sleep. Ailim put her on the bed.

Glancing at the windows, Ailim asked, "Where's Menzie?"

"She proceeds northwest. She stumbles often."

Toward the small fir forest, the boundary with T'Elder.

"Project a grid so I can 'port close, extrapolate her path and destination."

"It is noted that your energy levels are low."

"Project the grid!" She darted back to the closet and belted her emergency pouch around her waist. Digging out a knit hat, she jammed it on her head and swirled a travel cape around her. The layers and her fear made her sweat.

A topographical map of the grounds shimmered before her, along with blue gridlines that she could use to mind-fix a place for teleportation. A red, weaving dot denoting Menzie wavered northwest. Toward the big black jagged line.

"She's heading toward the fault in the earth." Ailim's hands shook as she pressed the fastening tabs down the front of her cloak. "Residence and ResidenceLibrary link, I have a question."

"Here," said the deeper voice of the combined entities.

"Does Menzie's amulet have the power to affect the earth fault?"

"Unknown."

"Hypothesize, please, the worst case scenario if the amulet was dropped into the weakest part of the fault."

"Difficult to determine."

Ailim closed her eyes and grit her teeth. This was worse than dragging answers out of culprits in JudgmentGrove.

"Could—the—power—of—the—amulet—trigger—a—breakage—in—the—fault."

"Probable."

"Could the fault cause the earth to slip and endanger the passage to the HouseHeart?"

"Probable."

Fear sliced coldly down her spine. Her eyes blurred as she watched the staggering red dot of Menzie.

"Also a probability that the Residence island would be undermined and compromised," the Residence said.

"How compromised? Is there danger to the Family?"

"The Residence would be damaged but the interior structure would hold, as designed, until help could come."

For an instant Ailim mulled over evacuating the Family, wincing as she thought of the ensuing scandal. There would be no way to stop the rumors, or the loss of face and even the estate itself if the FirstFamilies Council decided to consider this mad act of Menzie's as proof the SilverFir Family should die.

"Show the weakest point of the earth fault."

A white starburst appeared on the black line. "She's not quite on-target. I'm going," Ailim croaked, pulling on thin, worn, riding gloves, wishing they were gauntlets. "Discreetly notify Caltha as soon as possible. If I don't send word or return by third-bell, Caltha is in charge of the Family." Though if the amulet caused land to slip, they'd know soon enough.

With that, she inhaled deeply to subdue her fears and quiet her mind. It had never been so difficult. A second breath, exhale; a third breath, release. She checked the status of the Menzie-dot, dangerously close to the fault now, and the gridlines in her mind. Gnawing her bottom lip, she thought of the best landmarks she could envision completely near that point—the ones she recalled were too far from Menzie for her liking, but she shook her head, sucked in one more breath, and ported.

*A*re we going to that place Ship said? asked Samba as she trotted beside Ruis.

"Yes." A trip he dreaded, but which the Ship had convinced Ruis to make for his mental health. Ruis was to visit the T'Elder estate, the small cottage where he was raised, and even infiltrate the Residence itself. Ship postulated that if Ruis saw the place of his tormented childhood through adult eyes, it would help free him of past anger. Ruis sincerely doubted it.

The wind whipped up and blew dark clouds over the evening sunset, drenching the world in gloom. The cottage was on the edge of T'Elder land, a few meters from a cliff facing the GreatPlatte Ocean. Though directly south of the Ship a few kilometers, in memory, age, and tradition the cottage was light-years from the great Earth artifact.

The little house wore an air of decrepitude, looking as if it had been abandoned far longer than the twenty-one years since he'd run away. Ruis blinked. It was much smaller than his earliest memories, even shabbier and tinier than the last time he'd seen it, at fourteen.

A spurt of anger blew the depression from his veins. He tugged a little at the stylish silver torque circling his neck that held the Ship's communicator.

The appearance of the cottage spurred the realization that Bucus had never put a sliver of gilt into maintaining the structure, not through all the years Ruis had been living there with a caretaker, and not since.

*Thud. Thud. Thud.* His blood thumped in his temple with the cadence of memory—the roof leaking in several spots, dropping into strategically placed pots when spring rains thundered over Druida. A minor spell could have weathershielded the building. Ruis's Nullness hadn't been strong enough to negate the benefit. It had never been done.

Ruis knew now that Bucus must have hoped the defective Ruis-child might die of a chill, or the condition of the building would somehow harm him fatally.

He drew in a shaky breath. Dead and dried weeds surrounded the cottage, the door planking had buckled and gaped widely. He didn't want to go in, but he'd promised the Ship. Ruis strode up to the door and yanked at it. It stuck. He took a small multitool sphere from his belt and pressed the red button. The lazer sliced through rotted wood and the door fell apart in his hands.

Samba minced to the threshold and sniffed at the dim mustiness and some other awful, choking odor. She wrinkled her nose. *Nasty*. With fastidious steps, she entered. Ruis followed, flicking the blue switch on his multitool for the lightbeam. He swept the light around the rooms. The few sticks of furniture were as he remembered. The first room held a table, a stove, two chairs.

"Rrrowwww!" Samba jumped back from the partially open bedroom door to the left. She hissed and spat. Her calico hair stood on end. She rocketed from the cottage.

His own hair rising on the back of his neck, Ruis went to the door. The smell was stronger here. He gulped, then forced the door wider, screeching it across warped floorboards.

His lightbeam pierced the suffocating darkness and pinpointed the face of a horror. Ruis gasped.

*A*ilim *stumbled and fell to her knees, jarring her bones and* snapping her teeth together. The night was darker than she'd expected. Clouds covered the last of the sunset, draping over the moons and swathing star-bright sky. The wind whisked around her and she gave thanks for her heavy cloak.

She jumped up and visualized the path to Menzie. Ailim ran faster than ever before in her life to burst from the trees and half-fall, half-slide into the ravine that marked the fault-line in the earth.

Blinking, she swiped dust from her eyes and peered ahead. Menzie shambled along the rift, dressed in a thin indoor dayrobe. Ailim blinked again and swore. Menzie walked as if under a spell. The evil amulet controlled her aunt.

Ailim caught up to Menzie and grabbed her arm so

fiercely the older woman spun around. Her wide eyes showed the whites, her mouth was slack. One hand clutched the baneful charm.

"Stop this madness!" cried Ailim.

Awkwardly the bespelled woman battled Ailim. She ducked the blows, slapped her aunt across the face to wake her, a futile action. Menzie hit her hard on her ear and Ailim winced, dizziness engulfing her, ringing shooting through her head. A hard blow to her chest pushed her back down on her bottom.

Ailim strove to sense the spell consuming her aunt but failed, unskilled in such Flair. As she scrambled to her feet, she searched her memory for counter-spells but gave up, knowing the spell enveloping Menzie was too devious for an easy answer.

Menzie turned and lurched toward the weakest point in the fault. Ailim's only choice was to grab the amulet. She muttered defensive spells, hoping they'd be sufficient against the evil.

Three strides and Ailim joined Menzie. One more stride put her in front of the woman. This time Ailim went for the leather thong that suspended the amulet. "Break!" she cried, sending the Wordspell with all her might and yanking hard.

The necklace broke. Menzie's head jerked back and the red, blistered line around her throat bled. Ailim grappled with the heavier woman, forcing her fingers from the little bag.

Pounding shock sizzled up Ailim's arm as she touched the charm. Menzie fell on her and the bane slipped from Ailim's grasp. They rolled a meter.

"No!" screamed Menzie. "No!" She crawled back toward the amulet. Menzie's old, white fingers reached for it. Ailim jumped and scooped it up. Even with a corner of the cloak wrapped around her gloved hand, pain shot up her arm.

Menzie stared up at Ailim, confusion masked her face for an instant before her eyes cleared. "What? Where?" Then her gaze sharpened on Ailim's clenched fist. "No, that is MINE."

She struggled to her feet and flung herself at Ailim. "My lover's token, my—" Her words stopped as she pummeled

Ailim. They fell again. Menzie was heavier, taller, her reach longer. She stripped the charm bag from Ailim's grasp.

"I must, I must, I MUST . . ." Menzie chanted, turning.

Ailim leapt to her feet and grabbed at Menzie's arm, missed, and watched Menzie throw the evil thing several meters toward the stress point of the fault.

*R*uis *stood, gathering courage and strength, then stepped* into the bedroom of the cottage. Skin had dried and tightened over her cheekbones, and though her nose was gone and the side of her skull shattered, he knew it was the woman who had halfheartedly minded him.

Mostly she looked like a bundle of sticks wrapped in gray, tattered commoncloth. The fleshy parts of her had been nibbled away. Wild housefluffs, mice, perhaps even celtaroons had dined on his old nursemaid.

When he'd been tiny, before he understood she could never return the emotion, he had loved her. Had sought comfort from her before he learned she would not wipe his tears away. Had sought protection, before he knew she'd find him in any hiding place and turn him over to Bucus. Then he had hated her.

Now he didn't know what he felt. He hadn't thought of her in years. Something surged through him and he took time to examine it. Pity. Pity the old, stupid, poor-relation Elder with small Flair who'd been assigned to watch the boy, to minimally care for his needs.

She'd feared for her life. Bucus had indulged in emotional torture with her as much as he'd physically tormented Ruis.

Old Hylde had been right to be terrified. A small, dark red pattern was centered in the middle of the fragile skin over the depressed hollow of her wound. The pattern showed the imprint of a ring, the T'Elder crest of a raven and the initials *B* and *E* on each side of the bird.

Ruis stared. He could imagine the scene all too vividly. He'd run away. Bucus no longer had use for Hylde so he'd struck her. One blow would have done it, if Bucus had been angry and backed the blow with killing Flair. Flair could cause a mark like that on her skin.

Bucus might not have waited to see her fall before leaving. His villainy was obvious. The nobles would punish a murder such as this with death. Killing a dependent, a relation who had sworn a Loyalty Oath to you and to whom you owed protection with that oath, was the depth of dishonor.

Wheels started rolling in Ruis's mind. Wheels of vengeance, of fortune, of fate. He wondered how he could preserve this evidence, present it to the FirstFamilies Council. How he could make this work for him.

He could force Bucus's punishment for his crimes against Hylde and against himself. He could ensure Bucus's removal as the head of the household, as T'Elder. Ruis might, possibly, even be able to convince the NobleCouncil to restore his lands and title.

That thought brought him from his daze. He snorted. The NobleCouncil would never allow a Null within its ranks. A Null could not participate in the power-building, Flaired rituals that governed Celta. A Null could eventually wear down, then destroy spells in the Guildhall, the GreatCircle Temple. A Null would be welcome in no Residence, socially or otherwise.

He didn't want to be T'Elder. He wanted to continue as Captain of *Nuada's Sword*, and he wanted Ailim D'SilverFir.

He could, perhaps, keep the Captaincy. He doubted he could ever have Ailim for more than the briefest of affairs.

Ruis found himself staring into the sockets of dead eyes and abandoned the hut to find Samba.

She'd left a sinuous path through brittle high grass and sat on a boulder, staring at the distant T'Elder Residence inland to the southeast. A sole window shone with light.

Glancing at it, then away, Ruis felt the old fury and helplessness overwhelm him. How often had he crouched here, behind the large rock, and hoped for his uncle Bucus's death? How often had he prayed that Bucus would forget the small outcast on the estate's edge?

All too often, Bucus had caught him here. In daylight old

splotches of dark red would show on the stone, his own blood.

His fingers hurt; he'd curled them tight into fists. Digit by digit, he straightened them, then shook his hands out.

*Ship says we should go there*, Samba said, lifting a paw in the direction of the T'Elder castle.

"Yes." Ruis breathed deeply and evenly, counting seconds while inhaling through his nose, pausing, and exhaling through his mouth, an exercise the Ship taught him.

The Residence was beautiful. Made of white stone, built of piers arched over a river, it was fanciful with small round rooms protruding from the first floor, towers, a chapel, little peaked gables in the roof with round windows. Ship said the Residence had been modeled after an old Earth French castle called Chenonceaux.

His chest hurt as he looked at it. The Residence could never be his; he'd ruin the ancient spells that guarded it and the T'Elder Family if he ever lived there. It hurt that, beautiful as it was, he could never love it. It would never be more than an object on the horizon for him—evoking memories of the childhood when he gazed at it with many emotions.

The Ship was his Residence now. His home.

*Let's go play.* Samba's voice held a gleeful note. *Never played in that place before. Looks like good hide-and-seek. What's best way in?*

Ruis grimaced. "Follow me."

As they hiked to the Residence, Samba slipped off on side trips to chase rodents, and Ruis pondered how he could bring the murder home to Bucus. No one entered a noble estate without the notice and tacit permission of the owner.

None except Ruis, the Null.

Guardsmen couldn't step foot on a noble estate without backing by the NobleCouncil. Ruis wondered how many enemies his uncle had made. If there were enough to send an inquiry team. He shook his head. He didn't know of his uncle's enemies—or allies. The only way to get the information to the Council would be to give it to Ailim D'SilverFir, but he didn't want her confronting his uncle. He was a dangerous man.

Wind whipped the cloak from Ruis, revealing him; he

struggled to keep it closed and continued trudging to T'Elder.

$\mathcal{M}$enzie's amulet hit the ground. Earth shivered under their feet. A small crack opened in the fault near the bane.

"What have you done?" screamed Ailim, running. Menzie's heavy steps thumped behind her.

The crack widened. The charm slipped into it, fell a third of a meter, rocked on the lip of a hole that opened beside it.

Menzie grabbed Ailim. "What? What is going on?"

They fell against the side of the gulch as the ground ripped open under them.

"Release me!" The spell made Menzie drop her hands and cradle them to her body.

"What's happening?" Menzie sobbed, her eyes wild and staring at Ailim.

"That filthy thing you cherished has opened the earth fault. You have doomed the Family, the Residence." Ailim found her feet and quick-stepped along the shifting land. Rocks tumbled about them, pebbles struck with stinging force.

"No! No! It was nothing but a love token, something to keep you from bullying me."

"It's a curse upon our House!"

"No!"

"Who gave it to you? Who is our enemy that would harm us so? Who? Speak and tell me no lies!" Another spell, one that Menzie couldn't deny, traveled the link of the loyalty bond Menzie had sworn to Ailim.

"Bucus," Menzie gasped. "Bucus T'Elder. The Captain of the Council. My love."

"Our enemy!" Ailim turned in disgust and dropped to her hands and knees to scrabble the last meter to the charm. Just as she lunged for it the hole cracked meters wide, the amulet toppled into it.

Ailim followed. "Go get help!" she shrieked to Menzie, then formed a powerful spellcry in her mind. Before Ailim could speak a rock hit her head. Pain rammed through her.

Darkness below and around and above swallowed her
whole.

*A* *half-septhour later Ruis and Samba reached the T'Elder*
Residence's trade entrance, an unadorned door in the last
pier which was anchored on land. Ruis leaned against the
door and it fell open. He stumbled in, shocked the shields
had yielded easily. He hesitated, Samba came up and sat
next to him, curling her tail around his ankle. The door
whispered shut. At the end of the warehouse-room a torch
lit and glowed next to a huge, iron-strapped door leading
to the inside of the Residence. That door sighed open and
a rosy glow from the hallway beckoned.

Samba twitched. *Whiskers warn Me of Great Flair.*

"Ruis Elder," the Residence said in a vibrant bass voice.
Ruis froze.

"FirstSon of T'Elder. Welcome."

Ruis closed his eyes, mind spinning in confusion. It was
almost like the first time he'd spoken to the Ship. The words
from the Residence held nothing but respect.

He cleared his throat. "You acknowledge me?"

"Indeed." A slight creaking came, as if a mighty head
bent a bit. "Welcome, ResidenceFam Samba."

"Rrrowww!" She flicked her ears back, sat up proudly. *I
am Ship's Cat.*

"Nevertheless, you will always be welcome here, too.
This Residence has not felt the paws of a Fam in a long
time."

Samba sniffed and inclined her head.

Ruis crossed the room and into the next, closing the large
door behind Samba. The long gallery that linked to the main
building stretched before them, buttressed by five arches
set in the river. Windows on each side of the gallery let in
the bright starlight and twinmoonslight. Lamps that simu-
lated torches of dark red flickered as he went by. Thick rugs
muffled his footsteps, paintings he couldn't see filled the
walls between the windows. At least this wasn't the T'Elder
Portrait Gallery. That was a floor above him. He'd been
there once when he was about five, rump and palms stinging
with welts from Bucus's switch. The faces in the paintings

had intimidated him, looking at him with accusing eyes, knowing he was a defective "Null."

"Where do you go, FirstSon?" asked the Residence.

He forced the words from his mouth. "The ResidenceDen." The few times he'd been allowed in the Residence, it had usually been in the ResidenceDen. Words and blows had pummeled him there, but Bucus had saved the cutting and bloody beatings for the hut or outside, where the furnishings and ambiance of the Residence could not be harmed.

Samba explored, unaffected by his mood, poking her nose around the furniture, sniffing at the carpets, sitting and curling her tongue to use her sixth sense.

*House right. No pets for many lifetimes, no Fams, and no CATS.* The tip of her tail flicked in contempt of the shortsighted T'Elders and D'Elders. Ruis smiled.

"Had the previous D'Elder lived, Toria, she would have brought pets." As the Residence spoke a breeze wafted down the corridor like a sigh.

Ruis stopped in his tracks. "My mother."

"Yes, a GrandMistrys from the Black branch of the Oak Family. A good woman. A good HeartMate," Residence said.

Words strangled in Ruis's throat. Samba had stopped beside him, plopped down on her bottom and cleaned her forepaw. *House, you have holos?* she asked between licks.

"Yes." There was a long pause and Ruis heard a window rattle. "I will forward all holos of the late T'Elder and D'Elder to *Nuada's Sword.*"

Samba hopped to her paws and hissed. *You know where We are?*

"*Nuada's Sword* issued a tentative probe. I responded. We have continued contact."

"Then you know of my circumstances," Ruis said.

"Yes. Upon my inquiry, D'Elder admitted she and Bucus Elder had seen you in Druida. She avoids him, fearing his anger." Bucus liked to hit whatever was near when he was angry.

As Ruis approached the tall gilded doors to the main building, they opened. The gallery lights behind him faded.

"I'm affecting your spells," he said to the Residence.

"True. You are much more powerful now. The Ship has calculated that you would not breach my most ancient and basic of spells unless you lived here for approximately two Celtan years."

"I'm sorry."

"No worries. Until you reach your full strength and power at late maturity at ninety, you will be welcome to stay as long as two eightdays with minor effects. When you are ninety only an eightday will be possible."

Ruis's lips twisted. "I doubt I'll live that long."

"An Oracle was present at your birth, as is customary, and saw three futures for you."

Ruis shuddered.

*Light hurt her eyes.* Ailim blinked and blinked again, breathed and sucked dirt into her mouth, coughed. Struggling, she freed an arm from the pressure around her and wiped her mouth, smearing grit around her lips.

Touching the big lump on her head made her whimper. She moved fretfully, ducking light that shone into her eyes. Once in shadow she looked up and up. And remembered.

About two meters above her a slice in the earth showed a large round moon. From the patterned craters in the shape of the ancient earth letter *R*, Ailim knew it was Cymru. She moaned and wriggled. Dirt pressed in around her. Her entire body ached. When she tentatively moved, wrenching pain in her left foot sent her back into unconsciousness.

Finally she rose above the pain and the darkness of insensibility into full wakefulness. Cymru had slightly moved across the sky.

Ailim carved out more room around her face. Dirt sifted down to close tighter around her lower body and insinuated into all the gaps in her clothes.

She unfurled her Flair to seek Menzie. The task was long and difficult so she knew she was hurt badly and at the last of her energy. The tremors hadn't reached the Residence. Her aunt huddled on her bed, her mind pattern one of deep sleep.

Ailim extended her Flair to touch other SilverFirs. Cona rode the throes of passion with Donax. Ailim recoiled. No help there. With the last of her strength she reached Caltha, but her strong shields were up. Ailim pushed. Her head pounded, felt like it split, and her Flair failed.

Nausea clutched and Ailim fought it. She'd soil herself if she vomited.

With every shallow breath the hurt and dizziness diminished. Her head injury had destabilized her Flair. She couldn't save herself with her psi power. Not right now.

Tears of weakness and pain filtered through grit down her cheeks. The cold sweat that filmed her body also attracted grit, dampened it, and made her itch and suffer.

The earth quaked, squeezing the breath from her, then cracking further open so Ailim fell sideways and down, banging against the new wall.

The ground settled. Ailim sent her mind questing for the amulet. Since it had been made to thwart her, she could find it. Eventually she noticed a building pressure in the fault surrounding a small point. Soon the force would escalate and explode, ripping the earth wide, shifting D'SilverFir land until the HouseHeart corridor collapsed and the Residence's island tilted into a new shape.

The hole would close, crushing her bones.

With exquisite care, she flexed her left foot and bit her lip as pain roiled through her, spun her wits. Her foot was caught and wedged tightly immobile. She was trapped.

*R*uis licked dry lips. "*An Oracle was at my birth and proph-*esied my future?" he repeated.

"She saw three futures: In one you can live to a great age and father two children," T'Elder Residence said.

"And the others?" He waited a moment or two, but the Residence didn't answer. Ruis laughed bitterly.

"I will withdraw," T'Elder Residence said stiffly.

*Good,* said Samba. *Residence talks too much. Other Residences don't talk so much.*

Ruis considered this tidbit. The sole other Residence he'd been in was D'SilverFir's, which hadn't addressed a word to him.

"The Ship talks more."

*Ship is Ship,* said Samba with cat logic.

They passed doors to round towers on each side and continued down the main hallway. The door to the ResidenceDen on their right creaked open. Samba entered then stopped. *Bad smell.*

She exaggerated. The scent, composed of Bucus's cologne, body odor, and medicine wasn't rank or heavy. Ruis wouldn't care to live with the smell, but it was tolerable for a visit. Rather like his presence in the Residence.

"I think you have your answer as to why the Residence talks so much," he said to Samba, who moved her bulk daintily, taking care not to brush against the heavy furniture that might contain more of the bad smell. "Bucus must not talk to the Residence."

*Yes, We are good listeners.*

Ruis surveyed the small semicircular room with distaste. It was exactly as he remembered. It occupied the joint between the gallery and the main house. The bookshelves were pristine, all spines perfectly aligned. Ruis grit his teeth. He had Ship's whole library to read, and Ship printed out "classics" for him to study, but the language challenged him. Bucus looked at the books and only saw the gilt such valuable objects would bring. Once Ruis yearned for stories of Old Earth, where he would not have been unique; now he'd like tales all Celta knew, those contained in these volumes. He didn't dare touch them.

And he didn't dare stay long.

"The current T'Elder retired early sleeps restlessly," the Residence whispered, confirming Ruis's unease.

He looked at the desk. Now it was only a large piece of unremarkable furniture, not a towering block intimidating a young boy who knew all his sins were noted down there.

He glanced at the round arm of a green plush chair and shuddered at memories that had enlarged it. Now it was only a chair that Ruis's small body had been rounded over for the whip or the switch.

Ruis crossed to the wall and jerked open a corner cupboard. His gorge rose. There, freshly peeled, terrifying in their flexibility and the crown of thorns on the end, were lengths of Celtan roserods. Who did Bucus beat? Ruis touched one. He swallowed hard and slammed the cupboard door shut.

"Residence," he croaked.

"Yes, FirstSon?"

"Can you dispose of these rods?"

Hushed silence answered him. While he waited, Ruis noted the overall proportions of the room, the delicacy of the windows and the wooden molding. Beautiful. T'Elder Residence was one of the most beautiful on Celta, yet Ruis would always think it hideous because of the evil it harbored.

"There are certain spells that will destroy the rods without harming the room." The Residence's voice sounded very faint.

"Standard maintenance spells that can be programmed for—say—every day?" Ruis asked.

"Yes."

"Will you do so?"

"You must order it."

"I can order you? Why? I'm not T'Elder."

The Residence kept silent. All Ruis's suspicions about his early life, that he might once have been confirmed as T'Elder, with Family oaths sworn to uphold all of his rights, grew. Had Bucus added betrayal, treason, and the most serious of oath-breaking to his crimes?

"I am forbidden to tell of your status. Or discuss any events of your past with anyone," the Residence finally said.

*A*ilim steadied her breathing, whispered a mantra to calm the pounding of her heart.

After a few minutes she wriggled, trying to enlarge her prison. It worked; she could reach her belt pouch. She fumbled with the tabs, then opened it with her thumbnail. Sliding her fingers in, she touched a matchstick and sighed. She pulled it out and pushed it firmly into the earth above her head, then tilted her head to squint at it. With a tiny spellword, one that even someone with the least amount of Flair could say, the little light could last a septhour.

Ailim rolled her tongue in her dry mouth, summoning dampness to ensure her voice would work. "Light!" she croaked.

The matchstick ignited, burning red.

Ailim sighed and closed her eyes, tired from the effort.

The pressure filling the fault went up a notch, threatening to blow. The earth slid around. Ailim screamed as her foot wrenched. Cracks spiderwebbed. The stress of the earth eased. Then began growing.

When she'd gathered her strength she encased her emotions in an impenetrable tube so they wouldn't affect logic, wouldn't deter her from what she had to do.

Her hand found the rough hilt of the knife in her belt pouch and withdrew it. She cut a strip from her cloak, put the knife between her teeth, and tied the fabric as tight as she could around her lower calf, a few centimeters above where her ankle disappeared into rock.

Taking the knife from her teeth, she breathed shallowly, but filled her lungs. There was enough light to see the knife gleam as she raised it near her face. She studied it dispassionately. Glanced down at her ankle that disappeared into craggy, pulverizing rock. Brought her gaze back to the knife.

It looked sharp enough.

# Fourteen

A̶ilim bent and set the knife against her boot, near a line of worn leather, and began to saw. A little while later she felt the prick of the blade against her skin.

She ripped the slit in the boot wide.

She panted and thought the surrounding earth moaned with her. A fall of dirt cascaded down the right-hand wall and a pink snout poked through. *Who is there? Who is there?*

Ailim clenched the knife. It bit her ankle. She pulled it away. *D'SilverFir,* she projected.

The chink widened and the snout elongated as it appeared, wiggling with sensitive whiskers. *Light hurts. Hurts.*

"Dark!" Ailim said. Her matchstick died. She hoped she'd done the right thing.

*The earth moves. Moves. Right here. I came to know, know. This is not good. Not good at all,* the being said.

The slow soft mind-speech was on a wavelength she easily understood. Tears backed behind her eyes. *Who are you?*

*I am a mole, the mole. Called Tal, Tal.*

The tension in Ailim's neck released. Her head fell forward as blissful relief washed through her. Like dogs, cats, and horses, moles had become sentient and telepathic on Celta.

Tal's damp nose touched her, grazed up her cheek. Tal snuffled. *D'SilverFir-Fir, in-deed. In-deed.*

*Can you help?* She held her breath.

*You are friend of pup-py Prim-rose. Friend of Sam-ba Fam,
pup-py Prim-rose, Sam-ba Fam friend is D'Sil-ver-Fir, D'Sil-
ver-Fir.*

*Samba! Ruis Elder.* Her joyful thought escaped with her
breath.

*They are out tonight. Not far a-way. Not far at all.*

*Can you get them?* Renewed hope dazzled her.

*Yes. Yes. Yes. I can speak to Sam-ba, Sam-ba Fam.*

*Go, please go! Please hurry, hurry!* Ailim fell into the cadence of mole-speech.

More dirt fell as Tal withdrew. Ailim sensed her hurriedly
digging away, shooting toward Samba and Ruis, and rescue.

*R*uis repeated *T'Elder Residence's words again, trying to*
make sense of them. "You're forbidden to tell of my status.
Or discuss any events of my past with anyone." He wondered what Residence's punishment would be if it diso-
beyed Bucus's orders—if it could disobey. No doubt
something vicious and inventive.

"Correct," confirmed the Residence.

"But you can destroy the rods if I order."

"Yes."

"I so order," Ruis said.

"It will be done," the deep bass of the Residence intoned.

*No fun playing here. Let's go play elsewhere. House is
gloomy.*

"I have many windows to let in starlight and twinmoonslight. My architecture is light and airy. I am not gloomy,"
Residence said stiffly. "An observation," it hesitated.

"Yes?" Ruis asked.

"The current GreatLord's temper is—unreliable."

A ripe stench filled the air. Samba jumped from Bucus's
comfortchair behind the desk. Ruis coughed and headed for
the door, Samba following.

"What is that?" Ruis asked.

Samba gurgled beside him. *I left present for T'Elder.*

The clock bonged the septhour. Samba, who'd taken the
lead, looked back, her whiskers gleaming silver. *We go to
D'SilverFir's. You need her and Me. I will tease puppy.*

"Lady and Lord keep you, FirstSon Ruis," said the Residence.

"And you," Ruis said. He, too, wanted happier surroundings.

When Ruis reached the outside, he shifted his shoulders. Samba was right, T'Elder Residence was gloomy. He inhaled the fresh, crisp air of an autumn night and lifted his face to the sky. The splash of stars against the black depths of space made his heart sing and ache at the same time. Samba gamboled in fallen leaves. "Let's go play," Ruis said.

She ran ahead, toward the D'SilverFir Residence. After several moments, she angled from the path. Ruis lengthened his stride to catch up with her. "Samba!"

She yowled. *Something comes.*

A couple of meters ahead of them something popped out of a hole. Whiskers quivered, forepaws gestured. It looked at Ruis and popped back into the ground.

Skidding, Samba stopped. Ruis halted. She put her paw on his boot. *You wait here.* Her nose wrinkled in emphasis.

Curious and amused, Ruis watched Samba lope to the hole. Her front disappeared down, leaving fat rump and tail elevated.

He chuckled.

The ground trembled under his feet and he sucked in a shocked breath. "Samba!" he yelled.

She wriggled out and headed back. The ground beyond the hole curved upward and sped away as the creature tunneled just beneath the surface.

*Is mole Tal. D'SilverFir hurt, trapped, needs help.*

Ruis's gut twisted. Fear galvanized him.

*Tal leaves Us a path to show the way. Evil thing makes big bad bubble in earth. It will pop and make earthquake.*

"Lord and Lady!" The "evil thing" must be Menzie's amulet. "Is Menzie trapped, too?"

Samba made a disgusted sound. Ruis took it to mean no.

They followed the burrow until they came to a ravine; at the bottom was a large crack in the earth and an ominous hole.

"Ailim?" called Ruis, sliding into the gulch.

"Don't come close! The ground is very fragile!" Ailim's shout sounded thin and thready.

That she could answer soothed his fears—a bit. "Samba, can you go?"

She lifted her nose. *I will be careful.* Testing every paw-step, she padded toward the dark maw of the fault. Twenty centimeters from the lip, the ground crumbled under her forepaws and she saved herself, hissing.

Ruis checked each step until he stopped three-quarters of a meter from the hole. Then he circled the crevice until he found sound footing. He lay down on his belly and inched forward. A few moments later he looked into inky black-ness. Brittle clods fell into the pit. Ailim coughed.

"I'm sorry, dear one. But I'm here." He switched on the multitool lightbeam and shot it down the cavity. A couple meters below he saw her pale face and blond hair.

Ailim said, "We need to get help, fast. Can Samba go?"

"Tell me the situation." He'd gotten used to hearing problems from the Ship and solving them. "Samba said something about an evil thing causing a quake."

"The amulet," Ailim choked. "Its bane-spell triggered this. It continues to decay the earth around it and build pressure along the fault."

"Where is the amulet?"

"I think I'm on top of it," she said matter-of-factly.

Ruis's blood chilled. A rumble came and the earth shud-dered under him. He froze at the strange, horrible feeling of quavering ground beneath him. "Ailim? Ailim!"

He thought he heard harsh breathing. He rose, shed his cloak and tossed it to the lip of the fissure above him, pulled off his shirt, and began tearing it into strips. "I'm making a rope"—a fine word for a flimsy tool—"where's the mole?"

*Tal went to warn her family,* Samba mewed.

Ruis cursed. "Ailim!"

"I'm here." She sounded weak. "A rope won't do any good. My foot's trapped beneath a lot of rubble. I was—was about to cut it off when Tal came. I—I hurt my head and can't use my Flair. Maybe, maybe in a little while . . . Send for help, Ruis."

All the blood drained from Ruis's face. The wind was

cold on his naked torso, but he sweated. He thought of the Ship and the gardening machines, the other earth equipment that had built the earliest Celtan castles. "Just a minute," he said.

"Please, Ruis, send for help." He thought he heard her sob.

His danger didn't matter; he'd go for help in an instant if he thought he'd be believed. Samba could run to D'Ash or T'Ash. If they were available, they could help. The ground shivered again, and he knew he could only, as always, rely upon himself.

He donned the rags of his shirt and scrambled up the slope, leaving Samba murmuring cat assurances to Ailim. He touched his throat communicator. "Ship!"

"Yes, Captain."

"We have a dangerous circumstance here—"

"We mark you at the epicenter of the D'SilverFir Fault, sir. We respectfully insist you vacate the area at once. An unknown stimulus triggered volatility in the fault. Our seismic readings show the pressure continues to escalate—"

"How much time do we have? D'SilverFir is trapped in the fault and I won't leave without her."

The Ship hummed against his throat. "We calculate approx a septhour—"

"And if the source of the pressure is destroyed?"

"With proper venting the immediate problem can be resolved; with proper equipment the fault can be completely stabilized."

"I need a machine able to dig D'SilverFir from a hole approx four meters in depth. Activate sick bay. Is that possible?"

"You repaired a small airferry a few days ago that can carry machinery. The largest garden robot you repaired is sufficient to the task and programmable by voice and touch."

Ruis remembered the airferry. It looked like a large, flat raft and traveled over a cushion of air like gliders. It was dull black.

"Camouflage it the best you can. Load the machines and send it out the west portal over the ocean. Set a course avoiding D'SilverFir or Elder Residences. Get me the equipment fast."

"Proceeding. Approx arrival is eleven Celtan minutes."

"Add medical diagnosis apparatus for—ah—feet, bones."

"Understood. Approx time of arrival is now sixteen minutes."

"Good. What is the area currently affected by the tremors?"

"Estimated at twelve—"

"Put it in terms of the Elder and D'SilverFir estates."

"The tremors do not reach the Elder Residence."

Ruis thought of the gloomy Residence and found himself unexpectedly relieved.

Ship continued, "Nor would the Elder river or Residence experience any harm if a quake occurs. D'SilverFir Residence is in the line of the quake. We do not know the state of the corridor under the lake, but since it was built as a temporary—"

"What corridor?"

"D'SilverFir was one of the first Residences built. We provided equipment to construct a corridor from the Residence on the island in the lake to another chamber. We—"

"What of the tremors?"

"We do not know how they are affecting the hall. Presently they are not reaching the lake or the island. If the quake occurs, it is likely the hallway will collapse. This will undermine the Residence foundation."

"Enough. I need to get back to D'SilverFir."

"Captain, we protest. We believe—"

"Follow my orders, out." Ruis disconnected the call and slid back to Ailim. He didn't like the tingling in his spine.

Samba paused her cat-talk, only half of which Ailim understood, and she knew Ruis had returned. Now she wished he hadn't come. She would die here and she didn't want to take him with her. She put a fist against her mouth to stifle her sobs of pain and fear.

The dark closed in on her with the suffocating scent of ancient earth. Pebbles and chunks and rocks pelted her. With the last ripple, her prison had shrunk. The worst was the growing pressure in the ground entombing her and the atmosphere. When Ruis had come and stayed, the psychic pressure of the amulet had lessened as had her own shields. When he'd gone away, she'd measured her strength and her Flair, and thought she might have enough power for an alarmspell broadcast. If she could gather her energy. If she had time.

Her fingers left her mouth to find the travelfood bar in her pouch and break off another piece. She barely had room to lift it to her mouth. Nuts and oats and a bit of dry fruit lay on her dusty tongue. With effort she chewed and swallowed.

"Ailim?"

"I'm here."

The hole above her darkened, and Ruis looked at her. Thank the Lady and Lord he couldn't see her condition.

"Tell me about the corridor under the lake," he said.

She stiffened and coughed and dirt rained. "There's a hall from the Residence through the lake to the HouseHeart."

"And where's the HouseHeart?"

Something only D'SilverFir and the Heir should ever know. "On this side of the lake," she admitted.

"What's the corridor's state of repair?" he asked. He sounded so sure and confident, she couldn't quite grasp it. Totally in command and in charge.

She inhaled slowly to keep her voice from trembling. "Not good. Much of our gilt goes to maintaining it. I noticed cracks near the ends a few hours ago."

"If the hallway collapses the D'SilverFir Residence foundation will be compromised."

"I know." Her voice shook.

"On the other hand," he said softly, "if we rescue you and destroy the amulet, I can refurbish the corridor and stabilize the fault."

His words made no sense. How? "What?" she choked out.

"The colonists made the corridor?"

"Yes."

"What the colonists made, I can fix," he said with patent confidence. She remembered the Earth toy zooming around the pavilion. The idea wrenched awful hope within her.

"Ruis, I want you to leave. I'm getting my strength back. In a septhour or two—"

"We have about fifty-five minutes before the pressure in the ground generates an earthquake."

Her gasp echoed up and down the tube of her prison until it repeated again and again in her ears. She wiped her nose with a fold of her cloak, licked dry lips with her dry tongue. "I want you to go. I can use my Flair for an emergency Broadcast. It may ruin the Family, but it will save the Residence."

"I want you to trust me," he said. "I have a machine on the way that can free you. You know I can negate the amulet."

She shuddered and dirt pattered from above her head to her shoulders.

"I can't," she said. Trust an ancient Earth thing that didn't work with Flair? Trust something so incomprehensible? That she had never experienced and never known? "I can't. Please go. Save yourself and Samba and let me—"

More dirt fell on her as opening widened. He flicked on his strange light and she winced.

"Look at me, dear one." He angled the light up in his own face. Lit that way, and with the odd shadows from the cave-in, he should have looked like a demon. Instead he looked like her lover.

But his eyes were more intense than she'd ever seen them, his face sterner.

He looked like a nobleman, a GreatLord secure in his power—but not arrogant. Assured but not imperious.

His voice continued, soft and persuasive. "I can do this. Let me. I can get you out of there, destroy the amulet, repair your tunnel, and stabilize this fault."

Why didn't she laugh at his unbelievable claims? Why did she even imagine he could do as he promised?

Ruis's gaze turned shrewd. "You don't look like you have much Flair. What would an emergency broadcast alarm cost you? Do you know who'd hear, who'd come? How long would they take to get here and organize a rescue? You can't teleport with your foot caught in the ground."

"Bucus." The name escaped on a gasp. Bucus T'Elder

was her nearest neighbor. What would happen if he found her first?

"What!"

Ailim bit her lip to stop a whimper from the grinding pain of the rocks on her foot. "Menzie is your uncle's mistress. He gave her the amulet. He was at D'SilverFir this afternoon, visiting his nephew, Donax—and her, too. I believe he gave her orders to throw the amulet in the fault. She acted as if she was bewitched."

The angle of his jaw sharpened in the wavering light.

"Bucus! Donax isn't his nephew by blood. He's my aunt Calami's. I'm Bucus's nephew. He's your enemy, too."

"Yes." She sighed and collapsed against her prison walls.

"Ailim, my dear one. You know I'd never hurt you."

She didn't answer.

There was a moment of silence, and when his voice came it was full of suppressed emotion. "If you want me to leave so you can use your Flair, I will. I'll stay near to help in any way I can, at any cost to myself."

"No." She could hardly envision the tumult a broadcast alarm could cause, nobles 'porting here, confusion, the capture of Ruis. "You must not be found in Druida."

She stared up and they locked gazes. Her face crumpled. "Will you coerce me by saying that you will stay and be caught if I don't do as you wish?"

His breath hitched, his expression froze. Pain ripped across his face. "No. That would be blackmail." He spoke, words jerky. "If you insist, I'll go and watch from afar. Not come near you."

She heard the echoes of a lifetime of rejection in his undertone. She tried to clear her mind. His ideas were fantastic; she couldn't imagine how he could do as he said. His solution was inconceivable. She couldn't weigh her choices. Except to consider the man himself. She had to decide whether to trust the man himself. Her heart cracked at the amount of faith he was asking, how vulnerable she'd show herself to be if she trusted him—having so much trust in him that she would believe him able to achieve the impossible on his word alone.

But she loved him.

"I'm your lover." He echoed her thought, his words dropping as softly as tears. "Can't you trust your lover?"

Ailim surrendered. Stripped to her core, she knew herself, knew she loved Ruis. Love demanded trust and faith. "Yes." She shifted to be as comfortable as possible and closed her eyes to his scrutiny. "Bring on your Earth machines."

Her eyes flew open a moment later as clinking sounded above her. Her mouth slackened as a long gray tentacle slithered down the hole. She didn't know how the machine had gotten there, hadn't heard a sound.

The cylindrical thing slid against her body as it burrowed. She screamed.

"Easy now, dear one, nothing to fear," Ruis said.

Ailim glared up at him. "You aren't the one being fondled by an unnatural snake!" Watching in fascinated horror, she had second thoughts as the tentacle flexed and poked.

Snick! Four shiny metal prongs sprang out. Ailim tried to crawl out of her hole.

"Easy!" Ruis said.

*You fine*, Samba mewed.

The snake angled down toward her ankle, probed around the compacted dirt and rock. With a whir, it drilled into the stone. Ailim panted. Sweat from fear and the heat the tool generated coated her body. She moaned.

"Ailim!"

"Yes, Ruis?"

"Take this." He tossed an odd little ball down and Ailim caught it. It fit in her palm. The upper half was metal with switches and buttons. The bottom was encased in soft fabric and snuggled into her hand.

"The red button is a lazer. Don't press it," he said. "The blue switch is a light, the green one is a little scry. If you turn on the scry and the light, I can see what the digging machine is doing."

She blinked. The amulet's evil waves were much less noticeable. "Ruis?" she asked.

"Yes?" He sounded preoccupied.

"This object you gave me—"

"The multitool?"

"Yes." She held it up to her temple and tried a small telepathic spell to Samba. She'd been able to sense Samba's thoughts just a moment before—nothing! She looked at the tool in wonder, turning it over and over. "This sphere has a small energy field that works much like your Nullness."

"What?" He sounded startled. His head darkened the hole, his eyes round with curiosity.

She held up the tool. "It dampens my Flair. A pity it's too strange and large to carry in my pockets." Ailim studiously avoided glancing at the writhing tentacle near her ankle. She tried not to speculate what the loud noises were. She realized the snake-arm smelled familiar, like that additional tang of Ruis's personal scent.

Ruis frowned, examining the multitool. "Interesting."

The pressure on her foot vanished. Ailim moaned as a tide of numbness, then a different pain from her foot flooded her.

"Ailim?"

She knew she needed to attempt to move her foot, but had to regain control. A couple of minutes, maybe.

"I'm all right," she said through gritted teeth. "I'm free."

"Wonderful! Lift!" Ruis ordered.

Before she was ready, the arm curled around her waist, squeezed too tight, then relaxed as if sensing her weight and its surest grip.

It dragged her up, and her useless foot bumped against rock. Ailim clenched her hands tight around the tentacle to keep from crying out. The snake-arm didn't compress under her grip. After a meter, there were no walls close and she dangled in space, inching up. Ailim panted, then Ruis's arms reached for her, drew her close to his body.

He held her too high for her to set her good foot down. His strength and warmth and the pounding of his heart overwhelmed her as much as sheer relief. She couldn't prevent a steady oozing of tears.

"Shhhh. Shhhhhh. I've got you. Almost over." He cuddled her close, then lifted her and walked.

Ailim blinked, unable to comprehend what she was seeing until she was on a floating raft with strange machines.

Ruis gestured to a squat white one with a red cross painted on it. "Scan GrandLady D'SilverFir's left foot for harm."

The little robot waddled up and extruded a soft white

cradle. Ailim decided she was supposed to put her foot in it. She bit her lip when the weight of her foot hung in the cradle. The robot hummed as warm yellow lights flashed on her foot. She turned to ask Ruis what was going on. He wasn't there.

Squinting, she saw him being lowered into the hole, holding another little machine. Terror jangled her nerves. The robot peeped.

"Ruis!"

He lifted a hand. "I'm getting the amulet!"

"Don't! Forget it!" Nothing was as important as his life. Not her estate, not her Family, not her own life.

He disappeared. She tried to move, but her foot was trapped again, this time by an infernal machine. She felt a sting and her gaze shot back to her ankle. A long shining needle-like instrument slowly withdrew from the slit in her boot. At the end of it a single red drop of her blood beaded.

Her mouth fell open, dizziness overcame her. She battled the dark, but it won.

$R$uis's lips peeled back from his teeth when he found the amulet. The charm bag was filthy, the smell disgusting. The odor comprised the well-known stench of his uncle when in a torturing mood: high excitement, sweat, and his cologne. There was the stink of rotting corruption like when he faced Hylde's body; the sickening aroma of a woman, and a note of frantic, rough sex. Ruis struggled to keep his gorge down. He sipped the hole's air shallowly through his mouth.

Pulling a ragcloth from his belt, he dropped it over the thing and gingerly scooped the shrouded amulet up, treating it as if it were the decaying corpse of a small animal.

"Up full speed!" he shouted.

He was whisked from the hole in less than ten seconds. He glanced at the raft—Ailim was sleeping. Good, the best thing for her.

On either side of the main hole other machines were venting the crust at intervals to dissipate noxious Flair-energy.

He walked along the ravine, away from the epicenter of

the faultline, and crossed into Elder land, discernable by the lack of fir trees. He found a barren spot and dropped the revolting amulet. The ragcloth opened. The bag had shriveled into a small dry lump. Getting his lighter, he flicked it and looked at the clean orange flame. He calculated the amount of time he'd been close to the bane, whether his Nullness would have allayed the evil spell. He glanced at his watch. Twenty minutes before Ship's deadline. After his watch ticked away four minutes, he torched the rag. Black flames spewed up. Ruis jumped back. The thing burned gray, then purple, then blue, and finally vanished in a cracking white flash.

When Ruis touched the ash mummy of the amulet with his boot toe, the bane flaked to nothingness and drifted away on the wind.

Ruis grinned and dusted his hands. He threw back his head and laughed, triumph rising in him. He'd beaten his bastard of an uncle. He'd won!

This battle. This first battle, he'd won!

*S*ensations slowly filtered into Ailim's mind—an acrid smell that made her wrinkle her nose, the sense of lying on a hard pad, her ears filled with a humming and breathing of more than one set of lungs. Her mind quested—nothing.

She jerked upright and opened her eyes. Her vision blurred and she fell back into Ruis's strong arms. He pulled her close and she heard his heartbeat's steady *thump-thump-thump*.

Ailim touched her skull where she'd had a lump. It was gone now. Daring pain, she pushed her fingers against her head. Nothing. She wiped dirt from her eyes and looked down at her feet. They were bare, looking pink and healthy and freshly washed. She rotated her left ankle and flexed her left foot. No pain.

She opened her mouth to comment, then noticed the strange surroundings. The walls were a mixture of brushed metal, glassy panels, and woven tapestries. The bed she slept on was nothing like she'd ever seen before—an inset mattress filled with a firm but supportive substance that didn't feel like permamoss. She poked it. "What is this?" she said.

A rumpling purr came from near her right foot, and she lifted her head. At the end of her bed Samba sat on a—tray? "What? Where?" She was stupefied.

"Welcome to the sick bay of *Nuada's Sword*," Ruis said, making no sense at all.

"What?"

"Pppprrrrrrruuuuuup," Samba rumbled as if coaxing.

Ailim peeked at the Fam cat again. Samba's whiskers twitched. *You in Our home. Ship!*

"Ship?"

*Nuada's Sword?*

Trembling started from inside her body and spread until Ruis pressed her against him again.

*"Nuada's Sword?"* she asked, certain she'd misunderstood the cat's mutterings.

"That's right." Ruis's low voice soothed her.

She braced herself. "You're living in *Nuada's Sword?*"

He nodded.

Ailim licked her lips. Ruis got a metal tumbler from the tray and handed it to her.

Of course she'd seen goblets made of precious metals, but nothing this utilitarian. It was cold in her hand. She looked inside, then back up at Ruis. "Water?" Her voice was still husky from all the dust.

"Yes."

She gulped it. Coolness slid down her throat with such soothing freshness that after she swallowed she let out a moan of delight.

She looked around—even though it was obvious that this was a place unlike any she'd ever seen, she still found it difficult to believe Ruis was actually living in the starship. She pressed the tumbler to her forehead as if the cold would penetrate her skull and stimulate logical thought, and enjoyed the beaded dampness of condensation.

*"Nuada's Sword,"* she whispered again. "Isn't there supposed to be a curse that drives a person mad if they spend more than a couple of hours here?"

Ruis's lips twitched. He lifted her to a full sitting position and dropped his arm from around her. She missed it.

"That's what they say," he said. He turned and stared over her head. She craned to see an indicator panel behind her. It appeared a lot like a Healing Chart.

"You'll do." His smile looked strained. He took a step back to a chair, sat down, sank his head into his hands, and threaded his fingers through his thick mahogany hair. "Lord and Lady, you scared me," he mumbled. "I didn't know what had happened to you or what to do."

"You are living on the Ship, *Nuada's Sword*," Ailim said carefully.

"Yesssssss," hissed Samba, bobbing her head, then lifting her nose in smug superiority. *I am Ship's Cat.*

She put the water down to rub her eyes. "Despite the fact that *Nuada's Sword* is on the cliffs on the very edge of the city, technically, you're living in Druida. If you were found here—" She couldn't go on. This was madness.

Ruis raised his head. "I didn't know Ship had sedated you and started the Healing program—"

"The patient GrandLady D'SilverFir is recovering nicely," said a deep voice from thin air that ruffled the hair on the back of her neck.

Samba sniffed. *That is Ship. We fixed it. Broke curse.*

"Ship," Ailim said weakly. She looked around again. Perhaps if she looked long enough, observed everything thoroughly, she would be able to think rationally.

"A simple matter of subsonics," said the Ship.

Ailim wasn't sure what subsonics were, but with one more scan of the room, everything fell into place, Ruis's words about his passion, his skill in fixing ancient artifacts.

"You're rehabilitating the Ship?" Her mouth wanted to fall open in blank wonder.

Ruis stood and walked back to her raised bed. "That's right. Now you know all my secrets." His smile didn't touch his anxious eyes.

She reached out both hands to him, noticing that they appeared clean while the rest of him was dirty. It didn't matter, she needed his touch. "Please, Ruis," she said when he hesitated, "come to me. Help me understand."

Samba snorted and jumped down from the metal tray, leaving it vibrating. She stalked to the door. *You sllllooooowwwww.*

Ailim winced.

The door slid open to the side, and Ailim felt her eyes widen even more. Samba exited, tail up.

Ruis remained beyond her outstretched hand. He put his fists on his hips and frowned. "I want you to stay here tonight."

"It is recommended the patient D'SilverFir stay for observation," the Ship said.

Ailim stared at her bare feet, which were getting cold. She shook her head in disbelief. "What did it do to me?"

Ruis's smile was lopsided. "I don't quite know. I'm sure it would explain everything in excruciating detail if you asked."

Ailim winced, then sighed. "Don't say 'excruciating,' please."

He took the final pace to her side, his hand curved around her face. "I don't know what happened. I just know that the whole mess was too risky for my blood."

Ailim raised her eyebrows and shook her head again. "I can't believe that's true. You are the most reckless man—"

He stopped her words, her entire train of thought, with his firm lips on her mouth. She moaned again and leaned into him, bringing her hands to his shoulders so he wouldn't escape her again. She needed him. Badly. Now.

When he looked up, his pupils had dilated and his expression was one of stark hunger. "I was so afraid." He brushed little kisses all over her face, then buried his face in her neck.

Tears tightened her throat at his emotion, his ability to express it, to be free with his feelings in front of her. "You saved me again," she said huskily.

Raising his head, he tapped her chin with his index finger. "You could have saved yourself."

"Maybe."

"You would have tried."

She met his eyes steadily. "Yes."

He smiled. "We're fighters, both of us."

"Yes."

"Survivors."

"Yes."

"Stay with me tonight."

"Yes."

He laughed out loud. "You're very good for me."

"You're good for me, too. Better than anyone I've known."

Ruis ran his hand through his hair and grimaced when it came back dusty. "I need to clean up. There's a shower-room in the corner. Will you wait here for me?"

She examined the unfamiliar room one more time. "I don't think I dare explore."

"It's wonderful here," he said, bending an intense look on her. "And the Greensward is beautiful."

Ailim tried a smile. "I'm sure."

He shook his head. "You'll see." With a flick of his hand he headed off to a corner, opened a door she hadn't noticed, and disappeared inside.

Ailim swung her legs to dangle over the side of the bed and stretched. She felt unaccountably good.

"GrandLady D'SilverFir," the Ship said.

"Yes?" As long as she pretended it was the voice of a Residence instead of a Ship, she'd be fine.

"We have reviewed all your personal and professional records—"

"What! How?" Her lips thinned.

"We have reconnected with the Public Archives and the D'SilverFir computer."

"What?"

"Ah, the D'SilverFir 'ResidenceLibrary,' " Ship said.

"Oh," Ailim said hollowly.

"You are noted to be a lady of great integrity."

"Thank you."

"Our Captain, Ruis Elder, is in danger Outside our skin."

"Ah."

"We must insist that you swear an oath not to betray him."

That sent anger spurting through her. "Of course I won't betray him."

"You are an official judiciary officer and have sworn to uphold the laws of Celta."

"You don't have to tell me that. I don't forget my vows."

"Yet you are breaking them," Ship pointed out.

# Fifteen

"*All human rules and laws must be somewhat flexible,*" Ailim told the Ship. "Extenuating circumstances must always be considered."

When the Ship didn't answer, she exhaled in relief. She didn't want to debate her honor, her oaths, or how she was flouting Celtan law. She licked her lips. The air in this chamber seemed drier than that outside, or in D'SilverFir Residence. "Ship, you said that you had a connection with D'SilverFir Residence." She kept her voice firm, with a deliberate authoritative note.

"Correct."

"I requested an alarm be raised if I were absent later than third-bell. I think—"

"Transmitting information to the D'SilverFir Residence that you are safe and unharmed. Additional data regarding the state of the fault and the Residence foundation broadcasted also."

Ruis stepped from the corner of the room. His oddly cut trous molded his muscles. Toweling his hair, he smiled at her.

She shook her head at him. "You are really living on *Nuada's Sword*."

"As I said, you know my secrets."

"You know mine," she whispered. "You know of the HouseHeart tunnel."

He hung the towel around his neck and strode to her. "Ship,

do you have diagrams of the corridor you helped build for the SilverFirs?"

One wall darkened, flashed, then schematics appeared on it. Ailim started. They were better than the ancient drawings she had. "The corridor. Built as a temporary passage. We were never contacted to finish the project. Had we been involved in the construction, it would not be at risk today."

"I'm sorry," Ailim said.

"Only the outer shell was poured for the route. The material is the least strong and flexible, fit to keep small animals and plant roots from penetrating the passage."

"What needs to be done?" asked Ruis, sitting next to her.

"An inner coating of self-mending polymer and two more layers should be assembled of carbon nanotubes—"

"We don't need the details," Ruis interrupted coolly.

Ailim goggled at him. She began to grasp the great power of the Ship. The fact that Ruis commanded it made her breath catch even as it stirred something deep inside her.

Her gaze fixed on Ruis's hands. Strong, with long, elegant fingers, but with small scars due to his work. She frowned. No, the scars were too many and looked . . . She gasped and grabbed one of his hands to scrutinize it in the bright light, recalling that he'd hidden his hands from her view more than once.

His breath stopped, too.

Her mouth thinned as she examined palm and fingers. She whipped the towel from him to study his torso. Horror flooded through her at the evidence that he'd been systematically tortured. She'd seen razorslit torture before. Her stomach lurched sickeningly.

She touched one scar, two, on his chest. He'd gone still, face set, not looking at her.

"Oh, Ruis." She slid her hands up his warm body to his shoulders. Traced the line of his jaw with her index finger. His face had been spared, thank the Lady and Lord. "Oh, Ruis."

He captured her hands and brought them to his mouth, kissing them. He finally met her eyes, his hurt like some wild thing that had been trapped.

"No," she said. "Not you. This should not have happened to you."

"Of course it would." His voice was harsh. "I'm a Null, of

no use to anyone, and in the charge of a person like Bucus—"

"That evil man. That evil, evil man! I will get him for this. Where's the amulet?"

"I destroyed it," Ruis said.

Ailim stared at him. "Why? If we had it we could use it as evidence against your uncle Bucus."

"What!"

"Your uncle Bucus, my aunt Menzie." Her hand fluttered as if pointing out the obvious. "They're lovers. He gave her the amulet, and primed her to use if. If we could prove it—"

"The damned amulet was affecting you *and* the earth fault. An evil thing that had to be destroyed. It withered up and—" The words stuck in his throat as he remembered the other thing he'd seen that night that had withered up and might have fallen apart with a touch. A nasty taste coated his tongue.

"What is it?" Ailim demanded.

Ruis just shook his head. Whatever his expression was, it alarmed Ailim. She grabbed his shoulders and peered into his eyes. "Tell me!"

His mouth pulled down in distress and disgust. He put his hands around Ailim's waist, feeling her soft and supple strength, the life that ran through her. He closed his eyes and savored the feel of her. It calmed him.

When he opened his lashes, her eyes held more gray than blue.

"As a child"—he cleared his throat—"Bucus put me in the 'care' of a low-Flaired, dense distant relative. Her name was Hylde." A corner of his mouth curled in an unamused smile. "She wasn't much of a person, but I loved her before—before she turned me over to Bucus to torment and save her own skin."

"Ahhhhhhhh." Ailim stroked his face. How he wished he'd had a loving woman to mind him. Someone like Ailim, emotionally strong, honorable, caring. Pressure backed up behind his eyes and he stared hard at the far wall.

"Ship thought it would be helpful to my 'mental health' to visit the old cottage and the T'Elder Residence. I was there earlier tonight." He knew he rambled, but the feathering of Ailim's fingers was distracting, and he wanted that diversion.

"And was it?"

He blinked and felt inordinate relief that nothing damp leaked from his eyes. "Huh?"

She smiled and pressed her lips on his, more for his comfort, he thought, than anything else. His heart rolled in his chest.

"Was it beneficial for you to visit the T'Elder Residence?"

He jerked his head in a nod.

"And what of Hylde?" she prompted.

"I found her body."

Ailim sprung to rigid attention, withdrawing her hands. Her brows snapped down over fierce eyes. "Body? I suspect that her death wasn't natural? Why would the head of a household leave the body of a dependent in a—cottage?"

"He hit her and caved in her skull. Whether he used Flair with the blow or not, I don't know, but the mark of his signet is blazoned on her skull."

"Lady and Lord," Ailim breathed. She hopped down from the table and began pacing around the room.

She hit the fist of one hand into the palm of her other and swung back to him, eyes gleaming stormy pewter. "We have him. The evil man. To think he's Captain of the Council. Oh, but I shall bring him down for this! I've ordered a murderer marked before. He'll wear the sign of his crime forever on his face."

In two strides he caught up with her and chained her hands in his own. His little bubble of fantasy had broken. If a woman like Ailim had been his caretaker when he was a child, she'd have been dead in an eightday. As she would be now. "No. Absolutely not."

Her head fell back as she matched her stare with his. "You can't say leave this alone, that it's past. There is no past for murder. Murder is always an open crime." Her gaze swiveled around the room. "Like it was for our ancestors, murder must always be punished."

"No. Think. The evidence of the amulet is gone, and I'd wager your aunt won't testify against Bucus, her lover."

Ailim's eyes narrowed. "No. I don't know if she even re-members what happened. He bespelled and befuddled her."

"All the evidence of Hylde's murder is on his estate." Ruis snapped his fingers. "One pouf of a spell and that cottage would fall in on her and bury that evidence, too. There's no way we can legally avenge Hylde!"

Ailim poked him in the chest. "We can get justice for you!

Look at your hands—razorslits! You have scars all over your body. Child abuse . . . the abuse of a dependent is a vile crime. And he stole your estate from you, didn't he?"

Ruis grabbed her twisting hands as he fought his own temper. He'd never seen Ailim angry, but her fury fed his and someone needed to keep a cool head or they'd both be dead. That thought chilled his temper to ice. "We can't prove that there was a Loyalty Ceremony to me as a baby and that Bucus later convinced the rest of the Family to renege on their words and be forsworn. We can't prove he stole the title and the estate from me."

"Yet." She bit off the word. "We can't prove it *yet*. As soon as we have proof I can initiate a judicial review. I know the law, none better, and I will get him for his crimes." She rolled the sentence around in her mouth as if with relish. "He has betrayed his sacred vow of fidelity to his wife, and I'm sure he's betrayed his vows of loyalty to Hylde and to you. A man who will violate one solemn vow will violate others. He needs to be stopped!"

"He's killed, he's bespelled his own lover. At what cost must he be stopped?" Ruis couldn't believe he was arguing against his own vengeance that he'd savored earlier in the evening, but the idea of Ailim in danger chilled him to his very bones. "Aren't you violating your vows to the JudgmentGrove of Celta in associating with me?" he asked softly and hated the words that sped from his mouth as she flinched and turned white.

When her words came they were low and carefully spaced. "I would argue that there is a difference between law and justice, and that in the final analysis justice must triumph, not the rule of law. Justice for you is paramount, and for that I will break my vows."

She lifted her chin. "I am willing to take the consequences of my actions. I have betrayed my oath to the JudgmentGrove to be with you. I know the consequences, and if I'm called to suffer them, I'll do so, as all oathbreakers would. *But* had you been treated the way you should have, neither of us would be in this situation—and that should be a consideration. I don't intend to break any other vows, not my Loyalty Oath, not my oath to the NobleCouncil, nothing else."

Her hands gestured fluidly. "Everything I do flows from what

I believe in, what I am in my deepest self." She nailed him with her gaze. "I consider myself an honorable woman and by all my actions I have shown myself to be so. As you have shown honor."

He'd gone as pale as she. "What will happen if you're caught with me?" he asked. He had an idea, but she'd know better.

"We've avoided talking about reality." She shook her head and smiled sadly. "I don't think either of us wanted to interrupt our lovely moments together with speech about the harsh consequences of our actions."

She cleared her throat. "My title would be taken away. My Family would disinherit me. The NobleCouncil, especially under your uncle Bucus, would probably call our million-gilt loan due. We would lose the ancestral Residence and estate." She closed her eyes and shuddered.

"And your judgeship?" he muttered, wanting to go to her but unable to after he'd said such terrible words.

She opened her eyes to stare at him in disbelief. "All honors I have with the legal profession would be stripped from me. Who would trust even a notary, let alone a Truth-Seeker or Judge who had broken her word?"

"Even if you gave that little speech about justice?"

She threw up her hands. "Who knows? I can help you, you have been the victim of injustice. But I made the decision to violate my oath freely. That's a big difference."

"Not to me."

She rolled her eyes.

He frowned, following the logic of the consequences. "If you were disinherited, how would you support yourself?"

Ailim shook her head, glanced away. He thought he'd seen the glaze of tears in her eyes. "I don't know." Her voice was thick. "I don't have skills like yours. My Flair has always been linked to the law. Everyone knew as soon as I reached adulthood I'd be a judge. That's what I trained for."

Ruis thought hard. "Usually everyone with great Flair has an 'art,' too. Bucus makes little animated puppets, simulacra." Ruis fumbled for words. "It's the art that goes into making a HeartGift. Didn't you make a HeartGift during Passage?" Another subject he'd never wanted to address—if she had someone who'd bond with her on an emotional and mental level as well as a physical one. He found a tunic and pulled it on.

She went to a chair and perched on it, looked at her hands, stretched and curled her fingers. "I'm a mediocre lace maker. As for a HeartGift, I thought you knew." When she raised her level gaze to him, her bluish eyes were clear. "A person with great Flair usually experiences Passage at seven, seventeen, and twenty-seven. I did have my first Passage when I was seven, but my next came at nine, my last at eleven."

Ailim took a deep breath, exhaled, then rose and walked to him. She stroked his face with her hands. Her eyes looked misty and loving. Her whole aspect softened and Ruis wondered how she could have forgiven him his words so soon. Because they were the truth, he thought. Hurtful as they might have been to be heard aloud, she'd already known and accepted them. Known and accepted him. He found himself achingly aroused.

"You should leave me," he said thickly.

"You, Ruis Elder, are the closest to a HeartMate I will ever have. Your Nullness enchants me."

His heart thumped so his whole body shuddered. "I need you."

She longed for him. "I need you, too." She grabbed and hugged him fiercely, joyful when his arms closed reflexively around her. "Take me to bed now, Ruis. I need you. I need to make love to you." All the night's events demanded that she celebrate life with him.

"I—"

She put her hand over his mouth. Her skin felt hot. She had to have him. Had to hold him tight within her, to reaffirm that he was strong and whole, that she was healed and whole, too. That they not only survived but they triumphed.

He stood and swept her into his arms. As they approached the door, it split in two and opened. He turned right and strode down a corridor that reminded Ailim of the passageway to the HouseHeart. Walls were a dull, brushed silver and slightly curved, with planters staggered along them at varying heights.

The hall went straight and she saw no end. Six kilometers, she thought in wonder. *Nuada's Sword* was no less than six kilometers long. She couldn't tell whether the floor was carpeted or not, what the texture might be. Her arms tightened around Ruis's neck, and she buried her face against him.

He laughed softly.

"This is so very strange," she mumbled, peeking.

Ruis stopped at a large, elegant but battered wooden door. Ailim blinked at the golden insignia, but couldn't read the words. Scary, a language that wasn't Celtan, that she didn't know.

"Voice recognition for automatic open," Ruis said.

"The Captain is acknowledged," replied the echoing tones of the Ship, coming from nowhere and everywhere. Ailim clutched at Ruis harder, looking down at the small puncture in her foot and the darkening bruise surrounding it.

The door split in the middle and slid into opposite sides of the wall.

Ruis bent down and brushed his lips against her temple. His warm breath slid against her skin, carrying his scent, and she relaxed.

"These are my quarters."

Her eyes widened when she saw the large sitting room, with doors on each wall. She barely registered the furnishings before Ruis strode to the left, into the den with her. He crossed to the corner and another door whisked open at his approach. He stepped into a little room. "We're in an omnivator; it moves us through the Ship. To the Greensward," he said.

Ailim gasped when she felt movement. She bit her lip. "We're going somewhere?" Her words sounded shakier than she wanted, but they gained an unexpected benefit, Ruis cuddled her closer, dropping little kisses on her forehead.

Ailim concentrated on the solid body of her lover. Her life began to resemble a surrealistic dream. She rubbed her face against Ruis's muscular chest. The texture of his clothing felt strange, but his body rooted her in reality. This was his life. His new life, and she could only wonder that he managed so well.

The room stopped and the doors opened. A scented wave of humid verdancy rolled over her. Her breath stuck in her throat as paradise beckoned.

Chirping birds welcomed her with sweet song. Before her was a lush carpet of lawn in a green she'd never seen before but which resonated in her very bones. Flowering bushes framed small trees, then larger trees. She heard the buzzing of bees.

"It's light! And—summer?"

She felt Ruis's deep chuckle before she heard it. "The Greensward has its own time and seasons. It has various zones of plants and animals, based on Earth climates."

She pushed against him to see better and he put her down. "But how does it exist?

He shrugged. "I don't know, exactly." Again he chuckled and Ailim's gaze focused in wonder on his lips. He was smiling, truly smiling with real amusement. She caressed his cheek. He angled his head until his mouth turned into her palm and he kissed it.

"Welcome to *Nuada's Sword* and the Greensward of Earth." Now his voice was gruff.

Wonder and tenderness welled up in Ailim as she glanced around at the representation of her ancestors's home planet. Her eyes dampened and her mind spun at the odd liveliness of the scents and sights, the feel of the atmosphere against her skin.

"Lie with me," Ruis said.

She almost didn't hear him. So she lifted her face to study his expression. Dark passion sharpened his eyes, his jaw looked set, yet behind the flames of desire she thought she saw deep pools of loneliness and vulnerability.

He took her hand and ran it down his body, placing her fingers over his stiffening sex. With just that gesture, her own body primed for loving. Tingling bloomed between her thighs and her breasts ripened. She molded her hand against his shaft, rubbing. Lust overwhelmed the yearning in his eyes, his chest rose and fell unevenly.

Her own breathing quickened.

"Lie with me."

"Yes."

Ailim framed his face with her hands, her fingertips skimming his cheekbones, her stare locked with his. She smiled. "You are the most amazing man. So unique. You dazzle me."

His eyes flashed surprise as he rocked backward, breaking contact. He shook his head as if she bedazzled him, and she couldn't suppress a flutter of laughter—didn't want to suppress the laughter. She let it break from her, loud and free.

She saw hot desire roll through him, tensing his muscles, putting a predatory male attitude in his stance. He reached for her and she caught both his hands, gripping them tightly. "You make me forget who I am, what I am. With you I can be simply a woman."

"Not simple," he grated.

She lifted his fingers to her mouth as he had so often done to her and kissed them, one hand, then the other. Then she inhaled his scent—man and mint and the tang she now recognized as Earth machine or *Nuada's Sword*. Her tongue curled around one of his fingers. He shuddered. She smiled again. His hands gripped hers, and she knew he'd take charge of the love-making—as he had always done—if she let him. If she let him, he would swamp her senses with such delicious sights and scents and sexy phrases and sensual touches that she'd lose herself. If she let him, he would pleasure her.

But she wanted to pleasure him.

He pulled away.

"No," she whispered.

He jerked and stiffened and she knew he would instinctively believe he was being rejected. She could teach him to trust her—his body, mind and most of all, his emotions—had she the time. But she didn't think they'd have the time.

Too long, she'd thought too long instead of acting, and his face had frozen. He inclined his head.

She flung herself at him, grasping his shoulders and dragging herself against his hard aroused body to taste him at the base of his throat.

His arms circling hard about her. "What?"

"My turn. You've always given to me, Ruis Elder. It's my turn to give to you."

"Huh?" He took a couple of steps backward, looking stunned.

She tapped a finger into his chest and grinned, lifting her chin. "It's my turn to pleasure you, to make you dizzy with delight, to give you the night of your life."

Heat flared in his eyes, and a flicker of disbelieving wonder. "Just the thought of you makes me dizzy with delight."

Her mind was swimming again. She took a deep breath. She wanted to do this. His glance fixed on her breasts.

She slid her hands up his shirt, once more feeling the odd weave of his tunic. She plucked at it. "What is this stuff?"

He shrugged and encircled her wrists with his fingers, remaining silent.

With a finger she touched the insignia on his shoulders. "Captain of *Nuada's Sword*." Laughter escaped her again. "I am seducing a starship Captain. Ooooooooohhhhh!"

"You do that just by being you."

She shook her head, glorying in the feel of her hair loose from tight braids. "You won't distract me."

"No?" His teeth gleamed.

"My turn to play with you."

He scanned her and his features sharpened. He licked his lips. "Do it, then." It was almost a dare. His insouciant attitude again.

Her hands dipped to his waist. He sucked in his breath. She savored the view of him first, his lean waist with a red-brown line of soft hair that disappeared into his trous below. She gulped, then searched the waistband of his trous for fastenings.

He breathed raggedly. Her own nipples peaked. She glanced at his face and found his intent gaze fixed on her, studying her expression and reactions.

"I want you," she said starkly.

Ruis's eyes closed. "We want each other."

How could Ailim have deserved such a tender lover? A man so giving, one with noble blood who played no noble games. For a wild moment she wanted to fall on the grass and pull him with her and have him on her and in her and moving hard.

She took a long, deep breath to slow her wildly beating heart, and continued her study of him, marveling at his sculpted biceps, muscular shoulders, strong neck. His head was set at a proud angle, but there were small white scars all over him.

"Oh, no!" she cried out, touching one.

He flinched. "Don't think of it. They're the past, they don't matter. Over and done with."

She tried. Told herself to dismiss the past, live in the moment. "Bucus will pay for hurting you," Ailim whispered. Bucus should have paid long before.

He flinched again at his uncle's name.

"Now is time for loving," she said, moving her palms up his solid body and over his nipples. Her whole mind focused on him. She rubbed his nipples and he stiffened, braced his stance. She smiled again.

When she took her fingers from him, his breath caught on a groan. She chuckled. She wanted to feel his biceps, the inherent sinewy curves that were less marked than his chest. She caressed his hand, each finger, then inserted his index finger into her mouth.

Now he groaned. She swirled her tongue around it, sucked it hard, letting the taste of him fly and circulate through her body and make her ready for loving.

"Have mercy, woman!" Ruis said, face taut.

She kept the suction of her mouth tugging at his finger as she withdrew it slowly. "No."

"Ailim!" He clasped her hands and placed them firmly at his waist.

She looked down him, at where he'd placed her hands and then further down his body. And smiled again, delight unfurling. "Oh, yes," she said, cupping his thick sex, "I'm learning how to play."

His chest gleamed now with a trace of sweat, and she liked it. She'd had power all her life, the power of a noble woman, a FirstFamilies GrandLady, a Judge whose decisions changed lives, but none of this power made her as giddy as she felt now.

The power of a woman who was sexually desired by a potent man.

He reached up to curl her hair around his fingers, tug gently. "We're wearing too many clothes," he growled.

She'd never noticed the nerve endings in her scalp before— how they tingled when a man played with her hair. A sparkling sensation spread like champagne bubbles through her. Sweet, hot anticipation prowled at her core—an ache that she welcomed, knowing this special man would bring her relief and release as no other.

"Too many clothes. Oh, yes." Her voice sounded breathy. She wasn't sure what to do. She wanted to explore his bare skin thoroughly, but his shaft lengthened and pulsed with every second that passed. She hadn't ever spent hours learning a lover, and Ruis was so fascinating already without the additional benefit of magnifying her senses, that she didn't know where to start. The crinkly hair of his chest and little velvet nipples—her free hand swept up his torso to experience those textures once more. When she grazed his nipples, he groaned and his sex jumped in her other hand.

Feeling his sex turn steel-like was so intriguing—the heat of it, the throbbing pulse, the shape of it emphasized their differences—man and woman.

"Here." He guided her hands to his waistband. "The fastenings are a lot like our tabs."

She glanced up and knew she'd made a mistake. His mouth looked hard, his eyes burning. For the first time he appeared like a real outlaw, a banished man with no respect for rules or law or gentler things. It excited her beyond belief and she couldn't understand it. Craving was stamped on his features and his nostrils flared as he caught her feminine scent.

With one glance he amplified her need to addiction.

His fingers guided hers in opening his trous. They fell away. Though the material had appeared and felt thin, the garment was lined and he wore nothing underneath.

She stared at his erect flesh. He enthralled her. She pressed her thighs together to ease—or stoke—the yearning.

She licked her lips, her glance fixed on his member. "Step out of your trous." A fine trembling gripped her and she knew she wasn't going to be able to do all the things she wanted to do to him—trace him with her fingertips, taste and lick him. No, that ambition was beyond her tonight. With jerky movements she tugged off her blouse and trous, shimmied out of her breastband and pantlettes.

They stood naked in a green paradise, in a place she never knew existed.

"Now?" It was more a question than command. Sharing. She'd wanted to give, but this time, as the times before, they would share in the loving. When she raised her gaze to his, it pierced her and her knees weakened so that she had to grab him to stay standing. "I can't pleasure you the way I want, not tonight. Maybe next time."

His teeth gleamed in a wicked grin as he curled his hand around her wrist and drew her down to the grass with him. "Next time."

Ailim fell on him and the masculinity of him swirled her wits away. Only sensation existed, only her most primal instincts guided her. She slithered up him, skimming her skin against his. She moaned and stopped to taste the bulge of his arm, his nipple, nip the cord of his neck.

She caressed his hair as she rubbed herself against him, letting the contrasting textures stroke her, heat her, incite her.

When the pressure between her legs became insistent, she swayed against his hardness, teasing them both with rocketing anticipation. The scent of their damp bodies readying for mating made her breathe deeply, making her wetter.

His shaft slid against her—outside, and then outside wasn't enough. He had to be in. And he had to be on. She rolled off him and little, cool grass stalks tickled her back and she moaned with delight. Her hand fisted in his hair brought him with her, and with one smooth glide he was hot and throbbing inside her and she exploded.

Not enough.

"More," Ruis said. His eyes had darkened to black. His tongue invaded her mouth and she opened wide, letting him take whatever he wanted, so he would move in her and fill her and flood her with exquisite sensation.

He slid in and out of her. Easy, quick. Not enough. "More!" His legs tensed and he plunged into her. Fast friction, hot throbbing, pleasure spiraling high, but not enough.

"MORE!" he yelled.

She arched under him, felt his fingers clench around her bottom as he thrust.

Release burst upon her and she screamed.

"Ailim!" One more lunge against the very depths of her and his groan matched her scream. He pumped against her, his seed spilled, and they collapsed together.

For long moments they stayed together. Ailim blinked and tears rolled from her eyes. The shattering ecstasy had been beyond anything she'd ever imagined, and she knew he'd stolen another large piece of her heart. How was she going to survive this—this enrapturing freedom of her senses and return to the shields and stiff responsibility of her old self?

She inhaled brokenly. He pushed up on his arms to move off her, and she couldn't bear it. "Stay with me." At least for a moment longer, deep inside her body.

"I'm crushing you."

She shook her head and more tears leaked from her. She stroked his back, tensile with strength. "A woman likes to feel a man's weight on her sometimes," she said.

He braced himself on his arms. When he met her gaze, the tender lover had replaced the primitive male claiming his mate. "Does she?"

His words made her understand that he hadn't had any great relationships with the opposite sex, either. Another thing in common—their inherent talents ruining regular sex, let alone anything richer that involved the heart as well as the body.

*HeartMate*, she thought.

They lay there like that for some moments, until Ruis finally rolled off and cradled her next to him. "And sometimes a man needs to sleep with a woman close," he said huskily.

She grazed her head against the hollow of his shoulder, then settled into his arms as if there was no other perfect place on the whole planet. "Is that so?"

"Hmmmmm?" In the next breath he was asleep.

Ailim could have stayed awake and thought about the night, all the ramifications of her own and Menzie's actions, all the weighty responsibilities that awaited her with the morning sun, but instead she closed her eyes and cherished the feel of her lover, letting the quiet beat of his heart lull her to sleep.

"*WARNING!*" boomed the Ship. A screeching siren jolted them awake. "Potential intruder alert. Warning. Potential intruder alert!"

Adrenalin poured into Ruis and he jumped up. "What?" He pivoted but saw only the peaceful Greensward. "Stop that alarm and moderate your tones!" he commanded.

The signal ceased, but Ship continued with its warning. "Potential intruder alert, Captain Elder."

Ailim rose to her feet and rubbed her face. "What's wrong?"

He kissed her, briefly, hard. "Ship, what do you mean by potential intruder?"

"There are life-forms moving through one of my disabled sections, the lowest level of my northwest quadrant. Those are the farthest environs from our current working area. To conserve energy for our online systems, the Captain and crew, we have not powered that zone up. We speculate that these intruders are from Outside. They could be detrimental to you and to the Ship."

"Yooowwwwwwwwlllllllllll!!!" The new screech came from Samba on her saucer, rocketing through the Greensward. The vehicle halted to hover before him at chest level.

Ailim stood in her undergarments, outer clothes forgotten

in her hand, mouth open. "Lady and Lord, what is that?"

Samba angled her ears in pride. *Samba's Saucer.*

Ailim scowled at Ruis and shook her clothes as if admonishing him. "Did you build that for her?"

He raised an eyebrow. "No. She found it herself and had one of the droids fix it. Ship had put her on an exercise program."

Samba sniffed. *My toy. Mine. Mine. Mine. Mine. Mine. Mine. Best toy in whole world.* She lifted her nose in smug queenliness. *My sire Zanth now always beneath Me.*

"The intruders!" Ship's tone rose in volume and pitch.

Samba growled. *They followed Me. ME! They dared.* Her vocalizations grumbled so that Ruis couldn't comprehend them.

"Who?" he asked sharply.

Samba twitched her mouth and Ruis knew she was forming her words with care. *Holm Holly. Tinne Holly. They come in through one of my best hidey-ways.*

# Sixteen

❦

"*Fligger*," *Ruis swore. Ailim flinched beside him and put* on her clothes. He cursed more luridly under his breath and nailed his Fam with his stare. "Did you go out of the Ship in that saucer when I told you not to?"

The fat calico wouldn't meet his eyes.

"You did, didn't you." His heart started pounding as his mind scrambled for ideas.

Samba sniffed and looked away. Her silver collar gleamed in the light. *Best play is with the waves on the Ship beach.*

"I thought I told you not to go out of the Ship in that saucer, so you wouldn't call attention to yourself, to me, to the Ship."

Samba's back rippled. *Rules. Rules everywhere. Celta rules outside. Ship rules inside. Your rules. Me do what I please. Like you. You ignore rules outside. Me ignore all rules.*

"Here." Ailim shoved his clothes at Ruis. "You need to leave here and Druida at once. The Ship is part of Druida proper, and you have broken your banishment edict. Go, and I'll take care of this."

"No. I won't go. The Ship is my home, and refurbishing it is my calling."

"Just go for now!" She started waving her hands in a pushing motion, her face creased with worry.

"I won't let you handle this for me."

"If you don't leave, you could be caught and executed!" She was almost jumping.

"And the Hollys are just the sort of men to shoot their blasers first and deal with the mess later." Ruis thought of his workshop. He had a couple of knives there. But no blasers, or long-distance weapons. Hell, he couldn't even use a sword with any competency. The Holly brothers could carve him to pieces. "Ship, what sort of personal weapons do you have for Captain and crew?"

"Crew can use her saucer as a ram." Ship's speech sounded flat and atonal. "The Captain has an armory closet in his quarters, but the pieces have not been utilized for four hundred years."

"Great." He grabbed Ailim's hand and hauled her toward the omnivator. "Time for you to go."

She dug in her heels. In an action he'd never thought himself capable of, Ruis hefted her up and over his shoulder. She squealed and pounded on his back. It hurt a little, but not enough to deter him. She poked her fingers into his butt.

"Youch!" He set his teeth and kept on walking.

"You listen to me, Ruis Elder, Captain Elder. I am not going. I can cope with the Hollys."

He reached the omnivator. Samba's saucer bobbed in with them. It was crowded. "Captain's quarters," he ordered. He let Ailim slide down his body, tantalizing him, reminding him of hours before and the loving that might never come again. His jaw ached from gritting his teeth. He pushed her against the soft wall and cupped her face between both of his hands.

"You won't leave?"

She shot him a lightning-blue glare. "No."

He shook his head in amazement. Even mussed and with wrinkled clothes, she looked every inch the GrandLady.

She crossed her arms.

Ruis realized he was grinding his teeth again and stopped. "All right. I'm not sure what we'll do. But you can stay."

"Thank you," she replied in a cool voice.

"Ship, where are the Hollys?"

"They found an omnivator. It took them to the top level of section 42, passage 390. That section is slightly southerly from their entrance and has adequate reserves of power."

The door to the cubicle opened, but Ruis didn't get out. "Take us there at once."

"This omnivator does not attach to that level and section."

"Wrong. It does." Ruis pounded a fist on the wall. "I am the Captain. If you want me to remain here in the Ship as Captain, you will follow my orders."

The omnivator lurched and zoomed upward at such an angle that Ruis and Ailim were thrown to the corner of the car. Samba's howl was earsplitting as her saucer bounced against the walls.

The cube jerked to a halt and the doors opened. No sooner had they disembarked than the doors snapped shut and the omnivator whooshed away. He didn't know what the Ship was up to, but his foreboding increased.

He strained to hear. Nothing. The hallway was dim and shadowy. It stretched only a few meters both before and behind them before turning. The scent of ancient dust and Ship metal was strong.

Ailim leaned against a curved corridor wall, her face pallid. He set his hands on her shoulders and gave them a little squeeze as he kissed her brow. "Go home, dear one."

She snapped upright, raising her chin. In the indistinct light her eyes were more gray than blue. Her lips firmed, the SupremeJudge demeanor trickling back into her. "No." Simple and soft, it was still irrevocable.

He leaned his forehead against hers. "Please?"

Her shoulders quivered under his hands, but remained straight. "I would like to do what you want me to, Ruis, but I couldn't forgive myself if I could have helped you and didn't."

There was nothing more to say.

Samba had circled around them in laps, then her ears rotated and she whizzed off down the hallway ahead of them. Ruis heard muttering voices and a clank or two as if the Holly brothers kicked decrepit 'bots or other debris out of their way.

"Yow! What was that?" a lighter male voice called, getting closer with every step—Tinne Holly.

"It's that damned cat from the Opera House. Silver collar, calico, daughter of Zanth, just like T'Ash said. Yes, I'd wager she's Ruis Elder's Fam." Holm sounded as if he was cheerfully anticipating a fight.

"Ah, the outcast. We'll get him," Tinne said with rising excitement. "Wait, that looks like Samba."

"Samba?" asked Holm.

"I didn't see her well before. She's the daughter of one of our estate cats," said Tinne.

"Huh," said Holm. "We'll get her too."

Adrenalin flooded Ruis's veins.

The Hollys loved a fight. Ruis looked around for a weapon, but nothing looked usable. He firmed his jaw. Maybe he had a chance to convince them of his use in rehabilitating the Ship.

Samba's saucer tilted as she took the corner.

*ZZZZZZssssssst!* A blaser sizzled.

Samba growled.

Ruis and Ailim broke into a run.

*Boom!* Ruis recognized the sound of an antique airlock opening, then a low, powerful hum followed by the thin clicks of a robot. The sound of the belt-tracks of a fighting robot. He inhaled sharply and choked, doubled over coughing from the stirred up dust.

"What's that?" Tinne asked.

"Behind us!" Holm said.

"Lord and Lady!" Tinne swore.

Ailim looked at Ruis in concern, but her eyes narrowed. She darted around him.

Ruis didn't have the breath to curse, he couldn't stop coughing.

"It's big and it's a little clumsy, but pretty heavily armored," Holm said. "It moves on tracks—more stable than wheels. It's reach is long and those weapons in its claws look nasty. That cowardly bastard Ruis Elder set it on us."

Anger kindled in Ruis's gut.

"Do you hear something else?" asked Tinne.

"Coughing and running. There's two ahead of us, one's smaller," said Holm.

Ruis heard the slide of a sword being drawn from its sheath. His anger chilled and his brain cleared when he thought of Ailim running toward the Hollys. He sped flat out.

Ailim rounded the curve in the corridor.

"Judge D'SilverFir!" Tinne shouted.

The resonance told Ruis that the men were farther away than he'd thought.

"Greetings, GrandLady. We heard there was trouble on your

estate last night and you'd gone missing," Holm said politely.

"D'SilverFir had ground tremors, an earthquake was barely averted. Ruis Elder saved my life."

"Ah. Tell me, can you do anything about that war behemoth behind us?" asked Holm.

"Ship!" Ailim called out.

No answer.

Finally Ruis slid around the corner. A few meters away, Ailim walked with the grace of a GrandLady toward the men. The Hollys were about halfway down the long corridor, and Ruis was outside blaser range.

As soon as the fighting 'bot scanned Ruis, it rumbled quicker after the brothers.

"Hollys, sheath your weapons and I'll stop the robot," Ruis called.

He received a flashing smile from Holm. "Sorry, but I can't really trust you, outcast."

Ruis let the hurtful word pierce him, then pushed it aside. The dire circumstances demanded he keep control of his temper.

"Ship, slow the robot," Ruis commanded.

"Captain, we disagree. You are in danger. We postulate these native Celtans can kill you summarily."

"They're honorable men. They won't do that," Ailim said, her tone calm. She flicked a glance at Ruis. "Stop where you are."

"No. I won't hide behind you," Ruis said.

Red flared on her cheeks.

"Ship, I gave you an order," Ruis reminded. The robot slowed fractionally. "Reduce the speed of the fighting robot by half." The rattling noise of the robot's track diminished, but didn't stop.

Samba hovered in front of the Hollys, blocking them. Two friends—Ailim and Samba—were determined to protect him. Welling affection helped Ruis vanquish his anger.

"You have several options, Captain," said Ship. "We can hold the two native males in the brig five levels below."

The Hollys stopped smiling.

"Our preferred choice is for a memory wipe of the Celtans," said Ship.

The horrific concept froze everyone. The Holly brothers went
pale.

"What?" asked Ruis.

"With the medical information at our disposal, through a
mixture of hypnosis, drugs, and brain-laser we can remove the
knowledge of your presence here on the Ship in Druida from
the natives."

"Can you, Ship?" Ailim sounded cutting. "How selective can
you be? How delicate is this procedure? What ancillary damage
could it do to their minds? How long has it been since you
practiced this?"

"Very good questions, Ship," Ruis said. "Have a report answering them on my desk by this evening." If he was still here
and not in chains in the gaol again, he'd read it.

"We will not allow you to be captured," Ship said. The robot
caught up with the Hollys.

The brief commotion was too quick to see. A black hole
opened in the wall, the robot's silver tentacles flashed, shoving
the Hollys into the hole. Then the corridor was empty.

A revving hum started.

"What's going on?" Ruis barely got the words out before
Ailim screamed as the robot scooped her up and barreled toward him. Pounding came from the closed door. Then the fighting robot picked him up and bolted to the omnivator.

"Crew, follow with maximum speed," Ship said.

Samba did. Within instants they were in the omnivator and
hurling away from the hallway that had begun to vibrate with
noise and power. "We think you should supervise from the
Captain's Quarters," Ship said.

"Supervise what?" yelled Ruis.

The doors of the cubicle opened and they were dumped out.

Ailim gasped. Her eyes looked wild. Samba shot from the
'vator and whizzed down the hallway to their quarters. Ruis
heard her yowl her cat-passwords.

He grabbed Ailim's hand. "We can see what's going on in
my quarters. Can you run or should I carry—"

She ran.

As they arrived in the study a holo shimmered into view. It
showed the topside of the Ship, in the northwest quadrant where
they'd just been. Curls of smoke seeped out, tracing a square
metal hatch that faced the Great Platte Ocean.

"Lady and Lord, Ship's not burning them?" Ailim choked.

Prickles raced up Ruis's spine. "I don't think so. Ship, explain!"

A door raised from the curve of the Ship's hull, and a great cannon-like snout protruded. The Ship shook.

*Boom!*

He only heard the sound in speakers and not through his ears; he couldn't feel the shot, but Ruis's stomach dropped as he saw a round, reflective orb shoot from the Ship arcing away across the ocean.

"Lifepod!" Ruis shouted. "The Hollys are in a lifepod! Ship, maximum lifesupport. Sacrifice anything to ensure safe landing for them."

The projected trajectory on the screen arced over a quarter of the planet. Ruis winced. "Abort flight immediately, minimum flight and maximum security."

"We were only protecting you," Ship sulked.

"You have contact with the pod, correct?" Ruis had never felt more determined.

"Correct," Ship answered at its lowest audible volume.

"Then you will ensure that the lifepod will land at the soonest possible moment. You will instruct the pod to provide the maximum amount of assistance to the Hollys. This is not negotiable. If my orders are not carried out now, I will leave this Ship within the septhour and never come back."

"Aborting the pod at this moment would cause it to land in the Arctic Sea. Recommend that the pod finish an orbit."

"Yes, ensure their safety!" Ruis ordered.

"Commands are being sent to the lifepod with a program for automatic start up and translation of pertinent data for the Celtans. Calculating new landing," Ship grumbled, adding clanking sound effects.

A bar graph flickered on at the bottom of the holo, showing the progress of the systems Ship was sending to the lifepod.

"Flight being aborted. Landing program engaged. Set down at the northeastern edge of this subcontinent will be in ten Celtan minutes."

"Maps!" Ailim shouted.

"Transmit maps," Ruis confirmed.

"Our maps have not been updated in two centuries," Ship gloated.

Ailim muttered under her breath. Her phrases sounded like real swearing.

"Can you establish a scry—a visual and/or audio link to the pod?" asked Ruis

"The pod is not responding," Ship said.

"Tell the Hollys to prepare for landing. Broadcast instructions and repeat until the pod sets down."

More clanking. "Done," said the Ship.

Ailim licked her lips. "This lifepod, what does it have in it?"

Silence. Ruis rolled his eyes. "Answer GrandLady D'SilverFir's questions now and in the future."

A rattle.

"The pod is fully stocked with Earth medical supplies, space and atmosphere suits, emergency rations, and water," stated the Ship.

The minutes as the orb circled Celta passed in agonizing slowness. Finally the pod's arc passed Druida again and began to flatten. The little orange icon with two twinkling stars inside plummeted. Ruis held his breath for the final minute of the pod's dive. Ailim grabbed his biceps and squeezed. "Is it going too fast? Will they be hurt?" Her voice rose in near panic.

"Landing will be acceptable for strong Celtan men," Ship said. That didn't reassure Ruis. Ailim's nails bit into his arm. "Death probability is two percent, major injuries is five percent, minor injuries ten percent, bruising fifteen percent—"

"Enough!" Ruis said

"The Celtans are strapped in and ready for landing," Ship said.

"Lady and Lord," Ailim whispered as she wriggled under Ruis's arm so that he held her. The closeness comforted him.

With fifteen seconds to spare, the orb slowed.

"Final descent initiated," Ship said.

"Show us where in Celta they are!" Ruis commanded.

The view angled. Ruis blinked, trying to understand the geographic details from a unique viewpoint. When he comprehended the land markers, he wondered if he could hustle Ailim from the room before she deciphered them. The escape pod carrying the Holly brothers streaked down to the most inhospitable part of the continent. He looked at her. Her eyes had widened in horror.

"Oh, no," Ailim gasped.

"I think it'll miss the 271 mountain range." The peaks rose rugged and proud.

"It's going to land in the Great Washington Boghole! We're all doomed. They'll be dead and we'll be murderers," Ailim said.

"If the boghole doesn't get them, the mellyck will," Ruis said, giving in to momentary pessimism. Ailim shuddered. A fierce and unpredictable screaming wind scoured the landscape on a daily basis.

The orb met the ground.

"Touchdown," Ship said.

Ailim's panting rasped. "They're still there. The little star-bursts in the orb."

"Vital statistics of the Holly brothers, Ship," Ruis ordered.

"The pod's transmitter was damaged in the landing," Ship said. "We cannot send nor receive."

"But we can see them!" Ailim poked a finger through the hologram at the lifepod icon.

"The holoview is a result of distant satellite transfer."

Ailim blinked. "What?"

Ruis patted her hand. "A satellite is a large scry orbiting the planet. I believe Ship is linked to three."

"Oh."

Two little blinking white lights wobbled from the orange orb. "They're all right!"

"For now," Ruis said, thinking again of the vicious landscape the Hollys faced.

The room doors whooshed open. Samba flew loop-de-loops, glee quivering her whiskers. *The Holly brothers on great adventure*, she said. *No longer in Druida City. They are gone, gone, gone.*

Ailim shut her eyes. "And we are doomed."

"Doomed?" Ruis said. "Not necessarily. If the Holly brothers survive the boghole, they can rest at Lake Meraj. The way to Ragge Town isn't bad from there."

"In Ragge Town they should be able to hire guides to help them teleport in stages back to Druida." She sounded hopeful.

Ruis frowned. "I don't think they have much gilt. The pod is full of valuable ancient Earth relics, but there's not much of a market in Ragge Town."

"They both wear jeweled daggers."

"Tinne has a smoky quartz in his main gauche, and his scabbard is plain with cloisonné ivy leaves set in black. They both carry plain swords, but—" Ruis sighed in relief. "They both have Celtan silverstones inset in their blasers! And the sheath of Holm's main gauche alternates silverstones, emeralds, and pearls."

Ailim raised her brows. Ruis lifted a shoulder and smiled at her. "I'm an *ex*-thief."

"If the Hollys make it back, they'll know you're living in Druida despite your banishment. They'll know you're restoring the Ship." She stepped back from his arms and grabbed handfuls of his shirt and tugged, as if trying to shake him. Her stark face held eyes dilated in near terror. "You have to go, now. Leave. I'll give you gilt. You can go to—"

He kissed her. "No."

"No!" she shrilled.

He winced. "No. You're here in Druida. Ship's here. Shade's here and I can't give up on him—"

"Take him with you!"

He sent her a sardonic glance. "He's a man, he doesn't trail after me when I say 'come.' If you think I'm going to leave you at the mercies of your crazy aunt and my uncle Bucus, you're wrong." Summoning his gentlest touch, he surrounded her hands in his own and warmed the chill from them.

His brows lowered. Her fine trembling worried him. He lifted her and took a stride to the Captain's Chair behind the desk, then settled in it with her on his lap.

"Lady and Lord," Ailim repeated, resting her head against his chest.

Samba amused herself flying through the holo screen where the two silver starbursts had reentered the orb. Probably stripping the pod of anything that might help them on their journey. They'd know immediately where they were. No mistaking the jagged peak of Mount ZWZ or the rest of the 271 Range and the black, sucking boghole.

Ruis smoothed a hand up and down Ailim's back. The tension marring her suppleness gradually diminished. "Everyone knows the Hollys are tough and smart. Tough enough and smart enough to make it through whatever nature throws at them." He prayed it was true. "We'll see if we can help. Ship, listen!"

"We are attending," Ship grumbled.

"Can we launch another pod or some unit with supplies?"

"No. Nothing bigger than a peeper can be repaired and sent."

"A peeper?" Ruis asked.

"You would call it a 'scry,' a distant camera that can show the Celtan's progress. With several man-hours by you, a peeper can be repaired, readied, launched and set into a tracking pattern."

Ruis let out a breath. "Good."

"I need to go," Ailim said.

Ruis kept his face expressionless. "Yes. It's better if you disassociate yourself from me. You can think up a good reason for being here by the time they return—"

She stopped his mouth with her palm. "I'll walk to the north end of the Ship. There I'll try and contact the Hollys telepathically."

He kissed her palm and kept it. "You can do that?"

Ailim returned the caress of his fingers. "Distance doesn't matter, whether I can link with them is—doubtful. I've only been connected with Holm Holly in a formal ritual and a blending of many minds." Her mouth turned down. "If I were in their position, I'd have my mindshields up. The mellyck is known for screaming nasty things—undermining confidence and morale."

He tipped her face up and kissed her. She tasted sweeter than anything ever had. Every single time it was better, just as with their loving. Every time the bond between them strengthened, she reached inside him with her caring and stirred his life into a new shape.

He broke the kiss to speak. "We now have a deadline. It won't take more than a week for the Hollys to return."

"No," she said, her gaze unwavering. "We'll need to be prepared to demand a new trial for you, and set in motion retrieving your estate, and request a panel of judges—"

"We need to plan the upset of Bucus T'Elder, Captain of the Council. Quick and final. As Ship says, consider several options."

Her hands curled over his shoulders and squeezed. "Legally and publicly and right." She searched his face. From the shadow that crossed her own, he guessed she hadn't found what she'd wanted. She stood. "Samba, you will come with me. I want to talk to you."

Samba growled and whizzed her saucer a centimeter over Ailim's head. Ailim didn't flicker an eyelash at the angry cat, but turned elegantly on her heel and began lecturing. "There are reasons for rules—and laws. . . ." Her voice was cut off by the thick outer doors of his quarters.

She was dedicated to Celtan law. Ruis's heart stumbled and he wiped his palms on his trous. He should feel triumphant that she intended to stay with him, wouldn't deny him to others as her lover. But they hadn't spoken of many things. They hadn't talked of her danger, his rising fear for her and his equally burgeoning emotional demand for vengeance against his uncle—preferably with his own hands. His heart picked up beat. Somehow there must be a way he could have it all.

"Ship," he said, "show me the brig."

*Ailim convinced Ruis to stay safe in the Ship and work on* the "peeper" while she walked home. As she had anticipated, her attempt to reach either of the Holly brothers mentally had been futile. The last she'd seen of them on Ship's holo, they plodded along the narrow strip of land between the mountains and the boghole.

She shivered in the cold autumn dawn and sped her pace until she passed through the greeniron gates and down the drive to her home.

D'SilverFir Residence's round red towers picked up the rosy light of dawn and seemed to glow with peace and solidity. Ailim let out a quivering sigh. The castle was safe, ruddy towers capped with copper aged green, sitting whole on the small island, with the blue lake waters lapping around it.

She blinked away sudden tears. She'd never wanted to give the estate up, but at the time it seemed the only way out of the Family's gilt problems. If she kept the Family in line for six months, the loan would be permanent and the estate forever safe.

The wind nipped color into her cheeks, and she strode across the drawbridge, probing the inhabitants with her mind. Everyone was asleep, while the Residence initiated the daily housekeeping spells. Far too few to maintain the estate properly.

If Bucus Elder had been encouraging Menzie to be a spendthrift for years, no wonder the Family lacked gilt. Ailim's mother and Mother Sire would never have questioned the propriety of Menzie's expenditures, or her loyalty. Ailim's boot heels snapped against the stone drawbridge, the great doors burst open at the push of her mind. When she entered the Greathall, a swirl of autumn leaves joined her.

She swept up the stairs and to Menzie's rooms. The door was unlocked. Ailim knocked perfunctorily and entered. Fetid air hit her. With a snap of her fingers and a Word, the drapes before the paned window clicked aside and the windows opened to fresh air. Another gesture sucked the odor from the room.

Menzie sat up and squealed. "You have no right, Ailim D'SilverFir, none, to—"

"Menzie SilverFir Cohosh. Your disloyal actions have brought shame upon this GrandHouse and have endangered the Family and the Residence. You have three minutes to defend yourself before I order your belongings packed and your transfer to the D'SilverFir Farm on the Ruby Ananda River." Ailim folded her hands at her waist and donned her judge's impassivity.

"You can't—"

"I will. What I can't do is afford any more actions on your part that could ruin the Family."

Menzie gaped. "I don't know what you're talking about!"

"Look at yourself, your torn clothes, the lack of your evil amulet! Residence?"

"Here, D'SilverFir."

"Replay any scrys you have of Menzie SilverFir last night."

A holo scry flickered on, showing Menzie clutching her amulet and slipping into the twilight. Unlike the holo screen of the Ship, the scry projected sound. "Throw the amulet into the earth fault. Throw the amulet into the earth fault. Return to the Residence," Menzie muttered.

The holo changed viewpoints, then the grid Ailim had watched showed up. The scry went dark, then flickered as Menzie staggered back to the Residence in full night, clothes ripped and caked with dirt, spittle flecking her lips, the whites of her eyes showing around large pupils. She wrung her hands. Again she muttered at every step, "I tried, sweet lover. I tried. The amulet into the fault, the bitch, too." Ailim flinched inwardly. "I tried. Your sextoy tried. Back to the Residence. Await the tremors. . . ."

It wasn't enough for evidence against Bucus T'Elder! Ailim grit her teeth. Menzie hadn't named him.

"Residence, was there any damage to the foundations or any part of the Residence because of the earth tremors triggered by Menzie's amulet?"

"None, GrandLady. It is evident you prevented the tragedy."

Menzie started keening. "I didn't do it. No! I couldn't have! Not me!" She swung her head to fix a stare on Ailim, her eyes feral. "Lies, you made that up. You concocted a plot." She began screaming again.

"Silence spell!" Ailim ordered. Menzie wouldn't be able to speak. "Listen. Who do you think the NobleCouncil will believe, a properly dated Residence scry and the word of a SupremeJudge, or a member of the Family who's been known to spread spiteful gossip, who refused to give up a bane that harmed the Family, who went so far as to challenge the confirmed head of the household after swearing loyalty? Donax will support me on this." Since he was still in bed with Cona, Ailim felt he'd shown what he wanted. "As will the D'SilverFir Heir, Caltha. So you think, and decide what you want to do. Consider this: Your lover let you set a trap that might have resulted in your own death."

With a slash of the hand, Ailim said, "Release Spell."

Menzie only gabbled, "He would not abandon me. He will support me."

Ailim raised her brows. "Oh, will he? He's married, so he violated that oath, too. You're the only witness that he wants D'SilverFir for his own?" She snapped her teeth shut before she said what she really thought about the stupid, mean woman. "I will have a Healer attend you."

"Yes, yes!"

"Think of who owns your loyalty. Think of what you have done to this Residence *for years* in your greed and your lust. When you're stronger, I will have a certified

Truth-Verifier question you. Until then you are confined to this room and allowed no visitors."

"What about my daughter, my Cona!" Menzie wept.

"Your Cona is in the first flush of binding Donax Reed to her sexually. You think she will have time for you?" Ailim shouldn't have said it, but her temper had taken far too much strain. Menzie's gaze darted left and right, and she crept back into the corner of her bed to huddle.

"I will accompany Cona if she wishes to see you." Ailim turned on her heel and left—anger singing in her veins, energy flowing through her.

*S*napping a tiny power connection into place, Ruis stood back from the peeper as it began repairing itself. He'd "graduated" to working on delicate and complex apparatus.

"Calling crew," said the Ship. "Please report to the Captain's Quarters."

Ruis's eyebrows rose. "Why do I need Samba?"

"The peeper will be finished with its self-restoration by the time it is ready to be launched."

"Really?"

"Estimated time to launch is five Celtan minutes."

Samba zoomed in, nose lifted. *I'm here!*

Ruis carefully set the peeper, a cam as big as Samba's head, on the saucer. "If you take this to the northwest lifepod cannon, you can watch it launch."

Her eyes grew big. *Me? Me watch it launch?*

"Anticipated effect on the crew is her fur standing on end," Ship said.

Samba's tongue darted out to touch her nose as she considered it. *New adventure. I'll take now!* Out she flew.

Ruis flexed the stiffness from his shoulders and grinned. "She's very handy to have around."

"She is not losing weight," Ship grumbled.

Ruis shrugged and surveyed the workroom. Tidy and with only two other projects on the benches, the ambiance pleased him.

His gaze lodged on the multitool that he'd carried the night before during his visit to T'Elder Residence and he frowned. The little device had affected Ailim's Flair. Whistling, he called up diagrams of the multitool and began to dismantle it, carefully noting where each piece fit.

"Peeper launched!" Ship said, drawing Ruis from his labor.

"Holo screen, please!" He was just in time to see a final glimmer disappearing into the deep blue of the Celtan sky.

"Correct trajectory and orbit of the peeper will be achieved in two Celtan minutes."

"Fine," Ruis said absently, more interested in peering at the core of the tool. The centerpiece looked like a huge model of an atom—about the size of a boy's marble—with spinning nucleus and an orbiting electron or two. It glowed green. "Ship, tell me about this object and speculate as to whether and how it could depress Flair."

"One moment, please. De-archiving material regarding the gyro atom to analyze for hypotheses."

While he waited he thought of the DepressFlair bracelet that had driven Shade to cut his own hand off. As far as Ruis knew, the bracelets consisted of layers of thin metal irradiated with Flair that disrupted the use of psi by those who wore them.

Ruis studied the buzzing gyro-atom. It must operate by an entirely different set of rules. His heart started thumping fast. Ailim cherished being with him because he negated her Flair which in turn expanded her physical senses. What if he could give her a gift she could wear whenever she wanted?

Moving closer, he examined the little device. He rubbed his hands. He couldn't get the object that small, not on his first attempt, but it was a pretty thing and he bet he could craft a pendant the size of a walnut she could wear.

He'd encase the lovely thing in a crystal. He could inset a button in the back so she could regulate the field, too. Ruis could do no better than follow T'Ash's—the master jeweler's—design, so he gave Ship the dimensions he needed and ordered it to carve him a heart.

When the gyro-atom was inserted into the crystal, the heart would glow and sparkle with energy. It would make the T'Birch emeralds look like cheap glass. Ruis grinned.

He shook his head at the irony. He'd stolen T'Ash's HeartGift, a necklace the GreatLord had designed to attract his HeartMate. Ruis's smile died and his fingers curled into fists. He'd be upset if someone stole his gift to his lady.

HeartGift and HeartMates. He was a Null—never to know what those words truly meant. He could put all his skill and talent and heart into that gift and it would still fall short of a HeartGift that enticed and bonded. Regret coated his thoughts at never being able to reach any standard by which other people of his class were measured.

*Ping!* "The peeper is deployed and working at optimum capacity. Holo screen initiated to your right."

Ruis glanced up. The Holly brothers appeared rough and tattered already. Ruis winced.

He looked around his workroom and sighed. Here he was, skilled and successful. He had a lover who melted his bones and fused his mind, an affectionate Fam who always amused. Why did he envy the Hollys?

Because their achievements were based on solid ground, and Ruis's own were built on shifting sand that could be lost at a word from them that he still lived in Druida.

# Seventeen

❤

'The next morning Ailim hurried to the Ship an hour before she was due at JudgmentGrove. Samba had slunk into Ailim's bedchamber the night before, sulky because Ruis had ordered the Ship to restrict her saucer flying within *Nuada's Sword* unless it was a dire emergency. Apparently there were force-fields on Samba's exits that upended her saucer. Ailim thought the cat had been dumped four or five times.

Samba had dropped a little note written in Ruis's spiky pen-manship informing Ailim that the "peeper" was operational and the Hollys were alive and traveling southwest. Waiting to see what had happened to them, trying to figure out how to help, had preyed on her mind, distracting her from her Family problems so that she'd simply ushered an apprentice third-level Healer into Menzie's room after handing the youngster written instructions.

Primrose had acted foolish for a good quarter septhour before Samba deigned to play with the puppy. Ailim had watched them in silent contentment until her thoughts turned to her love for Ruis and their dark future. Then her eyes had stung.

When she neared the Captain's Quarters on *Nuada's Sword*, the doors parted and she ran into Ruis's den. He was there, sitting in the Captain's Chair as Samba napped on one side of the desk.

The holo screen stretched from ceiling to floor. Holm and

Tinnc Holly appeared nearly life-sized. Digging her feet into the carpet, Ailim stopped abruptly.

"The Hollys look terrible!" she said.

"Yes, Holm and Tinne look bad," Ruis said.

Ailim shot a glance at Ruis and knew he felt as bad about the Hollys as she did herself. It relieved her.

"I never truly wished Holm harm," he said, rising.

She went into his arms, closed her eyes at the love that shivered through her at his touch. She tried to keep her mind on the topic. "Of course you didn't plan to harm them."

"But it happened." His warm breath touched the top of her head.

"Yes, we can't change that. We can only go forward. Together."

His body rippled against hers. "Together? It would be best for you—"

She stepped back so she could gaze up at him. "I won't let you face this alone."

He set his fingers in her hair and slid them down her tresses. Her braids unraveled. "Look what I do to you."

She took one of his hands and placed it on her breast where her heart quickened and her nipple hardened. "Feel what you do to me."

A slow smile curved his lips. "That doesn't help me deny myself. I'm a very selfish person."

Two blond heads caught the corner of her eye. "No time for loving now," she said regretfully. "The Hollys are breaking camp and moving out." She scowled at the green-gray coating of their clothes. "Both of them look as if they fell into the bog!"

Ruis's hand dropped from her breast. He turned to watch the silent show. "Yes. There's strain between them, too. Something serious happened."

"I see what you mean." Her eyebrows lowered. "Even relationships have—rules. Obviously the parameters they'd formed as brothers before this adventure have changed or are in flux. They look stiff."

Ruis tipped her face to his with a finger. He pressed a kiss on her that made her knees weaken. "Holm Holly wouldn't cherish you the way I do."

She'd forgotten his prickly jealousy of Holm. "No," she agreed.

The tension in his body relaxed a bit. "Holly has all the advantages of the highest of nobles."

"Holly is lost in the wilds of Celta," she pointed out.

Ruis flashed a real grin. "It will do him good."

Ailim took hold of Ruis's wrist and tilted it to see his watch. "I have to go or be late for JudgmentGrove."

Ruis brushed her forehead with a kiss. "I'll see you this evening. We need to plot strategy to overturn Bucus." His smile showed a lot of teeth. Ruis adopted a stance every bit as arrogant as any Holly.

"Yes." She searched his face. "We'll do this together, right? Work on ways of undermining his authority and gather evidence against him." She made a face. "I must spend more time at gatherings, cultivating alliances."

"I can take a cam from the Ship and record the evidence in the cottage."

Ailim pushed her hands through her hair. "I don't know if that will be admissible evidence—" When she saw his jaw clench, she hurried on "—but it can't hurt."

Ship hummed. "We can translate the images from our cam and transmit them to all the other Residence computers—ah, ResidenceLibraries—and the PublicLibrary."

"It would be better in JudgmentGrove if the Ship was a disinterested party." She shook her head. "Ship is completely biased in your favor."

He caught her hands and lifted them to his lips, skimming kisses over her fingers. "As you are?"

"As I am." A smile tugged from her at his demand for assurance, even as a curl of heat unfurled deep within her. How she wished she could spend the day with Ruis—in his bed, or the Greensward, or anywhere!

She pulled her hands from him. "I have a healer with Menzie and an appointment for a Truth-Verifier next week when she's better. Since I'm partial toward you, and against Menzie, I must make sure not to prompt her. With care and a little time we will get the whole story from her about the amulet." Ailim's smile turned wry. "More expenses, which means I have to get to JudgmentGrove and earn my pay."

Ruis walked with her to the portal slightly south of the one in line with JudgmentGrove. "This morning I rewarded Tal the mole with plenty of earthworms *and* I ordered repairs on your corridor between the HouseHeart and D'SilverFir Residence."

Admiration and a touch of awe surged inside her. "Be careful, be very, very careful."

He just smiled down at her and touched a finger to her lips, pressed and released. "The machines aren't large. They trundled to your corridor's service entrance last night." He tilted his head back toward the Captain's Quarter's and his den. "I have a holo screen running on the progress. It's slow, but thorough. The first layer of outer sheathing is being laid. With a couple more, there's no doubt the corridor can be stabilized."

All the energy the D'SilverFir spent maintaining the hall could go to more mundane spells. She licked her lips and forced the real question out. "So the corridor will be secure? Without any more spells?"

He touched her eyelids and his finger came away wet. "You humble me with your gratitude."

"You aren't really a very arrogant man."

"No? When I think I'm better than the nobles, more honorable? That I can steal for my own purposes and not get caught?"

Ailim embraced him. "You are as honorable as the best noble, and more honorable than many." Lifting her face, she examined him as she did every time they met, trying to see behind his eyes at the man beneath, and how he was changing.

He pressed her hand on his chest flat, and she felt his steady heartbeat. "I had no reason to live except for my little Earth machines, and even that passion wasn't enough to overcome my resentment and anger, not then." His watch chimed and he glanced down at it. "I'm working with Shade at FirstGrove this morning."

"Are you sure?"

"He, too, deserves a chance to fulfil his potential as a man."

Her brows dipped. He caught her close and brought her against him, and the sensation of his hard male body, a body that satisfied her momentarily but left her aching for more, wiped every thought from her mind.

*A*s the week wore on, things proceeded with near normality, but Ailim felt she was living in an altered reality and definitely on borrowed time. It was a toss-up what would expose them first—the Hollys' return, Zanth's nosing around, Samba's prowling, or the rumors that streaks of light and booming came from *Nuada's Sword*.

Every night she'd go to the Ship with Primrose. She and Ruis would study old records, have Ship integrate with other noble Residences, and ask each to review and submit any archived memories they had about Bucus Elder's accession to the T'Elder title. There was precious little. Still, she worked hard to compile an air-tight case against Bucus.

Now and again, Ailim would arrive at the Ship late and alone, having attended a noble gathering. Subtly she tried to widen the breach of doubt that many felt for T'Elder. She wove a complex web of alliances, expected of any head of a Family. But this web was to trap T'Elder, and on behalf of Ruis more than the D'SilverFirs. She introduced Caltha, and helped her and her spouse make the transition to being integral to noble society.

At the Ship most of the time Ruis and Ailim worked in grim silence, but the loving through the nights seared Ailim's soul. Ruis would be sensitive and tender, or so wild, needy and demanding that orgasms shuddered through her again and again until she broke free of any constraint and became a being of pure sensation.

Ailim knew Ruis tried to bind her to him physically and emotionally, but the true binding was to her heart, giving her love as no one else in her life had.

At the end of the work week they'd compiled enough information to tentatively prove Ruis *had* been confirmed in the title and estate. The Elder Family had confirmed him as the next GreatLord and sworn loyalty to him. Bucus convinced the other Family members to all break their oaths when Ruis's Nullness grew evident. Bucus, by breaking his oath and covering it up, violated the most fundamental law of Celta.

"Proof!" Ruis shouted in exultation. He shoved back from the office desk and stretched. "Proof!" His hands fisted and his face grew hawkish. "Oh, yes, Bucus, we've got you now!"

Deep foreboding infused Ailim. She looked at the stack of papyrus. It would take a month or two to build a solidly undeniable case against the Captain of the Council. A month they didn't have.

The Holly brothers had survived the boghole and the mellyck, to the great relief of Ruis and Ailim.

"Ruis—"

He picked her up and spun her around, whooping. Samba trotted over from watching *History of Cats*. "Prrrrrrrrr-oooooph!" she purred, stropping Ruis's legs. *I am Ship's Cat. I am GreatLord Fam, too, now.* She lifted a regal paw. *I always knew.*

Ruis flung back his head and laughed. Then slid Ailim down his body, his eyes darkening. "I am legally T'Elder. Your match in status and wealth." He snorted. "Knowing Bucus, T'Elder has *more* wealth than D'SilverFir."

"That wouldn't be hard," Ailim said, suppressing a shiver.

"I can clear myself and court you."

"Let's do this right." Fear chilled her bones. "I'd rather do this right and *final* and have you, than sloppily and quickly and lose you. Can't you consider leaving Druida for a little while?"

His expression hardened. "Run? As I've run all my life? No." He cut the air with his hand. "No. I will get my uncle and I'll get him soon!"

He gestured again, then lifted his hands to study them, as if seeing the scars. In his eyes old pain echoed and Ailim flinched. She couldn't deny he'd been hurt badly, badly enough to crave vengeance, but she'd hoped he'd risen above that. She'd sensed he carried a destructive anger, but she had been sure that he was overcoming it. Now she didn't know.

"You've told me time and again that you weren't interested in vengeance against your uncle," she whispered.

He sent her a fulminating stare. His entire face tightened—the noble bone structure evident. A sinking feeling settled in her stomach.

"Because of several things. First, I've always been on the run, with hardly any time to stop, think, or plan." He raised his index finger. "Next, I had no power. All of my life the balance of power was in his hands—my life was in his hands. He wanted me dead—still wants me dead, but he got me banished."

Ailim's lips felt stiff. "You allowed yourself to be caught and banished because of your own actions."

Fury twisted his face, then he smoothed it out, jerked a nod. "Right, as always, SupremeJudge. My anger at my circumstances and the injustice of my life scoured me like acid. It blinded me. Do you know, Ailim, my lover, that you were the first person to ever treat me with kindness?"

"I know—"

"Shade learns from me. Sometimes I think he trusts me, sometimes not. Just when I think his mind and body are Healing, he gets a mad glint in his eyes. Shade doesn't welcome my touch, and when he stays for my company we walk so my Null field doesn't bother him as much. So it's true that I let myself be angry, that I acted on that anger." He shook his head. "The little records we have about Nulls is that they went mad or committed suicide. My anger was preferable." His chest expanded in a deep breath and his lips moved as he held the inhalation, counting, then exhaled to another count.

Ailim knew all about anger-management techniques—ones she used, and ones she saw people use in her JudgmentGrove every day. She wanted to go to him, but didn't know if he'd welcome her touch.

"Bucus had control of the Elder Family. He had the title and the gilt, and later even became Captain of the NobleCouncil. Captain." Ruis barked a laugh. "I had nothing and no one. That isn't true anymore. I have Samba, my Fam, I have the Ship. And I have a beautiful, Flaired noblewoman who has been willing to fight for me since the moment we met." His eyes looked bright as he reached for her.

Samba sniffed and stalked away.

Ailim grabbed him close. Then he was kissing her with fierce hunger—a need she sensed was as deep or deeper than his anger. Their joining was fast and turbulent and shatteringly satisfying.

They panted together. "Forbidden and dangerous loving is so incredible," Ailim said, "but I wish it was open and safe to make love to you anywhere, anytime."

"You worry too much."

"There's a lot to worry about. We can't escape discovery for long."

"You haven't heard the latest update. The Holly brothers have reached Lake Meraj," Ruis said.

They rolled apart.

"Thank the Lady and Lord!" Ailim said.

Ruis stood and pulled up his trous. His expression still brooded. "They'll be back in Druida in an eightday." He wrenched at the waist tab until it was tight. When he looked at her, his determination was set like armourcrete. "I won't run. And Bucus will pay. Much as I don't want to continue this discussion, much as I would like to ignore it or let it rest, or ride it out, I think you need to hear what I have to say. You asked why I didn't move against my uncle before, I gave you some good reasons." He shook his head and smiled and for an instant humor moved in his eyes. "We were speaking about power. Lord and Lady knows that what we generate between us is nothing but pure power. You have power over me. You always have."

Ailim rose stiffly. "I would never betray you."

"I know that, and it comes of your own sense of honor as a lady as much as it does your indignation at injustice. But I like hearing the words." He swept a hand around him. "No one can deny I have power now."

All the pleasure from their lovemaking drained from Ailim. She shook out her skirts. "That's correct. Do you plan on kidnaping Bucus and firing him off in an escape pod to the 271 Range?"

Ruis's lips curled. "And let it hit the crags of ZWZ? A very tempting idea. But there isn't another lifepod ready. Ship lured the Hollys to the only viable escapepod. I'll try hard to wait for you to work within the law."

He paced the den, "But I'm impatient. I didn't know before that Bucus had actually stolen my birthright. I thought it had been a Family decision, done legally and lawfully." The flames of injustice burned in him. "Bucus is evil. He has no honor. He'll do anything to gain glory or gilt or power. It isn't right that he's allowed to hold a title or public office. That he's allowed to pursue his plans at the cost of my lands and estate and yours. It isn't right that he goes free."

"And you stay trapped," Ailim ended quietly, setting her hands in their opposite sleeves cupping her elbows.

Ruis's gaze pierced her. "My life has been miserable. Much of that I've brought on myself, but most . . ." His tone turned low and deadly, matching the lithe movement of his body. "Most of my life was miserable because of one man. One man who used the system to ensure my life was as wretched as he could possibly make it. Bucus *must* pay. Soon. I'll give you until the end of next week to bring him to justice. Then I'll act."

"I don't like ultimatums. And I don't like how this predicament is changing you. You're bitter."

He laughed. "I've always been bitter. When I'm here, or with you, or even with Samba, I can put it aside."

She tilted her head. "I recall you told me the Ship crafted a psychological anger management program."

"That was before I knew."

*T*he next dawn Ruis jogged through the dead grass of the paths and parks on the way to JudgmentGrove, not heeding Samba's puffing whines. After experimentation, Ruis had found a large oak tree branch where he could lay, seeing and hearing Ailim well, even if her bailiff invoked the weathershield. Ruis only had to climb and settle himself in the oak just outside the sacred circle before anyone else arrived at JudgmentGrove.

Ailim hadn't come to him the night before. In the evening she'd left a message that the Hollys had called for allies to attend a ritual to seek their lost sons. Later, Ship had relayed that T'Holly had called in his nephew, Straif Blackthorn—GrandLord T'Blackthorn of the FirstFamilies, the noted tracker, to find Holm and Tinne.

That Straif Blackthorn would soon be trailing his cuzes disturbed Ruis. Blackthorn had great Flair, but how much would his psi talent tell him? How much of Ruis's Nullness would affect the Hollys's route?

Ailim hadn't come to him. No loving arms had cradled him last night. No comforting words had been whispered in his ears. No sensual woman had wrapped around him in ecstasy. They'd said goodbye the previous morning with bitterness between them, and Ruis hated that.

He pulled his cowl low and kept his head ducked to stop it from whisking away in the cold autumn wind. His hands were protected by the light-bending gloves and his boots were grass-stained and mud-splattered for camouflage. The fierce autumnal winds had started, and every step was a struggle to keep the light-bending cloak hiding him. Lately he hadn't been out in the day. Danger seemed to swarm around him.

He needed to see Ailim. To talk with her. He laughed inwardly at his lie. He needed to look into her clear eyes. He needed her to touch him. He was in deep trouble. Heart trouble that could crush him.

At JudgmentGrove he hefted himself up into the oak, careful not to tear his cloak. With grumbling and the jingling of her collar, Samba followed him up, climbing a bit further so she was higher than he—a sop to her pride. She'd catnap until something snared her curiosity, then she'd jump from tree to tree until she was several meters away and finally descend to the Grove to poke her nose into whatever interested her. He scanned the Grove once more before letting himself fall into pleasant fantasies of being with Ailim.

When the breeze wafted her voice to his ears, he jerked awake, sending his gaze questing for her. Occasionally she'd walk the JudgmentGrove before her official day began speaking with visitors, nobles and commoners alike, as she did now.

Ruis glanced at his watch. A half-septhour before JudgmentGrove began. He looked up to find her talking to Bucus. *NO!* His knuckles tightened whitely.

Bucus and Ailim were intent on their conversation. Bucus held his head at a mocking angle, with raised eyebrows, while Ailim leaned toward him. She pressed papyrus sheets into his hands, pivoted on her heel, and walked to her tower.

Bucus's sneer changed into a scowl as he read the papyrus and crumpled them, shoving the wad in his pocket.

He examined the Grove with narrowed eyes, then stalked away.

What had Ailim given him? Ruis cursed himself again for their argument, torn between wanting vengeance and wanting Ailim. Until now, Ailim had been circumspect in her investigations, but he must have pushed her to move more quickly and with less caution. What had been on the document? Instinctively Ruis sensed that it concerned Bucus and the SilverFir Family and wouldn't draw attention to Ruis. He thumped a fist on the wide branch beside him.

Tension bathed him and he scrutinized everyone. The sacred circle was drawn and closed, the weathershield raised, the opening blessing invoked. A stocky figure in drab brown caught Ruis's attention. The man looked familiar. As he wandered the edge of JudgmentGrove, Ruis strained to place him.

Ruis kept watch all morning, his gaze returning time and again to the man in brown. It grated Ruis that his honed survival skills had faded.

The last case before break was called. "Return to the People of Celta and the Maidens of Saille against Antenn Moss, juvenile," Yeldoc announced.

Ruis jolted. Antenn Moss, Shade's brother. Ailim's concentration was focused on the people before her. Her body language showed how important this case was to her.

Ailim looked at the boy and sighed. "Antenn Moss," she said, disappointed to see him again. She'd failed the boy. She hoped Ruis was succeeding with Shade.

Antenn flushed. He'd wrapped most of his cloak around his young, scruffy tomcat.

The Prosecutor coughed. "The apprenticeship of Antenn to the Turmerics did not succeed. There was a—personality clash regarding the cat—Pinky." The Prosecutor shrugged.

Ailim raised her eyebrows. Pinky had a ratty ear and scratches on his nose, no doubt taking after Zanth. She scrutinized Antenn. His mouth set stubbornly. It wouldn't do to separate the cat from the boy.

"I have further results of Antenn's Testing by T'Ash. Witnessed and confirmed by Mitchella Clover," Danith D'Ash said, gesturing to a stunning and voluptuous redheaded woman who'd accompanied D'Ash to the center clearing. D'Ash ran up the steps to the stage and laid papyrus onto the desk with a flourish, then joined the other woman.

Ailim flipped through the documents and her spirits lifted. When she looked up, she smiled, knowing her relief was nothing compared to Antenn's giddiness. The boy relaxed his tight grip on the cat.

"An impressive Testing in architecture, Antenn. In sight of this new information, the Grove believes the previous placement with the Turmerics to be faulty. T'Ash states that he has forwarded a request for apprenticeship to GrandLord Cang Zhu."

The crowd chattered. D'Ash beamed, proof to all that a person could rise from commoner to GrandHouse through sheer Flair.

Ailim squared the papyrus and inserted them in a flexifile. "The Grove will augment T'Ash's request for an apprenticeship to Cang Zhu. I do not anticipate any problems with your new apprenticeship." Best to give a warning, though. She narrowed her eyes. "I do not wish to see you in JudgmentGrove again."

Again Antenn flushed and shook his head.

Ailim folded her hands. "The Turmerics had trouble with Pinky." The cat hissed at her. "The Cang Zhus might also have issues with the cat. Therefore, I do not think it wise for you to live with them during your training." She scanned JudgmentGrove, stilled for a moment when she sensed a blankness in an oak tree outside the circle. Ruis. Another lost soul that might be saved. With a jerk, she brought her mind back to work. "The Grove notes that the boy still needs a proper home."

People shifted on their blankets and shuffled their feet around her. No one met her eyes.

"T'Ash . . ." D'Ash started hesitantly.

"Fligger," Antenn swore. He and the Prosecutor shared an uneasy glance.

"I know T'Ash is an expert on Downwind boys," Ailim said smoothly. "But in this instance, I believe I would prefer another home, perhaps one with another boy his own age, or an extended family—"

"Mitchella!" D'Ash cried.

The voluptuous redhead beside D'Ash started.

"You can take him." D'Ash then addressed Ailim. "The Clovers are one of the few large families of Celta. There are several boys and girls in a wide range of ages. Mitchella always wanted to be a mother—"

"Fligger," Antenn said.

"Not this way, Danith," the woman named Mitchella said. She met Ailim's eyes, then lowered her gaze.

Ailim studied the boy and the woman. SilverFir had no matchmaking genes, but Ailim had been a judge long enough to weigh character. Though the solution sounded odd, some meshing of the auras of the lonely young boy and the woman—who Ailim realized was sterile, an awful fate—seemed right. Ailim saw clearly they could help each other and live together as family.

"If Mitchella Clover would accept the boy, Antenn Moss, into her home, the Grove would grant the placement," Ailim said, avoiding GentleLady Clover's gaze.

Antenn put Pinky down and they walked to Mitchella Clover. Antenn's brown hair stuck out in clumps all over his head. "You don't want me, either. Know guy—" He stopped, struggling to correct his Downwind shortspeech. "I can work hard, as apprentice and more. The man who runs one of T'Ash's Downwind Centers will trade bed for work." He darted a glance full of trepidation at Ailim. He didn't like that she could read him.

Ailim sighed. "If you will give me the name of the—"

"No. He comes with me." Mitchella stiffened her spine, causing her bosom to lift. Men caught their breaths.

Antenn eyed her figure. "What a great mother."

"I'm not your mother. You can call me Auntie Mitchella, like my other ten nephews."

"Yeah. I can do that."

She looked the boy up and down. Then held out a hand. He put his own into hers. "Yeah."

Ailim picked up her gavel and banged it. "Noon recess is called. Yeldoc, you may dismiss the weathershield and sacred circle."

Mitchella Clover and her new ward strolled in the direction of middle-class Druida, their cloaks billowing in the wind. They had dropped hands, but were talking. Their new

life might not be easy on them, but Ailim believed it could
work.

Ailim's lips curved in a gentle smile that tangled Ruis's
emotions as she watched Antenn and Mitchella Clover.
Then Ailim glanced at D'Ash, who dipped her head. Ailim
frowned and Ruis knew they mindspoke. Ailim rose from
her desk to meet a hurrying D'Ash near the front of the
stage.

"Die!" A silver dagger flashed to Ailim, then sparked
blue as it hit a protective shield. She fell from the impact.

"Bind!" Yeldoc ordered, pointing his staff at the assassin.
The man struggled.

Ruis gripped the branch to swing down, blinded with fear
and fury.

Samba lit on his back. Her weight forced air from his
lungs. He panted to get breath back. "Grrrrrrr," he managed.

His Fam flexed her claws, pricking him through his cloak
and tunic. "Samba!" he hissed, enraged.

*Stop! Think! I go see!* Samba leapt to the ground.

"T'Ash!" cried Danith D'Ash.

By the time his vision cleared, T'Ash had 'ported to the
stage. He grabbed his HeartMate and held her close, then
scanned Ailim.

Ruis gasped, still trying to inhale a lungful of air. Tremors ran up and down his body. He set his jaw. If the man
had been anyone but T'Ash, he'd have run to Ailim. A
moan of anguish at his helplessness tore from his chest.
Always outside, and Ailim would come second for T'Ash,
not first. Ruis was the only one who put Ailim first.

With a stride T'Ash reached the desk and slapped a palm
on it. "T'Heather!" he roared for the best Healer on Celta.
Enough Flair circled T'Ash that Ruis could see it. Much of
the crowd scattered.

GreatLord T'Heather materialized on the desk, bag in
hand. A disapproving frown crossed his broad farmer's
face. "Decorum, T'Ash. Not on such a blessed desk." Healers were used to emergency summonings. He hopped down
and stumped to D'Ash, put down his bag, and checked her.

"Desk's stationary. Whole JudgmentGrove needs puri-
fying." T'Ash reverted to his childhood Downwind short-

speech. " 'Cause of this filth." He strode to the trembling assassin, grabbed his shirt in one hand, lifted, and shook him. The culprit soiled himself.

Ruis stared at the prisoner, willing his own memory to jog loose.

"Why did you attack?" T'Ash demanded.

"Ruis Elder hired me!" the man screamed.

Ruis's blood turned to ice. He should have anticipated this. Another lie from Bucus. But he remembered the assassin now. The man had hunted Ruis in his old apartment, wearing Bucus's colors. Sloegin with the gambling problem.

Ruis stared at Ailim. She was looking in his direction, concern on her face.

"Ruis Elder, the thief?" T'Ash asked. "Odd problem. But I'm thinking Elders are a bad lot."

"It was the Null!"

T'Ash plunked the man down, touched something on the man's head. Sparks flew, the criminal screamed. Blood poured from his mouth. He sagged and died.

T'Ash stared down at him. "Mindblock band with destruct spell. Great Flair, not Null. Who knows? Dead guy, now." Scowling, he turned back to T'Heather, who ran Healing hands over Ailim.

Bile coated the back of Ruis's throat. Useless. Again. Unable to protect his woman because he skulked in a tree. Unable to defend himself or clear the new calumnies against his name.

Yeldoc's nose wrinkled as he stared down at the corpse. With a wave of his staff, he banished the body to a DeathGrove. Another pass of his staff encompassed the loiterers. "Move along. JudgmentGrove is closed. I'll have a statement for the newsheets in a septhour."

"Yeldoc, the Ruis Elder case was before my time. There's no reason for Ruis Elder to harm me. The attacker wore a mindblock but he sounded as if he lied. Make sure that's clear to the newsheets," Ailim said. "Also, Yeldoc, contact JudgementGrove's Chief Investigator GrandLady Lady-Mantle and ensure she finds the truth of this whole business." She gripped the desk as if she had trouble standing.

There was no reason to say that he'd hired the attacker

except to vilify his name, Ruis thought. No reason except
to load more crimes on him, to put barriers in his way. The
aftermath of anger, fear and shock churned inside him,
slicking him with cold sweat.

Samba streaked across the stage and ducked under
Ailim's robes. No one seemed to notice. Ailim stiffened.

T'Heather observed her. "I'll give you a restorative potion."

Ailim's trembling wave indicated her Chambers tower.
"There."

"Very well." T'Heather picked her up and carried her to
the square building. Samba was nowhere in sight. Yeldoc
hurried to open the door for them. T'Ash and D'Ash followed.

The door banged shut.

Ruis set his forehead on his arm and closed his eyes. She
was safe! For now. But he knew who'd ordered the murder
attempt and blamed him. Whether Bucus expected the assault to succeed or not, he'd sent Ailim a warning not to
mix in his affairs. Not to challenge the Captain of the Council. A slow and mighty burning began in the core of Ruis's
bones, gathering force. This anger, when it burst, would not
be denied.

The last stragglers crunched away through blowing dead
leaves, gossiping.

Samba reached the bottom of his tree. *Ailim 'ports to
Landing Grove as soon as T'Heather Healer goes.*

Ruis set his jaw. His heartbeat still thundered. "She's all
right?" he croaked.

Samba set her claws in the tree trunk and stretched, then
sharpened her claws. *You saw. Grove shield stopped knife.
She NOT hurt. No blood.*

Ruis jumped from the tree and ran to the Ship, burning
off the energy of his fear. All he could think of was getting
his hands on Ailim again, celebrating life with her after a
brush with death as he'd done before. All too often.

Rage simmered through him until his mind spun with
what he wanted, needed to do. Bucus must be removed.
Now.

He paced the corridor of the Ship inside the portal nearest

to JudgmentGrove. The wind howled outside. Half a sept-hour later Ailim stumbled into his arms.

He held her while she trembled and sobbed and freed her emotions. Stroking her hair, he murmured soothing words, and deep tenderness pervaded him. She'd come to him.

Because he wanted to ravish, to take her hard and fast and deep, like the last time they came together, he strapped down his wildness and set a gentle, cherishing pace.

He needed to savor every moment of their loving, so he slowed as he carried her to his quarters. His heart still stuttered with fear that he'd almost lost her. He'd barely begun to know her, to enjoy her, to love her. To have lost her now was inconceivable. Even with Samba and the Ship, he wasn't complete. Only Ailim fulfilled his innermost needs.

She pressed her face against him, for protection or comfort, he didn't know, only that he wanted to give her everything.

"That fliggering assassin he—you—" Ruis couldn't go on.

She rubbed her head against his chest. "I know you had nothing to do with it. I'll make sure you're cleared."

"That's not as important as the attack on you!"

"It's happened before. The desk has a shield, so does the stage, and so do I. Bailiffs add moving shields when JudgmentGrove is in session. Yeldoc isn't only there to keep order, but to guard."

"When before?" Ruis croaked, cradling her closer.

Ailim sighed. "A long time ago in a southern village. They'll find out who he is and what grudge he had against us."

"His name is Sloegin and he worked for Bucus. He had a gambling problem." Red anger veiled his vision.

"I thought so."

"I can't think about it. Don't want to speak of it," he said thickly.

She opened her mouth, searched his expression. "No, we'll plan later," she whispered.

He kissed her forehead, felt the softness of her eyelids with his lips, the length of her lashes. Ran his tongue over her tempting lips until her breath came quicker.

The tension in her changed subtly. When she placed her

fingers on his chest, she found his nipple and rubbed.

Ruis walked faster.

She felt infinitely precious in his arms. As he caught the rich scent of her, he bent his head so wisps of her blond hair would caress his face. Her curves were soft against him, welcoming him as no other woman had done, becoming familiar yet remaining exciting.

His sex hardened and throbbed until all he wanted was to get her onto a bed where his mouth could roam her skin and taste.

Ailim reached up and traced the pulse in his throat, trailed her fingers around the collar of his tunic. "You look like you taste good," she said.

Ruis's breathing went ragged. He strained to harness his passions. Today he yearned to show her all his tenderness, how he treasured her. More than anyone else had or would. Ever.

# Eighteen

*When* *they reached the door of the Captain's Quarters,*
Ruis opened it with husky passwords.

Ailim chuckled and skimmed her fingers along his jawline.
"It still amazes me that you use my name as a password."

Ruis grunted and hurried through the sitting room into his
bedroom. He placed her on the bed, then gathered his control.
She started to rise and he lifted his palm. "Stay. Stay there for
me, lady. Let me cherish you."

She lay back with a gentle smile but flushed cheeks. Her
daygown was elegantly cut quality brocade, three years out of
style, but made her look ravishing. She'd look even more ravishing—ravishable—without it. He sat on the edge of the bed
and caressed her body, reveling in her soft firmness beneath
the lush fabric. He stroked from shoulders to knees, paused to
grip her hips, then went back to hold her breasts. They rose
and fell beneath his palms, her peaked nipples evident under
the thick cloth. Her eyes gleamed sapphire blue.

With a shaky exhalation, he took his fingers from her breasts.
Heat crept up his neck, painted his cheeks with arousal. He
cuffed her wrists so he could study her hands. Long, fine, fingers; pretty, short nails. Lifting her hands, he put her palms on
his nipples and shuddered.

Exquisite, anticipatory tension wound tight inside him.

He touched her hair. As always one slide of his fingers freed her braids. She shivered, flexed her fingertips against his nipples until he joined her soft moan.

Lightly, lightly he caressed her face, following her hairline, outlining her eyebrows, stroking her lips, reacquainting himself with the dear structure of her face.

Her hands explored him and he wanted to close his eyes and savor her touch, encourage her with panting groans to pet him. But this special time was for her.

His heart thudded deep and low. His sex had stiffened until his trous constricted. This time was for her, letting her fly free of everything that bound her.

"Open your mouth," he heard himself say.

Her eyes widened, her cheeks flushed further but her lips opened slowly. He thought of warmth and moistness. Passion racked him. She needed to crave him, too. He plucked her nipples. She arched, hips thrusting upward. She closed her eyes, but her lips stayed parted and a long soft sigh escaped.

He moved his hands from her breasts to cradle her head, then he bent and took her mouth, plunging his tongue inside the damp cavern and claiming it. Claiming her. His tongue slid and stroked and dueled with hers. He set a carnal rhythm that anticipated their mating, his sex lunging inside her.

She sucked his tongue and he grabbed the unraveling threads of his restraint. He moaned into her mouth.

Never breaking the kiss, he covered her, trapping her hands between them, settling until his hard erection lay against her plush mound. She closed her teeth around his tongue and lust broke over him in a heated, overwhelming tide. He let himself rub against her once, twice, then pulled his lips from hers and froze to steady himself, to prolong the intense pleasure, to build it more for them both.

Now he buried his head in the curve of her neck, glorying in the tangled mass of her hair, breathing deeply of her dark, rich fragrance that made his mouth water. He touched the tip of his tongue to her neck. She surged under him, stroking his manhood long and hard. All thought darkened beneath a wave of velvet desire.

He stopped her rocking hips with his hands, rasped words from his marrow. "Stay. Stay still. For me, lady." He didn't look at her, didn't attempt to calm his rough breathing.

She kept quiet. A moment, then two passed. Bliss. Her body

under his, ready to take him, ready to welcome him. Ready to love him.

Intimacy spun between them, emotions as well as bodies. He raised himself on his elbows, twined their hands together to the side of her. He looked at her from under heavy eyelids. She matched his gaze as she matched him—or complemented him— in everything. Sensuality pulsed between them growing with every breath. Her gaze dropped and traveled over him, cranking the arousal up a notch, heating the atmosphere around them. He was achingly aware of the press of their bodies together. Each millimeter where they touched sent tiny flashes of stimulating sensation through his nerve endings.

Again their eyes met and passion cycled between them. Escalating with every heartbeat. Their hearts synchronized and his shaft throbbed in time with the vein in her neck. Blood pounded in his temples until he no longer saw her, all he knew was hunger.

He needed her naked.

With a harsh sigh, Ruis raised himself from her and stood.

"I need to touch your skin," she said.

For a moment he couldn't move, then he flung away tunic and boots. He kept his trous on as a link to sanity. His hands trembled as he reached for the tab-seams of her gown at the shoulders and separated the front of her dress from the back along the side seams. Even through her breast band and her shift her nipples were stiffened rosy crests. His scrutiny wandered to the apex of her thighs. Her blond hair was curled and damp from her excitement. His breath strangled in his throat. Once more he stopped to garner control.

The gauzy layers of her underclothes enhanced her beauty, making her something of dreams. "I want, I need—" He cleared his throat. "This time is for you. Let me please you."

Her mouth opened, closed and opened again. Her tongue darted out to wet her lips. Ruis embraced the shock of lust. "You could never do anything less than please me, Ruis," she whispered.

He absorbed the shock of love to the heart.

She kneaded the muscles in his shoulders and biceps, then put her hands by her sides.

With one strong pull, he opened the shift, then freed her from the breast band and pantlettes. He tossed the underthings over his shoulder.

He took time to stare at her. Drink her in now and keep the vision for all time.

Ailim said, "I will never forget the sight of you in this moment."

He blinked. She echoed his thoughts. He drew his palms smoothly down her body, pausing to increase her delight whenever she quivered under him, or moaned, or her eyes went misty blue.

Soon she chanted his name and *please*, twisting the craving for her higher than he'd ever known. Dimly he knew that when he came into her body this time, he'd be marked by her forever.

Her thighs curved delightfully under his palms. He resisted temptation to touch the dampness of her desire, but caught the scent of her and bit off a whimper of his own. She was rich and ready and he could almost taste her. Later.

Her calves were supple and he caressed their graceful muscle, lingering to steady his pounding blood.

Her feet flexed and arched in his hands when his thumbs found her pleasure points. She moaned and twisted in his grasp and as her thighs parted he got another whiff of her arousal and his sex pulsated.

Not much longer. He craved the taste of her now.

He jerked off his trous and let himself jut free.

"Yes, Ruis. Please, Ruis." She raised her arms and he had a moment's regret that he hadn't stroked them. Then he saw the pink heart of her and all thoughts fled at the lure.

He grasped her knees and opened her thighs wide, staring at her most intimate flesh. Damp and warm and enticing. Blood thundered in his ears. She pushed against his grip, but he was intent on his goal.

With strict restraint he moved onto the bed, pushing her knees wide and back to her chest.

"Ruis!"

Rich, dark, enticing. He kissed her. Her taste exploded in his mouth and surged to his marrow. More. He feasted until she screamed and shuddered against his tongue.

He lifted his head and looked at her, dazed. Her swollen womanhood spellbound him. That he could have made her so needy, given her a shattering climax!

The dark rose color was echoed by the crests atop her pale breasts. With a groan torn from the depths of him, he moved up her body. He put his mouth on one nipple and suckled, taking as much of her soft breast into his mouth he could. Her taste was lighter here, mixed with the film of sweat from her release. He changed to the other nipple, taking it deep, curling his tongue around it, flicking the first nipple with his fingers.

She cried and bucked against him, her silken skin brushing against his rigid staff aching with need.

Again he shoved her legs wide. This time he plunged into her. Her hot, wet sheath gripped his sex and the wisps of his control vanished.

He pounded into her, knowing only the tightness of her, the scent of her, the sight of her and the hoarse sound of his name upon her lips.

Tension gathered at the base of his spine, wound hard, presaging ultimate rapture.

Faster, harder, deeper. The orgasm hit him like a firestorm, igniting every nerve, inflaming every vein, engulfing him until he shuddered on the rack of delirious ecstasy, her name torn from him. She clenched against him and screamed, too.

He collapsed upon her sweet, cradling body, still merged, still whole.

Her trembling hands slicked over his back and the gentle touch wrung an exquisite aftershock from him. She shivered beneath him.

As he whispered her name, her voice broke on his.

A septhour later he woke and rolled from her, inwardly cursing his thoughtlessness. He'd been too exhausted to lift a finger, let alone summon the muscle control to leave her—the willpower to leave her.

He rose and went to the shower, letting hot water pummel him. When he left the bathroom, towel wrapped around his hips, he detoured to his den for the gift he'd made her—the Nullifying pendant. Ship and Samba had dug out a fancy little square box from somewhere. He walked into the bedroom and laid it on the bedside table.

She'd curled up, looking small, innocent. Vulnerable. Shadows lay beneath her eyelids. A scar on her ankle from her escape from the earth fault marred her skin.

Fear squeezed his guts at his terror for her this morning.

Almost killed! And he'd been helpless to stop it. Impotent to help her. Even more useless now that he'd been accused of attacking her.

He wouldn't lose her. That confrontation she'd had with Bucus before JudgmentGrove was her death warrant. Ruis understood that even if Ailim didn't. His uncle wouldn't give up.

Ruis looked at his own hands, remembering being under the control of Bucus: the lashes, the burns, the razorslits. Cold fury burned inside him. He couldn't leave Ailim to his cruel and merciless uncle. Bucus would soon find some way to kill her, especially with Menzie still in D'SilverFir Residence.

The only sure way to keep Ailim safe was to eliminate Bucus.

The coldness of fear and fury transformed into heat, storming fiery through his veins until his mind seemed light. It burned everything he'd known before—all his restraint and hesitations in not challenging Bucus.

Ruis wasn't running anymore. He wasn't letting the corrupt older man's power stop him.

He went to the closet where he'd stowed the weapon he'd restored—a lazergun.

Ailim woke to the sounds of Ruis dressing. She stretched luxuriously and laughed. Free. She'd been totally, completely free in her passion, and she knew she'd never forget—she'd take the experience and use it to be freer in the other aspects of her life.

She turned her head to see Ruis buckling on a strange-looking holster, and all her cheer fled. She licked her lips, found her voice as he handled an object that could only be a weapon. "What are you doing?"

He glanced up, grim-faced. Fierce battle glittered in his eyes. "I'm going to take care of Bucus."

"We'll clear your name."

"It's not my name I'm worried about. It's your life!" he gritted out.

Ailim heard her heart *thud-thud-thud* in her ears as if counting the beats until certain doom. "I'm fine. I'm safe now and will continue so. I'll buy additional spells, hire a Holly bodyguard. Going after Bucus isn't the right way to handle this." She found her clothes and donned them with trembling hands. Dread filtered through her.

He snapped the weapon into the holster at the side of his left thigh. "I can't wait any longer. He sent a man to murder you today. Going after Bucus is the only way. I get him and throw him in the brig and he's no longer a threat to you. As long as he's free, you're in danger. I want to protect you."

Desperation made her words sharp. "And you're in danger every moment you're here in Druida! Every risk you take outside the Ship can lead to your arrest and execution. Your— *our*—discovery is only a matter of time! Listen to me. I've initiated the legal case against Bucus. It will only take a few days before he's in gaol. Leave Druida for a few days until he's captured, you be safe. That way it's legal, it's done right, we win forever."

"No." His smile was wry yet tender. "We value each other more than ourselves."

"You won't go?"

"I won't run and abandon you to Bucus's cruelty."

Dread escalated until she could hardly breathe, hardly think. "I want you to leave and let me handle this by law. You want to protect me and handle it by force—kidnapping and vigilantism. You won't run but you'll skulk and kidnap and hide!"

He flinched, but his gaze stayed grim and steady. "I'll do what needs to be done. He's gotten away with too much already."

"Let me take care of this, please!"

"No."

"Why not?"

"You can't do it, especially not in a couple of days," he said brutally.

Knifelike-pain stabbed and twisted. She stopped herself from swaying, stiffed her knees as she felt the blood drain from her face. "What?"

"Bucus is the Captain of the Council. He has all the power. All the nobles will back him. Nothing you can do will bring him down."

"Even now T'Ash is doubting him. So are others of the FirstFamilies. I've started proceedings—"

Ruis shook his head. "We don't have the time. I won't delay when you're in danger."

"We don't have the time not to do this right. We do it wrong and we could lose!"

"So we do it my way." He patted his weapon.

"I can't," Ailim said. "I can't condone you kidnapping him. It's not solely justice at stake, it's honor. It's believing in life and having faith that universal truths will triumph. More, don't you see? It's not that it hurts Bucus, and puts you and the Ship and Samba in danger. It hurts you, too. This action harms your *soul*."

He stared at her. "You're too much a lady. I don't care about the state of my soul if your life is safe."

She hurled herself at him, grabbed his biceps in both hands. "I promise, I *promise* that the law will get Bucus in two days. I'll make sure of it!" Her mind scrambled at how she could do it right, but she knew she could. If she called in every favor she'd been hoarding to use to the benefit of her Family, she could have Bucus in jail in two days. "Just hide here, deep in the Ship, where only you know where you are. Let the Ship protect you for two days and I'll get him for us. For us!"

"He'll twist your words or laugh at your case or slide free or escape. Then he'll come after you with all the cruelty and power and evil that is in his rotten soul. I can't risk that, risk you."

She just stared at him. "So what it comes down to is that you don't trust justice."

"There's no such thing as justice."

Her breath came fast, her palms sweat. "You don't trust the law as I do."

"You could afford to trust in the law—until now."

"You don't trust—"

"I trust myself and the Ship," he shot back. Then realization jolted in his eyes at what he hadn't said.

"But not me."

"Of course I trust you—"

"You have no faith in my skills, in my life work as a Judge, in me. I tell you I can have Bucus in jail in two days, that I can protect myself, and you don't believe me. What kind of life could we have in the future if you only have faith in yourself and never in me?"

"It's not like that."

"It's exactly like that." She twisted her hands together. "Will you trust me to put Bucus in jail in two days?"

He hesitated. His fingers brushed the grip of his weapon. She saw the torment in his eyes, his *yearning* to believe, but his ultimate lack of faith. His jaw clenched. "I can't take the risk."

"You have no hope that we could win against your uncle the right way. No hope we could build a good future together," she whispered. "I'm leaving."

In a moment, when she was away from him, she'd be able to banish the tears welling in her eyes with a Word. She didn't know how she would ever mend her shattered heart.

Her last smile for him broke. "The man I loved. Odd how I trusted you, your skill and your knowledge. *I* had faith in *you.*"

"Love! Faith? What?"

She shook her head. "Loved, past tense. I trusted you to save my life with those Earth machines. You think that was easy?" She ran. Fast. Down corridors she knew well. She reached the southeast airlock and pounded at the square manual door-opener. The portal slid open and Ailim stepped out into the wind that whipped the tears from her face, the cold gray day and barren park.

"*Fligger!*" *Ruis swore and dropped to sit on the bed. The* scent of their intimacy mocked him. He buried his head in his hands. He had to protect her!

"Ship, watch for any threat to Ailim! Call Samba."

"Ailim D'SilverFir has left," Ship said in subdued tones.

"Watch her closely." He'd lost her. A cold clamminess invaded him, wisping from his bones to curl around his heart, sending streamers into his soul. Desperation paced like a ravening monster on the edges of his emotions, waiting to pounce if he lost control.

He'd lost her. Not because of the pressure of outside circumstances. He'd lost her because of who he was.

He saw in his mind's eye her white face, dominated by huge eyes gone gray, without a hint of blue. Her bleak expression. Trails of unacknowledged tears. The image duplicated another one of Ailim he'd seen before. That Ailim had been dirty, desperate, close to imminent death. She'd tilted her face up to him from a filthy hole where she'd been trapped.

His gut tightened, the beast despair came closer. She'd feared for her foot and her life and her Residence. But she'd shunted aside all that fear to trust in him and his skills in something she'd never experienced.

He hadn't done the same.

The argument reverberated in his mind.

Two days. In pride and fear he'd refused to give her a simple two days. Why? His hands trembled as he rubbed his eyes. He thought of the morning, her conflict with Bucus, the subsequent attempt on her life. Let his lady battle his nemesis for him? The most cherished person in his life confront the worst evil in his life? Out of the question. Better that he fight and die than Ailim be in the least besmudged by Bucus. He wanted to keep them apart. Forever.

He walked back into the bedroom. The little box containing his gift stood on the bedside table.

He'd been so proud of himself, fashioning a gift that would give her peace and serenity, surcease from the pressures constantly weighing on her.

Yet he'd forgotten to give it to her.

*"Samba!"* He yelled it with all the fury, frustration, and desolation he felt. He imagined his voice echoing down the deserted corridors, the empty halls of the past and the future.

Samba and the Ship. Not enough. They'd taught him, made him a better man, but he didn't feel integral to their well-being—another person could have filled the place in their lives.

Not so with Ailim—and she had given to him as much or more than he'd given to her. More. He picked up the little box containing his gift. His head began to hurt.

Samba whizzed in, scowling. *You yell at Me!*

He didn't have time to soothe her feelings. "D'SilverFir may be in danger, follow her. Ride the saucer—"

Samba's eyes widened. *In the day?*

"—but fly high and slow, to be as safe as we can."

She tilted her head. Her whiskers twitched as she considered. *I can do. I fly high and slow and safe. Someone threatens, I divebomb.* She grinned. One ear angled as she saw the box he held. *Why didn't you give her?*

Ruis shook his head, touched the lazergun at his hip. "I planned on kidnapping Bucus."

Samba snorted. *You crazy*. Her saucer dipped as she turned and flew away.

He took the weapon off and stowed it in the closet. He had to go after Ailim. It was the only way he could convince her that he *did* trust her, did believe in her.

He'd doubted her and his past and pride had demanded that he only rely on himself. If he wanted her, he had to put his—their—future in her hands.

He should let her go. Associating with him could cost her everything—her career, her title, her estate, her Family. But he couldn't deny himself the comfort of her. Having someone care for him was too wonderful. He was too greedy.

His mouth quirked as he mocked himself. He could give up his reckless anger and his vengeance—had given them up and started changing for his own sense of self-worth. He could give up his pride. But he couldn't give Ailim up—not even if he could convince himself it would be the best thing for her.

He hoped she could forgive him. That she'd give him another chance.

Even if Ailim couldn't forgive him—if she was wise enough to keep away from him—she deserved the necklace. The gift he created that would provide her with what she most cherished.

"Samba has left," Ship said.

"How's she flying?"

The Ship hummed. "My cams can barely discern her. She is flying high to avoid turbulent winds. She does well," it said grudgingly.

"Good." Ruis twitched his clothes in order, flung his cloak around himself. His optimism rose—he would win her back, somehow. Time to go claim his lady.

"Ship, do you see D'SilverFir? Did she teleport?"

"She walks with her head down near the reflecting pool in Landing Park."

"Good." He rubbed his hands.

Taking the quickest omnivator, he hurried to the airlock exit and pressed the button.

The door rose. Ruis ran toward the reflecting pool.

His cloak whipped from his grip, and he fought it back

around him. Too late. A tall, rangy man separated himself
from the dimness of a tree trunk.

Ruis stared into dark blue eyes.

"I'm Straif T'Blackthorn." The man frowned. "You're
Ruis Elder. You don't look like a deranged and dangerous
murderer."

Ruis froze. He should be trying to think himself out of
this fix, trying to talk or run or even fight. But all he could
focus on was Ailim. She walked slowly through the park a
few meters away.

"I've never murdered anyone. I've stolen to survive,
that's my only crime." He paid little attention to his words,
let his cloak flap free. He wanted to hasten after Ailim; he
never wanted anything more in his life. But he dared not
draw attention to her, could not destroy her life. He kept
his voice low and looked T'Blackthorn in the eyes, willing
the man to concentrate on him.

"I've tracked Holm and Tinne Holly to this entrance,"
T'Blackthorn said.

Ruis winced.

"You know something about their disappearance?" The
man's voice sharpened.

"They were alive the last time I saw them." They'd been
close to Tory Town this morning.

"My cuzes are alive?"

"Yes."

"That's the Null! You, guy, he's ours! We get the reward!"

Three guardsmen appeared from bushes and tried to
shove T'Blackthorn out of the way. With graceful ease and
Holly training, T'Blackthorn set two of them on their butts.

Ruis detached and tossed his cloak under a bush to hide
it and spun to sink a fist into the third guard's soft belly.

"Someone wants you bad, Elder," T'Blackthorn said.

Ruis grinned with all his teeth. "Bucus T'Elder." From
the corner of his eye he glimpsed Ailim staring at them.
She stood still for a moment, then her chin lifted and she
walked toward them. No! he wanted to cry. He never
wished for telepathy more in his life.

"Are the Hollys in *Nuada's Sword*?" T'Blackthorn studied him with narrowed eyes.

Ruis met the GrandLord's gaze and put a hand over his heart. "No. I swear it."

"Look, guy—" One of the guards grabbed T'Blackthorn. He disengaged with a quick move. And looked at the man. "You may address me at GrandLord T'Blackthorn," he said. "I have business with this man."

The guard stumbled back, eyes wide. "The tracker."

"No wonder we was told to follow him," the other guard mumbled.

"What reward?" asked Ruis.

"This here's Ruis Elder, the thief. He's in Druida City," the third guard explained. "That makes him violating his banishment and to be hauled to gaol, or we can execute him. Cap'n of the Council said. Preventing us from doing our duties is a crime. He's ours. We got chains." He hauled a heavy black chain clanking from a sack he'd dropped.

Ruis tensed. He'd never wanted to be chained again.

"Is there a problem here?" asked Ailim, joining them.

"It's the Null's bitch," one of the guards said.

Ruis swung and hit him. All the guards jumped Ruis. He took a blow to the head and the gut. Dazed, he struggled as they clamped manacles on his hands and feet. "No, no, not her—" he slurred. A moment later a rag was stuck in his mouth and another tied around his head to gag him.

"This isn't right!" Ailim cried.

"Sorry, Y'r Ladyship," one of the guards sneered. "But this here's a criminal, violating his banishment. Now, you bein' a Judge, you'd know about that, wouldn't you, Y'r Ladyship."

"Yes." Ailim's voice was strained.

Pain exploded in his head as someone kicked him.

"Stop that!" Ailim demanded.

"Maybe we will, if you come along nice. Cap'n wants you, too. As for you, T'Blackthorn, there's five of us now, and one of us has already reported to the Cap'n. By the time we reach the Guildhall a 'mergency FirstFamilies Council'll be in session. GrandLord, I'd advise you to let us do our job. If ya like, you can take charge of the lady."

The autumn ground was cold, but the irons were colder than the hard earth and chill enveloped Ruis like a shroud.

"Judge D'SilverFir. Will you accompany me to the

Guildhall so we can sort this out?" asked T'Blackthorn smoothly.

Darkness fringed Ruis's vision. Why couldn't T'Blackthorn get her out of here?

She should lie, should deny she had anything to do with Ruis, say she'd found him and was planning to do her duty as a judge and turn him in. Whether Straif T'Blackthorn believed her or not, he wouldn't contradict a FirstFamily GrandLady, not in front of the guardsmen and a despised Null, probably not even in front of the FirstFamilies Council itself.

"Ruis Elder was my lover. He won't get a fair hearing before the FirstFamilies Council. I must attend."

No! Ruis struggled to speak, but no one paid any attention to him.

"I sorrow for you," T'Blackthorn said.

The last thing Ruis saw was Ailim flinch.


*A*ilim strode into the CouncilChamber followed by T'Blackthorn. The FirstFamily heads and consorts milled around, talking. Only a few sat behind the table, like Bucus T'Elder and his wife Calami.

As soon as he saw her, Bucus banged his gavel, hard. "This emergency session will come to order. Sit down and let me ensure we have a quorum!"

He had more than a quorum. All the heads of the FirstFamilies were there, and most of the mates. T'Ash and D'Ash, T'Holly and D'Holly, D'Vine. Ailim's heart sped as she calculated who she might depend upon.

"I would like to address the Council!" She raised her voice over the dying hubbub.

"One question, first, D'SilverFir, if you please," Bucus said silkily. "Have you associated with the banished thief calling himself Ruis Elder here in Druida, despite your oath as a Judge to uphold the law of Celta?"

Ailim stiffened her spine. "As SupremeJudge of Druida, I am concerned with justice, not simply the letter of the law."

"Answer the question!" Bucus Elder snapped.

The rest of the nobles subsided in their chairs, fascinated by the drama.

Ailim thought fast. Ruis's case was vital, but violations against D'SilverFir might sway the Council more. Better to start obliquely, with T'Reed, Donax's FatherSire, then work up to threats and attacks against her. She turned to the small, prune-faced man. "Have you, T'Reed, FatherSire of Donax Reed assigned to my household, conspired with Bucus T'Elder to steal my estate? Did you associate with T'Elder when he suborned his mistress, my aunt Menzie, to embezzle gilt to him?"

T'Reed reeled back, his wrinkled face shocked and pale.

"Lies! All lies. The woman is mad!" Bucus said.

Ailim swept her gaze across the nobles, aware of their attention. She smiled. "I can prove everything I say." She backed the statement with dazzling truth-Flair. By the time she needed to, she'd have evidence. Her smile took on a sharper edge, she gestured widely to encompass everyone. "Surely you all have begun to note the true character of Bucus T'Elder—"

He stood in rage, red and quivering, and shook the gavel at her. "My character is not the point of this session! I called this meeting for the execution of Ruis Elder, who has been found living in Druida, violating his banishment and perpetuating his crimes—spreading his Nullness—"

"Ruis Elder," Ailim spoke over him. "Your brother's son! The man who is a thorn in your side. The man you've tried to kill all your life—"

"Hold!" Bucus shouted—hitting her with a spell at the same time. Her mind shrieked in pain. He smiled. She stiffened her knees. He shouldn't have been able to penetrate her shields, but he'd made the amulet—so he knew from Menzie of Ailim's weaknesses. And he'd used the gavel as a spell-weapon. Ailim had never contemplated her gavel as a weapon.

His spell should have been impossible, or caused an outcry by some of the others. Ailim could only guess that the spell slipped beneath the roiling emotions of the rest of the nobles as they contemplated ordering a quick execution.

Gauze seemed to fill her head—she shook it, grasping for clear thought.

Bucus turned to the two guards who'd accompanied her and T'Blackthorn in his glider. "Did you find her in the company of the criminal, Ruis Elder?"

They shifted their feet.

Bucus addressed T'Blackthorn. "T'Blackthorn, upon your oath of honor, of truthfulness, do you know if D'SilverFir associated with Ruis Elder?"

T'Blackthorn didn't look at her. "Not of my own knowledge."

A guard shouted, "She admitted they were lovers."

Gasps came from the nobles. They leaned forward in their seats.

At that moment the other guards marched Ruis into the chamber, clanking with chains wrapped tight around him, blood running down his temple, and a gag in his mouth.

Ailim's heart contracted as she saw he tried to stride with his old insouciance, but hobbled instead. How she loved him. How close they had been to having it all! She fought to speak, to no avail.

"T'Blackthorn, you found the Null, Ruis Elder, in Druida?" asked Bucus, moving the mockery of the proceeding down the lethal path he wanted.

"I followed the trail of my cuzes Holm and Tinne Holly to the Ship *Nuada's Sword*. It is my expert opinion that Ruis Elder has been living in the starship since he was exiled from Druida and that he caused the disappearance and/or death of my cuzes."

"Living in *Nuada's Sword*? With the curse? Impossible!" cried T'Reed.

Ailim nearly smiled.

T'Blackthorn raised his brows. "When was the last time anyone here toured the ship?"

Nobles looked at each other. Bucus T'Elder grinned until his fat cheeks nearly buried his eyes. "The repulsive Null is here, affecting the Records so we can't access them." He rubbed his hands. "I have not visited the ship since I was a lad, and then I stayed in the museum. Of course the defective hid in an old, useless hulk—both unnecessary to Celta."

Anger burned in Ailim, but Bucus's spell lay heavy on

her tongue. He wasn't close enough and hadn't been here long enough to affect her, yet.

T'Reed frowned. "*Nuada's Sword* is not an artifact of interest to me."

"It doesn't seem to be an artifact of any interest to anyone." The voice of Muin D'Vine, the old prophetess, was strong and vital. "I voted for freedom for Ruis Elder. I stand by that. The Wheel of Fortune has spun and he is now deeply involved in an aspect of Celta—"

"My sons!" D'Holly leaned over the table, fixing her gaze on Ruis. He watched as tears streamed down her face. She had sounded as if she truly cared, a mother's love. Behind his gag, Ruis's lips turned down, his mouth dried. He'd never experienced motherly love, so had never considered how the elder Hollys might feel at the disappearance of their sons.

"Tell me what happened to my sons, I beg of you!" she cried.

T'Holly stood and circled his arm around his HeartMate. His silver stare bored into Ruis. They both looked older than Ruis remembered.

The chamber fell silent. T'Blackthorn came and pulled the gag down.

"Wait!" Bucus shouted.

"They live," Ruis said.

D'Holly sagged into her husband's arms.

"Where are they?" commanded T'Holly.

Ruis cleared his throat and tried to gauge how much to tell and still protect the Ship.

The doors to the CouncilRoom slammed open.

"We're here!" Holm and Tinne said together, making a grand entrance.

# Nineteen

❦

*Hubbub rose.*

The two Holly sons swaggered in, fit and brown and covered with dust on their leather traveling clothes. They were followed by the Council's guardsman, Winterberry.

"Since you are involved in this matter, you may stay," Bucus intoned. "Shut the door and guard it, T'Blackthorn. Winterberry, gag the thief. His input isn't needed."

T'Blackthorn shut the door on the gape-mouthed guardsmen.

"Ailim, I—" Ruis only got out before Winterberry pushed the gag back into Ruis's mouth. He didn't know what to say anyway. It would be better for her if he kept quiet.

D'Holly ran to her sons, sobbing. They closed in on her with blatant joy and hugged her between them in comfort. T'Holly followed to complete the family embrace.

"The Ship, *Nuada's Sword*," D'Vine said, her voice loud enough to still everyone in the room, "is the key to this matter, the path of Destiny."

"Ah, yes." Holm Holly's mouth twisted as he patted his mother and gestured that she and T'Holly return to their chairs behind the CouncilTable. "*Nuada's Sword*, an interesting entity, that. Completely dedicated to Ruis Elder, here, whom it refers to as Captain."

"Captain!" Bucus said, infuriated.

More astonished and horrified looks came Ruis's way. He

slouched in his chains, raised his eyebrows, and smiled behind his gag. Death was imminent and inevitable—he may as well be as irritating as possible.

Holm buffed his nails on his shabby shirt, probably the only rough furrabeast leather shirt he'd ever worn, Ruis thought. Then Holm examined his fingertips while continuing his story. "The Ship took exception to our attempt to detain Elder and bring him before the Council. It transported us to the 271 Range and the Great Washington Boghole."

"The Boghole!" cried D'Holly. "How did you return so soon?"

Another off-center smile from Holm. "By freight airship, with great difficulty and promises of outrageous rewards." He sent a pained glance to his father.

"Any debt you incurred will be paid," T'Holly said.

Holm sighed.

"How did the Ship transport you?" asked D'Vine. "We, the GreatLords and Ladies of the FirstFamilies, could not accomplish as much," she pointed out.

Holm winced. Tinne joined him by his side and rubbed at the side of his head, where a large bruise was fading.

"A bullet lifepod," answered Holm.

Several gasped.

"Celtans have lost that technology. We have forgotten most of the science embodied in *Nuada's Sword*. We have not even had a slight interest in it. Now, before us, stands a master of that technology, someone the starship trusts. Who among us knows how to restore a starship, perhaps take it into space, pilot it? What will we do if we lose this knowledge again?" D'Vine said.

"That can't be allowed to impact the Council's Orders!" Bucus shouted. "He has *already* been tried and convicted. The judgment against Ruis Elder was death if he was found in Druida. All we need do here is administer the punishment! There is no other matter needing to be debated. You all voted for his banishment, and his punishment if he broke that banishment, which he has. Death it shall be!" Bucus hit his gavel on the table.

Bucus sneered at Ailim. "As for you, D'SilverFir. Do you deny that you aided and abetted this Null?"

When Ailim spoke, her voice was steady. "No, I don't deny

what you say. I *do* deny that his previous trial was legal."

*Bang.* Bucus's gavel came down. "You add lying to your own crimes. You will say anything to save your lover. In consorting with a known exile, failing to uphold her judicial vows, D'SilverFir has forfeited her Family Estate."

Ruis watched her lift her chin even as blood drained from her face. She must have already accepted the verdict, but hearing the words would have been a blow. He reeled from the disaster and bitterly hated the fact he could do nothing. As usual in his dealings with the nobles of Celta. How he yearned to hold her. Why had he ever denied her anything?

"Ruis Elder was found within the environs of Druida. He is subject to execution. Guards, take the Null away to the execution courtyard," Bucus ordered with relish.

Guards grabbed Ruis. His survival instinct pumped with fast blood through his veins. He struggled and jackknifed to kick his captors. T'Blackthorn faded back to speak with Holm Holly.

"He's been wronged!" Ailim cried out. "I demand a retrial!"

"Winterberry, remove SilverFir from the room." Bucus waved a hand at the guardsman. As Winterberry walked slowly to Ailim, Bucus towered over the table, waving his gavel at her. "You are a disgrace to your name and to your former profession. You have betrayed your class and your title."

"It is *you* who have betrayed your Family!" Ailim shouted. "I have proof!"

Ruis never admired her more, but the nobles at the table shook their heads at her wild appearance, hair flying about her. She continued, "You should all be receiving proof. Records from the T'Elder Residence, and the starship *Nuada's Sword.*"

Winterberry put a gentle hand over her mouth and circled her waist with his other arm, lifting her and slowly walking to the ornate doors. Fury bronzed Ruis's vision. Another man touched her—against her will. She looked small and fragile. Ruis fought harder, but was dragged step by step to the door now open behind the CouncilTable.

"The Council has judged the Null. He flaunted the Council's Orders, lived within Druida for weeks with immunity. He dies!" insisted Bucus.

T'Reed nodded. "The Council *has* already determined that, this whole affair has already reached the newsheets. We are laughingstocks, we, the most powerful nobles on Celta.

D'SilverFir's lapses will be discussed later." He swept a hand to the open door. It looked huge to Ruis, and he wondered that he'd never noticed it before. The slice of outside he could see looked black as death, not the pewter gray of the day he'd known an hour ago.

The petty guard hit Ruis on his head and he sagged. Then Petty looked at Bucus, hitched his belly over his belt. "We never done this. Our blasers don't work around him."

"The *Null* is in manacles and chains. Some of you hold him, and another run him through with your short sword. Go!" Bucus yelled.

Ruis turned his head and looked at Ailim, still being silenced and carried by Winterberry. If he had to die, he wanted to keep the image of the woman who'd loved him before him.

Her eyes showed torment.

He wished—one last jerk and his gag fell free. "None of this is D'SilverFir's fault. I muddled her wits, I forced her—" He tasted blood at the blow to his mouth. The clanking of his chains and cursing of the guards drowned him out. Gray dimmed his sight as he was carried half-conscious into the cold, stone courtyard.

Ailim heard the door boom hollowly shut behind the guards and Ruis. As hollow as her life, cutting off all the beauty she'd ever known, slamming on the hope for any joy in the future. For an instant she stood, stunned. Then she broke Winterberry's hold and ran after Ruis.

Before Ailim could reach the center of the room, Holm Holly caught her. "You don't want to see this," he said, grasping her wrists in his hands and pulling her close to his body, where she had no freedom to fight. Ailim struggled, but he was too tall, too strong, and too trained—the premier fighter of Celta.

She tilted her head back to meet his eyes. Heat from agony, anger, determination, and the gathering of her Flair raced through her body. Somehow she'd find a way to prevent it, but she said, "I will see this. I will witness the folly of this act, and I will never forget."

"Let her watch if she wants, I do. Winterberry, come with me," Bucus said, carelessly tossing his gavel down. He rolled his shoulders and grinned.

*       *       *

$\mathcal{R}$uis watched Bucus and Winterberry step into the courtyard. Bucus looked back to the doorway behind him then
shrugged.

He strolled with complete arrogance to a chair on a dais.
"I will witness the execution," he rumbled from smirking
lips.

Ruis was not surprised. In fact, he felt little. He frowned.
He was numb from shock, he supposed. His doom was here,
never to be outrun, present and inexorable. He hoped his
desensitized feeling wouldn't wear off before he was killed.

From inside he heard Ailim's voice cut off mid-phrase.
His emotions rustled. He didn't want to think how he'd hurt
her, whether his death might hurt her. Maybe she would
marry Holm Holly after all.

"Execute him," Bucus ordered, gesturing to Winterberry.

"No," Winterberry said coolly.

That little surprise almost jolted Ruis from his numbness.

"I am a guardsman, the son of a GrandHouse, connected
to the Hollys. I am not an executioner. I will not kill him."

"I dismiss you from the guard!" Bucus raged.

"Fine." Winterberry said a Word and nothing happened.
He looked disconcerted, shot a glance at Ruis, then peeled
his guardsman tunic over his head, dropped it on the cob-
blestones, and went back inside the Council chamber.

Bucus fumed and looked around at the rest of the guards.
Several who appeared of noble blood followed Winterberry's example.

"You"—Bucus stabbed a fat finger at a slack-jawed
guard—"and you"—then at another—"and you"—a third—
"come here."

They looked at each other, shifted, dragged their feet.

$\mathcal{G}$reatLady Muin D'Vine unbent her old, thin body. Her
eyes flashed silver with commanding Flair. Her voice thundered through the room. "You know not what you do! By
the power in me, as the oldest member of this Council, and
as the True Embodiment of the Crone, I command you stop
this idiocy! Countermand the execution. Bring that boy
back in here now."

At her intimidating aspect, the milling nobles stopped in shock.

"I agree," called Danith D'Ash. She tossed her head and walked toward Ailim and Holm. Narrowing her eyes at Holm, she started past him. "See how many women you can restrain, HollyHeir."

"T'Ash," Holm called.

The big man started toward his wife. "I'm not going against D'Vine."

"But he's a Null," D'Birch protested.

"And he's been ill-treated all of his life," D'Ash said.

"Too late, too late, too late," whispered the prophetess D'Vine, turning pale and running past them all to the doors, arms outflung.

Ailim wondered what visions she'd foreseen.

With a shriek Shade rocketed into the room. A sheen of sweat dewed his pallid face. He flashed glisten-coated teeth.

"Vengeance for Slash, Nettle, *Ruis*! Death to you all."

Holly released Ailim and spun to meet the challenge. She heard the rasp of T'Ash's blades, the slither of leather of unholstered blasers.

Too late. D'Vine threw herself into the first firebomb. It hit her in the chest, burned red, then black through her robe, sending streamers of flame down her dress. She ignited into a flaming torch.

Beside her, D'Ash's hem smoked and caught fire, crawling up her dress.

A scream of emotional torment ripped from Shade as he flung another and another of the explosives. "Flametree's firebombspell. Once it touches you, it will burn you to flinders! There's no stopping the propel spell—" Holm's knife stuck in the boy's chest. His eyes widened and glazed as he stared at the blood painting his shirt. He died.

Screams and shrieks rose throughout the room as clothing and furniture caught fire. As their shields faltered, Ailim heard the awful torment of thoughts. Overwhelming fear and pain buckled her knees. She clamped her hands against her head and reeled against a wall.

"Lord and Lady, no!" cried T'Ash. "Danith, rip your robe off! Don't let a micron of the firebombspell touch you. It killed my Family. One cinder will kill you."

Ailim saw T'Ash tear the heavy formalrobe from his
wife, saw an untouched D'Ash, saw her garments con-
sumed.

"Healers!" cried D'Ash.

"Can't. Healers can't stop this. It's a propel firebombspell. Nothing can stop the burning," T'Ash said.

As Ailim stumbled to the door, she saw T'Birch staring
at the fiery sleeve of her gown, T'Reed beating at flames
on the chairs with his sword. T'Rowan screaming and staring at a blackened hand. Others rolling on the floor in agony. Half the people in the room were afire. Slowly burning
to death.

Ruis flung himself through the doors, chains dangling,
followed by Winterberry. "We heard screams! Are you
hurt, Ailim? What's wrong?"

"Shields down. Not hurt," she gasped. "Flametree's firebombspell. Can't be stopped."

Ruis grabbed a box from his pocket, thrust it at her. "My
gift to you."

She fumbled the box open. Her fingers clenched around
an emerald heart. The emotions ravaging her from others
dimmed.

Ruis glanced around. "Firebombspell is pure Flair. Flair
dies near me. I can smother it." He gazed at the closest
burning person and fell upon her. They both screamed, Ruis
low, she high. Then she only sobbed and whimpered. Ruis
rolled off her and to another.

Healers ran through the doors. "Something's wrong. We
can't port here," one panted, taking in the scene with a
glance. Horror crossed his face. "What—"

Ailim jumped to a Healer. "A propel firebombspell. You
can't Heal the ones on fire." She shoved the Healer to
Ruis's first rescue. "Go to her, her flames are out!"

She snagged another Healer, Lark Collinson, and pulled
her into a corner. "Have one of your people leave the
NobleCouncil Hall, out of the Null's range—"

"Null?" The smaller woman blinked.

"Yes. He's stopping the firestorm. Stopping it. You can
only Heal those whose fire is out."

Lark nodded. "Right." She sped from the corner and took
charge. Healers and nobles rushed to do her bidding.

Ailim scanned the crowd for Ruis. The fire on the furniture had been extinguished.

A cindered man placed a woman gently on the floor. Brown eyes looked from a blackened face. Ruis.

He shouted, stumbled toward her, his stare sliding past her.

She whirled to see Bucus Elder, lips peeled back from his teeth in a mad grin, swinging a long curtain sparking at the end. Focused on her. Crazy laughter rolled from his belly.

"So you've been snooping, gathering evidence against me, using Menzie. Can't allow that. I'm the most powerful man on Celta. No one crosses me." He spit a stream of filthy curses. Ailim froze. It seemed like a nightmare.

He approached, eyes glittering. "If I go down, so do you. I'll get you." Another amulet dangled from between his fingers.

Ailim clutched her new necklace, wondering if it could protect her. Even if she flung the necklace away, she was too weak to teleport. Walls of the corner crowded her.

Ruis dived between them, ignoring the bulk of his uncle, the flaming fabric.

Bucus stumbled back, shoved Ruis to the floor, kicked him.

"No!" screamed Ailim. She threw the little box with all her might, hitting Bucus between the eyes. His head jerked back, he hesitated.

Ruis swept Bucus's feet from under him. The fiery curtain wrapped around them both. They all screamed, Ailim in horror, the two men in pain.

Ruis rolled aside, pushed himself to his knees with blackened hands. Ailim grabbed him and helped him rise. He moaned.

A ululating shriek tore from Bucus. His entire body flamed. His face was a rictus of agony. Ruis put out a hand, but flames reached the amulet and Bucus torched.

Ailim and Ruis swayed together.

"Justice," Ailim whispered.

Lark Collinson strode over with a burning man. Ruis grasped him.

Other nobles followed, pushing the worst cases toward Ruis.

Ruis had been her man, her love, her hero.

Now, he was Celta's hero.

He looked at her through eyes that were mere glimmers between the swollen, blistered skin of his cheeks. The front of his clothes hung in tattered, black shreds. Or perhaps it was his skin. He smiled at her and his lips cracked open and bled.

"Restitution for my crimes," he said.

"Too much!" She faced a terrified stream of burning nobles.

"Who else can do it?" He reached for the next victim, hesitated an instant before encircling D'Birch, who'd lied about him and her necklace. Then he embraced the woman.

Finally it was done, the last of the flesh-eating, Flaired, inextinguishable flames halted. Ruis had to be lifted and his patient removed from under him and taken away to be Healed.

He lay on his back, a cinder of a man, barely breathing. A circle of nobles surrounded him. D'Ash and T'Ash. T'Holly, D'Holly, Holm, and Tinne. T'Blackthorn.

"T'Heather! Where's T'Heather?" Ailim demanded frantically.

"Healing," T'Ash said.

"Get him or Lark!" cried Ailim. She'd long stopped noticing the tears streaming down her cheeks, only brushing them aside when they became troublesome.

"Let's move him to the pentacle," T'Holly said. "That's where the most ancient and powerful spells are. It might help."

He was placed reverently in the pentacle. The nobles parted for Lark. She only shook her head. "We can't Heal him." Tears welled in her eyes. "He's a Null."

"He will die," Ailim said dully. After all they'd been through, all they'd overcome with arguments and problems still unresolved between them, they had still not altered any fate. He would die.

Metal clanged against metal as Samba's saucer hit the doorjamb. "Waaahh. Rrrrowww, hhrrrr ruffff," *Listen to Me, I know what to do,* Samba said. *Take him to the Ship.*

*Where He belongs. Ship will fix him. Fast horses outside.* She sounded falsely hopeful.

The nobles glanced at each other. "She's his Fam, Zanth's daughter," T'Ash said. "I'll do it."

Samba tilted back through the doors. T'Ash and Holm lifted Ruis and started out. Everyone followed. Samba glanced over her shoulder and sneered. *T'Ash rides with FamMan. FamWoman Ailim rides, too. Everyone else stays.*

The Fam slitted her eyes. Contempt at the nobles showed in the twitch of her ears, the twirl of her tail, and every muscle in her body. *Stupid nobles sit and think how they owe FamMan. How they need him. How they need Ship.*

T'Reed came forward, a hole where his left ear had been, streaks of blisters down the side of his face. He nodded. "He saved my life, many of our lives. We'll consider everything. Later." His face paled and he weaved on the spot. He looked at Ailim and blinked rapidly with lashless eyes. "You—"

She drew herself up, and sent a cold glance around the nobles, gesturing for T'Ash and Holly to hurry ahead with their burden.

"Ruis Elder's been misjudged since his birth," Ailim said. "He was betrayed and abused by Bucus T'Elder, falsely tried by this Council." She allowed disgust to thread her voice. "Charges will be brought." It was the last word she could squeeze from her throat, the last coherent thought she had. She could only run at a shambling pace to catch up with T'Ash and Holm and Ruis. Still, behind her, she heard the whoosh of Samba's saucer and her hissing, *you, greatlords and ladies. you, pray.*

*R*uis awoke feeling awful. *The dimness in his vision that he* recalled from other times he'd surfaced still plagued him. The pain was better. Memories descended in colorful chunks. He moved his lips. They felt rubbery. He hadn't been capable of asking questions before.

A warm, solid presence lay along his side vibrating with a purr that barely reached his ears. "Samba?"

*I am here.*

"Ailim?"

*She left when Ship told her you were waking up and that I could care for you by Myself.*

He wasn't surprised. He'd cost her everything: her title, her career, her Family, her home. Her very honor. More, he hadn't trusted or believed in her enough to save a future together.

He groaned. He tested his muscles, flailed spasmodically. "How long have I been in sick bay?"

*Two days. First you in a heal tube. Ship says it gets you well fast.* Samba snorted. *You supposed to be able to get up tomorrow, all better in three days.*

Physically he seemed whole. His eyes, half-open, closed in deep emotional hurt. Ailim had stayed long enough to ensure he would heal—perhaps that was her sense of duty to an ex-lover.

He moaned.

A little snick sounded by his left ear. *Ship gives you more pain meds. You on bed not in tube, good for both of Us.*

His mind seemed to float, all his aches, mental and physical, separated themselves from him.

"What happened?"

*Evil uncle caught you.*

"I remember that." It still didn't seem possible, but then, he should have been dead.

*You were hurt bad. Uncle got Ailim, too.*

"Yes." He knew he should feel anguish, the anguish that had pummeled him when he realized that she'd lost everything due to him.

*Took you to Guildhall and FirstFamilies Council.*

Those memories unreeled in brilliant color and clarity. He licked his lips. Something brushed his mouth.

*Straw. Drink.*

The tang of citrus juice exploded with exquisite sweetness in his mouth. He drank until sated. He opened his eyes to the arched metallic silver ceiling of sick bay.

"Lady and Lord, Shade! The firebombspell! The First-Families Council!" He tried to jackknife up, but his muscles only twitched.

*Shade is dead. Boy went mad. Used your Nullness to get into CouncilChamber. Set off nasty spell. Holm Holly killed Shade.*

Ruis remembered his shock and grief at seeing Shade dead on the CouncilChamber floor, lips peeled back from his teeth in a mad grimace. "The FirstFamily nobles?" His lips stiffened as emotions filtered back. He didn't want to remember the hideous pain of stopping the firebombspell with his body.

*Many burned. Five die. One HeartMate died, T'Rowan, D'Rowan not burned bad, but she's HeartMate, will die soon.*

"Six," his stomach roiled. "Six of fifty. More than ten percent. D'Vine, the old prophetess?" Though he had visions of her body flaming and crisping before him, a tendril of hope—

*Gone to cycle in Wheel of Stars.*

Hurt was coming back. Ruis shook his head on the pillow.

*You Hero. You saved them all.*

"They must think Shade conspired with me."

Samba snorted. *They know Shade used you. Used your Nullness. Followed you. Who could know when you get caught?*

"T'Blackthorn usually finds the trail of whatever he hunts."

*Straif Blackthorn wanted to talk about Hollys. Bucus's men get you.*

"Yes."

*Shade nowhere around you. You couldn't call him. He comes by himself for himself.*

Shade. A tickle behind his eyes became an ache and his throat closed. "He wouldn't have done it if they hadn't caught me. He was reforming," Ruis whispered.

*Who knows?* Samba said. *Big FirstFamilies Council meeting tomorrow. Ship will show Us.*

Ruis blinked. Shade was gone. And Ailim. Ailim. He needed her more than ever now. But he had cost her everything. He had committed the crime of his life. He had driven her away.

His mind swirled with color, he tried to roll onto his side. Sharp pain vanquished him.

\*       \*       \*

*Ailim* 'ported from *Landing Park* to the *D'SilverFir gates*. Her eyes filled as she trudged up the gravel path and her breath caught at the first sight of what had been her home.

Gone. All gone. Her title. Her estate. Her career. Her lover.

She could barely look at the proud Residence she cherished. Only her work on Ruis's case and her own self-discipline had stopped her from falling into despair in the last few days.

She had broken laws and her oath as a Celtan Judge. Ailim stiffened her back. She didn't regret her choice, even when she realized she'd played the fool for love—loving a man who had no faith in a future together. And then he proved himself a hero with such self-sacrifice that he humbled everyone in the chamber that day.

He was a good man. When the time for action came, he had risen above his childhood abuse and his flaws to reveal a man of truly noble character. He just hadn't been capable of taking the last step of trusting her against all the evils of his past.

As soon as Ailim stepped through the door, Cona ambushed her.

"How could you do this to us? How could you ruin the Family? I always knew those self-righteous manners of yours hid a sordid streak." Cona waved newsheets at Ailim.

Ailim stared at her. "Cona, shut up."

For a moment Cona's mouth hung open at Ailim's rudeness, then Cona continued her rant. "We are ruined! The scandal is dreadful. We have lost the estate!"

"Cona, shut up." Ailim saw Donax in the shadows. She rubbed her eyes, her shoulders slumped. "Ah, Donax, I've lost the Residence and its estate. You should have played it safe."

Donax dipped his head, an odd expression on his face. "Even if you did lose this Residence and the lands that go with it, we still have several holdings, all of which are prospering. So are our investments. We'll see this through."

"How could you, Ailim?" Cona screamed.

Ailim winced, then rounded on her. "Cona, I'm tired of you. Of your whining and your airs. You're a pain in the ass."

Cona sputtered. "You can't talk that way to me!"

"Of course I can. I'm not a GrandLady anymore, I'm not a Judge anymore, either. That means I can act as I please. I've already disgraced myself."

"Yes, you have!" Cona shrilled.

Ailim rolled right over her. "Everyone already believes the worst of me. I've had some very bad days and I don't have to stand here and endure any more snottiness from you." Her hands itched and she eyed Cona. "Lady and Lord, I've always wanted to tear your perfect braids out."

Cona squawked, clapped her hands to her braids and ran up the stairs. Donax's mouth twitched as he followed.

"Well done, lass," said Caltha, walking into the great hall from the den. "Go upstairs and rest. The special First-Families Council meeting tomorrow will be a challenge for you." She put her sturdy hands on Ailim's shoulders and squeezed. "I'm proud of you, as is most of the Family. Don't you worry about your own future. We'll take care of you, just like you took care of us."

Ailim shook her head and bolted to her rooms. When she got there, Primrose yipped in pleasure and radiated joy. *Love You!*

"I love you, too," Ailim muttered, falling onto the bed.

Primrose hopped up and licked the tears from Ailim's face.

*A*n urgent bonging woke Ruis. He stretched, winced, and sleep cleared from his head at the Ship's announcement. "Transmission of FirstFamilies Council Meeting on holo-screen."

Ruis blinked as images formed.

A tall, older, ascetic man strode into the CouncilChamber and faced the FirstFamilies. He was accompanied by an ancient man with wrinkled face and hands who walked with a cane reminding Ruis of old D'Vine. Ruis gulped as a burst of grief swept through him. Three others strode through the CouncilChamber doors, two women and a man, all in Judges's purple robes. Excitement and anticipation made Ruis's pulse beat faster.

Then his gaze fixed on Ailim as she and her Heir entered.

His mouth tightened when he saw she was dressed as a commoner. Longing and despair inundated him. It wasn't his Nullness or his past that had separated them. It was only his own sheer stupidity and lack of faith.

Finally a fat calico tail waved in the holo. Samba strutted in and sat beside Ailim. Ruis shook his head.

"As acting SupremeJudge, I, GrandLord Goldenseal, can convene a FirstFamilies Council, as I have done. And as SupremeJudge, with the consent and knowledge of my predecessor, former SupremeJudge Orris, and the current other Judges of Celta"—he indicated those in purple robes—"I can rule on any action of this council."

"This has never happened before. I object to this hasty meeting. I object to this so-called investigation of the FirstFamilies Council's action in banishing the thief Ruis Elder," T'Hawthorn said.

Goldenseal swept the table of FirstFamilies with a gaze that made many shrink. "Is Celta ruled by law or by whim?" he asked softly. "Does this council want to compound its illegal acts?"

# Twenty

T'Oak rose. Ruis's throat closed. T'Oak was his mater-
nal uncle, an uncle Ruis had never known, a man who had
helped him. "I stand with the SupremeJudge. All the acts of
any council must be ruled by the laws set by our ancestors."

"Laws are what separate men from feral beasts," T'Ash rumbled, standing.

"Justice must be done," agreed D'Grove as she joined the
men.

"This is an unpleasant duty that must nevertheless be endured," T'Holly said. Hand in hand with his HeartMate, they
both stood. Ruis winced. They looked older than they had a
few eightdays ago at his trial—before their sons had been lost.
Ruis knew who and what was the reason for their aging.

Each member of the council came to their feet, a pinch-faced
T'Reed the last.

The power should have been with the nobles behind the im-
posing table, but instead it emanated from the tall man standing
on the mosaic pentacle. As it would have been with Ailim, Ruis
realized.

She'd been right.

He'd been so wrong, blinded by old wounds until he couldn't
reason straight. Doubtful of her belief in the law. Untrusting of
her knowledge and her power. Untrusting of her? No! But unable to trust her against Bucus. If he'd reined in his impatience

and given her more time, at least given her the two days she'd asked for, would Shade still be alive? And the others? Nausea clenched in his gut.

"Yeldoc, the record, please," Goldenseal said. The JudgmentGrove bailiff stepped forward, not looking at anyone.

Goldenseal sent his gaze up and down the table. The only one he didn't seem to linger on was T'Ash, Ruis saw. T'Ash stood stoically, and Ruis suddenly remembered that T'Ash, too, had once stood trial before the FirstFamilies's council.

"Yeldoc, please read the entry of appearance of the advocate for Ruis Elder," Goldenseal requested, his voice softer than before.

Ruis shivered at the memories and the emotions that gripped him. He leaned back, weakened, on his propped pillows.

Obvious tension surged through the CouncilChamber. He wondered how Ailim must feel, if she was wearing his gift. He looked at where she'd been, but now she was outside of his vision. Worry fretted at him.

Yeldoc rustled papyrus, cleared his throat, drawing Ruis's attention back to the main players. "There is no entry of appearance."

T'Oak shuddered. "Bucus T'Elder, the Captain of the Council, stated that Ruis Elder had waived a lawyer to defend him."

"Yeldoc, please read Ruis Elder's Waiver of Advocacy," said Goldenseal.

More flipping of pages. "There is none, Your Honor."

"Bucus T'Elder lied." T'Oak words sounded like ice hitting hard pavement. "I took the Word of the Captain of the Council. The Word of a GreatLord. The solemn and sworn Word. And. He. Lied." T'Oak's fists bunched.

"That is not the only time T'Elder betrayed his vows. All know of his crimes now." Ailim's clear voice cut through the silence of the room. She handed a stack of papyrus to Yeldoc. "The betrayal of his loyalty oath to the infant Ruis Elder. That oath is the foundation of our House and Family system. The illegal usurpation of the treasury and estate of Ruis T'Elder; the beating of a dependent, his wife Calami Reed D'Elder; the torture of a dependent child and Family member under his care, Ruis Elder; the murder of a dependent Family member, the woman Hylde, nurse to Ruis."

She hadn't mentioned any of his uncle's crimes against her

or the D'SilverFir Family, Ruis realized. Only those that had hurt him and the Elder Family. He went cold. With effort he pressed a button to increase the heat of the bed beneath him.

Ailim retreated beyond the holo screen, and Ruis yearned with every atom of his being to see her pale, heart-shaped face again. His vindication diminished next to the desire to have her with him.

Goldenseal swept the council with a look. His lips curled. "I resent being called out of retirement due to the prideful bungling of this body of noble FirstFamily Lords and Ladies. You made a mistake, several, and you did not rectify them. Instead you piled error upon error until the whole of Druida wonders at your judgment. You've denied one of your own sons his basic rights. You didn't listen to a divinely inspired revelation by a confirmed prophetess. You stripped the rank and career from one of the best Judges I have known without consulting the law or glancing at the facts of the matter.

"But the first crime was the worst. You denied a Celtan his inalienable rights, you violated the basic tenet of our culture: DO NO HARM. You tried him and sentenced him and would have summarily killed him. That can *never* be allowed to happen again. You've seen the charges against you.

"Yeldoc, read from page forty-three, line twenty through page forty-four, line ten of the charges against this FirstFamilies Council," Goldenseal asked.

Yeldoc cleared his throat. "The late GreatLady D'Vine addressed the FirstFamilies Council and said: 'I have nineteen decades of using Flair, and not even a strong, young Null can suppress my wisdom. I am old, a crone—close to the cycle of death and rebirth—and my sensing of Mysteries is great. I have had visions of this young man—and of the fate of our Council, so I must speak. Events have already been propelled down a specific path. Be wary of trying to control the wishes of the Unknown, of usurping the strong Fate now in motion. Not everything is predetermined in this matter, but be assured by seeking to punish Ruis, you will turn the river of Destiny to flood yourselves.' "

Goldenseal studied D'Grove. "GrandLady D'Grove, you are now acting Captain of the Council. Do you remember those words?"

"To my great shame, I do," she said, blinking rapidly.

"Is it often that this august body ignores a prophecy of a renowned seer, a GreatLady or GreatLord of the House of Vine?"

D'Grove bit trembling lips. "Never. We never did before or since."

"Oh? And in this case?"

She shook her head, raised and dropped her hands. "The man is a Null, he affected us—" She audibly inhaled. "No, that is not worthy of me. We ignored her. We condemned him. I voted for banishment. When he came before us again, I agreed that he should be executed. He is a Null."

"He is a Celtan!" Goldenseal thundered, the volume of his voice all the more startling for its previous quietness. "Yeldoc, read—"

"Let's get this over with," T'Holly said. "You sent us a massive document, but I, for one, read it all, and know every indictment against us, against me, is true."

"Do any of you wish to go over the record that we Judges of Celta presented you? Do any of you need clarification?" asked Goldenseal.

No one answered.

"How do each of you plead?" asked Goldenseal.

"I'm guilty," T'Ash said.

"Me, too," said Danith D'Ash.

He scowled at her. "You wanted to free Ruis, both times."

She sniffed. "I let your opinion override mine and let you vote our one vote. I stand with you. I am to be punished as well."

Ruis smiled, saw the faintest curve of Goldenseal's lips.

"What would you have us do?" asked T'Holly through white lips.

Goldenseal raised thin gray brows. "It is the ruling of the panel of Judges that every individual who voted in the trial of Ruis Elder, be he or she householder or consort—"

T'Ivy sighed and murmured, "My HeartMate is spared, she wasn't here."

The SupremeJudge admonished him with a look, and T'Ivy sat upright.

"The next new twinmoons is in four days. An appropriate time for casting off old faults and initiating new, better habits. On the twentieth day of Reed, Ioho, midmorning bell, every individual who voted in Ruis Elder's trial will wear penitent brown common cloth and walk barefoot from this chamber to the starship *Nuada's Sword*."

Most shivered.

It was going to be cold, Ruis thought.

Goldenseal continued. "At *Nuada's Sword* the offenders will kneel and formally request forgiveness from Ruis Elder."

Kneel! Ruis felt his mouth fall open.

"Kneel!" D'Birch screeched.

"The crime is prejudice that would lead to taking the life of an innocent man. A grievous crime. For such a grievous crime, the punishment and humiliation must be extreme."

Ruis rolled with laughter until his aching body made him still.

"But the curse of *Nuada's Sword*!" cried D'Birch.

"I have been informed by the Ship itself and my Residence that the curse is a thing of the past. A problem Ruis Elder remedied.

"After that vized ceremony, the penitents will proceed to the public SacredGrove," Goldenseal said. "There they will acknowledge their wrongs to the Lady and the Lord and all of Celta and take part in a Purity Ritual."

"We're FirstFamily nobles, we need a council member to officiate," D'Birch whined.

"I can do that." GrandLord Straif Blackthorn stepped forward from the shadows, a wry smile curving his lips. "I can't say that I wouldn't be in your place had I been here. But I was absent. I can officiate."

D'Birch snuffled.

"To also officiate, I appoint the new acting T'Vine, young Muin; the former GrandLady D'SilverFir, Ailim; and the acting GrandLady D'SilverFir, Caltha. To make the couples even, I designate GrandLord Sage, though he is not of a FirstFamily. Are there any objections to this ruling of the Celtan Panel of Judges?" asked Goldenseal.

After a moment D'Grove spoke in a small, gruff voice. "No."

Silence.

The council members began shifting in their chairs. Goldenseal raised his voice. "Yeldoc, distribute the recommendations."

The council stilled again. Yeldoc 'ported blue papyrus booklets before each person.

"These are our recommendations in the matters before this JudgmentGrove. First, Ruis Elder is to be acknowledged as T'Elder. We believe that he may be amenable to waiving the title and accepting the honor and rank of Captain of *Nuada's Sword*, with full membership in this council by scrystone."

Ruis's mind swam—T'Elder, acknowledged the Captain of *Nuada's Sword*! It could only be Ailim's doing. She knew him so well. Not only had she cleared his name, but she had restored him to his rightful place in Celtan culture.

"Ruis Elder should be awarded his entire outstanding noblegilt from his birth to the present day. The entire Council will then decide the value of his services to society in restoring and caretaking the starship, and determine his annual noblegilt accordingly. That is the recommendation with regard to Ruis Elder.

"Now, with regard to the former SupremeJudge, former GrandLady Ailim D'SilverFir, it is acknowledged that she associated with a condemned person, that she violated her oath as GrandLady and as SupremeJudge to the laws of Celta."

Ruis frowned. He hated this. What would she do? He hadn't trusted her even though he knew she was breaking her oaths to be with him. His self-disgust grew.

"Yet she is human and makes mistakes. It is the considered opinion of the distinguished panel of Judges that in her misguided actions she did no harm; therefore, we advise that the Council reinstate her appointment as SupremeJudge as well as her title of D'SilverFir, and restore the ancestral estate to the D'SilverFir Family."

Ruis let out a breath of relief and studied Ailim. Her expression was impassive, but her fingers trembled. He was glad for her, but it would have been more satisfying for him if he could have helped her as she had helped him.

The great discrepancy of wealth and title and rank between them had vanished. That left only the awful barriers of distrust and pride and stupidity.

One last time Goldenseal scrutinized each noble. "I suggest you be very careful and informed about the laws of Celta in the future, FirstFamilies. The Judges of Celta do not want to interfere in such disgraceful matters again, though we are prepared to do so if necessary. For the good of all, I bid you blessings, and remind you of your engagement on Ioho, the twentieth day of Reed."

There was silence for a long time as the Judges, Straif Blackthorn, Ailim, and her beaming Heir filed out. Samba's tail flicked with triumph. After a few moments D'Grove banged her gavel. "This meeting is ended," she said. "Merry meet, and merry part, and merry meet again. Blessed be."

*The* next evening Ruis glanced at his watch again, huffed out a breath, and stopped his limping pacing. Finally it was time for him to leave so he could reach the Guildhall after Ailim's reinstatement ceremony.

He set his jaw. "I'm going to get Ailim."

Samba sniffed. Rotated an ear, but did not turn her attention from *History of Cats*.

*About time,* Samba said.

Ruis shook his head. He donned his new red silkeen shirt, his highly polished boots of the latest fashion, and flung a cape around himself for warmth. He no longer needed outward trappings of his worth. He knew bone deep that he made a vital contribution to his culture in restoring the last Starship.

Better than that, everyone from D'Grove as Captain of the Council down to the lowliest shoemaker's apprentice knew it, too. But wearing good clothes still made him feel better, and he couldn't imagine going to Ailim in less than his best.

He left the Ship and strode through Landing Park and the streets of Druida, head high and tread firm. The only stares he received were those still interested in the insignia embroidered on his cape—ancient symbols, venerated symbols.

He had triumphed. He'd proved his humanity and his skill and his worth through his own actions during the carnage in the Guildhall. But Judge Ailim D'SilverFir had exposed the negligence and abuse of the nobles in their dealings with him.

Ruis stood before the large embossed brass doors of the Guildhall.

He squared his shoulders and laid fingertips on the door. The heavy handle felt cold and solid beneath his fingers. He gripped it and pushed hard to release some of his tension. The door swung wide.

As he stepped inside the lights faded until only the skylights lit the gloom. Looking down the corridor he saw the distant lights flicker and dim.

Then, with a little hum, light spread. He went over to a torch bracket and scrutinized it, grinning when he realized a nanotech bulb was there, glowing with energy from a power source that the colonists had originally installed in the building. Ship must have sent instructions to the Guildhall library.

He kept grinning. Perhaps the lights and other technological backup systems were in place because the Guilds hated the thought of being without power, or helpless, but to Ruis it meant that he had been accepted. That Nulls had been accepted as integral to Celtan life.

Words carried to his ears. "Your reinstatement ceremony was lovely, Judge D'SilverFir. Sit here and calm yourself while I put my robes away in my cache." D'Ash's voice floated from around the corner, where the Council room was.

Irritation spurted in him. How often had Ailim heard those words in her life—"just calm yourself"? She didn't need to be calm anywhere except in the JudgmentGrove.

As he neared the waiting benches outside the CouncilChamber, his palms began to sweat. His knees felt weak. His stomach clenched and he began to doubt whether he'd get his tongue around the words he wanted to say. He shoved his hands in his pockets and rubbed them dry, but found that his fingers trembled, so he left them there. He hadn't been so nervous the first time he was here . . . but then that had all been about his past.

This was all his future.

He licked his lips, swallowed, and with a deep breath he rounded the last corner.

She sat straight, hands folded, on the bench. She looked small—she'd lost weight—and pale, the epitome of serenity. Around her neck she wore his gift, and he didn't know what that meant. Would she be able to forgive him?

At the sound of his footfalls, she turned her head and faintly raised her eyebrows. The knot in his stomach twisted. She looked every inch the noblewoman, every inch the cool judge—her hair confined in a silver net, her gown exquisitely simple and elegant.

He sat next to her and she turned her head away to stare as if absorbed in the mediocre mural on the opposite wall. His mind froze, all the words he'd planned on saying evaporated, gone. He cleared his throat. "I see you are the only case on the FullCouncil's agenda this evening, Supreme-Judge."

She didn't even bother to lift her shoulder a millimeter.

Ruis winced. He closed his eyes. He wanted her so badly his entire body shook. He didn't think he could live the night through without her. He opened his mouth. Nothing emerged.

Finally, in an act of pure desperation, he slid from the bench to his knees before her. He put a hand over her twined ones. They were ice cold. He jolted at the sensation of pure desire that raced through his blood, then folded his fingers over hers, hoping to warm them, warm her into just looking at him.

"I have come to beg."

She flinched, and he caught her gaze sliding toward him. He sucked in a breath and went on. "I am desperate, lady. I stand convicted of pride and stupidity and distrust. I have been banished from the most important place in the world—by my lady's side." He fumbled for phrases. She tilted her head and met his eyes, then glanced away.

He brought her hands to his lips, kissed them, inhaled her scent. It made him dizzy, but didn't stop the words that finally flew from his mouth. The right words.

"I love you. Tell me that you will be my wife, my lover, my—HeartMate." His voice cracked on the last word. What could he know of HeartMates? They'd never join mind-to-mind like other HeartMates. But if there was ever one woman for him, the woman, it was she.

He shook with futility. How could she prefer him over others? Now that her Family estate was secure for the future, how could she find any reason to return his love after he had scorned her so?

"Ruis." It was a breath, but he heard it. His blood pounded through his veins, his muscles warmed with joy.

He bent his head over her hands. He couldn't look at her. He'd made too many mistakes. She couldn't forgive him.

She slipped her fingers from his, and he felt stricken, executed. Then her small hands framed his face and tilted his head up. When he met her eyes, her own were warm, her lips smiled, her cheeks tinged with a blush. "Yes, Ruis."

"You'll marry me?" he asked and waited an eternity.

"Yes."

He shouted in triumph and picked her up and spun her around until her shrieks of laughter bounced off the severe marble walls of the Guildhall.

Then he slid her down his hardened body. His lips found hers, tongue plunging in her mouth to claim it, as he would claim her body and her heart. HeartMate.

Her arms went around his neck and her fingers played with his hair on his nape. He shuddered and moaned.

She molded herself to him, her tongue tangled with his. Her little moans ignited his blood so he thought he'd explode.

"Ahem!"

*Cough.*

"Damn it all. We go through hell and he gets the girl," a young male voice said.

Ailim giggled and broke the kiss. She tapped his shin with her foot, and Ruis reluctantly put her on her feet, pulling her back against his body. He scowled at the interrupters.

The Council Herald, Danith D'Ash, and the Holly brothers stared at them.

"Merry meet, Captain Elder." D'Ash dipped a curtsy.

Ruis frowned. "Merry part, and merry meet again. Forgive us, but we have business to attend to."

Tinne snickered. Holm nudged him in the side. "Merry part and merry meet again, Captain Elder." Holm bowed.

Ruis gazed down at Ailim who raised her face to him. Her blue-gray eyes were dilated and her lips were red and swollen with passion. He swallowed, then managed a wink. "Let's go home to the Ship."

She smiled.

"Let's go play," he said.

She threw back her head and laughed, waved goodbye and echoed, "Let's go play!"

Turn the page for a preview of
the next futuristic romance from
ROBIN D. OWENS,

# *Heart Duel*

*Coming May 2004*
*from Berkley Sensation*

## PRIMARY HEALING HALL, DRUIDA CITY,
### Summer

*First*Level *Healer* *Mayblossom* *Larkspur* *Hawthorn* Collinson faced the gold-inlaid door of NobleRoom One. She inhaled deeply and battled a sense of injustice. Primary HealingHall NobleRooms held all the best furnishings and equipment. Privacy and luxury for the privileged class. NobleRoom One was the best, reserved for FirstFamilies Lords and Ladies.

She shunted aside a contrasting image of the barren wards of AllClass HealingHall, where she also worked. Noble or common, an injured person needed her Healing skill. This thought came easier now than it had when her Healer husband had died trying to help in a streetfight between feuding nobles.

When she entered the room, Holm Holly rose from a chair, his expression serious. "How's my kinsman Eryngi?"

"He'll recover."

Holm's eyelids lowered for an instant. "Thank the Lord and Lady."

"Yes." She glanced at her patient, Holm's brother Tinne. He lay on the Healing Bed. He winked at her. ThirdLevel Healer Gelse, who was administering pain relief, nodded.

Lark turned back to Holm. She studied him, telling herself she scrutinized him for hurt, nothing else. He looked immaculate, every silver-gilt hair in place, not a smudge on his bloused shirt and trous, not a tear in his elegantly woven cloak thrown over a chair. "You were in the fight, HollyHeir?"

His jaw muscles flexed. "An ambush."

He said nothing about her Hawthorn name or Family—a Family feuding with the Hollys—and she admired his courtesy. She raised her chin. "You don't appear any worse for wear." There weren't even perspiration marks on his clothes, but then there wouldn't be; the cloth would carry a spell to erase those. With the thought, Lark became aware of his scent, musky and attractive.

"I don't look roughed-up because I'm the best at my skill," Holm said. He dipped his head. "As are you, Mayblossom."

She gritted her teeth. She hated that name, but hadn't corrected him when they'd had their first real conversation about a month ago—after a planning session for the charity ball to fund AllClass HealingHall. He'd escorted his mother, D'Holly.

The way he used Lark's given name reminded her that no matter how she denied her class, she had grown up his equal and he still considered her that, even though she was the widow of a common man.

Crossing to the Healing Bed of layered permamoss covered in silkeen, Lark took Tinne Holly's hand. She nodded to Healer Gelse and smoothly made the pain-relief transfer.

"My heartfelt thanks, GraceMistrys Gelse," Holm said, flashing a charming smile.

Gelse looked like she might melt. Then she shook her head as if to disperse bemusement and left.

Lark stared down at the handsome blond youth of twenty. "Well, GreatSir Holly. It's been a while since I treated you."

"Three years ago, my second Passage, when I fought my death-duels in the slums of Downwind, when I helped T'Ash."

"When T'Ash saved your hide," Holm said.

Tinne grinned, and Lark couldn't suppress her own smile. She lifted the poultice off Tinne's thigh. His trous had been cut from the injury, but the ends of the fabric appeared melded. The burn was bad, a third-degree streak from his knee to the outside of his hip. From the amount of relief she'd been applying, she'd thought it was a first-degree burn. He must have a high pain threshold. She wondered if it ran in the family and glanced at Holm, only to meet his intense scrutiny.

His gaze switched to Tinne. "You'll wear a scar from that one," Holm said to his brother.

"Really? That makes six," Tinne replied with relish.

Lark set her teeth at the sentiment, but built a layer of Healing energy between her hands and the burn. "So, what have you been doing, GreatSir, besides playing blaser-target?"

"Not my fault. Those fliggering Hawth—"

"Tinne," Holm said.

"Ah." Tinne pinned his gaze on Lark and smiled winsomely again. She had the unmistakable Hawthorn coloring of blue-black hair and violet eyes. "Sorry, GreatMistrys Hawthorn."

"It's GentleLady Collinson. Call me Lark." Lark carefully repaired the muscle, intertwining lengths of sinew, siphoning more energy faster.

"Ah. Yes. I'm grateful for your skill. I don't feel a thing, and it's looking much better—" Tinne raised his torso.

Even as Lark jerked her head at Holm, he was pushing his brother back to the bedsponge.

"GreatSir Tinne, I'm sure your family has an estate and an occupation for you," Lark said, trying to distract his mind while she Healed his body.

"Ah, yeah. Second sons always get the fighting and fencing salon, The Green Knight." He sounded pleased. "My G'Uncle Tab is teaching me, so I can become a Master and train young-bloods for the duel, street fighting—"

"Exercise and entertainment. Sport. Exhibition bouts," Holm continued easily.

Tinne's gray-blue gaze went to his brother. "Huh?"

Lark used a spurt of anger and disgust to Heal. The muscle glowed with health. The flow of the ALL through her picked up some of her own energy, tiring her. She concentrated harder at sloughing the dead skin away, bringing new skin to the top, transforming the cells to the proper shape and thickness for an outside layer. She quickened her pace, but didn't forfeit an atom of care. In a few seconds she was done. "All finished. Send the record to Primary HealingHall Library and T'Holly Residence."

"Immediate payment authorization of all Holly charges to the HealingHall," Holm commanded.

"Funds transferred," acknowledged both the deep male tones of T'Holly Residence and the comforting feminine voice of Primary HealingHall.

Tinne sat up. With a pretty, rhyming verse, Lark placed a spell on the injury, keeping it clean, but letting the flow of air through to the wound. "The bandage spell will gradually diminish over a week. Have your GreatHouse Healer examine the burn daily."

"Despite the fact that we are the Family that needs one the most, we have no HouseHold Healer. Perhaps you would be interested in the position?" Holm asked.

Shock forced Lark to look into Holm's gray eyes. She felt a tiny jolt. Small though it was, it was still a little stronger than the quiver she'd experienced the last time they'd met. She found speech. "Impossible."

"Huh?" Tinne asked again, his puzzled glance on his brother, then his lips curved. He stood and picked up her hand and kissed it. "My thanks, GentleLady." He glanced at his brother, hesitated, then said, "We would be pleased if you joined GreatHouse T'Holly. As you know, ours is a line of fighters, not Healers. We have no Family member who is capable of Healing. You would grace our halls."

Lark smiled at him. "Quite impossible."

Tinne put a hand over his chest and sighed. "You have anything for heartbreak?"

Lark laughed and shooed him out. He left with a bounce in his step.

Holm reached out and grasped her hands before she could follow Tinne. A shudder rippled through Holm's body. For an instant Lark imagined fear dawning in his eyes, then the odd expression vanished and he smiled as he cradled her hands in his own.

"Such power and Flair and beauty. T'Holly GreatHouse would honor and respect you, Mayblossom."

She stiffened. His palms were hard but gentle, his warmth and vitality astonishing. She tugged at her hands. He didn't release them.

"HollyHeir . . ."

"You know it's Holm. Even though the proper Heir name should be Tinne, for the Hollys it has always been Holm, after the first colonist who landed on Celta. I'm Holm."

She tugged again.

He waited an instant, kissed one of her hands, then the other. The press of his mouth was firm, yet held a note of tender determination. His lips against the backs of her hands sent a sensual tingle throughout her body, which she took as a warning.

Slowly, he released her fingers. "Merry meet," he said.

"And merry part," she replied automatically.

"And merry meet again." He shot her a brilliant look. "And we *will* meet again, Mayblossom. Soon."

Her mouth curved in a bitter smile. "I hope not. The feud, the injuries, death." A picture of her slain husband rose to her mind.

Holm's eyes narrowed. He grasped her shoulders and placed a short, hard kiss on her mouth. "We'll meet again."

"I don't associate with fighters," she called as he strode from the room, squelching the intimate memory of those firm lips on hers and the unexpected rush of desire. She buried the new sensations under old bitterness, hurt, and anger, muttering to herself, "I don't *want* to associate with fighters. I hate and despise fighting." And if her appointment as the head of Gael City HealingHall came through, she'd be gone from Druida before the month was out.

She yanked a cord to begin the Flair-spell-technology that would refresh and sterilize the room. Visualizing her bedroom, she gathered her Flair and teleported home.

*V*oices mumbled, swords swirled and clashed with discordant blows. Holm fought Hawthorns, spinning, using sword and dagger. The flash of a sword thrust at him. He hesitated. Tinne fell. Holm riposted and pierced the Hawthorn's heart.

Screams hit his ears. Words he couldn't distinguish. She drew his glance. Mayblossom Hawthorn, FirstLevel Healer. His HeartMate.

He woke on a shuddering groan. Dew coated the long grass a few centimeters from his nose. He'd curled defensively in his sleep—but only small night animals and birds rustled around him.

Not again! Sleep-teleporting again. The fourth time in two months.

Holm staggered to his feet, his breathing a harsh rasping. His arm ached all the way to his shoulder from his fierce grip on his dagger.

The night's chill breeze dried the cold sweat on his body. He shivered. He was naked. And alone.

The horizon was at eye-level. He looked up, past the branches of a great ash tree, and found the bright starry skies of Celta dimmed by the light of two waxing twinmoons. Once again he'd 'ported to the crater north of Druida that held the ancient Great Labyrinth—a meditation tool.

He didn't want to meditate or recall being trapped in a blood-colored dream of fighting and death. Or think of the ragged shroud of the previous nightmare where he'd failed his brother. Tinne hand sunk into the black, sucking swamp of the Great Washington Boghole—a dream based on unfortunate truth. Holm had floundered helplessly to save his younger brother, but Tinne had managed to rescue them both. Holm suppressed the groan that echoed in his chest, just as he'd suppressed the memory and ignored the dreams since the incident nearly three years ago. He'd hoped he'd banished those forever.

His mouth flattened. No doubt his subconscious thought he needed to consider some problems. He was at the center of the labyrinth and it would take a septhour to reach the end where he could 'port out. A person could teleport in, but never out.

He loosened his grip on his dagger and switched hands so he could wipe his sweaty palm on his thigh, wondering what he'd do if this plague continued into the windy autumn and snowy winter, whether he'd have beaten whatever caused the dreams by then.

Stretching, he worked his muscles and steadied his pulse from the dream's divulgence of his HeartMate.

Holm wasn't surprised. He'd known the minute he'd touched her earlier in the day. The dreams had primed him, her touch had triggered the revelation.

His thoughts unwillingly trailed back to the nightmare. His brother had died. He'd failed again. Holm scrubbed his face.

The forcelines of the labyrinth pulsed with rainbows of energy. He sighed and started the long walk out. Somehow he was sure that, as always, he'd fail to quiet his busy mind or find the core of serenity inside him that everyone said was there.

\* \* \*

"*Please, sit, son,*" T'Holly, Holm's father, rumbled and gestured to one of the large, comfortable wingchairs stationed in front of his desk.

Holm stared balefully at the chair. It represented all the reprimands of his childhood. When he became T'Holly and succeeded to the title and the estate, that chair would go.

When Holm saw his mother perched on the side of his father's desk, her hand in her husband's, Holm tensed for the emotional blow.

He grumbled inwardly. He'd known someday this moment would come, but, as usual, they'd surprised him. He'd just run out of time. And he needed time. He wasn't ready to start his wooing. She wasn't ready.

He reminded himself that he respected his parents and had sworn a loyalty oath to T'Holly as GreatHouse Lord. But Holm's mind sharpened as he sat. He had to play this game of wills smoothly.

His father cleared his throat. "Your mother and I have been talking. . . ."

Holm's gut tensed. The worst news always began: "Your mother and I have been talking." Whether it had been problems with manners, responsibilities, his tutor, his psi power—his Flair—he'd always sat in this chair and heard those words. Though his father said the words, Holm knew who prompted the little talks. He stared at his Mamá. She didn't meet his eyes.

His teeth clenched in dread.

His parents exchanged glances, then his father turned his pewter-gray gaze again onto Holm. "You're thirty-seven, and while that isn't the great age here on Celta as it was on Earth, it is time you married."

Holm would have given a great deal of gilt for a stiff drink right then. He sucked in a deep breath, trying to keep his face impassive. "None of my three Passages, the emotional storms that freed my Flair, indicated a HeartMate. I want what you have." Maybe that would earn him a little more time.

His Mamá looked at him with sorrow in her turquoise eyes and moved closer to his father.

"We know you don't have a HeartMate, dear."

Staying expressionless and meeting her eyes was hard
But the stakes were too important for anyone except him
to know the name of his HeartMate. He hadn't had time to
strategize how he'd win Mayblossom Larkspur Hawthorn
Collinson.

D'Holly sighed. "Many don't have HeartMates." She
nodded with determination. "But it's time you wed. A fine
marriage can be had with a good woman. Love can follow,
I'm sure." Her voice faltered at the end, since being a
HeartMate, she couldn't know personally. She swept her
hand wide as if encompassing the city. "The Alders have a
perfectly happy marriage, and my sister Nata loves her husband. . . ."

T'Holly continued for his HeartMate. "We need to know
the Holly line will continue. We need heirs. At least two
sons from you." His father was being less than his usual
diplomatic self. The fact that T'Holly found the topic dis-
tasteful didn't stop Holm from resenting him.

"A few daughters would be nice, too," D'Holly murmured. She flashed the charming smile Holm had inherited.
"As many as you can engender."

A growl rolled from Holm's lips before he could stop it.

His father raised winged silver brows and looked down
his nose. "We expected this reaction."

He tapped a crystal set into the desk. A calendar-moon
holo materialized between Holm and his parents.

The ResidenceLibrary spoke. "An appointment with the
matchmaker, GreatLady Saille D'Willow, has been made
for Holm, HollyHeir. The meeting was expedited for two
days from now, on Quert. It is to be a full session, no gilt
limit."

Holm winced at the expense. The globe spun faster until
it disappeared in a flash of blue-white light.

"We want you to be happy, dear, that's why we're sending you to the foremost matchmaker on Celta. D'Willow
won't have any difficulty finding you a suitable wife." His
mother sounded troubled but determined.

"But you don't want me to be as happy as yourselves,
with a HeartMate marriage," Holm said.

His father snapped into straight rigidity. "You know if

you had a HeartMate we would do everything in our power
to welcome her to the Family."

Holm narrowed his eyes and let a faint smile play on his
lips. "Would you?"

"Of course," D'Holly said.

Holm lifted his brows. "By your Words of Honor?"

T'Holly scowled. D'Holly furrowed her forehead. "Yes,
by our Words."

"By our Words," T'Holly echoed. "Not that it is appli-
cable. D'Willow's matchmaking ability is the best. She
doesn't personally see very many." He cleared his throat
and handed Holm a sheet of papyrus. "Perhaps this will
help her, and you."

Holm didn't have to read the papyrus to know what was
on it. "A list of eligible women from Families with whom
it would be advantageous to form a close alliance?" he
mocked.

"Don't take that tone with your father," D'Holly said, in
reflexive defense of her husband. "I'm sure several of the
ladies listed are women you could come to love. I quite like
Hedara of GreatHouse Ivy and am very fond of Gwylan of
D'Sea."

Holm had heard such names before in the form of
dropped hints. He stood. "Speaking of alliances, I trust that
this appointment with the matchmaker didn't also include
an alliance."

"It's a straight gilt payment," his father gritted.

"Good." Holm went to his mother and lifted her free hand
to his lips. "I will follow your wishes in this." But he didn't
smile at her like he generally did.

He'd go to the matchmaker. Better to keep his parents in
the dark about his mate. A situation they didn't know about,
they couldn't meddle in. He'd have to move quickly now.
"I trust you will be satisfied with my choice of a wife."

They wouldn't.

He squeezed his Mamá's hand and dropped it, then left.

**To read the entire first Chapter of *Heart Duel* go to
http://www.robinowens.com. The first chapters of *HeartMate*
and *Heart Thief* are also available at the site.**